...a of Michael

He is sin and satisfaction, lust and damnation, a lethal weapon created from the greed of man. A human soldier injected with alien DNA, he is one of many, yet none are like him, a legend within this new race, split between good and evil. Untamable, he has walked on the dark side and returned to the light, but it matters not, for he is feared, misunderstood—lethal in all ways possible. Women desire him, lust for the mysterious warrior, hungry for the raw passion that touches his every breath. Men envy his stature, his power; they lust to control him. But there is no controlling a creature such as he, no taming the primal fires within him. He is the past. He is the future.

He is Michael.

THE *Legend* OF
MICHAEL

LISA RENEE JONES

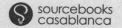

sourcebooks
casablanca

Published by Sourcebooks Casablanca, an imprint of Sourcebooks, Inc.
P.O. Box 4410, Naperville, Illinois 60567-4410
(630) 961-3900
FAX: (630) 961-2168
www.sourcebooks.com

Printed and bound in the United States of America
QW 10 9 8 7 6 5 4 3 2 1

This book is dedicated to Diego Harrison.
Your support is impossibly unlimited.
"Thank you" seems inadequate.
One day I'll pay you back in comic books.
For now, you'll have to settle for love.

Glossary

Area 51—Another name used for Groom Lake.

Blood Exchange—A part of the lifebond process done by choice, after the lifebond mark appears on the female's neck. This completes the female's transformation to GTECH and links the two Lifebonds in life and death. (See Lifebond Process.)

Dreamland—Though Groom Lake/Area 51 is often called Dreamland, in The Renegades series, Dreamland is the fictional military facility opened eighty miles from Area 51 by General Powell to take a stand against the Zodius who overran Area 51.

Green Hornet—Special bullet that is so powerful it not only shreds human muscle and bone, it permeates the thin bodysuit armor that the GTECHs—both Zodius and Renegades—wear when no other bullet can do so.

Groom Lake—Also known as Area 51, this is the military base where the Project Zodius experiments with alien DNA took place, which was later taken over by the Zodius rebels.

GTECH—The Super Soldiers who were created under Project Zodius and who divided into two groups—Zodius and Renegades. GTECHs are stronger, faster, and more agile than humans; they heal rapidly and have low fatality rates. They can wind-walk. Over time, many are developing special gifts unique to them, such as telepathy, ability to communicate with animals, and more.

GTECH Body Armor—A thin bodysuit that fits like a second skin. Extremely light and flexible. The material is made from alien technology recovered from a 1950s crash site. Until the Green Hornets were created, no standard issue ammunition could penetrate the suits.

GTECH Serum—The serum created from alien DNA that was gathered at a crash site in the 1950s and then used to create the GTECHs. The original sample was destroyed. Since the alien DNA will not allow itself to be duplicated, there can be no new serum created without new scientific discoveries. The remaining serum disappeared the day Area 51/Groom Lake was taken over by the GTECH Rebels known as Zodius Soldiers. The GTECH serum cannot be created from GTECH DNA. This has been tried and failed.

Lifebond Mark—A double circle resembling a tattoo appears on the back of the female's neck after the first sexual encounter with a GTECH, but only the female meant to be that GTECH's Lifebond. After the mark appears, the female feels a tingling sensation whenever the male Lifebond first approaches.

Lifebond Process—A Lifebond is a male and female who are bonded physically for life and death. If one dies, so does the other. This bond allows the GTECH male to reproduce, and it offers the females the same physical skills as their male Lifebond. The lifebond mark, a double circle resembling a tattoo, appears on the back of the female's neck after the first sexual encounter. A blood exchange is required to complete the physical transformation of the female to GTECH, if the couple makes that decision. There is physical pain and illness for the female during conversion.

Neonopolis—The Las Vegas satellite location for the Renegades, covertly located in the basement of the Neonopolis entertainment complex off Las Vegas Avenue.

PMI or "Private Military Intelligence"—A company run by General Powell, the officer who created Project Zodius. PMI is used as a cover for top-secret military projects that the government doesn't want to officially show on the books.

Project Zodius—Code name for the government's top-secret operation—two hundred Special Operations soldiers who were assigned to Groom Lake (Area 51) and injected with what they believed to be immunizations, but which was, in fact, alien DNA.

Red Dart—A red crystal found at the same UFO 1950s crash site where the GTECH DNA was discovered. The crystal creates a red laser beam that enters the bloodstream and creates a permanent tracking beacon that is sensitive to sound waves. These sound waves can also be used for torture and control of the GTECHs. Thus far, U.S. military attempts to use Red Dart have been fatal.

Renegade Soldier—A GTECH who protects humanity and stands against the rebels known as "Zodius." The Renegades are led by Adam Rain's twin brother, Caleb Rain.

Shield—A mental barrier that a GTECH uses to block their psychic residue from being traceable by Trackers.

Stardust—An alien substance that is undetectable in human testing and causes brain aneurisms.

Sunrise City—The main Renegades facility, an advanced, underground city located in Nevada's Sunrise Mountain Range.

Trackers—These are GTECHs with the special ability to track the psychic residue of another GTECH or a human female who's been intimate with another GTECH. If a female possesses this residue, then only that female's Lifebond can shield her from a Tracker.

Wind-walking—The ability to fade into the wind, like mist into the air, and invisibly travel far distances at rapid speed.

X2 Gene—A gene that appears in some, but not all, of the GTECHs by the fifteenth month after injection of the GTECH serum.

Zodius City—Still known as the top-secret U.S. military facility often called Area 51 or Groom Lake, located in Nevada, it was taken over by the rebel GTECHs led by Adam Rain. This facility is both above and beneath ground level.

Zodius Soldier—A rebel GTECH soldier who follows Adam Rain, the leader of the rebel movement. Adam intends to take over the world.

THE *Legend* OF
MICHAEL

Part 1

And so it began…

Chapter 1

NEVADA'S AREA 51 WAS NOT ONLY THE SUBJECT OF government conspiracy theories; it was now, officially, her new home. A good hour before sunrise, Cassandra Powell pulled into the military parking lot outside the launch pad leading to the top-secret underground facilities where the launch of the Project Zodius GTECH Super Soldier Program was a year under way. The ride from her new on-base housing had been a whopping three minutes, which considering the inhuman hours the military favored, she could deal with. The simplicity of a standard green army skirt and jacket—required despite her contract status—seemed to be working for her as well. The cardboard bed, not so much. It had, however, made a great desk for her laptop and all-night reading.

And considering she was only three days on the job—taking over for the former head of clinical psychology who'd transferred to another department—she had plenty of work to do. The prior department head hadn't done one fourth of the studies that Cassandra deemed critical to properly evaluate these soldiers. And while the counseling aspect fell outside her clinical role, she wasn't pleased with what was being offered. She'd certainly be nudging her way into that territory.

Files in hand, she exited her red Volkswagen Beetle and pushed the door shut with a flick of her hip. She walked all of two steps when the wind whipped into high gear, fluttering her suit jacket at her hips and tearing to pieces the blonde knot tied at her nape.

She shoved at the loose locks of hair and drew to a shocked halt, blinking in disbelief as four men dressed in black fatigues materialized in a rush of hot August wind at the other side of the long parking lot next to the elevator. She drew a breath and forced it out, trying to calm the thunder of her heart pounding her chest. Apparently she wasn't quite as prepared for the phenomenon of GTECH Super Soldiers as she'd thought she was. Or at least not this skill her piles of paperwork referred to as "wind-walking." It was one thing to be inhumanly strong and fast, even to be immune to human disease, but to be able to travel with the wind was downright spooky—and suddenly, so was the dark parking lot as the four men disappeared into the elevator.

Eager to get inside, Cassandra started walking, but made it all of two steps before another man appeared beside the elevator, this time with no wind as warning. Good grief, she hadn't read about that stealthy little trick yet. Special Forces soldiers were already called lethal weapons, but these men, this one in particular, were taking it to a whole new level.

Still a good distance away from the building, Cassandra slowed her pace, hoping to go unnoticed, but she wasn't so lucky. The soldier punched the elevator button and then turned and waved her forward. Oh no. No. No. Not ready to meet anyone yet. Not until she had a few of her ducks in a row. Cassandra quickly juggled her files and snagged her cell from her purse as an excuse to decline joining him, holding it up, and waving him off. He hesitated a few moments as the doors opened before he finally stepped inside and disappeared.

Cassandra started walking instantly, determined to get to the darned elevator before another soldier appeared. By the time she was inside, she had her file on wind-walking open—a good distraction from the entire underground, bomb-shelter-style workplace that made her more than a little uneasy.

Absorbed in her reading, head down, Cassandra darted out of the elevator the instant it opened, only to run smack into a rock-hard chest. She gasped, paperwork flew everywhere, and strong hands slid around her arms, steadying her from a fall. It was then that she looked up to find herself staring into the most gorgeous pair of crystal blue eyes she'd ever seen in her life.

She swallowed hard and noticed his long raven hair tied at the back of his neck, rather than the standard buzz cut—a sure indicator he was Special Ops. He could be one of the two hundred GTECH soldiers stationed at the base. *A Wind-walker*, she thought, still in awe of what she'd seen above ground.

"I'm sorry. I wasn't watching where I was..." She lost the final word, her mouth dry as she suddenly realized her legs were pressed intimately to his desert fatigues, and her conservative, military-issue skirt had managed to work its way halfway up her thigh. "Oh!"

She quickly took a step backwards, righting her skirt in a flurry of panicked movement. Three days on the job, and already she was putting on a show. She pressed her hand to her forehead. "I know better than to read while walking. I hope I didn't hurt you." He arched a dark brow as her gaze swept all six-foot-plus of incredibly hot man, all lethal muscle and mayhem, and knew that was unlikely. She laughed at the ridiculous statement, feeling uncharacteristically nervous. She was five four in her bare feet—well, on her tip toes—and she bet this man towered over her by nearly a foot. "Okay. I didn't hurt you. But, well, I'm still sorry."

He stared down at her, his gaze steady, unblinking, the chiseled lines of high cheekbones and a square jaw, expressionless. Except deep in those strikingly blue eyes, she saw a tiny flicker of what she thought was amusement. "I'm not sorry," he said, squatting down to pick up her files.

She blinked at the odd response, tilting her head and then squatting down to face him. "What do you mean?" she asked, a lock of her blonde hair falling haphazardly across her brow, free from the clip that was supposed to be holding it in place. "You're not sorry?"

He gathered the last of her files, then said, "I'm not sorry you ran into me. Have coffee with me."

It wasn't a question. In fact, it almost bordered on an order. And damn, if she didn't like the way he gave that near order. Her heart fluttered at the unexpected invitation. "I don't know if that is appropriate," she said, thinking of her new position. She stalled. "I don't even know your name."

The elevator behind them dinged open, and Kelly Peterson, assistant director of science and medicine for Project Zodius, appeared. "You're early, Cassandra," she said, amusement lifting her tone. "Morning, Michael." She continued on her way, as if she found nothing significant, or abnormal, about Cassandra being sprawled across the hallway floor with a hot soldier by her side.

Cassandra popped to her feet, appalled she'd made such a spectacle of herself. Her sexy Special Ops soldier followed. "Now you know my name," he said, and this time, his firm, way-too-tempting mouth hinted at a lift. Not a smile, a lift. God... it was sexy. "Michael Taylor."

"Cassandra," she said, unable to say the last name, dreading it more with this man than with the many others she'd been introduced to in the past few days. What was she supposed to say? *Hi. I'm the daughter of the man who changed your life forever by injecting you with alien DNA without telling you first, and then claimed it was to save you from an enemy biological threat? Now you're a GTECH Super Soldier for what we think is the rest of your life, but who knows what that really means long-term for you. But hey, I promise I'm one of the good guys, here to ensure you aren't used and abused just because you're a macho, kick-ass, secret government weapon? And did I mention I'm nothing like my father?*

"Cassandra Powell," he said, handing her the files, leaning close, the warmth of his body blanketing her in sizzling awareness. "I know who you are. And no, that doesn't scare me away. I never run away from anything I want." He leaned back, fixing her in another one of those dreamy blue stares. "So how about that coffee?"

She nearly swallowed her tongue at his directness, but, a true general's daughter, she managed to recover quickly, remembering her duty in a painfully responsible fashion. "I... don't think that's a good idea."

He studied her a moment before stepping into the now open elevator doors. "I'll ask again," he said as he turned to face her. She found herself lost in those addictive crystal blue eyes—eyes that had promised nothing, but somehow, promised everything—until the steel doors shut between them.

Cassandra inhaled, the scent of him still lingering in the air, and she bit her bottom lip. Too bad she'd sworn off soldiers years ago, because he was one heck of a man. Oh yeah, he was. But she'd seen her mother fret and worry over a man who was gone too often and might never return, right up to the day she'd died two years before, and Cassandra already had her father to worry about. So why was she wondering when he would "ask again"?

Forcing herself to shake off the encounter, Cassandra headed to the lab attached to the tiny corner office she'd claimed as her own on her one previous visit. The area should have been vacant this early in the morning, but Kelly was waiting eagerly for her entrance. They'd had a casual friendship for years, having met at a military seminar. Which made it easy for Cassandra to recognize that though Kelly looked every bit the scholar with her light brown hair neatly piled on top of her head, her lab coat already in place, and a pencil tucked behind her ear, the mischief in her expression meant she didn't have work on her mind.

"It's a shame those blue eyes of his are really black now, isn't it?" she asked.

"Hello and good morning to you too," Cassandra said, piling her things on top of one of the ten empty lab tables and turning to her. "And what do you mean his eyes are really black?"

"I see someone is behind on their homework," Kelly said, claiming one of the stools beside Cassandra to sit down. "All of the GTECHs have black eyes, but they can camouflage them to their natural color. Well, except with their bonded females. It's kind of freaky and amazing at the same time, like about everything else around this place."

"Clearly I'm way behind on my homework," Cassandra said, perching on a stool herself, "because I don't know anything about camouflage and changing eye colors. And what do you mean by bonded females?"

"To date, three random women have experienced pain on the back of their necks shortly after their first sexual encounter with a GTECH. Immediately afterward, a mark appears on their neck resembling a tattoo—a double circle with intricate design work around the outer line. For now, and for lack of a better term, we're referring to those couples as 'bonded' since the mark is clearly some sort of link between the two, though frankly, our understanding of what that means is weak, at best. But the very fact that the GTECHs can't camouflage their eyes from the female they gave this marking to supports some sort of unique bond."

Cassandra blinked in amazement. "You're sure these marks aren't tattoos and the three women—maybe even the GTECHs—are in on his together—trying to get attention?"

"That was my first thought too, but there's no ink, and we've attempted surgical removal unsuccessfully. The mark regenerates immediately."

"Wow," she said, blown away. "Just wow."

"You can say that again," Kelly agreed. "One thing about this job—it's never boring."

That was an understatement. "Aside from the immunity to the camouflage—what kinds of effects are these marks having on these women?"

"In the women, some specific blood work changes that appear to be nonmalignant. None in the GTECHs involved. Interestingly enough though, the couples are quite attached to one another, and the men quite protective of the women. Now—is that because of the marks? I don't know. Obviously, these couples were having sex, so they were already attracted to one another. Did the marks occur because of a deeper emotional bond, or did the deeper emotional bond occur because of the marks? I have yet to answer those questions. But, needless to say, we'd prefer to avoid further incidents until we know more. The men weren't happy when I handed out condoms en masse to the troops. Not needing a condom was a bit of cold comfort for being made sterile by the GTECH injections."

"You can't be sure they'll take precautions though," Cassandra objected. "What about the dangers to the general population? What if this tattoo marking comes with dangers we don't know about yet?"

"Two hundred GTECH soldiers and who knows how many sexual partners, yet only three women have been marked. Laboratory studies are inconclusive, but we've run test after test, and we've found nothing environmental, no set of stimuli, that re-creates that mark. And believe me, we've tried thousands of combinations. The odds of this mark spreading across the general population, even with unprotected sex, are next to zero. Even lower if at least a portion of the men actually use the condoms." She eyed her watch. "The weekly department-heads meeting starts in an hour. It's always... interesting. Why don't we grab some coffee, and I'll brief you before heading in that direction.

Bring your files, and I can answer any questions." The suggestion of coffee sent her thoughts darting to Michael and his words. *I'll ask again.* Disconcertedly, Cassandra shook off the memory and cleared her throat, not used to being this distracted unless it was with her work. "Yes. Okay." She pushed off the lab stool and reached for her files as they headed toward the door.

"You know," Kelly said, mischief creeping back into her voice as they headed toward the door. "I've seen many a woman drool over Michael, but I've *never* seen Michael look at anyone the way he looked at you by that elevator."

The out-of-the-blue comment took Cassandra off guard, and she cut Kelly a sideways glance. "What look?" she asked, with a delicate snort. "The man was all emotionless steel."

"Oh, he had a look," she said. "How does it feel to be wanted by 'The Dark One'?"

"The Dark One?" Cassandra asked, shaking her head at the strange name.

"That's what everyone here calls him. You know — because he's all dark and intimidating." She laughed. "They're afraid he'll kill them if they look at him the wrong way."

Cassandra gaped. "Kill them?"

Kelly chuckled. "I'm kidding, or mostly kidding. The stories of Michael are darn near legend, though half of them are probably not even true. The whole lethal-in-battle and lethal-in-bed kind of typical soldier talk. They say he's different than the other GTECHs." Before Cassandra could ask how, Kelly wiggled an eyebrow and added, "He's certainly got that tall, dark, and sexy thing going on, doesn't he?"

Cassandra shook her head. "Oh no. You aren't luring me into saying he's sexy. I'm here to do a job, not drool over the soldiers." Though silently, Cassandra wasn't sure "sexy" even began to describe Michael's appeal.

"You don't have to admit it," Kelly said. "I saw the look on *your* face, too, at that elevator." She grinned. "Just use a condom."

Heat rushed to Cassandra's cheeks. She didn't need a condom! Or a soldier to fret over, especially a man who apparently had plenty of other women to do it for her. No way. She was *not* having sex with Michael.

———

Late that evening, Cassandra sat at her simple steel desk in her still barren office—now her home away from her not-so-comfortable home—trying to focus on the GTECH file and failing. She grimaced, giving in to the temptation driving her to distraction, and punched in Michael's name. He was thirty-four, five years older than she was. Of course, who knew how the GTECH serum would affect his aging process. She could turn into an old lady, and he'd never age a day. She didn't like that thought much and moved on. He was from California and... holy moly. His family owned Taylor Industries, one of the largest weapons manufacturers in the world.

She sat back in her chair. There was no way his being here was a coincidence. Her father, of course, had to know. She'd bet her weight in chocolate that Michael was here because her father believed he could be useful in the future, if not already. Cassandra sat up, keyed again. Sure enough, Michael had been the only soldier pulled from his Special Ops unit and brought to Groom Lake. Her father was nothing, if not strategic. He'd wanted something from Michael beyond his battlefield skills. He wanted that connection to Taylor Industries.

"What are you up to, Father?" she whispered. "And why do I know it's not a good idea?" Frowning, she stared at the computer screen. And what made someone like Michael, who had to be filthy rich, join the military? Family trouble was the usual answer. She'd seen it plenty of times. Cassandra tabbed down the computer screen, reading the details of how Michael's father had died in a small plane crash in Saudi Arabia when Michael was twenty-one. She checked the record. That happened a year after he'd entered the Special Forces. Michael had been on a mission and didn't hear about the death until after the funeral. His mother now ran Taylor Industries. So even after his father died, Michael had stayed in the army, which meant he wanted nothing to do with the family business. Or his mother didn't want him involved.

"How's my favorite daughter doing?"

Cassandra all but jumped out of her skin at the sound of her father's voice, finding him standing in the doorway, a smile on his face, looking sharp as always in his well-decorated uniform, his gray hair trimmed neatly.

"I'm your only daughter," she reminded him, wishing he'd share that smile with the staff at Groom Lake who feared him far more than they should. "And that joke is older than you, Father." She had no idea why she felt like a kid who'd been caught with her hand in the cookie jar.

"The old ones are the good ones," he said. "Remember that." In tip-top shape and looking far younger than his fifty-five years, he lent truth to that statement.

"I don't have to," she said. "You remind me often."

He studied her with a critical eye. "Why aren't you sleeping?"

"I'm a workaholic, like my father," she said.

"And if your mother were alive," he said, "she'd hang us both up by our toes."

Even two years after her mother's car accident, the reference to her passing made Cassandra's chest tighten uncomfortably. "As my psychology mentor, she'd be as nuts as I am over the incomplete evaluations done on the GTECHs."

"I have no doubt," he said. "But before you dive in and try to conquer a year of what you see as our deficiencies, I want you to focus on a specific list of ten soldiers of special interest to me."

"What kind of special interest?"

He shut the door. "They've all tested positive to a certain gene we're calling X2. We have animals in the lab also testing positive that are showing aggressive tendencies we need to be certain don't translate into our GTECH population. We need to rerun all baseline evaluations and whatever extra testing you deem necessary, then ongoing evaluation." He fixed her in a silvery stare. "The animals and the soldiers seem to be showing the gene growth somewhere in the twelve to fifteen months post-injection range."

Cassandra ground her teeth. The fact that he, and the government, had withheld the experimental compound of the immunizations from the soldiers was completely despicable. But she'd stated all her objections to how the GTECHs had been created before taking this job. Heard all the vows that the GTECHs were created by accident, when they—meaning the army, though she translated that to her father—were simply protecting them from a biological threat. Considering her father was all about protecting his country at all cost, and though he meant well, often went too far by her standard, she wasn't completely sure she believed that claim. She suspected she'd hear the soldiers voice the same concerns once she earned their trust, which she fully intended to do. In fact, it was her objections to how the GTECHs were created, and then how little emotional support they'd received regarding that creation—rather than her father's urging—that had finalized her acceptance. Her father wanted her for the job for her skill and the family loyalty her mother had often given him. But like her mother, who had often worked by her father's side, Cassandra wanted to help the soldiers he employed. So, like her mother, and out of character to her true self, she did what most people did around her father and bit her tongue.

"Let's have a father-daughter breakfast in the morning," he ordered rather than asked. Her father didn't know how to operate outside of giving orders, even when he simply wanted father-daughter time.

Knowing this, and seeing it as his form of affection, Cassandra smiled. She didn't always approve of her father's ways, but she loved him deeply. "I'd like that."

"I'll pick you up at seven," he said, giving her a nod before disappearing out the door, and leaving her with a sense of unidentifiable dread that lingered for the next hour.

Finally, tired and ready for food, she exited the building and headed to her car, only to be greeted by a perfectly flat, perfectly defeating, tire. "Great," she mumbled, setting her files inside on the backseat and then pulling the tight knot at the back of her hair free to release the ever-growing tension there. She glanced around, looking for the resource never in short supply on a military base—a soldier or two or three, who could be easily convinced to lend a helping hand.

Suddenly, her hair lifted around her neck, a soft breeze picking up momentary speed with a raw masculine scent touching its depths. A second later, Michael appeared before her, as big and broad and devastatingly "sexy" as he had been this morning.

"You really should come with a warning alarm of some sort," she said, fist balled at her chest to calm her pounding heart.

"So I hear," he said, his too-blue eyes flickering with a hint of unreadable emotion before he glanced at her tire. "Looks like you need help."

There was something overwhelming—perhaps decadent even—about this man that had her struggling to remember how to form a proper sentence. "I... yes, please." Cassandra brushed a lock of blonde hair from her eyes and glanced at the elevator, then him. "Was that you this morning holding the elevator for me?"

He kneeled down to inspect her tire. "Yeah," he said, tossing her an amused look over his truly spectacular shoulder hugged by a nice, tight black tee. "But apparently, strange men and elevators don't work for you."

Cassandra felt her cheeks flush. "I had a call," she said. The look he gave her said he wasn't buying it, so she added, "Okay fine. I'm not beyond admitting I was a little intimidated. You wind-walked without any visible wind. I didn't know that was possible."

He pushed to his feet and ignored her comment. "You've got a screw the size of a rocket launcher in that tire. It'll have to be replaced."

Cassandra wasn't letting him off that easy. "Can everyone wind-walk without any visible wind?"

"I can," he said, his lids half-veiled now, his jaw a bit more tense. "I don't pretend to speak for anyone else."

Kelly's words played in Cassandra's head. *The stories of Michael are darn near legend.* "You're the only one who can do it, aren't you? That's why people talk about you. Because you're different and it scares them."

He stepped closer to her, so close she could feel the heat of his body, so close she had to tilt her chin to look him in the eyes. They flickered and then turned solid black. "Do I scare *you*, Cassandra?"

Oh yeah. He scared her all right, but not for the reasons he assumed. This man reached inside her and demanded a feminine response she wasn't prepared to give him. In fact, standing there, looking into his eyes—she didn't care if they were black or blue—they spoke to her in a soul-deep way that told her far more than she thought he knew. He was showing her the GTECH, and instinctively, she knew he needed her to see the man. "I'll make you a deal, Michael Taylor," she said. "I'll be scared of you when you give me a reason to be. But just so you know, being all broody and showing me how well you can shift your eye color isn't doing the job."

Surprise flickered across his handsome features, and for a moment she almost thought he might smile. She wanted to see that smile, for reasons she couldn't explain, and hung on to a thin string waiting for it, until the moment was gone. Until he said, "Let me take you to dinner. I promise to work on being scarier while we eat. And for added effect, I'll replace your tire when we get back."

Warnings played in her head at the invitation. He had a slew of females. She didn't date soldiers. Her father wouldn't approve. But still, she found herself looking forward to the challenge of enticing that elusive smile. She playfully replied, "I'm up for the challenge if you are."

Those black eyes shifted back to blue fire, filled with enough heat to make her knees weak. "I guess we'll see about that." He fished his keys from his black fatigue pants. "I'm parked over in the corner."

"What?" she teased. "We have to drive? We don't get to wind-walk to dinner? Superman used to fly Lois all over the place."

"While I'm never against a little comic book fantasy," he assured, "I'm no Superman, believe me, and you're not Lois—not unless you're looking for a near-death experience. It's dangerous for humans. Sometimes even fatal."

"Oh," she said, surprised, walking with him toward a row of cars. "That's limiting. I thought you could just pop in and rescue someone and be done with it."

"Gives me an excuse to keep Carrie," he said, stopping next to a classic black Mustang.

"You named your car Carrie?" she asked, surprised yet again by this man. He was far more human than people made him out to be.

"She's the friend who has never failed me," he said, pulling the passenger door open and waving her forward.

"She's also a psycho demon character from a Stephen King novel," she reminded him. "Not sure that's a friend I want to have."

"You won't say that after you ride in her," he promised.

All too aware of his warm stare, Cassandra slid into the car, sinking into the soft leather surrounding her, a moment before he shut her inside. *The friend who has never failed me*. Someone had not only failed Michael in the past, they'd hurt him doing it. And that hurt was a part of how he defined who, and what, he was. Maybe it even made him as lethal as everyone seemed to believe him to be. Maybe she *should* be afraid of him. So why wasn't she opening the car door and getting out?

Besides, how could one little dinner date be dangerous?

Chapter 2

MICHAEL WALKED INTO THE KUWAIT CITY FISH Market off Arabian Gulf Boulevard in street clothes—casual jeans, a black T-shirt, and shades covering his eyes. It was two weeks after meeting Cassandra, and he was on a mission, but in one hell of a foul mood, never something that boded well for his enemies. After four casual dates that had somehow not ended up in bed, despite a damn near primal need to strip her naked and have his way with her, Michael had sworn off seeing her again. And not because he wanted to. He wanted that woman like he had never wanted anything. She was full of life and intelligent, like his mother had once been before his father had shredded every bit of soul she possessed. And as his mother often said—Michael was nothing, if not the spawn of his father, a man who knew way more about death than he did about life.

The foul scent of the dead fish flared in his nostrils, made worse by the heat radiating beneath the canvas roof that covered the displays, reminding Michael he had a little of that death to deal today. He hated the smell of dead fish almost as much as he hated the smell of blood, but sources said Raj Mustafad came here every Friday to buy his fish, which meant Michael had to endure the stench. Raj was their link to an Iranian terrorist group which was hell-bent and on their way to the annihilation of Israel by biological attack.

Michael knew the instant Raj walked into the market, having memorized his photos. Three tables of stinking fish separated them, which Michael quickly remedied, fading into the wind and reappearing beside Raj, not giving a crap about witnesses. Not in Kuwait City where people were afraid to speak their names for fear of being stoned to death in the streets.

He grabbed Raj by his long robe and flung him onto the center of one of the tables of fish, the slimy bodies smashing beneath him and flopping off the table. He pointed a gun at the man's head and spoke in Arabic. "Where are the canisters?"

Screams sounded behind him, as the fish market cleared. Shouts called out for the military forces nearby. The wind shifted, and Michael didn't have to look to know Caleb and Adam Rain, identical twins, stood behind him, covering his back. He trusted Caleb completely, but Adam, not at all. Adam was a loose cannon developing a God Complex who Michael might one day have to kill to spare Caleb the pain of doing it himself. He suspected that was why Powell kept him paired with the two brothers. Because he knew Michael wouldn't hesitate to kill Adam no matter how much he respected Caleb. But for now, the two brothers made an impermeable shield, and Michael had a job to do.

Raj continued to plead for his freedom as Michael cocked the gun. "I don't have time for denial." There were millions of lives on the line, with reliable intel from the Israeli government that the attack was planned for sometime in the next twenty-four hours. A week and a half of chasing their tails for the details had led to only one person—Raj. He was all they had.

Raj spouted more denials. Michael moved the gun to the man's ear. "I'll start here and move on." Michael fired a warning shot, and Raj screamed as the bullet intentionally grazed his ear.

Gunfire sounded behind him. Caleb shouted at him, "Anytime now, Michael."

Michael shoved the gun to the man's crotch. "Last chance."

Raj spilled his guts before Michael did it for him. Michael released him, and without turning, called out a second before he faded into the wind, knowing Caleb and Adam would follow. "We're a go." He wasn't worried about Raj talking—he'd be killed for being a traitor.

———⁓———

Near sunrise, several hours later, in black fatigues, Michael materialized from inside the wind behind one of the four terrorists, who was arming the unlit fishing boat, and silently snapped the man's neck. Only a few feet away, two more insurgents were taken out by Caleb and Adam, wearing dark caps to conceal their short, light brown hair. If Raj's claims were accurate, then in exactly three minutes, a supply jeep would appear on the dark, dirt path leading to the dock—that jeep would hold the live biological agent they'd come for.

Michael quickly scanned for the fourth man, previously missing, but finally located him on the edge of the boat about to jump. Michael simply thought himself beside the man, and the wind made it so. In a matter of ten seconds, he'd snapped the man's neck. Quickly, he lifted the dead insurgent, dumping him below deck where Caleb and Adam had already stored the other bodies.

The eerie sound of wolves howling ripped through the distant woods. The three GTECHs stood side-by-side, eyes on those woods. Barely audible, Adam said, "Two snipers. Another ten insurgents a half mile down the hill. Here for the same reason as we are. They want the shipment that's on the way to that boat."

Michael narrowed his gaze on Adam. "How the hell do you know that?"

"The wolves," Adam said without looking at him, his attention on the dark line of the trees barely a kilometer away. "They've started talking to me."

What the F? "And do you talk back?" Michael asked.

"Working on that," Adam said. "I'll handle the snipers." The wind lifted a second before he was gone.

Michael cut Caleb a look. "Did you know about this?"

"It started last week on that mission to Asia we went on without you," he said. "The freaking wolves followed us everywhere."

Headlights flickered down the dirt path, and Michael and Caleb instantly faded into the shadows, taking cover. Michael took scout position behind the cabin, keeping the approaching target in sight. Caleb crouched low in a dark corner of the boat. The engine grew louder; the canvas-covered truck halted in front of the dock. Doors slammed shut. Male voices rumbled through the air.

The instant the last of the five men stepped on board, leaving the truck and the biological weapons unattended, Adam spoke into his headset. "Go." He didn't say "clear," which translated to: Adam still had his hands full, but he had them covered.

Michael signaled Caleb, and Caleb faded into the wind, going after that biological agent and leaving Michael to deal with the five men. Using the edge of silent wind-walking that made him lethal in ways no other GTECH could be, Michael methodically took out the men. Like a ghost, he appeared behind each, snapping their necks, and then disappearing. In less than a minute, he wind-walked to join Caleb, appearing behind the truck.

Michael found Caleb standing on the back ledge of the vehicle, lifting the canvas covering, unaware that a young boy, maybe fourteen, held a machine gun on his back. Michael drew the semi-automatic at his side, finger on the trigger.

Time seemed to stand still in the three seconds that passed, and that black place he called home when on the battlefield, slipped away. Dealing with the kid soldiers messed with his head. They always had. It was likely that the boy was fighting, serving the terrorists, because his mother—and brothers and sisters, if he had any—had been threatened. The line between killer and victim, man and boy, was skewed, which was the case all too often, yet Michael had never gotten used to it. Today the boy could become a killer and a man, if Michael let him, but then Caleb would be dead. Because even as a GTECH, Caleb had little chance of surviving a machine gun unloaded in the back of the head.

Michael fired his gun, hit the boy with a bullet in each arm, for good measure. The boy fell to the dirt screaming as Caleb jumped to the ground, a grim expression on his face showing he felt the same trauma over the boy that Michael did. "Michael," he said, "you had no choice."

The wind rippled as Adam appeared beside the boy and shot him. Michael went cold inside, his gaze connecting with Caleb's in shared discomfort.

From the nearby woods, a scream cut through the air, and Adam laughed. "The wolves were hungry." His gaze flickered to the boy. "Piece of shit human." He kicked the bloody, limp body, and Michael flinched with the action. "They're all pieces of shit, weak in every possible way."

He reeled back to kick the boy again, and Caleb grabbed him a second before Michael would have done so himself. "Enough!" Caleb said, glaring at his brother. "He is only a boy. A child and a victim, Adam. Probably trying to save his family."

Adam grabbed a handful of Caleb's fatigue jacket. "Oh come on, brother," he ground out. "Humans are no more than animals. They kill each other. We stop them. And for what? So they can try again. Maybe they are supposed to die so we can thrive." He let go of Caleb and eyed both of the men. "We evolve as they turn more Neanderthal with every passing day."

"Damn it, Adam," Caleb said, scrubbing his day-old stubble. "Stop talking crap. Sometimes I don't even know who you are anymore. Let's just do our jobs." He yanked down the tail of the truck and slid the wooden box forward.

"You'll come around, brother," Adam said, and glanced at Michael. "Once you're a little less human, like me. And Michael."

That comparison shredded what was left of Michael's gut. *Like me and Michael*. Michael glanced between the two brothers, so alike and so different—Caleb, who Michael knew would die to save an innocent human, and who might well have chosen that boy's life over his own; and Adam, who would kick the child while he was down.

Caleb pulled open the lid and exposed three airtight canisters, small, yet lethal—able to kill hundreds of thousands. Adam reached in and roughly removed a canister. "Eventually there must be an end so that there can be a new beginning."

There was an evil look in Adam's eyes that said he was considering opening that canister. Michael readied himself for action as Caleb grabbed his brother's wrist. "Enough. Put it down, Adam."

Adam laughed. "Maybe I'll keep one of these babies for myself." The wolves in the distance howled as if joining in on the joke. Another glare from Caleb, and Adam returned the canister to the crate and sealed the lid. "I'll do the honors of taking these to Powell." He grabbed the crate holding the canisters and faded into the wind.

Caleb cursed and eyed Michael. "I'll deal with Adam. And Powell." He disappeared.

Michael felt no compulsion to follow. He just hoped Caleb was truly as prepared as he claimed for what was to come, for the day when Michael would be forced to deal with Adam. A day that was coming sooner than later. The GTECH serum had done something to him, turned him into a monster. Caleb was a good guy, the one who wouldn't break rules. The one who needed someone like Michael by his side, someone who would.

He glanced down at the blood puddle at his feet, the blood of the young boy, the sight all too familiar, and told himself that every life he had ever taken had been necessary. He wasn't like his father, who'd sold weapons to foreign countries without concern for who lived or died, or his mother who justified his actions for money and security. Who hated him because he dared to shake up her perfect little world. Nor was he like Adam who killed for amusement. Michael had devoted himself to saving lives, and sometimes that meant taking lives. The GTECH serum had nothing to do with his choices, or Caleb's, for that matter. Caleb and Michael were not X2 positive. Adam was.

And it meant nothing that Michael and Adam had both developed special gifts—his own ability to communicate with the wind and Adam's to communication with the wolves. Michael balled his fists at his sides. He wasn't like Adam, damn it. *But you aren't like Caleb either*, the wind seemed to whisper back. In that moment, without any conscious decision to do so, Michael faded into the wind. More and more, it seemed to communicate with him, almost speak to him. And it knew where he wanted to go. It knew he needed an escape, to pretend he was still human—when sometimes he wondered if he had ever really been human.

<hr />

An hour and a half later, Michael leaned against the back wall of Vegas's version of Coyote Ugly, known for loud music and hot women in Daisy Dukes and cowboy boots, several of whom were dancing on the bar above the rows of tables.

He had no idea why he was still here, pretending to watch the dancers, why he hadn't done his normal post-mission roundup of a woman—or two or three— and already gone and buried himself, and the hell of his mission, in their many pleasures. Or why he had to keep talking himself out of going to see Cassandra when he knew damn well that was a bad idea. "What can I do you for, Michael?" There was no mistaking the invitation in the sweet southern drawl of Becky Lee, the twenty-something redhead who'd sidled up beside him and pressed her ample breasts and a sleek body against his side. She knew why he was here as well as he did. A woman liberal with her sexual preferences, willing to try about anything, who didn't want a commitment, Becky Lee was exactly Michael's kind of pleasure, and this wouldn't be the first time she'd serviced his post-mission needs.

Michael eyed her, his gaze raking the curves of her bountiful cleavage, expecting that rush of raw, primal need, the need that beckoned him to seek female comfort and seemed to draw females to his side. That same rush that got worse with every return home since he'd become GTECH. But he felt nothing. Not one damn thing. Michael ground his teeth at the thought. Damn it to hell, what was wrong with him?

He tilted back his beer and downed it, wishing his GTECH metabolism didn't burn off the alcohol practically before he swallowed. There was no pleasure to be found from booze, just a reminder of exactly what he was trying to escape—that he wasn't human. But sex gave him escape—sex made him feel alive, gave him a release. Frustration churned in his gut, and Michael grabbed Becky and pulled her with him. He was damn sure getting his escape.

A few seconds later, Michael dragged a laughing, pleased Becky down the deserted hallway, by the restroom, and out the back door exit. The minute they were outside, he pulled her lush curves against him and slid his hand into her silky red hair in preparation to kiss her, but was unable to execute.

Breathlessly, Becky Lee whispered, "I'm dying here, Michael. Kiss me. I need you to kiss me." But she didn't need him, not really. She *wanted* him, wanted the rush of sex with someone who burned for the escape it offered as much as she did. And there was a time when that had been a perfect match for Michael, a time when that made her a short-term kindred spirit. A time when holding a woman and knowing he gave her pleasure made him feel like something other than a monster. But tonight wasn't that night. Or rather, this wasn't the woman, any more than any of the others inside that bar were.

Michael released Becky Lee and led her back inside. "What you need is a drink."

Several minutes later, he exited the back door alone, the need inside him nearly primal now, a need beyond resisting, beyond any form of denial. Michael faded into the wind and reappeared on Cassandra's back patio.

———

Near midnight, Cassandra sat in the overstuffed chair in her bedroom, a stack of research papers on her lap, the rare cool evening breeze, compliments of a hit-and-run August storm, drifting past the curtains covering her open sliding-glass doors. She'd dressed for bed and promised herself she'd go to sleep at a reasonable hour, knowing full well that fourteen-hour days were wearing on her. But this X2 research was wearing on her too. There had been five more soldiers who'd tested positive for a total of fifteen. Out of those, a third of them were displaying out-of-character aggression, and as a result, her father wanted all fifteen men turned into pincushions. Washington had supported his immunization program because he'd given them an amazing weapon in the GTECHs. He wasn't going to risk losing that support, no matter what he put these men through. It was a miracle any of the GTECHs were still sane, but she'd give her father credit, he'd picked soldiers who endured and thrived.

A breeze lifted the curtains ever so slightly, and her gaze shifted to the doorway. Her thoughts immediately went to Michael, wondering when, or if, he'd ask her out again. Every time they got a little steamy, he ran for the hills. With all the heat between them, and all those legendary stories of his conquests, she wasn't sure what to make of it, but she worried it had something to do with the disapproval she sensed in him when the subject of her father came up. Not that she wanted to be one of his conquests, but well, maybe he could be one of hers.

She laughed at the insanity of that idea and then laughed some more in memory of their second date to play Putt Putt mini-golf when she'd smashed a ball into someone's car—a BMW, of all makes. The owner had, thankfully, been generous in his forgiveness, but Cassandra had been horrified. That was, until Michael, "The Dark One," had smiled and kissed her on the nose—she'd forgotten her embarrassment. She remembered looking into his eyes, all twinkling with crystal blue amusement, and feeling a connection. There was something different about him in that moment, beyond the smile she'd finally dragged out of him. He'd let his guard down.

Suddenly, the curtain lifted with a full-out gust of wind, and Cassandra could have sworn it called her name. Almost instantly she shook her head. This crush on Michael was making her crazy.

She set her file on the table beside the chair and pushed to her feet, her sheer white gown settling just above her knees. She intended to shut the back door and go to bed, but was also more than a little eager to peek outside. Pulling back the curtain, she saw the dim glow of her porch light sprayed across the porch, illuminating a tall figure standing several feet away from the doorway.

Cassandra blinked, certain she was imagining Michael standing there, but no, he was actually here, looking as lethally male as ever—and a bit like a warrior of old, with his hair framing that strong face and broad shoulders. That thought sent her stomach on a roller coaster ride. Oh God. He was a warrior—or rather, a soldier who'd just returned from a mission. She knew all about these midnight visits and the bad news that came with them.

She shoved open the screen and stepped in her bare feet toward him, all thought of her sheer gown forgotten. There was only the certainty her world was about to crumble around her. "Tell me. Just tell me now. It's my father, isn't it?"

"No," he said quickly. "Everything is fine. He's fine." He scrubbed his jaw. "*Everyone* is fine."

"You're sure?" she asked, searching his face for confirmation. "Please tell me you're sure."

He nodded sharply. "Yes," he said. "I'm sure."

"Oh thank God," Cassandra said, letting out a relieved breath, her hand still pressed to her chest where her heart had darn near ripped a hole. For all her father's flaws, he was all she had, and she loved him.

"I didn't mean to scare you," he said, taking a step backwards. "Coming here was a mistake."

"Wait!" she said quickly, certain he was about to disappear, closing the distance between them and grabbing his arm. "Please. Don't go. You came here for a reason, and you haven't even told me what that is." But she could see from the tension in his expression, he'd already shut her out. She didn't want him to shut her out. "Talk to me, Michael. What happened? Was it a mission?"

He hesitated, and said softly, "It's always a mission."

So something was wrong. Something had upset him, and he'd come here, to her, for comfort. Her heart swelled with that knowledge. Michael, who shut out everyone, had come to her. Her fingers slid down his arm to his hand. She drew it into hers. "Can you talk about it?"

"I wouldn't if I could," he said. "It's nothing you want to hear."

"I'm pretty tough," she promised.

He pulled her close and held her, burying his face in her hair, the warmth of him surrounding her. "I know you are," he said softly. "And too good for the hell of my life. Which is why I feel so damn selfish for needing you."

He tried to set her away from him, as if he planned to leave. Cassandra held tight, shocked by his confession, by his vulnerability. "You aren't going anywhere without me. I won't let you push me away. I need you too."

The fire in his eyes was instant, the low guttural moan that slid from his throat, primal. She barely remembered the moment he lifted her, hands intimately palming her backside. There was only the passionate wildness of his kiss and the need to wrap herself around him, to get close and then closer. She didn't even remember entering the house—completely out of her conservative nature. He could have taken her on the patio, and she would have begged him to take her again. She just wanted him, and yes, needed him.

Somehow, they made it to the mattress, her on her back and her gown on the floor. But shyness jolted her out of her wanton abandon when he rolled to his side, still fully clothed, and flattened his hand on her stomach, his gaze hot in its perusal.

Cassandra tried to sit up, but his hand pressed her back in place.

"What are you doing?" she asked, suddenly feeling exposed, vulnerable herself now. Why wasn't he as lost in passion as she was?

"Admiring you," he said, his hand gently brushed her nipple, and she barely contained a moan. She didn't want to be out of control when he was not.

He slid back on top of her, as if he sensed she was ready to bolt, trapping her beneath his big body and spreading her legs with his knees. Long raven hair framing his shoulders, reminding her again of a warrior— a wild, wicked warrior. *Her* warrior. It was a crazy thought, as wild and wicked as the man. But for tonight, he was hers, for tonight there was only the two of them, only the need that she saw in his eyes, tasted on his lips as they brushed gently over hers.

"This is the part where you relax and let me show you how beautiful you are." He kissed her neck, her ear. "So very beautiful." And so he did—slowly, seductively, perfectly. She lost herself to pleasure, lost time, lost coherent thought, as Michael's mouth found her breasts, her nipples, the aching V of her body. There was something magical about the way he touched her, the way he looked at her, that stole the inhibitions of her past and demanded she give herself fully to him. That demanded she lose herself and find him.

His tongue brushed her nipple, and her back arched, a soft moan slipping from her lips. He lifted his head, his crystal blue eyes touching hers, brimming with molten heat.

"I like it when you moan for me."

She touched his face, wanting so desperately to know the man beneath the warrior. "Your eyes," she said. "Show me the real color." She felt, rather than saw, his reaction, the instant tension in his body and responded. "The real you. That's who I want. That's who I *need*."

He stared at her, unmoving, barely breathing, until his mouth was on hers, hot and demanding, drawing her into a frenzied burn of pure hot sensation. Their hands were all over each other, their clothes vanishing. She never felt such an ache to feel skin against skin.

Time faded into moans, into sighs, into the ache of her body's need for him to be inside her that had her calling out when he pushed away from her to stand at the end of the bed—naked, rippling perfection, every bit as delicious as she'd imagined. Instinct sent her to the edge of the mattress, eager to touch him again, to feel him and look at him. He reached for her and pulled her with him as he sat down on the chair. "I need to be inside you, Cassandra," he said, easing her legs across him.

"Yes," she agreed breathlessly, letting him brace her

as she slid down the long, hard length of him until he was buried deeply, completely.

His hand tangled in her long blonde hair, gently tugging her mouth to his. "Do you feel how much I need you?" His hips shifted, his cock expanding within her, stroking her with one long, teasing caress.

"Yes," she gasped as he did it again.

His eyes shifted blue to black. "Are you scared now, Cassandra?"

She didn't want to fall for a soldier, didn't want to worry or be hurt, and her heart said it was too late. She wasn't falling for him. She'd fallen. "Yes," she whispered, leaning back farther, ensuring that he could see the emotion behind her words. "You scare the hell out of me, Michael Taylor."

"The feeling is mutual, sweetheart," he said, before he claimed her mouth in a hot, hungry kiss that paled to the wildness that followed. He let her feel the vulnerability and pain behind each stroke of his cock, each caress of his tongue. He needed her, and that didn't scare her. But how much she needed him… did.

―∾∾―

Michael wasn't good for Cassandra. He knew it. He was pretty damn sure she knew it too. But there was an odd feeling of peace inside him while he was with her, a feeling that almost—*almost*—as impossible as he thought it to be—made him feel human.

Michael had told himself to leave before she woke up, to make last night a mistake not to be repeated. But after getting dressed, he'd sat down in that chair where they'd made love and was still there when her alarm went off. And damn if he wasn't glad he'd stayed around because seeing her with her hair wild and her lips swollen from his kisses, was an invitation to a good morning that had him following her to the kitchen while she made coffee.

"I hope you like your caffeine so strong it'll peel your eyelids back," she said, a few minutes later in the kitchen.

"The stronger the motor oil," he said, leaning an elbow on the cabinet across from her, "the better."

She smiled her approval, turned to the cabinet, and pushed to her tip toes, trying to reach a mug. Michael would have helped her, but he was too busy admiring her cute heart-shaped butt, outlined in silk, and trying to talk himself out of setting her up on that counter and taking her right here and now.

She turned to face him, mugs in hand. "You GTECHs might not need much sleep, but I—" A gasp cut off her words, the mugs flying in the air, as her knees buckled.

Michael caught her around the waist, and she collapsed against him. "My neck," she whispered, barely able to speak. "It… hurts." She balled her fists on his chest, desperation in her pain-stricken face.

He lifted her and carried her to the couch, sitting down and cradling her shaking body in his arms. "Easy, sweetheart," he soothed, running his hand over her hair. He didn't have to look at her neck to know what was happening, any more than he imagined she did. He'd known to stay away from her, known he was treading dangerous waters, and now, he'd marked her.

Long minutes later, she eased off his lap onto the

cushion. "I'm okay. I think it's passing now." They stared at each other several tense seconds before she confirmed she was thinking the same thing he was when she said, "You should check my neck."

He nodded, and she slowly turned, lifting her hair to expose her neck. The instant Michael saw that mark on her skin, a rush of pure white-hot possessiveness flared inside him. He wrapped his arm around her waist and pulled her to him, pressing his lips to the double circle on her neck, wanting nothing more than to make love to her, to mark her yet again as his.

"Michael," she whispered, leaning into him, and he could feel her responding to his need, feel the passion turning damn near combustible. "Is it…?"

"Yes," he said, turning her in his arms, resting his forehead against hers. They were both breathing heavily, both barely controlling themselves. His fingers brushed her cheek.

Her hand covered his, holding it to her face as if she couldn't bear to lose the touch. "I should call Kelly."

"No," he said, fixing her in a stare, letting her see just how wild the fire was in his eyes. "No one can know about this. I won't let you get turned into a lab rat. Not because of me."

"I trust Kelly," she said. "She'll keep this to herself."

"Until something worries her and she feels obligated to tell your father," he said, releasing her, trying to get himself under control—feeling protectiveness fill the space that had been possessiveness and passion only moments before.

He pushed to his feet and ran his hand over his head, giving her his back, knowing he had to make her understand the importance of keeping their bond a secret. And so, he did the only thing he knew to do—he admitted to her what he had told no other—not even Caleb, who he trusted with his life. "You were right— that first day we met." He kept his back to her, avoiding any fear he might see in her eyes. "I *am* different than the other GTECHs."

"The wind," she said softly prodding. "You have a special bond of some sort with it."

He turned to face her, not even trying to mask the emotion in his face. She looked small, her long hair pushed behind her ears, exposing the uncertain emotion in her eyes. For a moment, he had to remind himself she might look and feel, even smell, like a delicate little flower in his arms, but she was tough. Otherwise she couldn't stand up to her father, as he'd already figured out, she did often. She could deal with the truth, just like she dealt with him. "Yes. Yes, I have some special connection to it, and who knows what else I don't know about yet. I won't let you end up under a microscope because of me. You have access to all the testing being done on the other marked women. You'll know what you need to know." He went to her then, bent down on one knee, and rested his hands on hers. "You can't tell Kelly or anyone else. I was selfish coming to you last night, and I will never forgive myself for that. But I'm telling you right now, I will do anything, and everything, no matter what cost to me, to protect you from any harm from this. This is our secret."

She hesitated, her expression cloudy, confused, before she nodded. "Yes. Yes okay. It's our secret."

He pulled her close, his relief at her agreement little

comfort, knowing that there was no known weapon, no GTECH skill, no drug that could undo what he'd done. He'd just changed Cassandra's life forever.

Chapter 3

CASSANDRA STOOD AT THE GRILL ON HER BACK PATIO, while Michael scavenged in the kitchen for some manly utensil he couldn't do without. It was an unseasonably warm day in November, six months since that day the mark had appeared on her neck, and she felt exactly the same as before it had appeared. But their relationship had not stayed the same—their bond was stronger, the passion, their *need*, so intense she could taste him on her lips just by thinking of him, feel his approach in the tingle on the back of her neck. This bond was something all the marked couples shared and the reason the scientific team now called the bonded males and females "Lifebonds," to signify a marriage by nature. But since the lifebond research had been classified beyond her clearance several months earlier, she knew little else. Ironically though, Michael's seemingly intense need to conceal their lifebonding from the rest of the world didn't leave him much room to protect her from the monster he considered himself.

"Step aside," Michael ordered from behind, a moment before he stepped to the edge of the grill with a fork the size of Texas in his hand, his long raven hair bristling in the light breeze.

"Oh good grief." She laughed. "That thing belongs on a battlefield, not at the grill." She'd barely gotten the words out when several cold raindrops splattered on her face. She eyed the dark line of clouds hovering above, ready to explode on their little outdoor adventure at any moment. She cast Michael a hopeful look. "I don't suppose you can handle the rain like you do the wind, and you just haven't told me yet?"

"No, but I cook a mean steak," he said, patting her blue-jean-shorts-clad backside. "And if I don't get them inside on the stove before the downpour, you might have to discover that talent another day."

Her stomach rumbled with the promise of a good meal, and she rushed into action by his side, grabbing the wine and two long-stemmed crystal glasses sitting on the steel patio table. Both the wine and the glasses were gifts from Michael, made more thoughtful and wonderful because they came after he'd learned she had a thing for trying new wines. Turned out, his mother had as well. It was one of the few tidbits about his family she'd managed to get out of him. But one day, she vowed, she'd unveil all the hidden pieces of the puzzle that was Michael.

He headed toward the door with the steaks loaded on top of a foil-covered pan, but on second thought, stepped backwards and snatched the Texas-sized fork off the grill. "Can't leave without my weapon," he teased, a smile lifting his lips a moment before he disappeared inside the house.

Cassandra stared after him, that smile warming her, telling her the walls were coming down, one by one. That only made the guilt she felt about keeping a secret from him all the more intense. Several months before, when tensions had risen between X2 positives and negatives on a mission, her father had sealed all the test results so that none of the soldiers knew who was positive and who was negative. But she knew Michael was on that X2 positive list, just like she knew what it would do to him if he ever found out.

———⁓———

Not long after the base had cleared for the evening, Powell walked through the animal lab, inspecting the cages riddled with dead, X2-positive animals after they'd finished attacking each other. He couldn't believe this had happened after he'd finally received the phone call he'd been campaigning for since before the first GTECH injection had been given—an invitation to the White House by the secretary of state. The president and chiefs of staff were pleased with the GTECH program and had high hopes for both it and Powell. But they wanted to be absolutely confident that the program could not backfire in their faces. It was his chance to show he was one of the great leaders of this country. But now there was this X2 gene problem.

"Their behavior," Dr. Chin said from behind him, "was not only widespread, but sudden and unexpected. This supports the theory of a trigger setting them off. There is no indicator of what that might be."

Powell's gaze lingered on one of the cages before he turned to face Dr. Chin, director of science and medicine for Project Zodius. Dr. Chin had proven to be admirably ambitious and loyal beyond the expectations of his employment by the U.S. government. "Who else knows about this?"

"Myself and my assistant, Ava Lane. The rest of the staff had already left for the day."

Powell eyed the curvy redhead on the other side of the glass panel as she studied a slide under a microscope; she'd made it onto his radar for more than her sultry looks. Ava had masterminded a blood exchange between one of the marked women and her male partner. The result was that the woman converted to GTECH without using the limited supply of serum.

Powell cut Chin a sideways look. "And Dr. Peterson?" he asked, well aware that Kelly Peterson often lunched with his daughter.

"Left shortly before the animals' erratic behavior began. I thought you'd want to know before anyone else."

"As it should be," Powell approved. "No one else knows." Especially his daughter. Cassandra had done her job as he knew she would—meticulously reporting the soldiers' mental capacities as slightly aggressive within normal ranges, despite her warnings this could change. A detail that had pleased the White House, but defied what he saw before him today in these X2 animals. She wouldn't understand why her tests were not enough. He motioned to the cages. "Do what you have to so that it remains that way. Is there any more 'kick in the teeth' news you care to share, Chin?"

"Not only is the marked female converted to GTECH, but the female will become X2 positive if her Lifebond is X2 positive. Early stage laboratory studies support a hypothesis that the 'Lifebonds' become capable of reproducing once the blood exchange is complete, though the men were previously infertile."

"Fabulous," he said, his voice dripping with sarcasm. "So now we can breed X2 monsters. That should please the White House." He walked toward the cages, scrubbing his palm across his face, all too aware he was backed into a corner. The X2s were simply too big a potential liability to be ignored. There was only one way to avoid long-term confinement of the X2s, and he knew it. Red Dart. Created by an alien crystal, the laser inserted a chemical into the target's bloodstream, allowing for both tracking and control by torture. It had been confiscated from an alien shipwreck some fifty years ago, but was never successfully manifested for use. When he'd seen the writing on the wall—that human law was no means to manage inhuman soldiers—he'd covertly confiscated the research.

He rotated to face Chin. "We're using Red Dart. Now. Today. I don't care how risky, how potentially fatal. I don't care. Just make it work."

"Science does not take orders, General," Chin said. "Nor will it be rushed. Again, as I've told you numerous times, Red Dart was designed for humans, not GTECHs. And even in humans, it's killing the carrier rather than torturing them. The GTECHs are another story. Death isn't my concern—they heal too rapidly. It's the application. Their immune systems destroy the tracking dart before it ever hits the bloodstream, which is necessary for it to function properly. It's worthless until I figure out how to trick their immune systems into seeing Red Dart as part of its normal operating system."

Silently, Powell cursed, using every profane word in the dictionary. And some that were not. Outwardly, he remained cool, collected. "If I double your funding, how soon can it be ready?"

"A year," Chin said quickly. "Maybe longer. Too long, considering we have no idea what set off the violence in these animals to begin with. The X2 positive soldiers could do the same thing at any given moment."

The words ground through Powell's stomach. Every fucking thing he'd worked for could be flushed down the toilet over this. "You're certain it's X2 related?" he asked.

"I am of the belief that all GTECHs are the unknown and thus volatile," Chin said. "Exactly why I'm willing to work on Red Dart. But specifically," he motioned to the cages, "this threat is directly linked to the X2 gene."

Confining those X2s, a group of nearly invincible soldiers, would take strategic planning, substantial manpower, and a creative story prepared for the secretary of state. His mind ran down a path that twisted and turned. Thankfully, the soldiers had never been told about the X2 gene, so there would be no connecting the dots. He'd tell the X2s they were being reassigned for further alien enhancements and given a new serum to make them bigger and stronger. They'd go willingly, then be lured to containment cells under the guise of protecting the medical personnel from potential side effects. The secretary of state would be pleased they were moving to another level of development with Zodius. This would buy him time.

A smile touched his lips. There was a reason he was headed for the White House. No challenge was too great.

Adam Rain lurked in the shadows of the parking lot outside the launch pad leading to the underground Groom Lake facility as the elevator opened and Ava exited. His eyes followed the sultry strut of her hips as she approached, admiring her long legs. She was the woman who secretly wore his mark. The woman who would one day, when the time was right, bear his child, a child who would be the future leader of a new superpower, the Zodius Nation. It would be a nation free of weakness and crude, human diseases. Adam's nation. And that day was almost here.

Ava approached, and Adam pulled her hard into his arms, his hand molding her soft, hot body against his, and kissed her, feeding the wild hunger inside himself before tearing his mouth from hers. "What was so urgent it could not wait? Or were you simply urgent to feel me inside you again, my little Ava?"

Her hands pressed to his chest, her eyes wide with urgency. "It's Powell." She panted past the kiss. "He's afraid of the X2 positives. He plans to imprison them."

Anger ripped through him. "When?"

"Tomorrow," she said, her eyes sparking with matching anger.

Adam cursed. The underground facility he'd funded through private investors with the promise of converting them to GTECHs wasn't ready yet, nor had they gotten their hands on the serum to mass produce it. Perhaps there was a bright side to this. His brother had been clinging to humanity's goodness, the same humanity that was about to cage the GTECHs and throw away the key. Perhaps even exterminate them, which is what he would tell his followers, accurate or not. Even Caleb would see the writing on the wall that humans corrupted everything they touched. It was us or them—and the stronger group, the GTECHs, would prevail.

"My following at Groom Lake runs deep," he said,

and not just with GTECHs. The human soldiers sent to battle in their natural, vulnerable form, resented being denied GTECH conversion. "We'll have no problem seizing control."

"The army will bring in reinforcements," she warned.

"The army will fear aggressive action that might alert the humans to an alien takeover," he said. "Any attempts to stop us will be weak, and we will prevail."

"Adam—"

His fingers wrapped around the back of her neck and pulled her close. "Do not fear, my beauty. Soon you will be the queen of a new nation that will grow and prosper. No one will stop us."

"No one will stop us," she whispered.

After eating their barbecue feast, an attempt to watch a movie was waylaid by passion. Hours of passion. Hours of *wonderful, amazing* passion. Cassandra lay curled on Michael's chest in the middle of a blanket on the living room floor, naked and only half-sated, the rain having long ago passed. She felt warm and wonderful inside, and she knew this was the moment—the time to share her past and tell him about her mother. She couldn't explain why, but she needed to do this.

But before she got the chance, he rolled her onto her back, his long raven hair tickling her cheeks, those black eyes piercing hers with emotion. "Cassandra," he said softly. "Do you know how much I—?" The wind gusted through the window, permeating the curtains and splattering rain onto the tiled kitchen floor.

Michael went ramrod stiff, the confession he'd

been about to make lost to the interruption, leaving Cassandra hanging on his words. A second gust of wind shot through the window, unnatural, like a demand. That gust confirmed in her mind that whatever was happening was created by "someone," not the "something" of Mother Nature.

Further confirmation came with Michael's reaction. "Stay here," he ordered, not waiting for a reply. This was the soldier she knew as part of him, and that soldier wasn't in "welcome" mode. He was dressed in seconds and out the door, pulling it shut behind him.

Cassandra slipped on her tank top and shorts, foregoing her shoes out of urgency. Unexplainable dread twisted in her gut, a sense of unease inside her that pulsed with life as she peered through the curtains. Adam and Michael stood outside facing each other, the wind whistling briskly around them—and as she had discovered these past months, the wind did not move, certainly did not whistle, unless Michael allowed it to do so. No one else had that power. Until now, she'd assumed his fellow GTECHs knew that, but she wasn't so sure. Because either Michael was concealing his ability, or he was too pissed to bother with controlling the wind. Or both. Adam set Michael on edge. She'd seen it when they were together, sensed it with the simple mention of Adam's name. Caleb was another story. Michael's admiration for him was clear.

Michael knew Adam was X2 positive, and he knew Caleb was not. If Michael knew that he himself was X2 positive, he'd think he was like Adam, and she wasn't going to let that happen. As much as she feared losing the hard-earned trust between them, she had come to know she loved Michael, too much to see him condemn himself unfairly. The wind shifted, pressing against the window. It was then that Caleb appeared, and Cassandra felt a sense of relief that was short-lived. Even without sound, it was clear from the body language and expressions that while Michael listened intently, Adam and Caleb were in a heated exchange. When finally Caleb and Adam departed, Michael walked back to her, his face grim, far more turbulent than the storm now passed; she felt her stomach twist with the certainty that something was terribly wrong.

Her hand shook as she opened the door to greet him. "What's wrong? What's going on?" She moved back into the kitchen to allow him to enter. He stayed on the patio, distant, and not just physically. "Michael?"

He grabbed her then and pulled her to him, hands laced in her hair. "No matter what happens to me," he said, "do not tell anyone you wear my mark."

"What?" she gasped. "Why? What's going on?"

"Promise me, Cassandra. No matter what. No matter how things seem, you stay silent."

"I… okay. Yes. We already agreed I—" He kissed her then, swallowing her objections in a deep, passionate, I-really-care-about-you, but I'm-saying-good-bye kind of kiss that ended with him fading into the wind.

Her eyes prickled, dampness clinging to her cheeks. Because wherever Michael had gone, he didn't believe he was coming back.

Chapter 4

MONDAY MORNING, DRESSED FOR WORK, HER PURSE ON her shoulder, Cassandra was in heavy pursuit of her keys, which she'd somehow misplaced, when she stepped into the slim hallway leading to the living room and stopped dead in her tracks. The scent, so uniquely Michael, laced the air.

A memory took shape in the shadowy recesses of her mind—of waking up with a tingle at the back of her neck that she'd only recently started to feel when he was near. Had he been here? While she slept? She shook her head. No, that was nuts. She hadn't seen or heard from him since Saturday night. She glanced at the clock on the wall and shook off the memory, cringing with her tardiness. She'd arranged to have ten lab techs begin a round of brainwave testing on the soldiers as of mid-morning, and she still had preparations to do.

Another ten minutes of searching for her keys, and she gave in and called Kelly to come get her. "You lost your keys?" Kelly said. "How very unCassandra-like of you."

Five minutes later, Kelly pulled her blue Camry to the curb and shoved the passenger's door open.

"Something is going on," Cassandra said the minute she slid inside, as she started replaying the events of the weekend.

"Adam's involvement is enough to make me nervous," Kelly said, cutting her a worried look. "I don't care what your profiles say about the man being within normal aggressive range. When you look into his eyes, pure evil looks back. I am betting these brainwave tests of yours are going to be far more revealing than discovering the X2 gene has been."

Cassandra's cell phone rang, and she fished it out of her purse, silently wishing for a call from Michael. Instead, it was one of her staff members. The call was quick, and she hung up more worried than ever.

"Okay, Kelly. Now I know something is wrong. My staff received a memo that all soldiers scheduled for the brainwave testing were indefinitely reassigned."

"Reassigned?" Kelly quaked, whipping into the main parking lot. "What does 'reassigned' mean? As in another military base? The GTECHs?"

"I don't know," Cassandra said, motioning across the parking lot as she spotted her father in deep conversation with a ranking officer. "But I intend to find out." The minute the car stopped, Cassandra was out of the door, purse over her shoulder. "I'll meet you in the lab." She slammed the door and took off across the pavement, her black high-heels pounding across the concrete slab.

"Father!" she yelled, making sure he knew she was here and wasn't about to let him get away.

With a barely-there glance over his shoulder, he offered a short wave of acknowledgement and continued speaking to the officer. About the time Cassandra reached the two men, the officer saluted and then headed across the parking lot.

"I'm on my way to a meeting," her father said. "Whatever you need is going to have to wait." He started walking away, dismissing her.

She double-stepped to keep up with him, firming her voice. "I just heard that some of the GTECHs in my studies have been reassigned. Why wasn't I told?"

"You'll get a briefing when everyone else does," he said, quickening his pace.

She grabbed his arm, drawing him to a halt. "Don't dismiss me like I'm one of your soldiers." He'd apparently forgotten she could be as dogmatic as her mother when she wanted answers. "You brought me here to do a job. I need to know what's going on to do it. I can quit. They can't."

"You try my nerves, Cassandra. You are my daughter, but you are also an employee of the base who will get the information as I deem it necessary."

"I can't do my job without proper communication. I had expensive, specialized testing scheduled this morning that just got flushed down the drain."

"Duty first, Cassandra," he said tightly. "I've taken command of a secondary base which required immediate high-level security. You'll find a list of soldiers removed from evaluation status is already in your inbox."

"How many soldiers?" she demanded.

"Fifty."

That was one-fourth of the GTECHs. "What about our research? We don't know enough about the GTECHs to simply send them off to duty like any other soldier."

"Dr. Chin left this morning with the troops," he said. "He'll oversee the scientific monitoring and research of the GTECH program. Dr. Peterson will be promoted in his absence."

Nothing about this felt right. "You relocated Michael, didn't you?"

"He met certain requirements for the assignment, yes."

Yet Michael hadn't said he was being relocated. Michael would have said good-bye. "What requirements?"

"He's a cold-hearted killer," he said. "Never blinks an eye at a command, no matter how bloody it may be."

She all but visibly flinched at both the tone and content of the statement. He knew she was seeing Michael and had made his disapproval known, but now he was going too far. "If you have something to say to me, Father, say it, but don't involve Michael. And don't judge him for doing what you order him to do."

"I don't remember saying I was judging him at all," he replied dryly. "I simply answered your question. You wanted to know what requirements Michael met for his relocation, to which I replied—he's a cold-hearted killer."

He'd said it again, and added even more bite. Her mind tracked back to the night before. To Michael's words. *No matter what happens to me, do not tell anyone you wear my mark.* And considering Caleb and Adam's visit had sparked the warning, she was beginning to piece this together. "Were Caleb and Adam also relocated?"

"Adam, yes," he stated. "Caleb, no."

That horrible feeling in her chest spread to her stomach. Adam, the man Kelly had just referred to as "evil," had gone with Michael. Caleb had not. And now her father was basically accusing Michael of enjoying the act of killing. "What have you done, Father?"

The question was swallowed as the humid Nevada wind rushed against them—unnatural, violent—a second before Adam Rain solidified in front of them and dropped a limp body onto the hood of the Jeep.

"He tried to lock me in a cage," Adam declared,

glaring at her father, black eyes framed by sculpted bone structure. His full lips twisted in contempt. "That's a good way to piss me off."

Shock held Cassandra, eyes riveted on the broken man on the truck, blood trickling from his mouth. The wind lifted again, tangling the loose hair around Cassandra's neckline and throwing dirt and rock from the nearby desert terrain at her feet. Relief washed over Cassandra as the mark on the back of her neck tingled with the certainty that Michael approached. Michael could control Adam, where her father could not.

Michael appeared beside Adam, and four more GTECHs formed a V formation behind the two of them—as if they were standing behind their leaders, as if Michael stood with Adam. Cassandra rejected the warning sizzling down her spine. Michael worked with Adam, ran missions with Adam. To see them together was not abnormal. But there was that warning, growing stronger by the second. And he wasn't looking at her. *Why* wasn't he looking at her?

"Michael?" she said, needing him to look at her, to reassure her everything was okay.

"Go inside, Cassandra," her father ordered.

"Yes," Adam agreed. "Go inside, Cassandra. That is, unless you want to watch your father bleed to death."

Cassandra's gaze rocketed to Michael, and she stepped toward him. The wind gusted, as if in response, pushing her backwards several steps. She stumbled and somehow regained her footing, only to be pushed backwards yet again.

Her chest tightened as she saw her father step toe-to-toe with Adam, and desperately she searched for help, finding that the parking lot had turned into a ghost town. Everything about this was wrong. Everything spelled disaster in the process. She forced herself to turn and run toward the elevator, telling herself Michael would protect her father, Michael would handle Adam. She had to warn the others on the base, to call for backup. She punched the elevator button and refused to look behind her, unable to face the prospect that her father might be lying dead on the ground.

"Michael will save him," she said, the verbal assurance allowing her to rush into the open elevator.

The minute the car hit basement level, she charged out of the doors. "Help! I need help!" But there was no one where there were usually many, and the red emergency phone was ripped from the wall.

"Kelly," she whispered and took off running, her heart in her throat. Please let Kelly be okay.

Cassandra burst through the doors of the lab where she'd told Kelly she would meet her and stopped dead in her footsteps. Ava Lane, with whom Cassandra had never shared more than an uncomfortable greeting, stood alone, arms crossed in front of her full bosom, the glint of evil in her pale green eyes enough to send a chill down Cassandra's spine.

"In a hurry?" she asked.

"Late for work," Cassandra said, trying to act nonchalant as she started to rush past Ava, with one intention—to call Caleb. Michael trusted Caleb.

"At one point I thought you were Michael's intended Lifebond," Ava said. "But no Lifebond would keep the secret you kept from him. I would certainly never keep any secret from Adam."

The biting accusation, along with the obvious proclamation that she was Adam's Lifebond, stopped Cassandra in her tracks. She and Ava were nearly face-to-face now, only a few steps separating them before Cassandra would have stepped around the lab table. "What are you talking about?"

"Michael knows he's X2 positive," she said. "And he knows you knew and didn't tell him. Did you know your father was going to lock him away because of it?"

"No," she said, her throat dry. "No. That's not what was supposed to happen. My father—"

"—should be thanked," she said. "He gave us a reason to act. Once we've claimed control of the base, we will begin to create a new world, free of weak, useless humans like yourself. It is the nature of evolution, a chance for a better Zodius race."

Cassandra pressed her hand to her temple, willing herself to think logically, to remain calm. Again, she replayed Michael's words in her mind. *No matter what happens, do not tell anyone you wear my mark.* It had been a warning—about this, about Adam and Ava.

Ava's cell phone buzzed, and she glanced at the screen. "Darn," she said. "Adam needs me. I was really hoping to stick around for the special treat Michael has lined up for you." She laughed. "Bet you can't wait to find out what it is." She waggled her fingers and headed for the door.

The instant Ava was gone, Cassandra bolted for her office to call for help, only to find her phone and computer ripped from the wall. She raced around her desk to the bottom drawer where she kept the Glock her father had taught her to shoot when she was twelve, only to come up dry again. The drawer was open, the gun gone.

She leaned on the desk, defeated. "Think Cassandra. Think. What now?"

The mark on her neck began to tingle, and she reacted immediately. "Michael," she yelled, certain he hadn't betrayed her. Certain he was here to save her.

But when she rounded the doorway and brought the lab into view, her hope and her world crumbled at her feet. Michael was, indeed, there, but he wasn't alone. He had her father in front of him, and he held a blade at his throat. Blood trickling from an open wound, no doubt the method used to keep him from warning her.

"Michael," she whispered, her eyes prickling with unshed tears. "Please don't do this."

The plea had barely left her lips when Michael lifted a gun and pointed it at her. Time stood still as she stared down at the tranquilizer in her arm, and then the world that had crumbled went black.

~~~

Cassandra woke abruptly, climbing through the darkness of a deep sleep to jerk to a sitting position, quickly registering that she was in a bed, steel rails on either side of her. An IV hung from her arm. Green curtains covered the windows to the right. She was in the hospital.

"Easy, sweetie," came Kelly's gentle voice, as her friend rushed out of the nearby restroom. "I knew you'd wake up while I was in there."

Kelly. Kelly was here. Cassandra cut through the tangled memories weaving through the blank spots of her mind. Michael's betrayal. The knife. "My father!"

she exclaimed urgently, adrenaline rocketing her heart monitor into a series of fast beeps. "Is my father—?"

"Alive and unharmed," Kelly said, sitting on the edge of the bed. Her eyes were red, her attire casual jeans, and an out-of-character, wrinkled T-shirt. "He had to fly to Washington to deal with the aftermath of Adam's take-over of Groom Lake." Her gaze took on a distant look. "I swear, that day was a nightmare I will not soon forget."

"That day?" Cassandra queried quickly, her hands going to the steel bars. "How long have I been out? What happened to me?"

A nurse rushed into the room. "You're awake!"

"Please," Cassandra said, holding up a hand. "I'm fine. Just give me a minute."

"Miss—"

"I need a minute," Cassandra said forcefully.

Kelly flashed the badge on her chest. "She's in good hands. Give us that minute." Reluctantly the nurse nodded and exited the room.

The moment she was gone, Cassandra asked again, "How long have I been out?"

"Three days," Kelly said. "You hit your head when, ah, Michael tranquilized you." She stood up and filled a glass with some water and handed it to her. Cassandra waved it off. Kelly stood her ground. "Drink."

Cassandra accepted the glass, the cool liquid soothing her throat, but not her heart. Michael had tranquilized her. That part she remembered all too well. She could still see his black eyes in that moment when he'd fired the gun—cold and calculating. She shivered and handed the glass back to Kelly before leaning against the mattress and crossing her arms over the hospital gown.

Her voice softened as she asked, "How did we get out?"

"Caleb," she said. "And thank God for him, though I cannot imagine what it must have been like to stand against his brother. Apparently, Adam had been planning a revolt for some time. Caleb had been working to head it off. But when your father suddenly decided to throw the X2 positive men into confinement, he forced Adam's hand."

"Michael…" A lump formed in her throat, and she had no idea what she'd wanted to say.

Kelly squeezed her arm. "He's alive, if that's what you want to know. With Adam, Cassandra. At least seventy-five GTECHs and almost the entire medical and military staff at Groom Lake followed him."

She remembered Ava's vow. "Did they get the serum?"

Kelly nodded and rolled the doctor's stool to the side of the bed before sitting down. "Enough to create two to three hundred GTECHs. That's a lot of GTECHs, but not enough for the world domination that Caleb says Adam has his sights set on."

World domination. This could not be happening. "Can't he duplicate the serum?"

"I'm sure he thinks he can," she said. "But he can't. And neither can we. The original sample was destroyed, and the alien DNA we are dealing with is nothing like human DNA. It protects itself from duplication. Almost as if it defends itself against imperfection. So once he hands out the serum that he has on hand, he'll have to find another way to grow the GTECH population."

Kelly grimaced. "It's easy to talk big, but execution is another story. Three hundred men is hardly a new race."

"Who says humans won't follow him, Kelly? The

GTECHs could become like royalty. The humans will hope to be made into GTECHs."

"Zodius," she said. "That's what the army is officially calling the GTECHS who are under Adam's command to distinguish those who follow him and those who follow Caleb. Caleb's followers are the Renegades because they're standing against Adam, but outside the veil of the government."

"That's because my father destroyed any hope Caleb will ever trust us again," she said, still reeling from what he'd done.

"Regardless." Kelly said. "Caleb is going after Adam, Cassandra. He'll stop him before he becomes a bigger threat."

"Surely we can end this with some sort of covert attack?"

Kelly sighed and reached for the remote control on the nightstand. "Once upon a time, I had a good bedside manner, but I don't seem to be doing the comfort thing well today." She flipped to the news where they were showing a Casino up in flames and then flashed to a high-rise in downtown Manhattan, also on fire. "That's how Adam managed to get Caleb to back down. He promised every attack on Area 51 would be met with double retaliation."

"You're right," Cassandra said. "You really aren't good at the comfort thing today. So if there is anything else, just spit it out, and let's be done with it."

"There's an inquisition into your father's actions. He may face court martial. And… there are guards stationed at your door in case Adam tries to kidnap you." Translation—Michael might try and kidnap her, but

Kelly didn't want to say that. "Not that anyone has any reason to believe he might. Caleb says Ava was planning to use you and me and any female they could get their hands on to re-create the fertility testing she's been working on at Area 51 by trying to find lifebond connections." She shook herself. "That woman was going to offer us up to their entire male population. Bottom line here is that you're safe. You were convenient, and now you're not. We're just being cautious until things settle down a bit, in case they try to use you to lash out at your father."

Cassandra's chest tightened. Michael had said he wouldn't tell anyone about their Lifebond, but he'd tried to kidnap her. That could mean only one thing. He must have told Adam. And if she had been captured, he would have used her to reproduce and build Adam's new Zodius race. Which meant he was going to come for her. It meant she should confess her lifebond connection to Michael and plan for protection. But even as she had the thought, she couldn't find the words. Cassandra wasn't ready to let go of the hope that everything wasn't as it seemed. *No matter how things seem*, Michael had said. No. She wasn't ready to let go of Michael or their vow of silence. The takeover of Area 51 might have been Kelly's personal nightmare, but Cassandra had a horrible feeling that this was only the beginning of hers.

<hr />

Inside a covert warehouse location, two weeks after his successful takeover of Area 51, Adam sat at a conference table with Ava to his right, and Michael, now his second-in-command, to his left. Also present, twelve of the country's most influential powerhouses—men who represented banking, technology, pharmaceuticals, even government.

"As you know from prior conversations," Adam announced, "we are here today because our government is failing our people, and you want to be a part of a better nation. You want a country free of corruptness, free of human illness." He tapped the table. "You want a Zodius Nation. Each of you is so close to a perfect world. I know you can taste it. All you have to do to ensure that you're one of the first one hundred conversions to Zodius is to dedicate yourselves to our success."

An immediate rumble of assurances quickly followed—promises of generous donations that bordered on begging. Adam leaned back in his chair, satisfaction filling him. He quite enjoyed having these humans—high-ranking amongst their race in power and prestige—beg for his approval. Let the bidding war begin.

Part 2

*All wars are civil wars,
because all men are brothers.*

—François Fénelon

Chapter 5

Two years after that dreaded day Adam Rain had overtaken Area 51, Cassandra pulled her wool-lined coat around her chilled neck, her heels clicking on the red-brick path that led away from the German military hospital where she'd worked for nearly two years. Her coworkers had left hours ago for the New Year's festivities she had no desire to take part in. She'd take her rented *G.I. Joe* DVD and microwave popcorn and be just fine. She didn't mind being alone. In fact, she preferred it, found peace in it. She simply hadn't been ready for relationships — neither male nor female. Not after the two people she thought she'd known — Michael and her father — had proven, despite all her clinical skills, that she was incapable of evaluating those closest to her.

Even now, she would catch herself replaying Michael's parting words, trying to understand why he'd been so adamant about hiding the mark if he wasn't trying to protect her, if he was really loyal to Adam and his Zodius movement. She shook herself, murmuring a word of frustration. She was doing it again, tearing herself up inside with the unanswered questions. Trying to make a traitor into a hero.

The few months she'd spent at a Texas air force base right after the Zodius uprising hadn't been far enough away from Groom Lake. She'd never considered herself a coward, but maybe she was — because she'd simply wanted out. Away. She wanted to forget. She didn't even ask what was happening with Adam. There wasn't any news of some massive Zodius takeover, and Adam wasn't coming after her. That was enough for her.

A snowflake fluttered in front of her. Another touched her nose. She loved the snow. She loved this job where she counseled rather than researched. She wasn't sure how she'd gotten away from that aspect of the field. She liked her life. She liked the food, especially German pasta—she adored spaetzle. And she liked—the rest of her thought was lost as the wind gusted around her, blowing her a step backwards. The snow began to fall faster, mixed with ice that pelted against the pavement. She cast a furtive look around the nearly vacant parking lot a few feet away. There was no sign of trouble. No GTECH—Renegade or Zodius. No Adam. No… Michael. God, would she ever stop looking for him in the wind? Hoping he'd come to her and explain everything, hoping everything wasn't as it seemed.

Quickening her pace, Cassandra clicked the lock on the silver Audi that had replaced her Beetle—a little luxury for once, a luxury she'd decided she deserved. She was about to get into the car, when a black sedan with dark windows pulled up. The back window rolled down. "How's my favorite daughter?"

Her heart stopped beating for an instant. She wasn't sure if she were more shocked just to see her father—who she had not seen since her move—or to see him out of uniform, in a designer-looking, black suit. "Father?" she said, questioning the obvious, reeling with disbelief. "What are you doing here?" The wind gusted again, snow and ice plastering her hair against her head and face, reminding her why leaving her hat in the car was a bad idea.

"Get in, sweetheart," he said. "You're getting wet." The door popped open.

She stood there, staring at the door, her heart randomly charging and stalling. Tears prickled in her eyes, and she was thankful for the snow. She hadn't cried since that first night in the hospital when she had faced Michael's betrayal. And her father's actions, both at Groom Lake and then in the aftermath, when she'd caught glimpses of a desperate man trying to save himself no matter what the expense. But she'd dealt with these things. Or so she thought. Yet now emotion filled her chest like a heavy block of steel, crushing her.

With a slow, calming breath, she forced herself to slide into the double-seated back, directly across from him. He reached for the door and pulled it shut, leaning back as he brushed the snow away from his jacket.

"What's going on, Father?" Even as she asked the question, a stark, cold memory filled her—of asking that same question that day at Groom Lake.

He arched a brow. "No 'how are you?' 'Happy New Year?' No hug for Dad?"

"I'd prefer skipping the part where we pretend everything is okay," she said. "We both know you didn't come to Germany to wish me a happy New Year."

He offered her a file. She ignored it, didn't want it.

"Take it, Cassandra," he said.

Her lips thinned. "Whatever you're up to now, Father, I want no part of it."

"Adam's Zodius Army has been attacking our naval

bases," he said. "They claimed a New Mexico base and another in Texas. Men are dying. Good men. And you can help prevent that. Take the file, Cassandra."

She didn't want to hear this. She didn't want to know this. But... now she did, now she couldn't pretend she didn't know. She took the file, her gaze flickering over the label "Red Dart" and underneath that "PMI Research," then back to him. "What is 'Red Dart,' and who is this PMI?"

"PMI is my private company, and Red Dart is a tracking device we've developed that will allow us to tag the Zodius during attacks, like we do animals in the wild. It enters the bloodstream and becomes permanent. It then alerts us to their approach. This program will allow us to save lives and capture the enemy."

"I still don't see what this has to do with me."

"I've got a meeting in Washington on Monday morning, and I've asked Caleb Rain to attend as the leader of the GTECH Renegades. I'd like you to be there as well."

She handed him back the file. "That's not going to happen."

He leaned forward and took her hand. "My daughter, the angel of my eye," he said, his voice rough with emotion, "I have made mistakes. I hurt you. I know this. But I swear to you that everything I did was meant to protect the country I love and the daughter I worship. I knew what Michael was—I knew he was using you."

Hatred laced his voice, and Cassandra couldn't blame him for that. Michael had tried to kill him, though knowing her father, the embarrassment of Michael making him look a fool was probably more like it. Michael—a man who'd stolen her heart, had almost ripped it out.

Pain knifed through Cassandra, and she squeezed her eyes shut. Every passing day, every day that he didn't appear, reminded her that he was Zodius, no matter how much she didn't want to believe it to be true.

"I have to fix the tragedy that Project Zodius has become," her father continued, squeezing her hand and willing her to look at him.

Cassandra opened her eyes, stared into the desperate plea in her father's face, so out-of-character, and felt her insides unraveling, felt him tugging her into his world again.

"Adam's Zodius Nation is nothing short of a cult," he said. "Some of those GTECH soldiers following Zodius can be saved. If anyone can make that happen once we have them in custody, it's you." He squeezed her hand again. "Stand by my side, daughter. Show the world you believe in me, and I will not fail you or them."

———

"In the six months since Powell's return to duty, I've been hearing these claims that he can control the GTECHs with Red Dart. And I've looked over the data Lucian collected from his White House informant with some excitement. However, there is absolutely nothing here that allows me to create the Red Dart program. Certainly nothing that even remotely indicates it works on GTECHs. In fact, just the opposite. The research shows Red Dart is destroyed by the GTECH immune system."

The announcement, made by Dr. Edward Reed, the frail, fifty-something scientist, displeased Adam. In fact, he was so fucking not pleased, he couldn't decide if he wanted to reach across the desk and wring Reed's scrawny little neck or turn around and grab Lucian Brody—the Zodius soldier who'd made this White House contact—and pull his balls through his throat. He grabbed Reed's laptop from his desk and flung it against the two-way shatterproof glass panel. The computer hit the floor with a thud, plastic pieces bouncing off the tiled floor.

Silence swelled in the room while the two other men, one GTECH and one human, stared at each other. Adam waited for one of them to say the wrong thing— that would let him know which one would die today. Because one of them needed to die.

"Red Dart is the reason Powell was reinstated—with I might add, a promotion," Lucian argued defensively, anger seething in his voice as he glared at Reed. "It's why they created the role of security advisor to the secretary of state and acquired funding for a new Nevada air force base twice the size of Groom Lake's Area 51. He is calling it Dreamland. The government is afraid of the GTECHs, all of us. They only pretend allegiance to the Renegades to gain their protection from us. Powell promised the joint chiefs of staff that his company, PMI, is no more than a few weeks from having Red Dart GTECH-ready. There are troops being transferred to Powell's new Dreamland facility to prepare for a full-scale attack on both the Zodius and Renegade bases even as we speak. I'm working on getting more details about his attack plans now."

Reed pressed his dark glasses up his nose and straightened. His lower lip quivered with fear. "While this information sounds quite daunting, nothing in the data Lucian has given us supports such claims. This file holds nothing but a detailed documentation trail of failed attempts to use Red Dart against enemies of the United States government. They were able to bind the alien chemical component to the humans' blood, which makes them sensitive to sound waves. When they activated the sound device for torture, it killed the humans. Painfully. It became a kill switch rather than a torture mechanism. Red Dart was ruled inhumane and terminated. The file was sealed fifty years ago."

Adam jerked around and leaned on Reed's desk, shoving his face into the other man's. "And what's wrong with a little inhumane?" he asked. "Fucking. Love. It. And I fully intend to use it on both humans and GTECHs. Do you understand?" Reed nodded, turning ashen, and Adam continued, "Then you get me Red Dart ready for humans while we wait on the GTECH formula, and you do it now." A little torture, a few high-profile dead bodies, and he'd own the White House—hell, he'd own every government in existence. Once he had the GTECHs fully controlled as well—there would be no stopping him.

"Red Dart is administered by a laser," Reed said, his voice shaking. "The laser is created by a crystal. I have to have that crystal or there is no Red Dart."

Adam pushed off the desk, ready to fling the doctor through the window this time. Already the man had failed to re-create the GTECH serum. The alien DNA protected itself from duplication, and they did not have the original DNA sample. Now, while Adam's scientists sought a way around the problem, Adam was forced to grow his following with lesser beings, with humans. But he was dealing with the problem the way all great leaders dealt with problems—creatively. If he could not convert the humans, they would simply have to become his pets.

"I still think we should ransom Cassandra Powell for the crystal." The female voice came from the doorway.

Adam looked dismissively past Lucian, to find his Lifebond, Ava, standing in the doorway, her long, red hair draped over her lab coat, and one of the many wolves Adam commanded at her feet. Adam's gaze traveled possessively to the beginning of a baby bump lifting around Ava's stomach, the heir to the kingdom he was building. One day soon, Ava would discover the secret to creating Lifebond matches who would produce GTECH offspring.

"Powell won't negotiate," he told her. "Not even for his daughter. No general worth his salt would."

She looked thoughtful, walking farther into the room. "Then send Michael to seduce her into getting the crystal," she said. "He had her once. I'm quite confident he can have her again."

"He tried to kill her father," Adam reminded her.

"But he didn't," she said. "Michael will tell her he never intended to either. That he always loved her. That he protected her. That he can no longer stay away. He'll tell her he wants to save humankind, and she can help him—by helping him locate, and destroy, the crystal. Once he has the crystal, I'm sure he can manipulate an answer as to how to use it on GTECHs. Though, I must say—human application of Red Dart might be enough. Once we use it on say, the president of the United States, and we hold his kill-switch, I find it doubtful Caleb will do anything but obey your commands."

A slow, satisfied smile slid onto Adam's lips. "I like the way you think, Lifebond."

Calmness overcame him, his mind finding the peace that only she could give. And with that came clarity. Michael would get him Red Dart. Michael had never failed him.

She was at a fancy Washington, D.C. party when it happened, wishing herself back to the comfy, secluded confines of the Vegas condo she'd rented upon her return from Germany six months ago. It was the moment that Cassandra had longed for, yet dreaded for over two years. That moment that, deep down, she had always known would come.

It started with a soft breeze that seemed to lift the sound of music and laughter and funnel it around her. Calling to her. Demanding her attention. Instantly, memories washed over her, of the fire of his touch, the spice of his kiss, the warmth of his body pressed close to hers.

Slowly, her gaze shifted from the displays of delicate finger foods and flocks of uniforms and elegant gowns to the sheer curtains caressing the double-paned patio doors. A familiar tingling sensation touched the mark on the back of her neck. Her hand shook as she set her champagne glass on the table and watched a waiter push the doors shut.

Michael. God, Michael was here. She could feel his presence as easily as she did her own breath within her chest. She'd hoped the mark would fade with time away from him, but it had not, and neither had the bond.

With a deep breath that did nothing to calm the racing

of her heart, Cassandra pushed off her chair, her floor-length, white chiffon dress clinging to her petite frame as she began weaving her way through the crowd, past elaborate floral arrangements, and a dance floor filled with perfectly learned ballroom dancing.

Her mind was already far from the purpose of the night's festivities, but she was forced to stop and shake hands with the daughter of the visiting Mexican dignitary they were honoring tonight. Cassandra's father, now a White House security advisor, wanted to nurture the relationship, considering Mexico's close proximity to Zodius activity. He'd managed an alliance—albeit an uneasy one—with Caleb's Renegades, and he was close to unveiling some cutting-edge technology, which would even the odds against Adam's Zodius soldiers. These were good things. Things that made her not regret her decision to return to the States.

Finally, Cassandra managed to break away from the crowd and paused as she reached the double-glass doors, pressing her palm to her fluttering stomach. Born of nerves, not fear. In fact, as more of that fanciful laughter bubbled up behind her, Cassandra was struck by the irony of the blissful party when a silent war against humanity was well under way. Michael was a part of that war, she reminded herself.

Angry now, Cassandra yanked open the door and stepped onto the patio, the hot night suffocating her with eerie stillness. Her nerve endings prickled, bristled, screamed with awareness an instant before the wind gently lifted, blowing wisps of her long blonde hair worn straight and to her shoulders, around her face.

A musical sound shimmered in the air, drawing her

attention to a wind chime hanging at the edge of a walkway. Michael wanted her to follow that path. And much to Cassandra's dismay, Michael's way of using the wind to communicate warmed her limbs, wickedly declaring she still wanted him. And that uncontrollable want, which bordered on need, delivered a dose of the fear she'd thought she'd left behind. In fact, it downright terrified her. But she was out here now, and she was quite certain that he wasn't going away until she went to him.

Shaking inside, Cassandra inhaled another breath and started forward, following the lighted walkway that twisted and curved and ended at a dimly lit gazebo. In the same instant she stepped inside the structure, he emerged from the shadows, potently male, a presence that expanded, consumed her, downright stole her breath. A presence more powerful than she even remembered. The scent of him—male, musky, uniquely Michael—flared in her nostrils and rippled a path along her nerve endings.

His long, black hair touched broad shoulders and framed that powerful square jaw she'd touched and kissed so often. He towered over her, reminding her of a sleek, muscled panther, hungry and ready to feast. On her. And Lord help her, as she stared into those intelligent, unnaturally black eyes that seemed to see straight to her soul, a part of her that she had no control over wanted him to.

"You look more beautiful than ever, Cassandra."

His voice swept along her nerve endings with a velvety smooth slide, licking at her limbs with fire. She hugged herself against the sudden heaviness in her breasts, the ache of her nipples—against the wanton reaction that had to be about the mark on her neck. This man had tried to kill her father. He was trying to destroy humanity. He was the enemy, and she was here for answers. And for anything they could use to defeat Zodius.

She drew her spine stiff. "Why are you here, Michael?"

"You're in danger," he said softly.

"If I'm in danger, it's from you," she bit out through her teeth.

"And yet here you stand," he pointed out, challenge etching his chiseled features.

"To protect everyone else in that building," she quickly countered.

He arched a disbelieving brow. "So you bravely put yourself in harm's way." One corner of his far-too-inviting mouth lifted. "Or maybe you simply remember I'm the kind of 'dangerous' you enjoy."

It was a familiar sensual taunt he'd used in the past, and unbidden, the words drew an image of Michael's hard body pressed tightly against hers, of his hand sliding up her dress. Cassandra squeezed her eyes shut and silently cursed. Her lashes lifted, and she cast him an accusing glare. How powerful had Michael become? Could he place such a thought in her mind?

He laughed and held up his hands. "Don't look at me like that, Cassandra. Whatever thoughts that wickedly lovely mind of yours conjured up were all your own. And don't tell me they weren't wicked. We both know you have a way with creative imagery." His hands slowly lowered, those sensual lips lifting at the corners ever-so-slightly. "I do believe I'd like to hear what you were thinking now."

"Oh, they were wicked thoughts all right," she said.

"And they were, indeed, full of creative imagery. I've had two years to contemplate all kinds of interesting ways to kill a GTECH as powerful as you."

"And I've had two years to dream of touching you again." He inhaled. "You still want me. I can smell your arousal."

"This is insane," she said. "I shouldn't have come out here." She turned, started to walk away, but quickly regretted the action. Damn him. Damn him! She would not retreat. She'd waited too long for this confrontation.

Cassandra whirled around to face him and sucked in a breath as she found him in close pursuit; she barely kept her hands from settling on his chest as she steadied herself. They were toe-to-toe now, so close her body ached, so close she could lean forward and touch him. She hated herself for wanting to.

"What makes you think you have the right to say such things to me?" she demanded, frustrated that her voice trembled. "You followed Adam and his Zodius movement. You tried to kill my father." Her words rasped deeper, her fingers curling in her palms.

"If I had wanted your father dead, he'd be dead."

Cassandra swallowed hard at the lethal quality in his voice, ground her teeth at the memory of Michael holding a blade to her father's neck. "I was there. I saw the blade at his throat. I saw the blood." The memory shook her, and she stepped backwards, a mistake when she was so close to the edge of the stairs. She stumbled, losing her balance and almost taking a tumble. Michael reached for her, steadying her, as if he were her protector. Thighs pressed to thighs. Hips pressed to hips. The world disappeared. The man and everything he'd meant to her reappeared. In those few seconds, she both reveled in the feel of him close to her again and silently cried at the loss.

"Let go," she whispered. He narrowed his gaze, defiance settling there. "Let go, Michael!"

Instead, he kissed her, one hand threading through her hair, the other molding her hips to his. His tongue possessively pressing past her lips, coaxing a response. Cassandra tried to resist, her hands pressing against him, her intention to push him away. Instead, heat seared her palms and spread warmth up her arms. And the taste of him, wildly Michael, rushed through her like a gust of hot, sensual wind. Consuming her. Melting her. Oh God, melting her resistance.

And just when she knew she was lost, when she could hold back no more, he released her, stepping away. Giving her space that she both wanted and hated all in the same instant. She hugged herself against the ache in her body and the heat of his stare.

"My response means nothing. It's the mark."

"You kissed me like that before that mark ever existed," he reminded her. "And we both know it." His voice softened. His eyes too. "I didn't betray you, Cassandra. When it was clear that the Renegades could not defeat Adam, we needed someone on the inside of Adam's operation. I was X2 positive. Adam believed I had reason to follow him."

She could barely breathe, barely think. "But you didn't tell me?" Emotions collided inside her, a desperate part of her wanting to believe his words. Another part reminding herself not to be naive, not to let down her guard. "What do you want from me, Michael?"

THE LEGEND OF MICHAEL

"I want *you*, Cassandra. Make no mistake about that." His words were firm, powerful. Possessive. "But if Adam had known you wore my mark, he would have demanded you be hunted down and brought to Zodius City. And there was no way in hell I was allowing you anywhere near Zodius City. You couldn't know the truth, Cassandra. It was too dangerous."

Her heart thundered in her chest. "Then why are you telling me now?"

"Project Red Dart," he said, dropping the term as if he were testing her knowledge.

Her chest tightened at his mention of the top-secret program. Oh God, he was trying to use her. This was all one big trick. "Red Dart?" she asked, feigning ignorance.

"Adam knows about it, Cassandra."

That was impossible. There were only a handful of people who knew about Red Dart for fear of leaks to Adam. "I have no idea what you're talking about."

He crossed his arms in front of his chest. "Red Dart is a laser beam created by a crystal that shoots a chemical into the bloodstream of the target. The target is then tracked," he paused, "and tortured, sometimes to the point of death."

Her mouth dropped open in a near gasp that she struggled to contain. He was wrong, but telling him so meant admitting she knew about Red Dart.

"You didn't know about the torture part, did you?" he asked, then softly added, "I knew you would never support such a thing."

He was serious. He really thought Red Dart was a torture device. "Of course, I wouldn't," she agreed. "You have no idea what you are talking about." There wasn't any torture involved with Red Dart. *Oh God*. Please let there not be any torture involved with Red Dart. The idea that a GTECH could be ordered to do anything—no matter how unethical or wrong—or risk torture, was not a possibility she wanted to consider. Please let her father really be making things right as he'd promised.

"Did you know he's promised the secretary of state that all GTECHs, Renegade and Zodius alike, will be under his complete control within sixty days?"

"Oh no," she said, shaking her head in instant rejection. "He would never act against the Renegades. And damn it, Michael, there is no torture involved with Red Dart. We don't even water board our enemies. We sure as heck aren't going to insert some sort of torture mechanism that would do Lord-only-knows what to them."

"Yet that is exactly what your father intends. Just like at Groom Lake, he is driven by a personal agenda that endangers innocent lives. There were two men on the military tribunal for your father, both ready to put him away for life. Both died of brain aneurysms. A very unlikely coincidence."

"What does that have to do with any of this?"

"There's a drug called 'Stardust' that was developed at Groom Lake. It causes brain aneurysms," he said. "It's an alien substance that won't show up in blood testing. I know this because Adam confiscated a supply when he took over your father's operation."

She gripped the railing. "I know all too well what my father did in the past." Her father was here, trying to fix the mistakes he'd made at Groom Lake. Michael had been gone two years. Michael had been with Adam. "He's trying to defend us against a Zodius takeover. He needs the Renegades to defeat Adam, and he knows that."

"Why then, has he told Caleb nothing about Red Dart?" he asked dryly.

"It's classified."

"Right. Classified. Well here's something else 'classified.' Both Adam and your father want to use Red Dart to control all the GTECHs. As for Adam, once the GTECHs are under his control, he plans to take it even a step further. He plans to use it on humans. On every government and financial powerhouse in the world. I need your help, Cassandra. We have to destroy that crystal so that no one can abuse it—not Adam, not your father. Because it can destroy the world."

She didn't know where Red Dart was even if she wanted to destroy it. But that wasn't the only problem... there was also that thing called trust. "How do you know any of this?"

"Like your father," he said, "we have friends in the White House."

He had a fast answer for everything. "You said my connection to you puts me in danger," she said. "So why are you here, and not Caleb?"

"That danger I spoke of," he said. "It *is* me, Cassandra. Adam sent me here to seduce you into helping him. And if I don't convince him I've done my job, he'll send someone else for you. And their method of persuasion will not be seduction."

Cassandra gasped at the same moment that her father's voice filled the air. "Cassandra!"

Michael reached for her, pulling her tight against his body, one powerful arm anchoring their hips together and rendering her immobile. "There will be a package at your hotel desk tonight," he said. "A phone you can use to contact Caleb without being traced. He'll confirm I'm telling the truth."

"Cassandra!"

Her heart kicked into double-time as her father's voice grew closer. "If my father finds you, he'll order the guards to kill you."

"We both know they would not succeed." His gaze dropped to her mouth, and then lifted, sensual hunger charging the air as if he were more concerned with kissing her than he was with his own life.

"You might be willing to take a chance with the guards, but I'm not." She shoved at his arm. "Go now, Michael."

A hint of satisfaction flared in his dark eyes, as if she had said she cared about him when she had not. He ran his hand roughly through her hair, his lips inches from hers. His breath, warm and tempting. He was sin and satisfaction, and damn him, she wasn't sure she could ever escape him.

"Don't go trying to save the world without me," he warned. "Trust no one, Cassandra. Especially those closest to your father."

"I've learned not to trust," she bit back, feeling exposed, vulnerable. "Thanks to you."

His eyes darkened, his mood shifting with the stir of the wind. "I know all too well what you think of me," he said, as he abruptly released her. "I'll return for you soon." The wind gusted in a powerful surge, as if he wanted to taunt her father with his presence. A second later, Michael was gone.

The absence of his touch and the promise of his return flowed through her as a deep ache. No matter how she had tried to deny it, she'd wished for the day he would come for her, that he would have a reason for having left her that made sense. But she was no fool. Despite their physical attraction, he'd come back for Red Dart. Not for her.

"Cassandra!" Her father's voice forced her to pull herself together, or at least try. The world felt like it was crumbling around her, but somehow, she painted on a calm expression and turned to find her father at the edge of the gazebo. "You shouldn't be out here alone," he reprimanded the instant he spotted Cassandra, his face etched with apprehension. If he had his way, she'd have guards by her side 24-7. He was certain that one day Michael would contact her, try to use her again. And tonight he had.

"I needed air, Father." She managed to sound nonchalant, but she could feel herself shaking inside.

"The wind, you shouldn't be out in the wind."

"The wind, Father, has been gusting all night," she assured him, walking down the stairs and latching her arm onto his.

His gaze skimmed the gazebo and then the surrounding area as the wind began to fade. "You're sure?"

"Quite," she said, urging him back to the party. "And I find the fresh *wind* far more appealing than the stuffy cigar smoke that drove me outside in the first place."

Slowly, he relaxed and smiled. "General Roberts?"

"Isn't it always?" She smiled brightly, her mind racing with the implications of all Michael had said. She squeezed her father's arm more tightly. She didn't want

Michael to be right about him. But she didn't want Michael to be lying. And even if Caleb backed Michael's statement, it still didn't mean they were right about Red Dart. It simply meant she had to prove them wrong.

"They are about to cut the cake," her father said, pulling her back into the moment. "I know how you love your sweets."

She smiled and agreed, somehow making small talk as they walked down the path, somehow presenting a façade of happy and lighthearted. But in the back of Cassandra's mind, she knew a storm was coming. And that storm had a name: Michael.

Chapter 6

WITH THE TASTE OF CASSANDRA STILL LINGERING ON his lips, Michael stepped onto the elevator leading to the underground world of what was once Area 51, but now known as "Zodius City," the first of its kind in Adam's planned Zodius Nation. Michael was shaking inside. And he didn't shake. He couldn't shake. It showed weakness, and weakness would get him killed and maybe Cassandra with him.

He'd been living the façade of being the second in charge to the most evil monster on this planet. Hell, he'd earned the reputation as the "Punisher" for his torture of any Zodius soldier who dared cross Adam. And he was fucking shaken. To the core. Because no matter how forcefully he reached for that black spot in his mind where he felt nothing, it was nowhere to be found.

There was only Cassandra, and that bittersweet taste of her on his lips. He could make her want him again, but he doubted he would ever make her trust him again. Which was for the best, he told himself. Nothing had changed. This place, his role in it, was proof; he was not the man for Cassandra. Hell, most days the darkness inside him made him doubt he was a man at all.

The elevator dinged its arrival, the doors sliding open to Adam's private corridor, a part of the never-ending expansion of the underground facility. A pair of silver doors, similar to those on the elevator awaited him, two armed guards on either side, both in desert fatigues, machine guns on their shoulders. Neither soldier dared to look Michael in the eye; there was a class system followed in Zodius, with Adam at the top and humanity below, under his foot.

The guard to the right used the wall phone to call Adam. Before he hung up, the doors slid open, and Michael stepped into a hallway resembling that of a hotel with doors running down its length. He headed to the one at the end—Adam's apartment that dripped of Upper East Side Manhattan luxury.

Ava appeared in the entrance before he arrived, draping herself over the frame, one hand over her head, her hip seductively cocked. She wore a sheer white bra and panties, displaying her rounded stomach and full breasts, nipples barely covered. Long red hair draped over her shoulders.

"Michael," she said, a taunting, sexual smile on her red lips, despite the fact that she had eyes for no one but Adam. But like her Lifebond, Ava was pure evil, and she enjoyed luring men into her web and then watching Adam catch them. Look the wrong way at Ava, and you ended up in the "coliseum," Roman style. There, the entire city watched as dozens of Adam's wolves savaged the offender, who couldn't kill one of the prized animals—at least not without further reprisal. The soldier would heal but not without disgrace and a hell of a lot of pain.

Ava was a bitch. "Where's Adam?" he asked shortly.

"In the shower," she said, inching the door open. "I'll keep you company until he's out."

"I'll wait in the hall," he countered, his eyes never leaving her face.

She pursed her red lips. "What's the problem, Michael?" she baited. "You afraid you'll be tempted to actually *look* at me if you come inside? Or do you simply find me unattractive because I'm pregnant with Adam's child?"

Such a fucking bitch. He gave her a heavy-lidded, cold stare. "I just want to talk to Adam."

The door opened fully and Adam—wearing a navy silk robe, his hair damp—stepped behind Ava and smacked her on the ass. "Stop taunting the man. You should know by now that Michael is not going to betray me."

That shaking feeling Michael had felt when he'd stepped off the elevator disappeared for a moment as Michael smiled inside. Ava was Adam's weakness. She made him blind and foolish.

Adam yanked Ava tight against him and wrapped his hand around her head, his lips close to hers. "Not even for you." He kissed her hard and then set her away. "Get dressed." He turned to Michael. "Come in."

Michael sauntered into the apartment filled with black leather and expensive art—stolen art. Adam wanted. Adam took. Ava wanted. Adam took. If the bank vaults weren't sealed tight from the wind, they'd be empty.

Adam sat down on the couch, waving a hand for Michael to join him, before filling two crystal glasses with brandy. You'd never know the man had been a "Bud" guy only two years before. Michael hated brandy, and Adam damn sure knew it. But every time he came here, he poured him a glass. And every time, Michael didn't touch the shit. Some sort of test, though Michael had no idea for what.

And as usual, Adam studied him, willing him to pick up that glass. "You are the only Zodius who would dare to snub my offer of anything." He seemed pleased with this, as if it somehow made Michael worthy of being "second." Yet anyone else would be beaten for such a refusal.

Adam set his glass down and spread his arms across the back of the couch. "Tell me about Cassandra. I always thought she was one of those preacher's daughter kinds of fantasies for you. Only it's the general's daughter." His lips twitched. "Did you kiss her broken heart and make it better?"

Michael had a fantasy all right, the same fantasy he had at least once a day, and not about Cassandra. The one where he slit Adam's throat and ended all of this. Only it wouldn't end. Adam had insurance on himself — a strategy he'd made clear to both the government and the Renegades. Upon his death, those three biological weapons they'd taken from Port Said years before would be released, among a string of other disasters that would escalate around the country.

He and Caleb both blamed themselves for that one. And thus far, only Michael knew where they would be released, but not by who — if he knew who, he could end this, end Adam, and end his terror.

Michael forced himself out of the fantasy and back to the conversation. He disliked talking about Cassandra with Adam. "She'll be cooperating," he said. "But she's been kept in the dark. I'll guide her through manipulating her father. She'll find Red Dart."

"Quickly," Adam said. "Guide her quickly."

Ava sashayed back into the room, wearing a pink

silk robe and draping herself over Adam's shoulder. "Did you tell him about the fertility testing?" She didn't wait for a response, excitement lifting her voice. "I injected six women with a hormone formulation from my pregnancy. Their fertility ranges immediately skyrocketed off the charts. Next step is to pair them with some of the soldiers and see if the hormones make them lifebond compatible." Ava lavished the women inside Zodius City with gifts and luxurious living quarters. These were the future mothers of Zodius children. Seventy percent of the nearly one hundred women inside the "Silver, Gold, and Twilight Quarters"—the female housing units—were brainwashed by the glamour and Ava's unique ability to mold nearly every female mind she touched. Only a small percentage were unaffected by her new gift. Despite the requirement of frequent, rotating sex partners, they wouldn't leave if given the chance.

"What Ava failed to mention," Adam said, "was the part where two of the six females she injected have died. The last thing I need is a bunch of panicked females worried about why women are disappearing. I want them all injected now, deal with the fallout, and be done with it all at once. There is no reason to wait."

Michael had gone ice-cold inside. This was where the buck stopped, where he exited Zodius. Because he was leaving with as many of those women as he could—and he was doing it tonight, while they still had a chance to live. And considering a woman who'd had sex with a GTECH developed a psychic energy that could be traced by certain skilled GTECHs while above ground, that wasn't going to be easy.

Ava curled up to Adam's side. "We'll need more women, Michael. You'll need to send a team out hunting."

Adam smiled. "If you didn't have to attend to the needs of Cassandra," he said, "I'd say we take the wolves out hunting for prospects. It'll be an interesting diversion. I love to watch their faces when the wolves go at them, and then we save the day by rescuing them." He laughed. "Priceless. They come willingly. We are their heroes."

An hour later, finally having leveraged himself out of Adam's company, Michael appeared inside Sunrise Canyon on a deserted dirt road eighty miles north of Zodius City. Only a few miles from the underground Renegade Headquarters, their version of Zodius City: Sunrise City.

A black Jeep waited by a mountainside, and with nothing but desert and darkness for cover, he wasted no time climbing into the front passenger's side. Caleb sat behind the wheel. Sterling Jeter, one of Caleb's closest confidants, sat in the back, his long blond hair loose around his shoulders. Wild, like his entire existence.

"The Dark One has arrived," Sterling joked, hitting Michael's shoulder. "What's cooking, Mikey?"

Sterling could crack a really bad joke at any given moment, regardless of circumstances. Michael ignored the jokes because Sterling's irritating need to be a comedian didn't change the fact that Sterling was not only both a loyal friend and confidant to Caleb, but also one hell of a soldier. None of which kept Michael from wanting to beat Sterling's ass. Often.

"What's cooking is my nerves," Michael said dryly, refocusing on Caleb. "If we rescue the women, he'll just kidnap more."

"Maybe," Caleb said, cutting him a sideways look. "But it will take time for him to find this number of women again. Time we can use to stop him completely. Time the women inside Zodius now do not have."

"If we do this," he said. "I'm out. Only three people have the codes to override the security to get them to the surface," Michael responded. "Myself, Ava, and Adam. He'll know I did this."

"Get me into the mainframe," Sterling said, leaning forward. "I can make it look like we hijacked Adam or Ava's security codes."

"Not even you can do that," Michael said. "There is a full-body scan to get into that room, and I'm not approved. Adam never fully trusts anyone. The bottom line here is, I stay in Zodius and a large percentage of those women die. Or I am out, and we save them."

Caleb's hands closed around the steering wheel in a white-knuckled grip. Obviously struggling with his choice. After several seconds, he slanted Michael a sideways look. "After two years of trying to get the name of the person, or persons, who would launch the attacks on our country upon Adam's death, do you have any reason to believe you can get that information now or in the near future?"

"No," Michael said. And he'd tried. Every which way and back.

"And you're certain those chemical weapons are not on site?"

"Positive," Michael assured him.

"Nor can you find out where they are?"

These were all questions Caleb had asked before, and he knew where this was heading. "No chance at all."

Caleb stared out the front window, tense seconds ticking by. "We can't let those women die. No. We *won't*. We'll get the women. Then, we're going to get Red Dart and stop Adam once and for all." He lowered his voice. "And you've been in that place too long, Michael. You can only play with the devil so long before you lose your soul."

Right. Soul. Michael almost laughed at that. He wasn't sure he had a soul *to* lose. But Caleb did, and Michael wouldn't let that happen. "01200 then," Michael said. "When the guards change."

Sterling rubbed his hands together. "A long night of kicking some Zodius ass," he said, excitement in his voice. "I live for this shit." And he meant it. He lived to die everyday. Michael saw that behind his jokes. It was a wild glint in his eyes. And when they invaded Zodius City he might just get the chance. Caleb started the Jeep engine and glanced at Michael. "Looks like you're about to walk into Sunrise City and stay this time," he said. "Where you belong."

Michael digested that like a well-placed bullet, right in the gut, with a hard bite. Not because he didn't want to be inside Sunrise City, but because this was the day he had always known would come, the day he'd become Adam's worst enemy. And Cassandra was right in the middle of the firing range. A prime target for Adam's vengeance, and he had no way to get her off the radar. Not when she was the best shot they had at getting to Red Dart—a technology that could hand the world over to a madman. His world was bleeding onto hers. He ground his teeth. But that blood always seemed to originate with her father. A man he'd once

had a chance to kill. And Cassandra had been right—
he'd wanted to.

—⁓—

Sirens shrilled through the intercom, blasting through
Adam's bedroom. "Oh my God," Ava gasped, her hand
cradling her stomach. "Are we being attacked? Our
baby. Adam, our baby."

A phone rang beside the bed, and Adam answered.
He listened a moment and cursed as he flung it across
the room. "The Renegades are attempting to remove
the females," he said, already standing, and shoving
his legs in the fatigues he kept near the bed for such
an occasion.

She was on her knees. "What? No! That will destroy
our testing. You can't let them take the women! How
could they even get to them? How?"

"Michael," Adam said vehemently. "Michael has
betrayed me."

She gasped. "No!" She shoved the covers aside. "I'm
coming. I have influence over the women. I'll—"

"You will not leave this room."

"But Adam—" She was shaking. Panicked.

"Ava," he said sharply, still dressing. "Control
yourself."

The phone on the wall rang. Adam yanked it off the
receiver. He listened a moment before the anger turned
to red rage and then to fury. He beat the phone against
the wall, fast, hard, pounding thrusts that didn't even
begin to release the rage inside him. He grabbed not one,
but two, MP5 machine guns and headed to the door. He
was going to blow holes in Michael and let him damn

near bleed to death. Then let the bastard heal and do it all over again.

The instant Adam exited the building he heard the Renegade choppers—to the east, west, and south sides of the complex. He faded into the wind and went west, appearing just as a group of his soldiers were about to fire a rocket launcher at a chopper. Awareness ripped through Adam—the kind he felt only for two people—his Lifebond and his twin.

"No!" he shouted, but not soon enough. The weapon discharged and time stood still. The dreams of a greater world—of his brother joining him to rule a new kingdom—threatened in the shadowy swampland of his brother's certain death.

A crackle of energy slid over Adam, much like the awareness of Caleb an instant before. Michael stood in the doorway of the helicopter—the wind shifting around him, seeming to take form. It was unlike anything he had ever seen before, nothing any other GTECH could do. Then suddenly, a powerful wall of wind thrust from where Michael stood and forced the missile back at the Zodius soldiers in his pursuit. Adam faded into the wind a second before the missile exploded, one of the few weapons sure to be lethal for a GTECH. He returned seconds later to see soldiers sprawled out on the ground, injured or dead, and the helicopter quickly traveling away. Those who had survived scrambled for their footing, murmuring about both Michael's betrayal and his ability to control the wind, an ability no one, not even Adam, had known about.

Fucking Michael had power he'd never disclosed. He could control the wind, use it as a weapon. Michael who had betrayed him and made him look like a fool. He sneered. The red rage part of him wanted to start blowing shit up until the government gave him Red Dart.

Adam paced, calming himself down, thinking. If Michael was working for the Renegades, Caleb knew about Red Dart and the government's intent to use it on all GTECHs. Caleb was smart enough to know that Red Dart in the hands of the government meant his demise as well. This was a race—who got to Red Dart first. Him or Caleb.

Adam grabbed the phone on his belt, hit the two-way radio, and called two of his officers to his side for immediate action. Within seconds, the two men stood at attention before him. Adam stopped, turned to them, his hands behind his back. "If I find out that either of you is working with Michael," he vowed, "I will start cutting out vital organs. Starting with your fucking eyes. Understood?"

"Yes sir!" they barked together.

He cut a look at Tad, the officer in charge of female recruitment. "How many did we lose?"

"Half," he responded.

Adam ground his teeth. "Replace them. Quickly."

"Commander, sir," Tad replied. "I respectfully request the added duty of killing Michael. Both to prove my loyalty and because I would enjoy drawing his blood."

"A dead Michael feels no pain," Lucian, Adam's third-in-command, countered. "I can give you Red Dart. Then use it to make Michael suffer. You will control him. Make him sit at your feet. Make him bark like an animal if you wish, so all of Zodius City may see."

Adam turned to Lucian, new interest in the soldier who'd always paled in Michael's shadow, often seeming weak. He studied the harsh slash of Lucian's mouth, the turbulent, black eyes set in a handsome face, unlike the doggish hardness of Tad's features. No one without physical beauty would be a part of his elite upper class. Exactly why the women recruited for their studies were all beautiful. Those who were unattractive would serve, not lead. Tad would serve. Lucian would prove himself to lead.

As for Michael, Adam now knew him to possess a lethal ability to control the wind so powerful he could direct missiles with it. That meant Michael was too lethal to be left alive unless Adam controlled him with Red Dart. "You are that confident in the man you have inside Powell's operation?" he inquired of Lucian.

"He's closer to Powell than his own daughter—who he keeps at a distance," he said. "Easily capable of creating doubt about where Michael's loyalty may lie."

Acidy warmth filled Adam as he contemplated a far better option. "If Cassandra Powell were dead, then her father will be distracted enough to let down his guard, which will allow your connection to get his hands on Red Dart." He sharpened his words. "Make it look like an accident. I don't want this connected to Red Dart. But I do want her dead." His lips twisted. "A car accident—the way her mother died. My gift to Powell. His dead daughter. That's what he gets for crossing me. Kill her. And get me that damn crystal and the method to make Red Dart work on the GTECHs. And I want them both now."

Adam faded into the wind.

Chapter 7

TWENTY-FOUR HOURS AFTER MICHAEL HAD REAPPEARED in her life and turned it upside down, Cassandra sat in the bar of her Washington hotel enduring the final items on her agenda before her return home to Nevada the next morning. She and Lieutenant Colonel Brock West—her father's closest confidant since her return from Germany—were hopefully wrapping up the first of two press interviews scheduled for the evening.

The press was eager to gobble up details about her father's new role as special security advisor and about the new facility he'd built eighty miles north of Groom Lake. And despite her best efforts to stay focused, Cassandra kept thinking about Michael and that kiss. God, that kiss. And the envelope with a phone inside that had been left for her—no instructions, no phone call yet—that she knew was the contact he'd promised. She told herself to throw it away. Told herself she didn't trust him, didn't want to talk to him, that she should turn him over to her father. But his words, his accusations about Red Dart, had burned like acid in her stomach, awakened more than the reality of her desire for Michael. They had made her feel doubt, made her realize that deep down she still didn't trust her father either. And truth be told, kissing Michael again, feeling those strong arms around her, had taken her by storm, made her realize why she had not dated. No one had ever lived up to Michael, and she had always secretly hoped beyond reason that there had been an explanation for his actions that was forgivable. Yet, his two years away and his time with Adam more than suggested he was the one not to be trusted, that he was manipulating her to get Red Dart. That idea twisted her in knots, and she shoved it away and refocused on what Layla Cantu, the raven-haired reporter from the *Sun Times*, was asking.

"Why would the army build this new Dreamland military facility less than eighty miles from Groom Lake rather than use Groom Lake?" she queried. "I mean— how much space does all that top-secret research at Groom Lake really take?"

Not liking the direction this was going, Cassandra opened her mouth to respond, officially back in this conversation with full attention, but Brock answered before she could. "Top-secret means top-secret, Ms. Cantu," he said with the same snotty arrogance he'd used on even her, despite his desire to please her father. He simply couldn't help himself.

Cassandra cringed, knowing full well you don't reprimand someone for interest without creating more interest. She eyed Layla and gave her a discreet eye roll that said Brock West—"Brock," as he'd casually, flirtatiously, insisted that she call him—was a pain in the backside. The eye roll was for show—well, not really. She couldn't stand the way Brock panted after her father, condescended to her one minute, and flirted the next.

"Groom Lake is a top-secret research facility," Cassandra agreed. "Secret because we don't want our enemies to have the upper hand with technology, if Lord forbid, we ever go to war again. Trainees coming and going from that facility would represent a great security risk. And Dreamland is going to be the most amazing training facility ever created. A place where every branch of military, and even nonmilitary law enforcement agencies, will send their very best to make them better."

Which was true. What she didn't tell Layla was that they'd be training to fight Adam. Zodius soldiers would be targeted with Red Dart while outside the protection of Zodius City, captured, and brought to Dreamland. How they planned to capture them she did not know, but she planned to find out. The truth was, her father had been hush-hush about the progress with Red Dart—claiming the secrecy was for her own safety. And she hated that Michael was making her question whether that was his true motive for keeping her in the dark.

Layla tapped a pencil on her pad, glanced between Cassandra and West with a look that screamed "I'm not buying it." "I don't suppose either of you would like to comment on the rumors that a nongovernment militant group has taken over Groom Lake?"

Cassandra all but gaped at the question, while West maintained his unflinching, stone-faced soldier persona framed by a buzz-cut and lots of attitude. Cassandra managed a reasonably realistic sounding laugh. "Next thing I know, you'll be telling me those nongovernment militants are big green aliens."

Layla didn't laugh. "Are they?"

West *did* laugh, the sound mocking, snide. "You've got to be kidding."

Layla visibly paled. "Yes," she said. "Of course." She closed her notebook. "Thank you both for your time."

Cassandra and Layla shared a few cordial words of

good-bye. West didn't bother. "I have no idea why your father thought I was the appropriate person to meet the press. I can't stand those UFO chasers."

"My father wanted you involved because you're in charge of the training operation," she reminded him. "And he had to return to Nevada a day early." Cassandra shifted gears. "Aren't you even a little worried about her questions regarding Groom Lake?"

He snorted. "Not in the slightest. She was digging for a reaction. If she'd had anything of substance, she wouldn't have stopped pushing."

Maybe. Hopefully. She let it go and focused on poaching him for information regarding Red Dart—"RD" for discretion. "The first group of Dreamland troops arrives next week. Reading through the training protocols, there is no mention of RD. The soldiers are being taught the same rapid-fire and heavy weapons techniques already in place to battle the Zodius. I thought Dreamland and RD were about capture and reform."

"So far the tranquilizers we've used don't work more than a few seconds, so it's imperative we train our men to survive at all costs," he said. "Trust me. We have a plan."

But she didn't trust him. "I know we have to survive." She lowered her voice further. "If they can wind-walk past our security gates, how will RD help?"

"Once their blood is bound with the RD chemical, we have weapons and sensors inside the gates that will be automatically triggered when they approach," he said. "Even in the wind."

That sounded dangerous, like an accident waiting to happen. "So it only works if they are tagged with RD," she said.

"That's true," he said. "But RD is a painless laser, easily used in confrontation. And it permeates their armor. We'll get them all tagged and captured in no time."

"When exactly will RD be officially launched?"

"Soon," he said.

"In time for the training?"

"Soon," he said again. "You know your father doesn't want you involved in RD. I'm not supposed to be telling you any of this."

Oh she knew. And she knew he wouldn't be telling her now without an agenda. "Then why are you?"

He leaned closer. "He's too protective, Cassandra. He underestimates you." His voice was low, seductive. His eyes hot. He wanted her. He'd made that clear on more than one occasion. "Why don't we finish up here? We'll go to dinner and talk. Plan a strategy to convince your father to ease up."

She recoiled inside, barely containing a tart response. He didn't want to help her. He wanted into her pants and further inside her father's good graces. If she were a vicious person, she'd tell her father. But she wasn't. So she didn't.

His hand slid over hers. "Perhaps if I promised to keep you safe."

Awareness rushed over Cassandra, her skin heating, her senses tingling with lethal warning. Michael. Michael was here. And she didn't know how she knew—but he was most definitely, angry, possessive, ready to rip Brock apart. And Cassandra was scared, not for herself, but for Brock. She yanked her hand away from him at the same moment that a bosomy waitress appeared at the table to refill their coffee mugs. Cassandra vaguely welcomed a refill, trying to calm her racing pulse, to get a grip on the whirlwind of emotions assailing her. The conflicting parts of her that both reveled in Michael's silent claim over her and felt angry that he dared flex a role he'd left behind two years ago.

The lieutenant colonel chatted with the waitress who was flirting outrageously with him. Cassandra took the opportunity to escape and pushed to her feet. "I'm going to freshen up before the second wave of press arrives."

She didn't wait for a reply. She had no idea what Michael might do if she didn't go to him. The government might not fully understand the lifebond connection, but she did. She knew full well how possessive, how consuming, that bond could be.

With quick steps and a racing heart, Cassandra walked toward the bar and asked for the location of the restroom. Then she walked toward the lobby knowing Michael would follow her, that he would find her. She entered a hallway, stepped toward the women's restroom. She hesitated before entering, pressed her fist to her chest, and drew a deep breath that did nothing to calm her. She shoved open the door. The instant she entered, Michael was there, stealing the very breath she'd just taken.

The door slammed shut behind her, her back suddenly pressed against the hard surface, his big body fitted over hers, a rough palm rasping over her thigh as he lifted her leg to his hip, and good Lord, settled his cock between her thighs. Heat rushed over her, fire like she had not felt in the two years since his departure, lust that threatened to consume.

"If he touches you, I'll kill him."

If you stop touching me, I might die. "You don't get

to decide who touches me, Michael," she hissed, the desire he provoked downright frightening.

He stared down at her, his long, dark hair wild around his face, passion harshly edged in his dangerously beautiful face. "You are my Lifebond."

She shivered at the possessiveness of his words, aroused when she should have been outraged. And damn it, she hated how he stole her control, how he could make her melt no matter how much time had passed. "Don't call me that," she proclaimed defiantly, reminding herself of his betrayal, telling herself this was nature at work, not Michael. She was over him. She would not fall for him and be hurt again. A hiss slid from her lips. "Don't act as if the mark gives you some claim over me. You don't have any. Not anymore."

"Ah, but I do," he said, his eyes alight with anger. "And we both know it." His free hand ripped open her blazer, his hand sliding beneath, palm branding her side as little silver buttons flew through the air, clattering to the floor. He tilted his head down and rested his cheek against hers. The heat of his chest framed hers, rushing over her like a warm, erotic blanket.

Her hands closed around his arms, muscles flexing beneath her touch. "Michael," she whispered desperately, a plea to stop, a plea to continue. "You can't just show up again and…"

His lips brushed her ear. "Your words deny me, but your body does not." Possessively, a man confident of her body, his hand swept up her side, fingers stroking her breast, teasing her nipple into a stiff peak. She should demand he let her go, but she said nothing for fear she would instead beg him for more.

"I remember how sensitive your nipples are," he whispered, a strand of his silky raven hair brushing her cheek, and she shivered with the featherlike erotic sensation even as he pressed onward, pressed her further under his spell. "Remember how much you like them licked and sucked." His warm breath touched her mouth, teasing her with the possibility of a kiss. "I remember everything."

"I don't want this," she whispered.

"Liar," he purred, nipping her bottom lip with his teeth, but denying her the taste of him she craved. She was lost in that craving, in her need for him—helpless to stop his hand traveling up her thigh and firmly covering her backside.

Cassandra gasped as he shoved aside the thin strip of her thong and ruthlessly sought the proof of her burn for him, stroking the sensitive flesh beneath. "Already you are slick and ready for me." His fingers slid along her core as little darts of pleasure shot through her body, her hips arching into his of their own accord. Arrogantly, he promised, "I can make you come right here and right now."

Yes. Please do. She grabbed his shoulders. Told herself to shove him away. She didn't have the will. She should hate him—she did hate him—yet, she wanted him, desperately wanted him. "Someone is going to find us," she offered weakly.

"Ask me if I care." Steel laced that statement; magic laced his fingers. She gave up, let her head fall against the door, let the pleasure roll over her. Allowed those nimble fingers of his to intimately explore, deftly pleasure. Let the waves of passion rush over her, the possibility of discovery set aside. "That's it, my sweet," Michael murmured, his lips dragging along her jaw, her neck. His finger slid inside her, caressing her. She was hot, aching with need. Her nipples tightened, her core gushed. The rise of release came on her quickly, embarrassingly so, but she could do nothing to stop it, nothing to hold back. Not with Michael, she could never hold back with Michael.

Cassandra tightened her hold on his shoulders, buried her face in his neck. She felt her core clench at his fingers a moment before she shook with the intensity of her release, waves of pleasure rushing over her, born of years of needing, fantasizing, longing.

When finally she calmed, the heat from her body flooded her cheeks. She didn't want to look at him, didn't know what to say. Michael eased her leg to the floor, but held her close. His hand slid over her hair, gently, tenderly, reminding her there were two sides to him, reminding her of the lover and the fighter.

She didn't want to remember. She didn't want to feel these things. Slowly, she lifted her head, tilted her chin upward to look at him, and defiantly lashed out. "This changes nothing. It proves nothing."

Torment flickered in his eyes a moment before an arrogant, hard look slid across his face, and his hands pressed on the wall on either side of her. "Word of warning, Cassandra," he said softly, lethally. "Seeing you again has ignited possessiveness in me like nothing I have ever felt in my life. When you deny wanting me, I have a sudden urge to prove you wrong. So if you wish to leave this restroom, I suggest you stop denying what we both know is true."

Oh good Lord, why did his words have her nipples aching again? She tried to calm her shallow breathing, to will her heartbeat to slow. She didn't know how to respond, and thankfully she didn't have to. He moved from personal to business, if that was possible between them.

"Now onward to that help you're going to give me with Red Dart." He reached in his jeans pocket and presented her with a silver flash drive stick. "Go through airport security—point two. Someone will be there to ensure your laptops get switched. Go to the restroom and insert this into Brock's laptop. You'll need twelve minutes to get a full hard drive copy. Remove it, and I'll come for it. There are cameras in your offices, so it has to be done in the airport."

Her gaze jerked from the flash drive to his face. "Why would I do that?"

"Because you don't want innocent people to die. And because you want to know who is lying—me or your father," he said bitingly, the words holding the harsh reality of cold, hard truth. "Otherwise you would have already told your father I came to see you. And we both know you didn't."

She didn't take the stick. "I received the phone, but no phone call. I won't be used or manipulated, Michael."

"Caleb has probably been trying to call you all day," he rebutted, snagging his cell from his belt and punching in a number before handing it to her.

"There were unavoidable circumstances last night, or he would have called," he said.

She swallowed and took the phone. "Hello?"

"It's Caleb, Cassandra," came the familiar male

voice. "Michael is one of us. He's always been one of us. I'll call you later tonight if you want to talk."

Her eyes connected with Michael's, a combination of relief and hurt washed over her. "Yes," she whispered in agreement, ending the call and offering the phone back to Michael.

He grabbed it and her hand. "Cassandra…" His voice trailed off, as if he wasn't sure what to say, his hand sliding away from hers. Still watching her with those black eyes—eyes that somehow darkened beyond the blackest of black as he stood there, silent, unmoving, towering above her. The mass of thick, raven hair draped over his broad shoulders only added to the primal charge clinging to his presence.

She didn't know what else to say, didn't know what he expected her to say. This man, this GTECH soldier, was her biological Lifebond no matter how much the pain of the past made her want to deny the fact. She longed for him as much as she ached to escape the pain that the longing had created. But a lot had happened. Maybe too much.

"I'll get the data from the hard drive," she finally said. "But I'm not handing it over until I look at it first." She wasn't allowing Red Dart to be destroyed until she evaluated what was really going on and who had what agenda. "Caleb might trust you, but you are too close to Adam to suit me."

The door jerked behind her, and in one long, agile step, Michael's palm flattened on the wooden surface, sealing it shut. He was close again, his body heat radiating around her, his eyes pinning hers in a hard stare. "There isn't time to explain, but the situation with Adam has become increasingly dangerous."

"Make time," she demanded urgently. "What does that mean?"

"Hello!" A woman's voice sounded from the other side of the door.

"It means I am no longer undercover with Zodius," he said. "And if I had any other choice but to have *you* get this data, I would take it. We have to find and destroy Red Dart before it's too late."

Her breath lodged in her throat. That meant... oh God. "You said Adam—"

"He'll never get to you." He took her hand and closed it around the stick. "I'll kill him, or anyone, who tries. I'll be close, Cassandra, watching you. *Protecting* you. Use the phone we left you if you need me otherwise. I'm programmed in the autodial." He brushed her cheek with his finger, a shiver racing down her spine with the contact as he said, "And don't let West touch you. It pisses me off. And I am really *good* at being pissed off."

He let go of the door, forcing her to scramble as it started to open. A second later, Michael disappeared, and a little old lady appeared in his wake, scoffing at Cassandra's obvious disarray. The woman huffed in disgust and marched to the stall.

Cassandra ran her hand down her flared black skirt, thankful the silky material didn't easily wrinkle. She wasn't going to crawl around for her buttons; she took off her jacket and marched to the mirror.

The quick inspection proved, indeed, she was a mess, her hair all over the place, a glob of smudged lipstick on her jaw and chin. She looked... Cassandra frowned, heart suddenly racing as her eyes dilated and changed, fading green to black, green to black. Cassandra gasped, trying to control the panic threatening to overtake her. She leaned on the sink as if a closer look would somehow change the reality of what she was seeing. But it didn't. Her eyes were definitely black now—so black, that against her pale skin, with her blonde hair pulled neatly back at the nape of her neck, they all but consumed her face.

She pressed her hand to her forehead. This couldn't be happening. She'd managed to get her hands on Ava's lifebond research after Adam's takeover, and she knew a blood exchange was necessary for her to be converted to GTECH and fully linked to Michael. Her mind raced with the possibility that the lifebond process had evolved, that Michael might know it, that he might be using their bond to get to Red Dart, to her father.

She grabbed the sink again with both hands, her knees wobbling with the thought. "What have you done to me, Michael?" she whispered.

Chapter 8

ONLY MINUTES AFTER LEAVING CASSANDRA IN THAT restroom, Michael appeared on the roof of the hotel where he was to meet Caleb and instantly began to pace, damn thankful Caleb had yet to arrive. He was coming out of his skin, reveling in the memory of holding Cassandra, tortured by the fact that he burned to claim her, his Lifebond, his woman. He ran a hand over his face, tension rippling through every muscle of his body. He told himself he was still a man of control, a man who, despite everything he'd faced with Adam, had managed to manipulate a fine line between right and wrong to serve the Renegades' cause. Yet when he'd seen Brock West touch Cassandra and felt the lust rolling off of that bastard, Michael had been ready to kill. Had Cassandra not come to him when she did... well, he did not know what would have happened.

The wind shifted ever so slightly, and Caleb materialized, quickly assessing Michael's edginess. "I assume you saw Cassandra?"

Michael forced himself to stop pacing, one hand on his jean-clad hip. "She's agreed to copy the hard drive."

Caleb narrowed his gaze. "Did you tell her you are no longer undercover inside Zodius?"

"I told her," Michael said. "And I swore to protect her. What I didn't tell her was how likely it is she is going to need that protection. She has plenty to worry about with Brock right now. And she's no fool. She knows she's on Adam's radar. She knows he'll send someone else for Red Dart in my absence. I figure she had plenty to digest right now."

"I'm sorry, Michael," Caleb said grimly. "I know you don't want her involved in this. If there was any other way—"

"You didn't do this, Caleb," he said, cutting him off. "Her father did. He's the reason that she is back on Adam's radar. Why the hell did he bring her back from Germany? I should have killed that SOB when I had the blade to his throat."

Michael started pacing again, replaying that moment inside Groom Lake. How much he'd wanted to kill Powell, rather than simply put on a show for Adam, how certain he'd been that Powell would be nothing but trouble. But damn the look in Cassandra's eyes... it had shredded him up inside. Staying away from her for two years had been hell, but he'd watched Adam's soul grow darker by the day, and Ava's with him. He was headed there—he knew that. And as long as he didn't complete their blood bond, he told himself, he wouldn't take her with him. He should have killed Powell. The world would have been a safer place, and Cassandra's hatred for him would have kept them both from feeling temptation.

Caleb sat down on a concrete block that surrounded an air conditioner and cast the sky a thoughtful inspection, seeming to know—as he did often these past few years— where Michael's thoughts had drifted. "Letting a man like Powell turn you into a murderer isn't the answer."

That stopped Michael in his steps. "How many people did we kill because that man ordered us to do it?"

"Because it was our duty," Caleb reminded him. "To protect our country."

"Knowing what we know now about Powell's personal agendas," Michael said, "I question every order he ever gave us."

"Regardless," Caleb said. "Killing him would have been the wrong choice."

"If I had killed him," he murmured disagreeably, giving Caleb his back as he turned to the skyline, "Red Dart would not be an issue now."

Caleb pushed to his feet and joined him, and for a few minutes they stood there, staring into the night. "I could have killed Adam hundreds of times over," he said.

Michael cut him a sideways look. "He's your brother," he said. "I'll do it for you."

"Let's figure out how to keep him from blowing up the world from his grave first, eh?" He patted Michael on the back—the only man alive Michael trusted enough to allow such a thing. "Once Cassandra is safe again, we should go have a long-past-due beer and plot his demise."

A beer with Caleb. A kiss from Cassandra. Her safety. If only it were all so simple. But it wasn't, and Michael knew it.

After Michael had left her in the restroom, her eyes black as coals, Cassandra had been sure she would miss the press conference—her black eyes would be a dead giveaway to Brock West that she'd converted to GTECH.

But a quick trip to her room, and she'd discovered that her eyes, thankfully, were already fading back to green. She had no idea what that meant and hadn't had time to think it through. She'd quickly changed her jacket, willed herself to calm, and managed to make her meeting.

Now, two hours later, back in the bar, Cassandra and Brock wished the final reporters farewell. And while the black of her eyes might have been temporary, the rage of hormones that Michael had created in her still thrummed within her body. A dull ache between her thighs punished her with awareness that had her squeezing her legs together.

Her reaction to Michael had always been physically intense, but nothing like this. It was as if her body were trying to complete the lifebond process on its own, and that terrified her. They knew so little about Lifebonds; the few who existed all lived within the Zodius compound, out of their reach. For all she knew, the more powerful Michael became, the more responsive she would be to their connection.

"You're an ace with the press," Brock commented, eyeing a text message on his phone. The slightest hint of irritation flashed on his face before he refocused on her. "Listen. I want to take you to dinner, but I have unexpected business to attend. Can we do it tomorrow night?"

Relief washed over her. Even without the threat of Michael nearby, she had no interest in this man's obvious intent on seduction. *Not that any man had a chance against Michael*, she thought wryly. "I'm tired anyway," she said, packing up her bag. "I'll meet you in the lobby at ten in the morning to head to the airport?"

He didn't move, his eyes fixed on her—hot, inviting. She felt as if he knew she was all wet and wanting, as if she were transparent. "You didn't respond to my dinner offer."

Her first instinct was to shoot him down, but

Cassandra checked her reaction. Michael was right—she wanted to know who was lying, and creating an enemy out of Brock didn't seem a smart move when she needed to snag his hard drive information.

She forced a smile. "Let's play it by ear. We have a long day of travel tomorrow."

"And we'll need to eat. We might as well do it together." His phone vibrated with another text message, and he sighed. "I better go. I'll see you in the morning." He pushed to his feet, and she stared after him. *Who was that call from*, she wondered?

Cassandra grabbed her things and headed to her room, her mind and body replaying Michael's touch. He was no doubt miles away now, but one call from that phone he'd left her, and he'd be with her in seconds. Part of her wanted to throw it off the hotel balcony for fear she'd dial it—dial it to scream at him, dial it to demand to know how he could have left her without one single word in two years. Dial it to beg him into her bed to make this ache and loneliness go away. "Damn you, Michael," she whispered, as she stepped into her dark room and leaned against the hard wooden surface of the door. "I don't want to feel this again."

A voice sounded in the hallway—Brock's voice, she realized. She'd known they were on the same floor, but not this close. "She's in her room," he said. "Where I was planning to be too, until you called." He listened a moment. "I told you I'd get it, and I will. And she's a part of my plan, which you are interrupting." A few seconds of silence. "Fine. I'll be there." A low curse followed as the door next to hers opened and slammed shut.

He'd been talking about her! Lord help her father

if that was him on the other line. And get what? Red Dart? Oh, no. Maybe that wasn't her father. Maybe it was… Adam. Or Michael? No, that was insane. Unless Michael was a really good actor. She bit her bottom lip. How could she be sure he wasn't after everything that had happened?

She flipped on the light and set her briefcase and purse against the wall. She considered a moment and then kicked her shoes off, unzipping her skirt in the process. She didn't bother to change her shirt and jacket, just quickly grabbed a pair of jeans and slid them over her hips. Sturdy boots followed.

Wherever Brock was going, she was discreetly going, too. She had to find out what was going on and who was behind it all. And who, if anyone, she could fully trust. She paused, a sick feeling coming over her. What if that had been Adam, not Caleb, on the phone with her today? Didn't twins sound alike? She inhaled sharply and forced herself back into action. All the more reason she had to follow West, and any minute now, he'd be opening his door again.

Too many had died at Groom Lake, and maybe, just maybe, if she had seen through her father sooner, then she would have saved them. She couldn't sit back and risk being wrong about his motives again. Nor could she risk trusting Michael and then find out he was really still with Zodius. Because Michael had been right on another point besides her need to know who was lying—Cassandra couldn't sit back and let innocent people be harmed if she could do something to stop it from happening.

And right now that meant trusting no one.

Cassandra was already fishing the rental car key from her purse when she heard Brock's hotel door open and shut. She listened for his footsteps to fade and then quickly did a hallway sweep before darting toward the stairwell. She raced down the fifteen flights of stairs to get to the parking garage, hoping that Brock's elevator had a good many stops on the ride down—enough time to make up for the delay her run downstairs required.

With her chest heaving, Cassandra finally reached the basement level and paused for both breath and caution. She eased the door open just in time to see Brock sliding into his rental two cars down from hers. Deftly, she slipped through the door and inched it silently closed then used a blue Ford pickup as cover while she waited for Brock's departure. The instant Brock pulled away, she took off running to her car, wishing for a security clicker rather than the stupid key entry that rental cars used. She fumbled to jam the darn thing in the lock and then fumbled some more to start the car, her adrenaline in overdrive. But she was moving and just in time to see in which direction Brock turned onto the street.

Only a few minutes later with her discreetly on his tail, Brock pulled into an alley behind a cluster of three white stone buildings near the National Mall District, with the Lincoln Memorial lit in all its glory a short walk away. It was nearly 11 p.m. now, and the streets were relatively bare but for a speckle of pedestrians.

"Damn it," Cassandra murmured, knowing that honking and waving her hands would be more discreet than following him down that alley. Instead, she whipped the car to a narrow side street that sat on the edge of the adjacent park and killed her lights, not happy about leaving the safety of her car. Instinct sent her hand to her purse for her weapon a moment before she grimaced over the realization that it was not there. Growing up a military brat, she'd been taught to use a gun about the same time she'd learned to walk. But taking a gun through airport security post-9/11 and into the capital city wasn't exactly approved—government employee or not.

Considering her options, Cassandra grabbed the cell phone Michael had given her, her chest tight with the thought of punching his programmed number. Not unless hell froze over, she vowed, but also knew she'd grabbed it at the last minute for a reason—she wasn't going to let pride get in the way of safety. If anything went wrong with this not so brilliant plan she was about to undertake, she knew clear to her soul Michael would protect her. The only person Michael was going to let hurt her was Michael himself. A little like her father, she'd decided grimly. Cassandra flipped the phone to vibrate and then slid it into her pocket, shoving open the car door as she did. Her purse would stay behind with the car door unlocked, precautions meant to ensure she could make a fast escape if need be.

She eyed the trees draping the street and the statues in the park, assessing a few possible escape routes and hiding places—more of her father's training—as she quickly crossed the two-lane street to approach the buildings from the front. She cut between the first two, keeping a tight line down the side of the wall until she found the grass divider outside the alley lined by shrubs. Muffled male voices lifted from the alley where Brock had pulled his car.

Bending down, Cassandra crawled through the grass

to the edge of the shrubs. "I'm starting to get pissed off, Brock." The voice was low, deep, familiar, though she couldn't quite place it. The kind of familiar that sent chills down her spine because she knew the man was one of the GTECHs from Groom Lake. "Adam wants the crystal and the protocols for GTECH use. *Why* is this so *fucking* difficult to produce?"

"I'm aware of what Adam wants, and I'm working on it," Brock snapped back, clearly not afraid of the Zodius. "Powell isn't keen on giving out that information to anyone. He insists it's still in the testing stages, not ready to be revealed, and after Groom Lake, he won't hand it over until he's certain it's ready."

"I'm beginning to feel we're being jerked around," the Zodius soldier countered. "You need to get this under control, and I mean now."

"Don't tell me what I need to do, Lucian," Brock spouted back. "Fucking around and moving too fast isn't going to do anything but screw this up. Once Powell is out of the way, I'll be the go-to man. I'll control the government's Zodius initiatives, meaning... *we'll* control those initiatives. But that means patience, which you, Lucian, have never had."

Lucian! Yes. Now she remembered the voice. He was one of Adam's most trusted Zodius. She sought confirmation, tweaking a few leaves enough to create a line of sight and managing to gain a visual—tall, muscular, bigger than life, with short, military-spiked, blond hair. She recognized Lucian instantly.

Lucian sauntered a few steps toward Brock, leaving the two Zodius who flanked him behind. Brock stood waiting, arms crossed in front of his broad chest, legs spread in a solid stance. He lowered his voice for Brock's ears only. Cassandra wasn't sure what he was saying, but she thought it was, "If you fail me, Adam will kill us both."

Yes, that was what he'd said she decided when she heard Brock reply, "I will not, nor have I ever failed you," his voice equally as low. "Powell demonstrated Red Dart on humans. His company, PMI, is testing it on GTECHs in his private facility."

"So he doesn't trust you," Lucian accused. "Or you'd be a part of his PMI staff."

"I'm close to becoming an insider," Brock insisted. "Getting close to his daughter would—"

"Michael has defected to the Renegades," Lucian said. "And as we all know, they are ex-lovers. We know they have been in contact. Cassandra Powell needs to be eliminated."

Cassandra barely contained a gasp. Dead. Adam wanted her dead.

"Are you fucking insane?" Brock demanded. "She is the only thing, besides himself, that Powell gives a shit about. If she dies, he'll go nuts. He'll put his guard up—and I'll never get to Red Dart before it's too late."

"Not if it looks like an accident," Lucian said. "And while he grieves, for a brief time his guard will come down. Use the opportunity to get me Red Dart."

"I want to talk to Adam," Brock demanded.

Lucian and the other two Zodius soldiers laughed. "Adam does not talk to humans," Lucian said, amused.

"I wouldn't be human if you gave me the damn serum."

"Earn it," Lucian said. "Get us Red Dart."

"Powell wants me to romance his daughter," he said.

"He's grooming me to be his son-in-law. His right-hand man. This is bigger than Red Dart. We'll know every move the government is making."

"We don't need to know what they are doing," he said. "We'll have Red Dart to control humans. We simply need the Renegades out of the way." Lucian's laugh filtered through the air, low and deep. "Besides, in six months you haven't gotten into that bitch's pants. I'm not placing any bets on you now. We already know she's susceptible to Michael's influences. She's a liability. You want the serum. To be one of us, you *will* kill her."

Cassandra had heard enough. She could barely breathe. She started to back away, realizing that being caught was a death sentence. A twig broke. She froze as she felt their attention shift in her direction. Her mind raced. She hadn't been seen yet, and she didn't want to be. She contemplated backing up slowly or simply charging to safety, to heck with noise—and the need to run won out. She sprang into action, straining with every stretch of her muscles to get around the corner of the building to the more public forum.

A motorcycle screamed in her ears as she rounded the corner, the headlights streaming in her face, blinding her. A second later she was swept off her feet as a powerful arm wrapped around her waist. Warmth washed over her, and a sense of security that defied the precarious way her feet dangled above the street. *Michael*. Suddenly, the questions and accusations about his motives didn't matter. He was here. That was all that mattered. And she had a chance to survive this night.

Chapter 9

THE TWO ZODIUS SOLDIERS TRAVELING WITH LUCIAN faded into the wind, leaving Brock with only one Zodius to beat his ass. Anger flashed in Lucian's eyes a moment before Brock was slammed against his rental car, the air walloped from his chest as his back hit metal. Brock flinched at the pain along his spine and vowed the day he was finally a GTECH he would kill Lucian. Rip him apart limb by limb. Oh, how he would enjoy every minute of that blood bath. And *he would* be a GTECH. He'd played his cards too well. Either Adam or Powell would give him that serum.

"You stupid sonofabitch!" thundered Lucian. "You were followed!" He glared at him suspiciously. "Or did you tell Powell you were meeting me? I swear to you, Brock, if I find out you're working both sides, I will rip you apart piece by piece."

"If anyone was followed," Brock grunted back fiercely enough to defy the truth of the accusation, "it was you. I wouldn't even be here if you'd left me the fuck alone. As of last night, you have the Green Hornet bullets. Those bullets are golden. They're the only bullets that can penetrate the Renegades' body armor and take them down, until you can use Red Dart on them. That is your proof of my loyalty, and it should be all you need."

"Once I test the bullets and they prove effective," he said, "perhaps it will."

"Damn it, Lucian," he ground out. "Those bullets are meant to be used with Red Dart. Use them to wound the Renegades. Tag them with Red Dart and capture them. Don't use the damn things until we have Red Dart. I'm the only person who could give them to you besides Powell. He'll know I betrayed him."

"Maybe that is what I hope for," he growled.

Sorry P.O.S. was trying to mess with his head, and it wasn't going to work. "Let me do my job, Lucian. And that job includes fucking Cassandra Powell, not killing her."

Lucian snarled. "The only person getting fucked is you if you've exposed our plans to Powell. Adam doesn't just want Red Dart out of Powell's hands, he plans to use it to gain control of the Renegades and force his brother to join him. You have no idea how pissed he will be if you screw that up. So I suggest you get me that Red Dart crystal with the GTECH method of application. That's the only way you can prove your loyalty. And turn the lights out on Cassandra Powell before I snap your delicate little human neck." The wind whistled around them a moment before Lucian disappeared.

Brock balled his fist and jerked his sore body off the hood, punching at the air. Damn it to hell, this was ending, and it was ending now. He had come too far from the shit hole, Chicago public housing where his father beat the crap out of him every day to allow Lucian or anyone else to use him as a whipping dog.

The writing was on the wall—GTECH was the future. He wanted to be that future. And he would not be played a fool by either Powell or Adam to get there.

Powell had promised that Brock would lead a new generation of GTECHs. Stronger. Faster. Able to capture and control those GTECHs already in existence. He'd find a way around Red Dart once he controlled all the other GTECHs. The most important thing was being the one at the top of the food chain.

He charged toward his vehicle, already removing his cell from his belt to call Powell. If the information he had to share tonight didn't convince Powell to step up the pace and give Brock the new, improved, GTECH serum that PMI had been working on, then nothing would. And then, Brock would know Powell did not deserve his loyalty, though he wasn't keen on being one of Adam's followers. But that would be better than remaining human. And following Adam would mean Powell's baby girl was going down. A little detail he'd keep to himself, of course, since he'd be Cassandra's assassin if need be.

Brock punched the autodial.

After turning in early Powell woke from a dead sleep at the sound of his cell phone ringing. He grabbed it from the nightstand and irritably eyed the caller ID before punching the answer key. "This better be good, West."

"Michael has left Zodius," he said. "He's now with the Renegades."

Powell sat up, instantly alert. Michael. The fucking bane of his existence. It was bad enough that someone in the White House had leaked Red Dart to the Zodius. Now, the Renegades would know as well. And now, if Michael was involved, Cassandra would be in danger.

No one was supposed to know about Red Dart until this was over with control back in his grasp.

"What exactly happened, West?" he demanded impatiently.

"Lucian demanded a meeting. Adam intends to use Red Dart to force the Renegades to join him. He also believes Michael is using your daughter to find it and destroy it before that can happen."

"That's insanity," Powell blasted through the phone. "My daughter is not helping Michael. Damn it to hell, West! The man tried to kill me. And the very fact that Caleb could trust Michael, an X2 positive that had been with the Zodius for two years, proves my point. All GTECHs must be controlled. We can't trust any of them."

"I agree, sir," West said. "Give me the serum, General. I'm ready to fight. I'll force the GTECHs back under your command."

Powell could practically hear the man salivating over the serum that few knew he still possessed. The government was afraid of the serum, afraid it would make more Adams. They wouldn't be afraid after they saw the results of Red Dart in action. But then, most humans were afraid; he was not most humans. And he could not wait until they got over their fear; he had to make more soldiers and properly protect this country.

"There are risks, Lieutenant Colonel West." Like death.

"Soldiers take risks, sir."

That was enough for Powell. He wanted to take risks—Powell would let him. "Get my daughter home safely, and we'll talk." Powell walked to the corner bar of his bedroom, poured a glass of bourbon, and sipped the amber liquid. "Put a surveillance team on my daughter," he said. "Make sure they are equipped to put down a GTECH. Michael Taylor is to be killed on sight." Powell wasn't going to allow Michael to use his daughter to get to him again. No one made a fool out of him and lived to brag about it. He ended the call and dialed yet another.

"Hello," came the smoky female voice that never failed to rocket heat through his loins. Jocelyn. One of the most knowledgeable weapons experts on this planet, and the woman who'd made both the Green Hornets and Red Dart possible.

His attraction to her was an unexpected complication that drugged him further upon each contact. He'd involved her for her resources and for the pain she could cause his enemies—a shared vengeance for one enemy in particular. Michael. She had a history with him as treacherous as his own. And a desire to see him pay.

Their shared desire to make Michael suffer had turned decidedly erotic, an aspect of their relationship untouched thus far, though that might soon change. He liked her as she was—angry and bitter, yet feminine. He saw no reason to tell her of Michael's shift to the Renegades. No need to risk her falsely seeing him as rehabilitated. She was, after all, a woman, and generally weak, unwilling to take certain risks. Unlike Chin, who didn't mind a fatality or two or three for the greater good.

Exactly why she was not involved in Chin's work. "We're ready to test Red Dart on a GTECH."

An excited squeal filled the line. This work was her pride and joy. And as such, she refused, despite his prodding, to hand it over until she could test it herself, though she'd granted him demonstrations.

"How wonderful," she exclaimed. "I can't believe this is finally happening. Chin told me it would be weeks before the soldiers were ready for Red Dart. When?"

"Tomorrow night," he said. "But I don't want the lab's location disclosed. Sedation will be required prior to the subject's transport to the facility."

"Of course," she purred softly. "Whatever is necessary. This is too important to take unnecessary risks."

Unnecessary risks. Yes. Exactly. She simply wouldn't understand the necessary ones. So he focused on what they both would understand. "You're certain it will work? You've found the right tranquilizer mixture to stun their immune system?"

"I can never be certain in the lab without a perfect test subject," she said. "But I'm as certain as I can be."

His lips thinned. "That is not the answer I want to hear."

She laughed, soft, silky. "You're very demanding," she chided. "It's going to work, General."

A smile touched his lips, relief easing the tightness in his chest. "We're going to save the world, Jocelyn. You do know that, don't you?"

"Oh yes," she said. "I know. And I can't wait to celebrate." There was a seductive promise in the words that tightened his groin. She aroused him, but not nearly as much as the power that would soon be his as the greatest general who'd ever lived. Never again would another country dare strike against America. The GTECHs were like the ultimate nuclear bomb waiting to explode. And he alone would hold the remote. It was absolutely fucking beautiful.

Skidding the motorcycle around a corner and to a halt behind a cluster of trees, Michael killed the engine to buy time and set Cassandra down on the pavement. He didn't dare take her all the way to her car for fear she'd be spotted before he could distract the Zodius soldiers who followed them. The Zodius would scout before attacking and evaluate their prey as human or GTECH, which bought him about three minutes max.

Flipping open his helmet, he growled, "Damn it, I told you to be careful. This is not careful."

"You also said trust no one, and I don't," she countered. "Not even you."

Anger coiled in his gut. "In case you didn't notice, sweetheart, I'm the guy saving your sweet little ass."

"Guess you still need something from me," she shot back sharply.

He ground his teeth against that remark, reaching for the Wesson strapped to his leg and handing it to her. It wouldn't do her much good, but knowing she had it made him feel better.

"Between the eyes or don't bother. They wear body armor now, since your father started popping them with tranquilizers for Lord only knows what purpose."

"Trying to keep from killing them," she countered, palming the weapon. "He doesn't want to kill them or torture them."

Right. Michael was buying that about as readily as he was Cassandra ever trusting him again, but now wasn't the time for arguments.

He watched her do a quick inspection of the weapon, taking comfort in her confident handling of the gun. She'd need that confidence if one of the Zodius confronted her.

"Go to your room and lock the door, and don't open it until I get there," he ordered. The wind's energy trickled down his spine, a charge he'd come to know as a warning. The Zodius were approaching. "Go now!" he hissed in a whisper. Instantly, Cassandra took off running, a good little soldier following orders, thanks to her father's mentoring. One of the few good things that man had ever done for her.

Michael flipped his helmet down and sat behind those bushes, waiting until the wind whispered along his spine with enough intensity to tell him he needed to act. The wind was his weapon, as much a part of him as the blood racing through his veins. It was a living being to him, able to communicate, and under his command at all times. No one wind-walked with Michael nearby unless he allowed them to. Not even Adam and Caleb.

Unfortunately, using his abilities wasn't an option. He had to convince them he was human with his helmet giving him the cover of anonymity. Anyone could be following Brock—certainly Powell had a track record of distrust that would support having Brock followed. A façade of humanity also meant they'd want him dead before they'd want him reporting back what they would believe he'd heard in that alley—which had been every damn word, including the part about Cassandra.

Revving the engine, Michael jerked the bike back into action, his intention to put himself in the path of the Zodius soldiers and give Cassandra time to depart unnoticed, while making them believe he'd been the sole person eavesdropping in those bushes. The two Zodius soldiers were instantly in his path, and he cut to the right toward the grass. They followed quickly on his tail, on foot, but he'd hoped they couldn't wind-walk without risking exposure in such a public place.

He hit the curb and took it with a hard thud that sent the wheel and then the bike flying. Instantly, his spine tingled; the two soldiers weren't being as cautious as he thought. Fuck! They were wind-walking, and though he could stop them, he didn't dare without giving himself away.

Michael spread his legs and let the bike go, allowing it to fly forward while he tucked and rolled to the ground. He came down hard on his back into a rock formation that jarred his ribs and muscles. But he didn't have time for pain. By the time he'd finished the roll, he'd drawn two guns—one with bullets and one with tranquilizer darts.

The soldiers were charging at him, a foot away at most, and he landed a tranq dart in both their foreheads, but not before one of them got off a silent shot of his own. Pain exploded in Michael's rib cage as the enemy's bullet penetrated what should have been his impermeable body armor.

The two soldiers stumbled and fell, giving him no more than a minute before their GTECH metabolism had them on their feet again. Ignoring his injury, Michael ground his teeth against the pain and kicked to his feet, feeling damn cranky and ready to get this over with. Sweat trickled down his brow, under the helmet, blood already matted to his T-shirt. He managed a quick sweep of the area even as he took aim at one of his targets. He'd noted no obvious witness, but he really didn't give a crap if there was one. Let any witness and the dead bodies be Lucian's problem.

Ruthlessly, he put a bullet into both their heads

right between the eyes. He didn't recognize either one of them, but that was no surprise. Adam's scientists had assured him they could reproduce the serum with Adam's blood, and hungry to grow his population of followers, he'd handed out the injections he'd confiscated from Powell's stock like it was candy. That was, until he found out his scientists were wrong—they couldn't duplicate the serum with his blood.

"You really shouldn't have pissed me off," he murmured at the dead soldiers, feeling no remorse for killing them. He was a soldier and a trained killer; it was all he had been his entire adult life. He did what others wouldn't and couldn't do, because somebody had to do it. And he didn't know how to be anything but those things—not even for Cassandra.

Michael purposely left the tranquilizer darts behind. The army used the darts to slow the Zodius soldiers down enough to get a fatal shot off, which was exactly why Michael had used them. To stay off Adam's radar as much as possible until he had Cassandra and the Red Dart crystal secure. Michael called the wind, fading into it as mist did into rain. His injury would soon force him to sleep in order to heal or risk collapsing. He had to get to Cassandra before he lost too much blood to protect her.

"Sonofabitch!" Lucian cursed, towering over the bodies of his dead soldiers, grimacing at the sight of the trademark army tranquilizer darts stuck in their foreheads right next to the bullet holes. Powell's army. Which meant Powell now knew Brock was working with the

Zodius. Lucian's Red Dart connection was gone. He balled his fists, punching at the air in pure fury.

Sirens sounded in the near distance. Fuck. Fuck. Fuck. The last thing he needed now was more humans. He grabbed his phone and called for a cleanup team the Zodius kept in hot pockets of activity, ending the call with a frown as his gaze caught on some blood several feet from the bodies. He walked to it and squatted, touching it, using his rare "tracker" ability to read the metaphysical energy that certain living organisms produced.

"Michael," he whispered. It had not been Powell's man here tonight. It had been Michael.

The wind shifted, and Lucian shoved to his feet. Tad appeared beside one of the bodies and bent down, grabbing the tranq dart from the soldier's forehead. "Defeated by humans," he said and snorted. "And you think you're capable of replacing Michael? Do you really believe Michael would ever be defeated by a human?"

"Fuck you, Tad," Lucian said.

The cleanup crew manifested near the bodies, and Lucian waved them into action. They grabbed the men and disappeared.

"No," Tad said. "Fuck you, Lucian." He made a growling noise meant to taunt. "You're nothing but wolf bait when Adam finds out about this."

"You're nothing but trailer trash. You think Adam will allow the likes of you inside his royal circle? My father was a senator, my grandfather, a five-star general. I am the reason we know Red Dart exists. What can you do besides hunt down weak females?" He sneered at him, looking the brawny piece of crap up and down. "You are nothing but one of Adam's pets. A dog who does tricks."

Suddenly, the wind shifted, wicked, hot, and wild, a telling sign that Adam approached and that he was angry. Tad's face transformed from pure anger to gloating arrogance. "We shall see who the 'dog' is now."

Adam appeared dressed in black leather, two wolves at his feet. Much to Lucian's distress, wind-walking didn't kill the little bastards. At least not when Adam transported them.

"Why has my evening of pleasure been disturbed?" he growled. Pleasure being a group of humans thrown in a ring and fed to his wolves. Whoever survived would get a dose of the highly in-demand serum. So far, no one had survived.

Tad held up a tranquilizer dart to Adam. "Lucian went and got two of our men killed by Powell and his army."

Adam arched a brow, his voice low, but tight. A deadly edge curled around the words. "Have you failed me, Lucian?"

The wolves turned on Lucian, growling as if picking up on their master's anger. Adam did not like to lose GTECHs. Lucian seethed with anger. Those beasts would never have growled at Michael, and it pissed Lucian off they had growled at him. One day soon they would not. One day they would respect him as they had Michael. Lucian held up his blood-tinged fingers.

"It is Tad's limited tracking abilities that have failed," he replied, cutting Tad a short, demeaning look. "Michael followed Brock West here, no doubt trying to find out something about Red Dart."

"In other words," Tad observed, "Michael now knows your contact Brock West to be a traitor."

"And that means what?" Lucian challenged. "To

expose West to Powell is to expose the Renegades' knowledge of Red Dart. They don't want Powell to bury Red Dart someplace impossible to reach any more than we do. Everything is as planned, Adam. West is close to Red Dart. Michael is injured. He'll be forced to sleep off his injury. By the time he is capable of approaching Cassandra Powell, she will be dead." And Lucian wasn't waiting for Brock to kill her. Not after tonight's close call. He'd do it himself.

Police cars screeched to a nearby halt. Adam's attention did not waver from Lucian. "Bring me proof she is dead by nightfall tomorrow or suffer the consequences." He cut Tad a sharp look. "I do not enjoy being interrupted. I suggest you find a way to repay me for lost pleasure before you return to the city." Adam faded into the wind, not even a leaf ruffling around him.

Lucian and Tad glared at one another, violence rippling between them, before they both wind-walked. One of them would die before this was over, but not before Cassandra Powell.

Chapter 10

SHE'D BE DEAD RIGHT NOW IF MICHAEL HADN'T SHOWN up, and surviving was all that was on her mind as she pulled the rental car into the same spot she'd left, feeling certain that a Wind-walker was going to show up at any moment. Adrenaline raced at high-octane speed through her body as she shoved open the car door and headed for the stairwell, noting the absence of Brock's car and praying that meant she'd beaten him back to the hotel. She wouldn't feel certain she'd dodged the proverbial bullet until she was inside her room.

Nerves twisted Cassandra's stomach in knots as she took the stairs to the main hotel level, trying to avoid the risk of running into Brock. The man wanted to kill her. She didn't want to run into him in a vacant stairwell. Shoving through the door, she rushed through the sparsely populated lobby and found the elevators, thankful when the doors opened instantly.

Stepping inside the car, she prepared a story to explain where she had been in case of a confrontation with Brock. But thinking was hard, her nerves working her over, clouding her mind. She was terrified over that order Lucian just gave to kill her, but she was also worried over Michael. He was in trouble; she could feel it in every inch of her body and practically taste it in every laden breath she drew. Which was nuts. She was the human with Zodius GTECHs after her. She'd watched his abilities develop and seen the mighty force that was Michael. But this did nothing to calm the worry creating a roller-coaster ride of emotions inside her.

The bell chimed as she arrived on her floor, and she rushed into the hallway, thankful it was vacant. The minute she approached the door to her room she had the sense of Michael being near, but it wasn't the same vibrant rush of awareness she normally felt. He was hurt—the thought came to her with a clarity she didn't question.

Anxiously, she swiped her entry card through the lock and was about to enter her room when the door next to hers opened, and Brock appeared.

"I wondered where you were," he said, walking toward her. "I was worried. I've been knocking for a while now."

A while, *her ass*. It was a miracle he'd beat her back to the hotel, and she wasn't exactly sure how he'd managed to do so. "And here I thought only my father worried," she replied, sarcastically. "I tried to find a twenty-four-hour pharmacy with no success. Looks like I'll be paying an arm and a leg for a toothbrush at the airport in the morning." She cringed at the horrible excuse when she could have called room service, but it was out now, and she had to live with it. He sauntered closer, too close. She didn't turn to face him, but still she could smell his cologne, and his scent turned her stomach—it never had before. This man who would be her killer if she allowed him to be. It was all she could do not to confront him. But she was smart enough to know she needed to think—to process what came next if she wanted to stay alive.

"It's late to go out alone," he commented dryly, suspicion in the depths of his eyes.

"I'm a military chick," she reminded him, trying to jest, but her voice sounded stiff even to her own ears. "We'll risk life and limb for a toothbrush."

He studied her a moment, looking none too convinced. But there was that lusty haze to his eyes that had her wanting to kick him right below the belt, especially after what she'd overheard. Did he want to bed her once before he killed her?

"We're both awake," he said, leaning against the doorjamb to her room. "Why not share a little nightcap?"

Her fingers curled around the metal knob in her palm a bit more firmly, ready to push her door open and make a fast escape, but found herself forced by his posture to turn and face him. She willed herself to offer a smile. "I'm exhausted, and we leave early," she said. "We said tomorrow night, if we aren't too tired. Let's leave it at that."

A heavy-lidded inspection followed, along with a thick silence that ended when he finally said, "Lobby at straight one thousand hours, then?"

"Yes," she said and made a disagreeable face. Ten o'clock was going to feel early tomorrow morning. She waved. "Night." And she didn't wait for a reply. She shoved open the door and quickly closed it firmly behind her. Immediately, she flipped the security latch into place.

"I'm going to really enjoy killing that sonofabitch."

Cassandra's heart skipped a beat as she whirled around to find Michael propped against the headboard of her bed, his dark hair hanging loose around his face where it had escaped the tie at his neck, long muscular legs stretched out across the bed, and a bloody red towel pressed to his side.

Her chest tightened. "Oh God." It was clear the towel he was holding against himself was drenched and that he was bleeding horribly. She rushed forward and crawled on the bed to his side.

"Why don't you have on Zodius body armor?" she asked, removing the bloody towel and trying to inspect his injury, but there was too much blood to see how bad it was, so she reapplied more pressure. "You're not invincible no matter what you think. You might heal quickly, but you can bleed to death just like the rest of us."

He tugged his T-shirt upward, displaying the thin suit he wore like a second skin. "Whatever they hit me with wasn't standard issue ammo."

Her eyes went wide at the sight of the thin bodysuit, impermeable to bullets, state-of-the-art technology that Adam's scientific team had somehow managed to manufacture and that her father was dying to get his hands on.

She pressed her hand to his stomach, memories of so many intimate moments shared with this man rushing over her. "How is this possible?" she asked. "My understanding was that no bullet should penetrate your armor. A grenade or rocket launcher, something more powerful, yes, but not a bullet."

"Clearly the Zodius have a new weapon," he said. "Once you cut the bullet out of my side, I'll get it to the Renegades' lab."

Her heart tripped. "The bullet is still inside you? Are you sure?"

Strain etched his handsome features. "Believe me," he said. "It's in there, and the sooner you get it out, the sooner I can go wipe the ground with Brock's 'night-cap' ass."

"You heard that?" she asked, shocked, recognizing that no normal person could have heard clearly through that door from the bed. It was an ability he hadn't possessed two years before.

"I heard everything," he said, shackling her arm with his free hand. The next thing she knew, he'd pulled her on top of him, pressed to that long, hard body. "Including the order to kill you."

Their eyes locked and held, and for just a moment, she forgot everything but how much this man had once meant to her. How safe and right he had felt. And she desperately needed to feel safe right now.

"Let me go before you hurt yourself," she protested way too late and far too weakly, her hand flexed on the solid wall of his chest. Adam had ordered her murdered; she was scared, and Michael's lips were close, so very close.

"You could have been killed out there tonight," he countered, his voice darn near a growl.

"But I wasn't," she whispered. "And I needed to follow him. I needed to know who I could trust."

"Because you don't trust me," he challenged and didn't wait for a reply—they both knew he'd nailed the truth. "I did what I did that day at Area 51 to protect innocent lives, yours included."

"This isn't about one day," she amended. "Two years, Michael. Two years of silence. You could have talked to me." She pushed up on his chest, trying to escape, but he held her firmly. "Let me up before you bleed to death." Seconds ticked by, his eyes were blazing, his jaw hard. And her heart—well, it hurt. Desperately, she whispered, "Please. Let go, Michael."

He released her, and she scrambled off him and to the edge of the bed, feeling like a doe-in-headlights that had barely escaped a head-on collision. Looking into his eyes always did her in. She felt a connection, felt she knew him. Yet, really—how much had she really known about Michael?

She reached for the phone to call the front desk. Without turning, she said, "I'm going to order some supplies."

—◦◦◦—

Michael lay on that bed only moments from holding Cassandra in his arms and listened to her phone conversation with the front desk operator. And he heard the quaver in her voice, the emotion that he knew he'd created. He wanted to protect her, but it seemed he knew only how to hurt her.

He blinked against the spots forming in his vision. Damn it, he could not pass out. Not until this bullet was out.

With all his will, Michael forced himself to move and somehow managed to remove the weapons strapped to various parts of his body, setting them on the nightstand. He took the utility knife from one of the straps around his thigh and laid it on the edge of the bed, deciding it was the best bet at removing the bullet. Then, with supreme effort, he heaved himself past the pain to a sitting position to remove his shirt. Somehow, he had to get out of this worthless armor.

Hanging up the phone, Cassandra turned to him and

gasped, "Are you crazy? You're gushing blood. Stop moving around." She scrambled to his side, her hand on his chest.

Their eyes locked, collided with the impact of a concrete slab right in his chest. Memories. Desire. She swallowed, and he watched that delicate little throat move. No amount of pain or blood loss could stop him from thinking of kissing it, of kissing her.

"Lie down, Michael," she ordered, her voice cracking, defying the steadiness of her stare.

"I need to get this shirt off," he said, his voice not much stronger than hers. He was powerful—a man people feared—yet what he feared most was this woman judging him unworthy. God, he never wanted to face that day. He wouldn't face that day. Damn. He'd left her so he wouldn't have to.

"Let me do it," she said quietly, a plea lacing the words. "Put aside everything between us right now, and let me do this. Michael. Please."

How many times had Michael wished to hear his name on her lips again and thought he never would? He longed to pull her back down on top of him—he didn't care that it was the wrong choice—that it would be dangerous to his ability to walk away. He didn't want to hurt her again, knew that was where this was going if he wasn't careful—if he didn't ensure that she stayed angry and distant. Despite this, raw possessiveness rose inside him. He had to make love to her one more time. And he *would*—soon, very soon. Maybe that made him selfish, but he didn't care anymore. He needed that one more time to survive a lifetime without her.

"Hold the towel on the wound," he said, his voice as tight as every muscle in his body. "Once I get the shirt off, you'll have to unzip the armor. You'll never get the bullet out as long as I have it on."

She nodded and quickly applied pressure to his wound. Michael yanked the shirt over his good arm and then over his head, letting it dangle off the shoulder near his injury. Cassandra helped him inch it down his arm and then tossed it to the floor. He reached down and held the bloody towel against his wound.

Cassandra winced at the blood running down his side. "You're bleeding way too much. We need to get this done. Hold on."

She reached forward, and their hands connected. A combination of pain and arousal rocketed through his body as she softly said, "I can't reach the zipper." It was the only warning he got before she climbed across his lap, using his shoulders to steady herself.

Again his eyes held hers—emotions, past and present, thick with implications and unspoken words. "And here I thought you were pissed at me," he commented in a low voice.

She cut her gaze, but not before he saw the sadness crossing her lovely face. "I got over being pissed a long time ago," she whispered.

"You seemed pretty angry at the gazebo," he commented.

She glanced at him, and then back down. "Maybe I'm still a little angry." She focused on working the zippers lining the top of his shoulders and his healthy left side. His armor fell free, connected only along his injured side, which he held in place with the towel, using what little energy he still had. His head was spinning, the blood loss taking a toll.

Cassandra eased her weight off his legs and took the armor and the bloody towel with her, quickly throwing it aside and shoving another towel onto his wound before applying pressure with both hands.

"Where the heck is housekeeping with those damn supplies?" she murmured.

His eyes were heavy. "We can't wait," he said. "The bullet has to come out now."

"We have nothing for pain," she fretted. "Nothing to sew you up with. No bandages. They're bringing everything. And I don't want to get started and then have them show up."

A knock sounded on the door, and she let out a sigh of relief. He willed himself to move, to grab a gun. Cassandra stared down at the gun, but said nothing, scooting off the bed and rushing toward the door.

"Just a minute," she yelled, stopping long enough to shrug off her soiled jacket and wipe off her hands before pulling on a clean shirt and tossing the dirty one aside. She grabbed her purse and the cash inside before discreetly cracking the door. He heard the attendant ask if she was okay, heard her murmur about falling and a make-believe trip to the ER to explain the bandages. A few seconds later, she'd gotten rid of the attendant and wheeled a tray inside. He set the gun down—it seemed suddenly heavier than normal.

Cassandra crawled to his side and handed him a bottle of vodka. "It's not much of a pain reliever, especially not with your metabolism, but it's something. Drink it down while I get some hot water. I know alcohol doesn't have much of an effect on you, but, well, maybe if you drink a lot and fast, it'll help some. It's worth a try."

He accepted the bottle of vodka as she scurried away despite his distaste for it.

With a low curse, he downed several long gulps, the clear liquor burning a path down his throat, the irony of Cassandra's unknowing choice of the vodka not going without notice. It was as if his father were laughing from his grave, reminding Michael that no matter what he did, where he went, he was still born of his father's blood, still of his birthright.

Cassandra returned and set the water on the night table, next to the supplies she'd laid out moments before. She drew a breath.

He sensed her hesitation and headed it off. "The sooner we do this," he commented, "the sooner I can start healing."

"I know," she said heavily. "I know."

He downed another long swallow of vodka, capped the bottle and handed it to her. There was no need to sterilize his wound; he didn't get infections. "Did I ever tell you how much my father loved a good vodka martini?"

A look of shock crossed her face. "You never spoke about your father."

Or the mother who hated his guts. Not that she'd said she hated him, but she didn't write, didn't call, didn't give a damn where he was or what he did. Sounded like hate to him. Michael offered her the knife, and she reached for it, but he didn't let go. Part of him wanted to try and explain why, but it wouldn't change who, or what, he was. He released the knife and turned onto his side, somehow keeping the towel in place. "I talked about my father," he said. "I remember precisely telling you he was a bastard."

She pressed her hand over the towel. "I've got it. And yes, now that you mention it, I do remember the bastard description rather clearly." She shifted to the matter at hand. "Okay. Let's do this. I'm going to try to see the bullet first." She lifted the towel for her inspection, and he felt her wiping and wiping at the wound, clearly trying to get a good visual. She let out a shaky breath, then, "I have to pull back the skin."

"Do what you have to." She didn't wait for another invitation, and he jerked and grunted as the bullet scraped his rib.

"Sorry," she whispered. "It's deep, Michael. I can't get to it. Not without cutting you." She pressed the towel down on the wound and leaned over him, staring at him, desperation in her face. "Call for help. We need a doctor. You have to have a painkiller, Michael. I'm insisting."

Using the last bit of energy he possessed, Michael reached up and laced his fingers through her hair, pulling her across his body. "Listen to me," he said, locking eyes with her. "You *have* to do this. There is no one else."

"A doctor—"

"The Renegades have only human doctors. Meaning they can't wind-walk, and I can't wait for them to take a plane. I need you to do this."

She inhaled and shook her head, her bottom lip trembling. "I hate this so much."

That made two of them, he thought, as he let her go and lay back down. His lashes lowered, his eyes heavy, the room suddenly spinning. He'd lost too much blood. How he'd kept going this long he didn't know. He swallowed against the nausea threatening to overcome him.

"Ready?" she asked.

Grinding his teeth, Michael willed his stomach to calm. "Yes."

She didn't give him time to change his answer. Steel cut through his flesh, the acid burn of radiating pain following. He was stiff. Sweat gathered on his back, his face, his entire body. In a distant corner of his mind, he knew Cassandra was crying, but still she worked, still she did what had to be done. And he knew the second she hit the bullet; his body jerked despite his best efforts to remain still, and he barely contained a scream as pain splintered through nerve endings.

"I'm sorry," Cassandra whispered a minute before he felt the blade slicing through his skin again and her finger digging inside him. Little pulses of light spread before his eyes, into his head, into his limbs, a moment before darkness pressed down on him. Panic formed— he never panicked. In his mind, he clawed through the darkness. If he died now, who would protect Cassandra? But it was too late—everything simply went black.

Hours after completing Michael's surgery, Cassandra sat on the edge of the bed, holding a cool rag to his head, scared for him, unsure what to do. She'd seen the GTECH healing process many times, which ranged from tingling skin for a small cut, to violent muscle spasms for more intense injuries. But never, ever, had she seen the kind of torture Michael's body was putting him through. He was burning up with fever, his muscles jerking and spasming. She could see them pulsing beneath his skin.

She rested her head on his chest, overwhelmed with worry. How much more could his heart endure of this kind of pain? What if the bullet had been poisonous?

She had to call for help, and the only person she knew to call was Caleb. *Cell phone*, she thought. Michael had to have one. Maybe it would have Caleb's number in it. She ran her hand over his pockets, and sure enough, another super slim phone was in his front pocket.

"Yes," she whispered, retrieving the phone and quickly tabbing through the saved numbers, her heart stopping as she saw one noted as "Adam." Her stomach clenched at that name, and unable to stop herself she thumbed through his call log. Her stomach rolled this time. He'd called Adam recently. Her mind raced as she saw the date and time. Oh my God. He'd called him the night he'd visited her in that Washington restroom. He'd told her he had already left Zodius that night. Who had she talked to on the phone? Caleb or Adam?

Suddenly, Michael sat up, and Cassandra gasped at this unexpected action, certain he was about to grab the phone. Instead, he was on his feet and headed toward the bathroom, hunched over—sick, she realized. She raced after him.

She found him hugging the toilet, throwing up. Cassandra grabbed the doorjamb, forced herself not to go to him, despite the instincts that told her to.

She held the phone, considering a call to Caleb again. Call for help or wait it out? She watched as Michael threw up over and over, so sick—too sick. Her mind raced, fear twisting her in knots. She'd heard Lucian clearly state that Michael was no longer with Zodius, but what if it was a setup? What if he hadn't left at all? That should make her more ready than ever to call Caleb, but Lord help her, it didn't. Because what would Caleb do to Michael if he were Zodius? And more importantly, why did she care?

Chapter 11

MICHAEL GASPED AS HE SAT STRAIGHT UP, SEARCHING the room around him and realizing he was in a bathroom on the floor, and holy hell, Cassandra was, too. He sucked in air as he tried to gather his bearings.

"Easy," she whispered, her hand going to his chest where he could feel the light spasms that meant his body was healing.

The scent of her—soft, female, deliciously Cassandra—insinuated into his nostrils and drew him back into the present. Memories rushed over him. The attack, the bullet. The hours hugging that damn toilet while Cassandra soothed him. "How long have I been out?"

"About six hours," she said.

"Damn," he murmured. He needed to call Caleb. He reached into his pocket and found it empty.

He started to push to his feet, and Cassandra grabbed his arm. "You were sick like I've never seen a GTECH sick before, Michael."

"I'm fine," he said, touching her cheek. Damn. "The healing sickness has been getting worse for a lot us. But once it's over, it's over." He pushed to his feet, moved his arms, felt on the mend. "I'm nearly healed, just weak, and in need of food." He offered Cassandra his hand and helped her up.

"What's the cause of the reaction?" she asked. She looked tired, the pale skin beneath her eyes now dark from lack of sleep. "It was bad, Michael. I was afraid your heart couldn't handle what your body was doing to you."

"The doctors don't know the cause, but they're working on it. The best they've come up with is an extreme vitamin C deficiency that is much more severe during the healing process." He patted his pockets. "Have you seen my phone?"

She stared at him a moment too long and then said, "Nightstand."

Michael frowned, sensing something in her that wasn't quite right, but shook it off and turned away, the need to communicate with Caleb winning his attention. He walked toward the bedroom, grimacing at the sight of the blood all over the bed, a mess he'd have to deal with before she checked out of the room.

Snagging the phone, he glanced at the clock, noting the early 6 a.m. He was about to hit the autodial for Caleb when Cassandra spoke from behind. "Which brother are you calling?"

Michael froze and turned to her, narrowing his gaze on her pale features. She looked fragile in an inexplicable way that drew his concern, because it was not natural for her. "What does that mean, Cassandra?"

"I was going to call for help, but I saw both Caleb's and Adam's numbers in your phone. I wasn't sure which one would help you and which one would kill you."

He inhaled at the implications of her words, anger climbing through his veins. "Maybe you should have just killed me yourself while you had the chance."

"Maybe I should have," she spouted back. "You called Adam the night you visited me. The night we…

you know—in the restroom. Yet you told me you'd left
Zodius. So who was I talking to on the phone? Adam
or Caleb?"

There was nothing he could say to Cassandra that
would matter. Instead, he punched Caleb's autodial
number on the phone and gave her his back.

The instant Caleb answered, he said, "We have
problems." He then relayed his concerns about the new
weapon technology and the connection between Brock
and Lucian. Finally, he said, "I need Sterling on the line.
Cassandra needs to be reassured that I am a Renegade by
someone who does not resemble your brother in voice or
appearance…" He hesitated. "And ask him to confirm
the last night I was undercover inside Zodius."

He turned and found Cassandra still standing in the
bathroom doorway. Their eyes collided, tension shimmering between them as he held out the phone. "For
the record, that would be the night before we were in
that hotel restroom. You looked at the caller ID wrong.
A little too eager to condemn me, I guess. But talk to
Sterling." She knew Sterling from Area 51 and had heard
he'd joined the Renegades. "Ask him whatever you want
to. Get that peace of mind that I can't give you."

Distress washed over her delicate features. "I don't
know what you want from me, Michael." Strain tightened
the words. "How can you expect me not to question you?"

"I'd consider you a fool if you didn't. Give your trust
to Caleb, not me." This was what he wanted. Her distrust, her hatred. A way to leave without hurting her.
He'd get her to Sunrise City, and he'd leave. Get the
hell away from her and keep her safe. Work for Caleb
from a distance.

She inhaled and walked toward him, taking the phone.

"Hello," she said. "Is this Sterling?" They exchanged a few words, her side of the conversation softly spoken, edged with discomfort. She ended the short talk and handed him back the phone.

Michael quickly confirmed that all was well with Caleb and ended the call. Preferring to save the confrontation with her over what was, or was not, between them for later—or better yet, never—he flipped the phone shut and shifted the conversation.

"Where is the bullet you removed?"

She shook her head. "Just like that? Where's the bullet? We aren't going to talk about why—"

"You needed to talk to Sterling," he said coldly, "because you don't trust me. And you *shouldn't* trust me. End of conversation."

Her jaw went slack. "That's it?" She inhaled, then forced it out. "I see. I get it. This is business. Talk to Caleb. Get Red Dart. Leave the personal out of it. Except when you think it might convince me to help. Anything to achieve your mission. Right? Kiss me. Touch me. Oh yes. Why not just *fuck* me while you're at it? Just to be sure I do what you want? Not necessary, by the way. I not only want to stop Adam, I intend to prove to you that you're wrong about all of this. Adam has manufactured this Red Dart torture story to divide the Renegades from the government. So please! Leave personal out of this. Stop… with us. With our past. Stop everything but business."

She started to turn away, and he knew he should let her go. He couldn't. "Cassandra. Wait." She paused, but didn't face him. Seconds of tension-filled silence swelling between them before he softly said, "You are my Lifebond, and I would die for you."

She half-turned, anger glistening in the depths of her green eyes. "I haven't seen or heard from you in two years, Michael," she said. "So don't give me that Lifebond crap, because it obviously doesn't mean anything. You're a soldier, Michael. You would die for your cause, and I am a part of that cause right now—though I have no idea exactly what that is. You were with me at Groom Lake. Then you were gone. You were Zodius. Now you're Renegade. I don't know who you are. I wonder if you even know." She didn't wait for an answer. "Your damn bullet is in the glass by the bed. It's green and spiked. Nothing like any bullet I've ever seen before. I'm taking a shower. I have a flight to catch." She disappeared into the bathroom and slammed the door.

Now probably wasn't the time to tell her she wasn't taking that flight, Michael thought, as the door shut. Nor was it the time to explain that he wasn't worried about "who" he was; he was worried about "what" he was. No normal person could communicate with the wind. No normal person felt the sense of unnamed power growing within them as he did, that might or might not, be about the wind. Nor was any other Renegade tainted enough to endure the brutality of living among the Zodius as he had.

But this wasn't a conversation for now, or ever, in his book. She hadn't slept, hadn't eaten; she was beaten up over his return. Oh yeah, and the little detail about Adam

wanting her dead. She was definitely not going anywhere but underground, inside the Renegades' Sunrise
City headquarters. She'd hate him for that, too. Which
sucked. But it was good. She needed to hate him. Then
he couldn't forget himself and throw her on the bed and
fuck her until there was no tomorrow, and then do some
stupid shit like admit he loved her.

And on that happy fucking note, he walked to the
room phone and called the lobby. His shirt was shredded, his pants bloody, and he couldn't leave without
replacing them, without drawing unwanted attention to
himself. As expected, an offer of a big tip scored him
the promise of new clothes. He added an order for orange juice and hung up. Feeding his metabolism so he
could fully heal had to be high on the priority list, as did
getting rid of all the blood—which unfortunately might
include the mattress. That would all cost money, lots of
it, but he didn't really care about the cash. His money
had been his father's, after all, and what he hadn't do-
nated to charity, he now used to fund the Renegades.
The Renegades couldn't depend on their own personal
resources or government funding. Not when Zodius was
recruiting from private sources in any way necessary—
be it promises of power or intimidation.

He reached for the green-spiked bullet in the glass beside him and went cold when he felt the rubbery texture.
"Hello Mother," he murmured, bitterly, all too familiar
with the technology he held. Upon his father's death,
Michael had inherited a chunk of stock from the company, which still ground his nerves. He hadn't spoken
to either of his parents since the day he'd found out his
father was selling to terrorist operations, and his mother

had defended him. She'd sworn his father hadn't known and sworn Michael was lying when he told her his father had admitted he had.

To the day his father had died, that man had been certain that Michael would come around, that Michael was a chip off the ole block. That the army would make a man out of him, and Michael would come back for the good life. Michael didn't dispute that he was like his father—he felt it, accepted it, knew on some level he removed emotions and acted when necessary in ways others simply could not. He didn't give that part of himself time to mature, to take root and grow into something that he would recognize as his father.

Michael had sold that stock like hot potatoes, but not without doing a good share of research on its operations and contacts. He'd seen the published data on the Green Hornets, including a number of manufacturing mishaps endured during testing that had gotten it—temporarily, it seemed—shelved. Oh yeah. Green Hornets came from Taylor, all right. Which meant his mother was the one supplying them to Adam. And if she took a clue from his father, she'd sell to the army as well. A bloodbath in the name of money was, after all, the Taylor legacy.

Cassandra stood under the hot spray of the shower, her hands pressed to her face, willing herself not to cry. More confused than she'd ever been in her life. Seeing Michael again was tearing her up inside. She was pretty sure she loved him and always had. And that probably made her insane.

She thought of his vow. *I would die for you*. She

laughed bitterly into the water. Right. Like the man didn't invite death to come for a visit every day of his life. She was his duty. It was all about duty to Michael. Exactly why soldiers equaled pain. Her mother had warned her, and she'd been right.

"Damn you, Michael," she whispered, thinking of that day by the elevator when he'd been so damn devastatingly hot. *I should have walked away.* She pressed her hands to her face again and then mentally shook herself. This was not about her and Michael. This was about protecting the world from Adam. How had she ever walked away and pretended something so big didn't exist?

She could only hope and pray that the accusations against her father were not true. He was all she had in this world. A little girl's hero, one she'd felt she'd lost after the Area 51 nightmare. She'd believed he deserved a chance to mend the past, and she'd wanted to help. And she knew there was no choice but to imprison the Zodius. They were now terrorists against humanity. But she wasn't okay with torturing them. That would be inhumane.

In their own way, all the GTECHs, Zodius and Renegade, were victims of the government's experiment. Unwilling ones too. They'd been told they were getting immunizations. No, they didn't deserve to be tortured, and her father wouldn't be a part of that. Yet... in the back of her mind, she admitted seeing glimpses of a power-hungry man, desperate to save himself and regain his position of authority.

Resolve formed as she reached down and turned off the shower. She was getting on that flight this morning and copying that hard drive. If Red Dart was detailed on

Brock's computer, she could prove there was no torture mechanism. That easily. One hard-drive copy. Then, the Renegades and the government could refocus together on defeating Adam.

Cassandra reached for her towel and started to dry off when she suddenly froze with a realization. She squeezed her eyes shut. Her clothes were in the exterior room—*with Michael*. Great. Wonderful. She could put her bloodied clothes back on, which really did not appeal to her. Or she could walk out into the room to her suitcase with only a towel to cover her. Flashes of herself and Michael making love, their bodies pressed close, the wildness they'd shared, flickered in her mind. Oh no. The towel was really not a good idea. Her robe made sense. She'd simply tell Michael to grab it from the suitcase.

Quickly, Cassandra towel-dried her hair and cracked the door open. "Michael?" No answer. "Michael?" Still nothing. A fizzle of fear raced through Cassandra. Had he collapsed? Fallen ill again? "Michael!" She yanked the door open, holding the towel tight around her body, scanning, heart pounding a wicked beat against her breast bone. The sheets and blankets were gone, the mattress changed or maybe flipped.

Her gaze swept the room, and still, she did not see Michael. He was not lying on the floor, dead or dying, which was a relief, but neither was he anywhere in sight. Her breath lodged in her chest. Had he left without saying good-bye yet again?

Suddenly, the patio door opened, a gust of wind lifting the dark floral curtains, the sheers beneath fluttering wickedly. Michael stepped into the room, and the wind died. He looked like a warrior, dangerous, primal. He was bare to the waist but for the bandages she'd wrapped around him, his jeans hanging low to display sculpted abdominals, his feet bare, his long, raven hair loose around his shoulders.

And despite the proof that he was not Zodius, that she had no reason to fear him, she did feel fear. So much that she could barely breathe. Fear of what she wanted. Of her inability to resist this man when she knew damn well he was going to hurt her again if she gave him the chance—a realization driven home as he cast her in a heavy-lidded inspection so intimate that her knees went weak.

Instant heat spread through her core and then sizzled like a wildfire through the rest of her body. Her nipples tightened, her thighs ached. In the midst of the flames burning her inside and out, there was relief that at least he had not left her again, no matter how much she *should* want him to.

She had two options. Refuse to be intimidated by her state of undress and march over and get her clothes, or turn and run back into the bathroom. She had a flight to catch, along with Brock's computer drive to copy, and Michael had already seen her in her towel.

"You didn't answer when I called you," she said, her eyes flickering to his, her fragile bravado already faltering under their heat, her voice raspy, unfamiliar. Her fists balled tighter around that terry cloth at her chest. "I was afraid you were sick again."

He stared at her, said nothing, an animalistic quality crackling off him, edgy, dark—powerful. Hot. So damn hot. She swallowed hard, the sensual touch of his dark eyes flustering her, arousing her. "Say something, damn it!" So much for keeping a cool head and acting unaffected.

And still Michael did not speak—he simply stood there, immobile, his eyes holding hers, sexual tension between them, magnetic, impossible to resist. The desire between them had always been intense; their lifebond connection simply turned up the heat another ten notches, transforming the desire to something darker, more intense—all-consuming. As if the desire had a life and mind of its own.

Desperately, she cut her gaze and charged toward the closet. Touching him would be a mistake. It would cloud her judgment and skew her ability to judge the man beneath the Lifebond. But she barely made it a few steps before he was there, pulling her into his arms.

"You didn't really think you could walk out here in a towel without this happening, now did you?" he half growled a moment before his lips came down on hers.

Cassandra lost herself to Michael in that moment, to that hot, hungry kiss, a mating of mouths that she longed for. The spicy male scent of him seemed to pour through her veins like an aphrodisiac. Her hands were all over him, his all over her. It was wildly exciting, intensely addictive. And there was no fighting it, no understanding it. His hands were in her hair, hers in his. Teeth nipped, lips caressed.

The towel disappeared, her breasts pressed against his bare chest, his hands caressed her body as he picked her up, one hand curving along her backside, the other laced through her hair. Her arms wrapped around his neck, her legs around his waist. She didn't resist; in fact, she clung to him, far more desperate to feel him close to her, to feel him next to her, inside her, than she had been to get away from him.

Somehow, someway, a semblance of real life slipped into her mind, and her fingers shoved into his hair, pulling his mouth from hers. "You left," she whispered hoarsely. "You left and never said a word."

Their eyes collided much as their passion had—wild, emotional. "You have no idea how many times I've burned to feel you like this again," he said, low, guttural. "How many times I was hard just thinking about it."

She shook with his words, shook with the magnitude of the passion between them, though it solved nothing, explained nothing. But her body didn't care; her body simply wanted and needed. *Don't ask a question you don't want the answer to*. She didn't ask. Not now.

"Prove it," she challenged. "Prove it now."

Cassandra couldn't get enough of Michael. She clung to him. Burned for him. Breathed him in as his mouth slanted over hers, punishing, hot, as dominating as the man. There was nothing gentle about the way he took that kiss, the way he claimed her. Raw, animalistic passion that burned away the past and left only this moment and then the next.

They went down on the bed, her on her back, his broad masculine frame commanding hers, his lips traveling her jaw, her neck. He pressed her breasts together, lapping at her nipples with his tongue, suckling and licking until her back arched. He rolled the stiff peaks with his fingers, tugged and nipped to the point of near pain, yet it was so much pleasure. She was panting, watching him in wonder, stunned that this was really happening.

He lifted his head, his eyes finding hers, her breasts still intimately molded to his palms. Time seemed to stop as the unanswered questions, the unspoken words, burned between them, a spell of sorts, holding them, compelling them to deal with more than the physical need. Michael pushed out of her embrace, standing up and reaching for his jeans.

Emotionally shaken, but no less physically enthralled by the sheer male power of Michael, Cassandra rested on her elbows, her legs still spread where she wanted him to return.

She watched as he shoved his jeans and underwear down powerful legs and bare feet and stood in all his naked glory for her inspection, his cock jutting forward, thick with readiness. Inhaling a lust-laden breath, Cassandra crawled toward him as surely as he was reaching for her. His legs touched the end of the mattress as they came together in a deep, frenzied kiss, one of his hands palming her backside as he picked her up, caressing along the cheek and intimately sliding along the cleft.

Again, Cassandra wrapped herself around Michael, her arms draping his neck. His erection wedged thickly between her legs, and she moaned into his mouth, the anticipation of having him inside her almost too much to bear. He reached between them, used both his fingers and his cock to stroke her sensitive flesh, before he pushed the pulsing head of his erection inside her and sunk deep to her core. Their lips froze in a caress. For several seconds, they clung together, bodies joined in the most intimate of ways, his powerful one wrapped around hers. Every inch of her body tingled with pleasure, a connection beyond anything she'd ever known.

Michael brushed his lips over hers in a long, languid motion, drawing his erection slowly along the inner walls of her body. Cassandra gasped into his mouth as he thrust hard and hit her core—gasped with pleasure, with fulfillment, with need. A wild rush of passion followed, a frenzy of hips swaying and pumping. And in one long, hard thrust of movement, they went down on the mattress, Michael's muscular legs spreading her in a V, demanding what she did willingly—open for him.

Their bodies moved in wild abandon, hands exploring, caressing, clinging. She lifted off the bed, hips pressed to his, meeting his thrusts, desperate for more of him, desperate in a way that she couldn't escape. Desperate for far more than the deep thrust of his cock, but for something she knew in the far reaches of her mind was part of their lifebonding process. It was a feeling she had felt before, but never like this, never so intense, never so all-consuming.

He tore his lips from hers, his hair draped around his shoulders, around hers. As he stared down at her, his dark eyes wild, hungry, tormented—she knew he felt what she felt—that he understood her burning need.

Slowly, Michael thrust into her—a long, deep, sensual stroke of his cock that had her arching into him, tilting her hips to take more of him. To get closer. She could never be close enough. And when she wanted more, he pulled back, teasing her as he traveled a slow, torturous path of pleasure along her sensitive core. With only the tip of his thick erection inside her, he paused, before he drove into her once, then over and over, until they were in another wild frenzy.

Riding on the edge of release, Cassandra wrapped her legs around Michael's, wrapped her arms around his back, moaning as he kissed her again. A deep, torturous, wonderful kiss that took her over the edge of bliss. The combination of his tongue and his hips shattered her control, causing her muscles to spasm around his cock, her body shaking with the intensity of her pleasure. With a guttural moan, Michael pushed deep into her core, buried his face in her neck, and she could feel the pulse of his release.

Time stood still for long moments as they held one another, their bodies vibrating with energy, until slowly, slowly, muscles eased and tension unraveled.

And with the unraveling of passion came the formation of another kind of explosion, and this one had nothing to do with passion. At least not the kind of passion made of pleasure. The kind made of confrontation. Confrontation that started forming in her chest, with the hurt of the past, with the hurt that was Michael.

"Let me up!" she yelled, suddenly claustrophobic. They'd had sex. Fine. It was good. She didn't want what came after; she didn't want to look into his eyes, to face the past or even the future.

"Easy, sweetheart," he purred near her ear. "What's the rush?"

He rested on his elbows and forced her to do what she didn't want to do—stare into his eyes. Those damn eyes that always made her think that nothing but the moment mattered. Made her think they had something real when she knew better.

Her throat went all cottony. Her tongue thick. "I have a flight to catch. I need to get ready."

His eyes glimmered with determination. "You aren't taking that flight."

He couldn't be serious. "Of course I am," she said. "We need that hard drive."

"We don't," he said. "Brock told Lucian he knows nothing more than we do."

"He could have been lying," she said. "We can't take that chance. The return flight is a perfect opportunity to get that drive."

"The only place you're going is to Sunrise City where I know you'll be safe."

Safe. *He* wanted to keep *her* safe. Right. She glared at him. "I can't find Red Dart in Sunrise City, and what am I supposed to tell my father?"

"Whatever you need to," he growled. "Be creative."

"And then we don't get that hard drive and the data on Red Dart!"

"We'll find another way."

"There is no other way, or we both know you would never have come to me in the first place!" Frustration boiled inside her. "For two years you didn't give a damn about where I was or what I was doing. What right do you have to tell me anything?"

He glared right back at her, his jaw clenched, his eyes glistening—looking as if he was about to explode—like he might actually, for once, yell back at her. And she wanted him to. She wanted him to say what was on his mind. To let her inside that hard shell of his. But it didn't happen. He rolled off her and leaned against the headboard.

"You're not getting on that plane."

He'd shut her out again. Damn him. Damn him to hell. With a sound of frustration bursting from her lips, she rotated to her knees, facing him. She didn't know if she was more angry at him for shutting her out again or for being a bossy, arrogant ass. "I am getting on that plane, Michael, and you cannot stop me."

"Watch me," he said with dark menace.

She shook her head, agitated. She wasn't going to argue with him. It wasn't even an argument anyway—he didn't talk to her. "No," she challenged. "*You* watch me."

She scrambled toward the edge of the bed and toward the closet. In a flash, he was sitting on the edge of the mattress, pulling her between his thighs. Awareness came instantly, her nipples inches from his face. His hands branding her hips. His brushed his cheek against one of her breasts, his lips against her nipple.

She shivered, and damn him, she struggled to retain her anger. To remember why she had to get dressed. His tongue laved her nipple. Her thighs tingled, her core ached. Need built inside her, and she fought it. She craved this man, his strength, even his damnable bossy, silent treatment. Which meant she was really in need of some counseling, because he was going to hurt her again. She knew it. She figured he did, too. Yet knowing she had a hard drive to copy, maybe even a world to save, she was seriously considering climbing back in bed with him.

Clinging to what resolve she had left, angry at her weakness, she shoved at his shoulders. "Damn it, Michael. I am not having sex with you again. This won't work. I won't be manipulated." He sucked her nipple, all that silky dark hair erotically tickling her skin. Desperate to stop him, before she no longer possessed the will, her hands went to his head. "Stop, Michael!"

He tilted his chin up, a challenge in his eyes. "Is that what you really want?"

She glared. "Yes. I do." Or she wanted to and that was what counted. "I'm getting dressed, and I'm leaving."

He arched a brow. "Care to bet on that?"

Chapter 12

MICHAEL HAD BARELY THROWN OUT HIS CHALLENGE when Cassandra's eyes flickered and turned solid black. Wild, uncontrollable need to claim her right then and there overcame him, like a mating call that demanded satisfaction, the need to throw her on the bed and bury himself inside her again almost too intense to ignore.

He cursed. "Your eyes just turned black, Cassandra." His gaze raked her naked body.

She said something to him, but he didn't hear her. His mind filled with potent, white hot need—his cock thick, pulsing. Whatever was happening to him, to them, was primal, powerful. Not at all the scientific lab version of bonding as he knew it. It was as if his body and soul believed if he took her again, the process would be complete. She would never want another. She would bear his children. She would die if he died. That jolted some sense into him. He set her away from him, nerve endings raw.

She stumbled with the unexpected action, and he started to reach for her and stopped himself. "Holy hell," he said, running his hand over the back of his neck. She was naked, and so damn hot. His woman. *His*. Fuck. Not his. Couldn't be his. He was X2 positive. He was… not what she needed. "I can't touch you." He snagged his jeans from the floor and shoved his legs inside. "Get dressed before I don't let you."

"I—"

"Get dressed, Cassandra," he ordered, balling his fists by his sides. He'd tried to do everything in his power to protect Cassandra.

A shaken look crossed her face, before she darted toward the closet and started to dress.

He tried not to watch. He failed. His gaze followed every inch of the pink silk panties as they slid up her long legs and over that little triangle of dark hair. He turned his back, inhaling a breath, trying to calm the sudden raging lust ravishing his body.

"They turned black in the hotel restroom after we… saw each other," she announced from behind him. "They changed back to normal in a few minutes."

Before he could stop himself, Michael turned to face her. Mistake. Big mistake. She was putting on her bra. Pink like the panties. Sheer. He wanted to rip it off. He jerked his gaze to her face. "And you didn't tell me? How could you not tell me something like this?"

"At first I thought you knew and then…" She slipped on a pair of slacks and reached for a crème silk blouse. "I would have told you."

"When?" he demanded. "I wouldn't have touched you again had I known we might become bonded without a blood exchange, Cassandra."

She made a sound of disbelief and slipped on her shoes. "Right." She crossed her arms in front of her, but not before he saw her hands shake. "Of course. Well, now you know. It happens when you touch me. So don't touch me."

The icy cut of her words rippled over him. Crap. "Cassandra. I didn't mean that how you took it. This isn't how lifebonding, as we know it, works. We have no idea what is happening to you or how dangerous it might be."

She held up a hand and waved him off, slipping on her shoes. "Oh my God, Michael. For a man who says so little, you are really good with excuses. The eye color changes back. So stop panicking. We aren't lifebonding. And believe me I don't want that any more than you do. Why would I want to be bound to a man who might decide to leave me again tomorrow and go another two years without talking to me? Oh wait. If we lifebond, long-term separation would make you physically ill, right? Isn't that what I read in Ava's research? No wonder you don't want this to happen. You'd have to commit. You couldn't leave."

Anger rolled off her in hard, biting surges of energy. It was all Michael could do not to go to her. He didn't know what to say. Everything felt wrong. He only knew how much he needed this woman, how much... he loved her. His voice hung in his throat, with the confession in his head he didn't dare say out loud. "I want you, Cassandra. I want you so badly I can barely breathe sometimes. I'm X2 positive. I contain what is inside me, while others do not, but that doesn't mean that you would. I've seen what Ava is. I will not let you become that."

She scoffed, looking away and then back at him, her jaw set firmly. Her words came out through clenched teeth. "We both know Ava was an evil bitch before she ever completed the bonding. If lifebonding is some joining of kindred spirits, then Ava and Adam's were tainted before they ever met. No more excuses, Michael. I don't need them. Nor do I need you if that is all you have to offer. When this is over, we part ways. Just don't touch me in the meantime, and we'll get through this just fine."

"Damn it, Cassandra," he growled. "You have no idea who I am or what my family is."

She drew back, the look on her face wounded. "You're right. I don't know because you never really let me inside, now did you?"

He scrubbed his jaw. "I was—I am—trying to protect—"

"Don't you dare say, 'protect me,'" she said, jabbing a finger at the air. "*Don't* say it. If you need to believe that to make yourself feel better, fine, but keep it to yourself."

Michael forgot distance, stepping toward her. "Cassandra—"

She retreated backwards. "I said, don't."

A knock sounded on the door. "Room service."

"Great," he mumbled. "Now they get here. An hour after I ordered."

"I'll get it," she said, turning toward the door.

He was there in an instant, pressing a solid palm on the wooden surface, stopping her from opening it. "If one of Adam's spies sees your eyes, he'll know you're my Lifebond. He'll use you to get back at me."

She paled and backed away, and he could feel the tension in her. Michael silently cursed his brilliant delivery of that information and quickly got rid of the attendant. He wheeled the cart into the room, his new clothes draped over the top. Cassandra stood in the center of the room waiting for him, a stricken look on her face. He wanted to say something, the right something, but his last effort had gone over about as smoothly as a tornado.

"So this is my life now? Hiding from Adam?"

His gut twisted at those questions, because there was no good answer. He had a sudden flashback of that first day they'd met at the elevator inside Groom Lake. Her smile. And that musical laughter he replayed in his head when that dark, empty place he hid in wasn't big enough to hold all the hell messing with his head. She'd been happy. Before her damn father stole it away. He grimaced at that. Who was he kidding? Until *he* stole it away. He was just as guilty as her father. He'd known not to get involved with her. She wouldn't have that mark, if not for him.

"You'll be safe in Sunrise City. We'll charter a plane home and get back without notice." And then he'd find a way to destroy Adam if it was the last thing he ever did.

She nodded, hugging herself. "Yes. Safe. Okay."

It was all he could do, not to go to her, to pull her into his arms. But touching her, daring to believe they could be together, was the very reason she wore that mark on the back of her neck. He had to fix this, not make it worse.

"I'm going to shower and change," he said. "Try and eat something." He forced himself to walk past her and managed to make it to the bathroom without reaching for her. But he stopped there for just a moment, guilt twisting him in knots. This was why he didn't do relationships. His life had a way of bleeding onto the lives of those around him. "I'm sorry, Cassandra. I never meant for any of this to happen. I'll make this right for you.

Somehow, I'll make it right." And then he disappeared into the bathroom.

The minute the shower turned on, Cassandra headed for the door and quickly zipped her bag. Of course, half her stuff was scattered and unpacked, but she didn't have time to worry about that. She'd forget the bag if it wouldn't look odd to Brock.

She snatched her purse and her computer case, and she was in the hallway in a flash, easing the door to a silent closure, and then darn near running to the elevator. If this was her life now, then fine, but Cassandra wasn't going to sit back and wait for Michael, or her father, to make it better. Nor was she going to tuck her tail and hide from Adam. She was going to be a part of the solution. And once she copied the hard drive on Brock's computer, she'd call Caleb for help.

Her and Michael… well, that was an emotional subject she refused to think about right now. To say they had history to deal with was an understatement, and she wasn't sure they could get past it or even if she wanted to at this point. He'd hurt her two years ago, and today in that hotel room. She didn't want to hurt anymore.

Halfway down the hallway, Cassandra managed to hoist her computer bag on her shoulder and dig her sunglasses from her purse. She slid them in place as the elevator opened, thankful to find several people inside. Michael would never be able to stop her now without making a scene. She would have been relieved if not for the sudden feeling of nausea that washed over her.

After a fast trip to the restroom to check her eyes and slap on some makeup, Cassandra nervously scanned the lobby, praying Michael wouldn't show up. She spotted Brock standing near the bell desk dressed in tan slacks and a button down with a military-issue, tan tie.

Cassandra walked toward him, forced to endure the far too intimate inspection of a man who wanted to kill her. She held her sunglasses in one hand, ready to put them on at an appropriate moment, because though her eyes were more green than black at present, they were also glossy and dilated. Just barely able to pass as normal. Right. Normal.

"Morning," Brock said, pushing off the bell desk as she neared. "You look like walking death."

Her jaw went slack at the comment—no doubt about the hidden meaning. And then she got mad, just barely taming her retort to below hostile. "I thought they taught you military men more manners than that," she said, shoving her sunglasses on her face, her nerve endings prickling with the sudden awareness that Michael was nearby. "Migraine," she complained. "And no, it's not a good morning. Not a good night, for that matter." She crinkled her nose. "I left my drugs at home too, so it won't be a good ride home either. Pity for you, sitting next to me. I'll try and use the doggy bag and not your lap." *She was definitely aiming for his lap*.

"You won't mind giving up the window seat then, I guess," he commented dryly. God, the man was a bastard. A lying, arrogant bastard. A fool, too, if he thought he would be using her father. No one got anything over on her father. They might think they did, but they always ended up playing his game, his way.

Brock flagged a bellman and handed him a bill. "We need a cab, ASAP." He shifted his attention back to Cassandra and motioned her forward. "Shall we?" He inspected her with suspicion. "Were you after pain medication when you went out so late last night?" Brock inquired, setting a duffel bag on the ground. You could take the honor out of a soldier, but never strip him of his duffel bag. Soldiers used them for life.

She had no pain meds, so she didn't want to claim otherwise. "Could have sworn I said toothbrush," she said, casting him a sideways look and offering nothing more, remembering her father's often spoken warning. *Your words can be the enemy's weapons.* In short, keep your mouth shut.

Well-timed, the cab pulled up in front of them, saving Cassandra from further prodding, and she quickly scooted in to the far side next to the door. If Brock dared sit too close to her, she might just use her *foot* as a weapon.

Thankfully, Brock kept his distance and talked on his cell phone for most of the short ride to the airport—to her father of all people; her stomach rolled the entire time, and she was glad for the distraction, to rest her eyes if only briefly.

Minutes later, standing at the curbside airline desk, she felt a twist in her stomach. She swallowed against the bitter taste in her mouth. Cassandra had no idea what was happening to her, but she didn't think it was lack of sleep.

It was becoming clear that she couldn't ignore the implications between her connection to Michael and her illness, not after the eye color change and not when she knew the lifebonding process included a short, violent, physical transition, nausea being par for the course. Much more intense than her random eye color shift and some mild nausea. And she and Michael had most definitely not exchanged blood. But now wasn't the time to let her worries, or her stomach, get the best of her. She had to get that computer hard drive copied before she keeled over and couldn't complete the task.

Inside the airport, Cassandra quickly stepped into the security line that Michael had designated for the laptop switch.

"That one is shorter," Brock argued, pointing to the next line over.

"This one is closer to the restroom," Cassandra countered, and with a grimace, Brock followed her lead.

Soon she was tossing her shoes in the plastic tray on the conveyer and then setting her computer in one as well. Beside her, Brock did the same thing. Nerves churned her stomach a little harder as she shoved her sunglasses into her purse, her gaze downturned as she worried about what her eyes might look like.

Quickly, she passed through the metal detector without challenge, but behind her, Brock set it off with a loud buzz. He grumbled, checking his pockets as she retrieved her sunglasses and slipped them into place. The female security guard behind the conveyer gave her a weird look.

"Migraine," Cassandra explained as the buzzer on the metal detector went off again.

"Wand check!" yelled the guard by the metal detector.

"Oh hell," Brock complained rather loudly. "I'm army. We *protect* the nation, not blow it up."

"Sir," the guard said. "I don't make the rules. I just follow them. Please step to the side." He walked to the plastic trays and motioned to Brock's computer and bag. "Is this yours?"

"Yes," Brock said grumpily. "Now can we get on with this?"

The male guard picked up Brock's bag and with a quick shift of his body to block the view, snagged Cassandra's computer rather than his. Adrenaline rushed through Cassandra's blood as she toed on the shoes she held in her hands and then stuffed Brock's computer, rather than her own, into her bag and zipped it closed. Shoving her purse and briefcase over her shoulder, she turned to find Brock's back to her, his arms outstretched as he endured the wand inspection. No doubt this would be when the guard would put her computer inside his bag so he wouldn't know there was a mix-up.

"I'll meet you at the gate, Brock," she called out. "I'm going to the restroom."

"Yeah, yeah," he said as the wand buzzed near his knee, indicating a need for further inspection. "You have got to be kidding!"

"Please raise your pant leg, sir," the guard said.

Cassandra didn't wait to hear more. She was already rushing toward the restroom sign, unzipping her purse as she did and retrieving the flash drive. Twelve minutes. She needed twelve minutes.

Rounding the corner of the restroom, Cassandra quickly noted the line of six stalls and went to the handicapped one, shoving the door shut and hunching over against the churning in her stomach as she unzipped the computer bag. She shoved the baby changer down and opened the computer, but a sudden need to throw up had her yanking away her sunglasses and leaning over the toilet. Thank God the toilet and floor were clean. Dry heaves followed, her empty stomach wrenching in hard spasms that felt like they were tearing her inside out, her hand still clenched around the flash drive. Finally, the nausea subsided.

Cassandra hooked her glasses on the top of her blouse and unrolled some toilet paper to dab her mouth, her hand shaking as she did. The flash drive slipped from her grip. Cassandra watched in dismay as it hit the ground and bounced under the door.

Inhaling a calming breath, she yanked the stall door open only to be greeted by a short, gray-haired woman, wearing a badge and holding a cleaning rag—clearly this was the restroom attendant. She was also far more attentive than Cassandra wanted her to be right now.

"Is this yours, honey?" she asked, holding the flash drive up between two fingers and peering over Cassandra's shoulder at the computer open on the changing table.

"Yes," Cassandra said, snagging the stick. "Thank you." She shut the stall door, hating that she had to be rude, but she had no time for politeness. She quickly inserted the stick into the computer, and it started showing progress.

The announcer's voice came over the speaker. Her flight was boarding. "Damn it!" she murmured. She was never going to have time to finish. Minutes passed like hours as she watched the computer tick off progress, but not nearly fast enough. Think Cassandra, think.

She looked at the toilet paper in her hand and placed

it over the latch on the computer, so it couldn't fully close and power off. She shut the lid over the paper and then shoved the computer back into the bag. She'd go straight to the airplane restroom when they boarded and then remove the paper and the stick before she took a seat.

Cassandra put the sunglasses back in place, wishing she had time to inspect her eyes. She grabbed her things and half jogged toward the exit.

She rounded the restroom entryway and came toe-to-toe with Brock, all but barreling into him.

"You have my computer," he said. "I need it back."

Her heart jackknifed. "I do not have your computer," she said, trying to step around him.

Brock moved in front of her. "Yes," he said. "You do. The security guard remembers mixing them up."

She motioned with her hands in defeat. "Okay, well, maybe they did." She patted her briefcase. "It's not going anywhere." She motioned to the gate. "And boarding call has already been issued. Besides, I'm way too sick to deal with this right now. You can switch them on the plane where I can sit down, before I throw up yet again."

He clenched his jaw, ignored the announcement and her suggestion, then he looked suspiciously at her glasses. "Since when does a migraine make you throw up? I thought it was a headache."

"It *is* a headache," she ground out between clenched teeth, thinking how offended her mother, a sufferer of migraines, would have been at that comment. Brock just dug himself deeper into jerk territory every second. And knowing that he wanted to take her to bed, she'd hate to think how he'd treat her if he did not. "Migraines are the volcanic eruption of headaches."

His probing attention continued, his stare so deep she thought he might see through her glasses. "I have a confession to make," he said finally. "After you declined meeting for a drink last night, my ego was a bit wounded. Then, this morning with the headache again, I was convinced you were faking a headache to get out of dinner tonight. I apologize. Male egos really can be monsters."

His apology reeked of insincerity. "No one fakes being this sick," she said. "Or looking like 'walking death.'"

He grimaced. "Sorry for that, too. Again. The ego monster." Last call to board sounded over the intercom, saving her from further argument. "We better get going." He reached for her bag. "Let me carry that for you."

"No, no," she said, trying to hold onto it. "Really. It's fine."

His hand remained on the bag. "I insist," he said, refusing to let go. "You're sick, Cassandra. I'll carry the bag. It's what any gentleman would do."

Cassandra reluctantly let him pry the bag from her hands, aware she'd just been well manipulated. He wasn't going to let her take that bag to the restroom, so how the heck was she going to get the flash drive out of the computer without him knowing? She was more than sick. She was drowning in trouble.

Chapter 13

CASSANDRA FOLLOWED BROCK ONTO THE PLANE MANaging to maintain a remarkably calm façade. Relaxed even. As if she were not about to be found out by her wannabe murderer. If she couldn't get to a phone and call Caleb, Michael would save her. Of course he would. He'd know the flight she was on. He'd wind-walk to her arrival airport and be waiting. He'd be pissed, but he'd save her. And if she was going to deal with two hundred pounds of pissed off, macho man, she was going to have something to show for it. She was going to get that copy of the hard drive. So think. Think! There was a way out of this.

She passed an enclave where a flight attendant greeted her when a plan hatched in her mind.

"Hi," Cassandra said, stopping to chat with the woman. "I'm battling a migraine, and it's really making me sick. Any chance I could talk you into bringing me a Sprite before takeoff."

The twenty-something female was quick to help. "Oh, my sister gets those, and they are hell. We're running late, so let me give it to you now so you have time to drink it." She motioned Cassandra out of the aisle so people could pass. She then popped some ice into a glass and filled it with Sprite. "Make sure it's empty before liftoff. What seat are you in? I'll check on you once we're in the air."

Cassandra searched her ticket and showed it to the attendant before accepting the drink. "Thank you very much," she said and then rushed after Brock, praying she got to him before he managed to open that briefcase. She arrived at her seat just as Brock buckled himself up, her computer case at his feet, ready to open.

With a silent prayer that this was going to work, she moved to sit, and accidentally, on purpose, dumped her Sprite in his lap. He cursed and jerked in shock, ice and cold liquid all over his pants and shirt.

Cassandra reacted with instant shock. "Oh no! Oh Brock, I am so very sorry. I am really not myself." She handed him the glass. "Put the ice in this." She reached for the computer bag. "I stuffed some tissue in here while I was in the airport restroom in case I got sick." She partially unzipped the bag and fumbled around, removing the flash drive and trying to conceal it with the tissue.

"Miss," a flight attendant said, stopping beside them. "The bag needs to go under the seat for takeoff. Oh no. Do you need help here?"

Brock crammed the ice into the glass and handed it to her. "You can take this and bring us some napkins."

Cassandra discreetly maneuvered the tissue and the stick to her lap and used the briefcase as cover as she slipped the stick into her pants pocket. "Here you go," she said, offering him the tissue as she zipped the case closed and then slid it under the seat. "I'm really sorry."

He accepted the tissue and started wiping down his shirt. "It's fine," he said, his tone saying it really wasn't. "I guess we can change the computers once we are in the air."

"I guess so," she said softly, leaning back in her chair and closing her eyes. She'd dodged a bullet. Now, if she could get away from Brock without getting herself killed.

—⁓—

With Chin by his side, Powell stood in one of several private PMI labs, their location highly secret. Together, they overlooked a dozen willing soldiers strapped to hospital beds, still several injections from completing their conversion to GTECH. All receiving the original GTECH serum—Grade 1—while Chin perfected a newer, faster-acting Grade 2 version. "You're certain we cannot use the Grade 2 serum to speed up their conversion?" Powell asked.

"Grade 2 is not ready, and to mix the two versions of the serum would mean certain death," Chin replied, hands in his lab coat. "There is no rushing the process. They are two weeks from being Red Dart ready and impatient to be liberated from those restraints."

"They'll be free when they are under Red Dart control and not a minute sooner."

"From what Jocelyn has told me this can happen twenty-four hours after the final injection," Chin assured him. "She seems quite certain she's found a way to overcome the immune function of the soldiers, but only once their bodies have stabilized in their new condition."

Yes, his little Jocelyn was quite the prize. "It's time we find out for sure. A dozen soldiers ready for battle two weeks from now is no longer enough. Not with the entire GTECH population trying to stop Red Dart from happening. We have no idea what they might do to stop us. Use the GTECH2 serum. I need an army of GTECHs, and I need them now."

Chin objected instantly. "General Powell, I must remind you that the GTECH2 serum is a conversion that is rapid and potentially lethal. Those that survive will not only be positive for X2, but the aggression will be magnified times ten. You are talking about a highly volatile soldier. One without a mind for anything but violence. I need time to alter this reaction."

"Will the GTECH2s be stronger and faster as you promised?"

Chin hesitated, "Yes."

"And at least half of those dosed will survive?"

"General—"

"I take that as a yes," he interrupted. "Both Adam and Caleb Rain are after Red Dart. Do you wish to see our country fall to the GTECHs?"

"You know I do not," Chin replied brusquely. "I need a human test subject."

"You'll have Brock West," he replied, pleased with Chin's agreement. "I've sent orders to have the several hundred recruits scheduled for next week report two days early. We'll have hundreds of test subjects in forty-eight hours."

"You do realize that West and anyone we dose before I perfect the serum will be little more than an animal on a leash?"

"The Zodius are animals, Chin," he said. "I *want* an animal who can face them and win, who is both powerful and in control of my troops," he said. "And in case you've forgotten, Red Dart is my leash. It's my method of control."

"Very well then," Chin agreed. "I assume I will have the Red Dart application immediately available?"

Powell gave a short nod. "Jocelyn is in the lab next door running final tests even as we speak. We'll bring West in tonight when he returns from Washington."

Soon this country would know it was safe and that he alone had kept it that way.

―∿―

After a long delay in Houston, it was early afternoon when Cassandra finally stepped off the plane in Nevada. She immediately tried to ditch Brock. "I need to drop by the ladies' room, and since I'm under the weather, I'm going to call it a day. No dinner for me tonight."

"Understood," he said. "But I'll wait. You'll need help with your baggage, and I should probably give you a ride home."

Not going well. Especially since she'd come to the realization she didn't have the phone Michael had given her and had no idea how to reach Caleb without the call being traced. Nor did she have her own phone. It had been on the nightstand in the hotel. Which explained why Michael hadn't been calling to yell at her. But neither had she felt so much as a tingle of awareness of him nearby. She could really use a tingle right about now.

"I'll be fine to drive," she said. "If you can just get my bags." She started walking toward the escalator.

"I thought you needed a restroom," he said suspiciously.

"Changed my mind," she said. "Rather just get home."

Twenty-minutes later, Brock settled her bag into the trunk of her new red Beetle that had replaced the fancy

German car. He grabbed his duffel bag, which was leaning against the bumper, casting a critical inspection over what Cassandra knew to be an appearance worthy of that "walking death" comment that still made her cringe.

"You sure you can drive?" he asked, though he didn't seem particularly interested in doing so.

Cassandra guessed he hadn't made any plans to kill her yet. Comforting thought, so she clung to it. "I'm fine," she said. "See you in the morning."

He offered her a two-finger salute and sauntered away. She watched him and frowned. Why had that been so easy? Didn't the man want to kill her? She turned to her car and got in, uneasiness in her stomach as she slipped the key into the ignition.

—∾∾—

Brock dialed his voice mail as he left Cassandra, hoping to find instructions from Powell regarding his first injection, but stopped short when his Chevy Blazer came into view. Lucian was leaning against it, all nonchalant, as if contact with a member of Zodius Nation wasn't a major fucking problem. Cassandra could drive by at any minute.

Brock charged forward. "Are you crazy? I can't be seen with you."

"That's not a very friendly welcome," Lucian chided.

Brock ground out between his teeth, "Get in the damn truck before someone sees us." He clicked the locks open with his key chain and rounded the bed of the truck, lifting the tarp along the way to toss his bag in the back.

Lucian didn't move. "It was Michael who followed

us last night," he said. "His unfortunate involvement demands aggressive actions. We've set plans in motion—Cassandra Powell will be dead within the next hour. I've arranged for the secretary of state to pressure Powell for Red Dart during his grieving. You will volunteer to deal with Red Dart and the government while Powell is mourning."

Brock's heart thundered in his ears. "Powell told me to look out for his daughter. If anything happens to her, he'll blame me. I will be the last person he trusts to take care of things while he buries Cassandra."

"That's why it will be a car accident," he said. "Just like her mother." He made a fist and twisted it in unison with his words. "That should twist Powell in the gut extra hard. And there is no way you could prevent such a thing."

"You can't be sure a car accident will kill her," he argued, trying anything to shut this down.

Lucian smiled. "You underestimate me, Brock. There's a little alien something we call 'Stardust' in her exhaust. It will cause a brain aneurism. It is undetectable in human testing. Her car will crash. She's dead regardless of cause. I suggest you get to work so you can be there by Powell's side when he gets the news. Be ready to take control." The wind lifted, and he was gone.

Brock stood there all of three seconds before he started running toward Cassandra's car as fast as he could. If anything happened to Cassandra, he didn't care what the cause, Powell would go ballistic. He wasn't taking any chances of losing his injections or even delaying them. He ran ten parking rows and one level up. By the time he got to her car, he was panting, finding her stupid little Beetle sitting where it had been with Cassandra nowhere in sight.

He let out a breath of relief. She must have forgotten something inside. He'd wait. He didn't want to risk missing her. Thirty minutes later, no Cassandra. Brock lifted the hood of her car and disabled the battery. Then, for good measure he pulled a pocket knife and discreetly sliced two tires.

He had to get to her house before Lucian found out she was alive and decided to kill her some other way.

Chapter 14

HER STOMACH TWISTED AND TURNED IN SUDDEN SHARP waves that, thankfully, remained dormant during the ride from the airport to her condo. Cassandra paid the cab driver and lugged her suitcase out of the car, balancing her computer bag on top, purse over her shoulder. She'd been about to turn the key in her ignition when it had hit her that in the movies a few too many of those who were knocked off ended up dead in their car. She hadn't liked her odds.

Nervously, she rolled her bag toward her condo and realized that going inside might not be smart—the second place that people got killed was in their homes. But she didn't know where else to go that she could be sure Michael could find her. She had no direct number for Caleb. If she called her office, she worried that her father would find out she'd asked for the number.

With her heart fluttering wildly in her chest, she entered the paved walkway with her residence to the left. She drew a breath and unlocked her door, then shuffled her bags inside. Cassandra felt the tingle of awareness spike the mark on her neck a moment too late. Suddenly, strong arms were around her, and she was inside the condo, the door shut behind her.

Michael leaned against the solid surface, pulled her hard against his body, powerful thighs molding hers, branding her. He slid his hands up her back.

"Michael," she gasped. His hair was pulled back so that she could see the anger etched in his beautiful face all too clearly.

He placed his hand over her backside. "I have a good mind to turn you over my knee and spank that pretty little ass of yours."

"You wouldn't dare!"

"Oh I'd dare, and you know it," he rebutted. "What part of… Adam wants you dead… do you not understand?"

"What part of, Adam has to be stopped before the world is destroyed, do you not understand? I had to get that copy of Brock's hard drive."

"And did you?"

"Yes," she said, chin tilted defiantly. "I did."

Dark eyes assessed her. That hand on her backside flexed, almost in threat. And damn it, that made her hot when she didn't want to be. He made her hot. "Did you know, Cassandra," he replied tightly, "that once a female has had sex with a GTECH there is a psychic residue that can be tracked? Unless that female is lifebonded, or underground, a skilled GTECH Tracker with the right motivation can find you anywhere. Even Germany."

Shock rolled through her. She had never been safe. Adam's Trackers could have found her. "You knew I was in Germany?"

"I've always known where you were. And I knew you were far enough away to stay out of sight, out of mind—off Adam's radar. I was furious when your father lured you back to the States, back onto Adam's radar."

A knot formed in her throat. "I… you knew I was there, but you never once came to see me." In that moment, she realized painfully that she'd used her time in Germany as his excuse for not contacting her. He couldn't find her. He couldn't come to her. But he'd found her all right.

His hands slid into her hair. "I came to see you," he said softly. "You just never knew I was there. You were safer that way. I've kicked myself a million times for not intervening when you were returning home. I should have made you stay there. But I also knew any contact with me put you at risk—and not just from Adam, Cassandra. I knew if I touched you again, there was no way I would ever let you go."

She sucked in a breath at that confession. He was touching her now.

His hand slid up her back, molding them closer. "Do you know how damn worried I was about you when you were on that plane?"

"No," she said, leaning back to search his face. "No, I don't." But she wanted to. God, how she wanted to. "I don't know anything about what you feel, Michael. Because you never tell me."

"Well, I'm telling you now," he said hoarsely. "I was going insane, coming out of my own skin. Barely able to stop myself from yanking you out of that airport and back into my arms." His mouth came down on hers, hot, passionate, and fiery, like a man starving. Cassandra clung to him, hungry for the comfort that his strong arms offered, the scent of him devouring her with... him. Yes. Him. He was what she needed, and she could feel the same hunger in him. He needed her. He'd always needed her. He'd always known where she was, always been near.

But… she tore her mouth from his, still clinging to him, unable to make herself let go. "What happened to not touching me, to being afraid we'll lifebond without a blood exchange?"

"The knowledge that in one instant you could be taken from me forever." Emotion cut deep in his tone.

This was what she'd wanted to hear from him, was it not? So why was there an empty gnawing feeling inside her? Confused, so confused. Her hands went to his chest, self-preservation kicking in. "No." Then stronger. "No." She shook her head. "One minute you push me away. The next, you pull me close. I can't do this. I can't."

"Cassandra," he breathed heavily. "I want you. I want you so damn much. But there are things about me you don't know." She was ready to reject those words, to shove away from him until he added softly, "Things… I don't *want* you to know."

Tenderness rushed over her, and Cassandra pressed a palm to his cheek. It was an honest, raw answer. The most honest he'd ever been with her. "I do. Tell me. Please. Just say whatever it is, and be done with it. Then the worry is over."

Abruptly, he set her away from him. "This isn't the time for this conversation. Adam's men will come for you. We have to leave."

They stood there, staring at each other. His face a stony, unemotional mask, yet hurt and loneliness spilled from him, seeping into Cassandra's pores. She felt herself become that hurt, that loneliness—his hurt and loneliness.

It made her angry. It made her want to shout at him to stop being a fool. It made her want to run to him. It made her want to run away. Nothing had changed from moments before, when she'd tried to push him away. He was still incapable of letting her inside himself. He would hurt her.

This was over. They were over. And she might have said just that—wanted to, needed to—but a sudden rush of nausea seemed to merge with her emotions, and her knees wobbled.

Instantly, Michael was there, his arm wrapping around her waist. "Cassandra." He picked her up and carried her to her oversized blue couch and laid her down. On one knee beside her, he studied her with those probing, black eyes. "The lifebond illness."

She nodded, the implications clear. She was having the lifebond illness. "I've been sick. Yes. All day. But before you start freaking out, it's not the violent, bedridden illness of lifebonding. And we still haven't done a blood exchange. So please. Let's skip the part where you do the brooding Michael thing you do, and tell me how dangerous you are for me. We both know we have no business lifebonding after everything that's happened between us. Let's leave it at that."

Michael's expression shifted. He looked shaken. "Cassandra—"

She shook her head. He pulled her close, pressed his forehead to hers. "I never meant to hurt you, Cassandra."

Her fingers curled on his jaw, her chest heavy, eyes tingling though she refused to cry. "I know," she said. Just as she knew he wouldn't mean to hurt her again if she let him. She wouldn't. Nor would she run. Not from Michael. And not from Adam. She'd spent far too much time watching rather than participating, making a difference. She'd accepted Michael's emotional distance. She was done accepting. It was long past time for her to stand and fight.

She leaned back and ran her fingers over his lips. She loved his lips. Loved kissing him. So she did. She pressed her lips to his and then leaned back, pulling the flash drive from her bra. He arched a brow, and she smiled. "I wasn't about to let it off my person. Care to do the honors while I pack?"

He took the flash drive from her. "Backpack or small duffel. We'll be traveling by motorcycle through Sunrise Canyon."

Fifteen minutes later, with a small backpack filled, Cassandra had changed to jeans and tennis shoes. She returned to the living room and found Michael sitting on her couch, laptop open. "Any luck?"

"Encrypted," he said with frustration, shutting the lid to the computer. "I just talked to Sterling. We'll meet him on the way out of town and give him the flash drive. He'll have it decoded by the time we get to Sunrise City."

A moment of trepidation fluttered through Cassandra at the lack of control that gave her. She knew Adam was after Red Dart; she also knew the Renegades were against her father. But they wouldn't be once she proved he was not against them. That hard drive might be the answer to doing that.

Cassandra nodded her approval. The sooner it was decoded, the sooner they could all work together.

<center>~~~</center>

Michael exited Cassandra's condo, pulled the door shut, and locked it. He took her hand in his, a silent promise everything was going to be okay. Her hand was tiny, soft. He wanted to hold it forever, and for a moment he couldn't remember why that wasn't possible. The instant they cleared the building, the stifling early evening heat wrapped around them, the smell of rain touching the air. A distant rumble of thunder promised the trip through the canyon would be a wet one. Reaching out to the wind for any warnings, Michael listened for the whispers only he could understand, and then ordered it to seek out trouble.

Glancing at Cassandra, he inclined his head toward the side of the building, to a row of parking meters that faced another building and more meters. "I'm over here," he said, leading her toward the less-than-discreet spot he'd parked the Ford F-150 he was driving, scanning the perimeter with feigned nonchalance and noting four vacant cars across the street. A fifth car sat two empty spaces in front of the truck.

He opened the passenger's door of the truck, and he settled his hand on her tiny waist, helping Cassandra climb into the cabin. "I can't believe you traded in Carrie for a pickup truck."

"Carrie is waiting at home for her next ride," he said as she settled into the seat, and then softened his voice as he added, "or ours," remembering all too clearly a night they'd made love in that car. That had been a feat, considering it was small, and he was big, but a pleasurable feat. From the pink flush on Cassandra's pale cheeks, he knew she remembered that night as well. "She's missed you."

Her lips parted, full, tempting, and the only thing stopping him from kissing her was the need to get her to safety. "Then why isn't she here?"

"We're headed toward some hard desert terrain. Carrie doesn't like hard desert terrain. I can't exactly wind-walk amongst the general population, so believe me I'd take her speed and agility any day over Frank here." He patted the truck's dash.

She snorted, delicately. Cute. Damn, he loved everything about this woman.

"Frank?" she laughed and shook her head. "You and your nicknames."

Good. Laughter. Keep her mind off danger. "I've been eyeing a white vintage Mustang. I need another Carrie."

He started to shut the door, contemplating the many ways to change her mind, when the wind whispered a warning. His gaze snapped upward and did a quick scan.

"What is it? What's wrong?" Cassandra's hand touched his chest, warm, insistent.

"Someone is watching us." He reached across her and popped the glove box open, displaying a Browning 9 mm pistol. "Lock the doors, and lie on the floorboard."

Cassandra grabbed his arm. "Let's just leave," she said. "Drive away. I don't want you to get hurt again."

His gut clenched with her concern. No one but Cassandra had ever worried about him. He grabbed her. Kissed her fast and hard. "I'll be fine," he said and shut the door on her before she could stop him, already following the wind's direction.

Abruptly, he turned to the blue Toyota 4Runner across and to the right. Someone was hiding behind that vehicle. He wind-walked behind it and found the crouching male behind the front bumper.

Michael grabbed the man by the neck and found his ineffective attempts at escape confirmation that he was human. The buzz-cut and stoic demeanor spelled out military despite his street clothing. If he worked for Adam and was here to kill Cassandra, he was dead. If he was here to spy for Powell, well… he was dead. Allowing Powell to know Cassandra was with him wasn't an option. That would shut her out of her father's trust and destroy her chances of getting to Red Dart. Probably the Renegades' chances too, as Powell would increase his security measures.

But before he killed the man, he needed to know for certain if Powell was suspicious of his own daughter.

Michael jacked the guy against the wall, holding all two-hundred-plus pounds of him dangling above the pavement. "What the flip is your problem!" the man demanded, indignant, unruffled when he should have been.

Michael dug his fingers into the man's flesh, giving him an idea of the amount of pain he could inflict. "Who are you working for, soldier, and why are you here?"

"Let me go," the man grunted. "I'm not working for anyone!"

"Right. You just like crawling around behind cars."

"I was checking my tires!"

"Don't fuck with me," Michael growled. "Who *the hell* are you working for?"

"You're flipping insane, man. I have no idea what you are talking about."

Michael ground his teeth, spoke tightly. "Did whoever sent you tell you who I am?" he asked, well aware of his reputation. "Did they tell you how capable I am of killing you without blinking an eye?"

"I told you, man," the soldier said, "I was checking my tires."

The wind gusted with warning, and Michael yanked the man to the ground and behind a car, bullets splattering all around them. But not soon enough. The man went limp, a bullet between his eyes.

Fuck! More bullets. *Cassandra*. Michael left the man behind, ordering the wind to surround his truck, create a windshield, a buffer that he was capable of holding no more than sixty seconds.

He wind-walked to the driver's side of the vehicle and held his position, listened for a message in the wind. The shooters were dead. That was the extent of what he understood. Often he didn't understand at all, but that was improving.

Michael popped the door handle and climbed into the truck, quickly turning on the engine. "Stay down until I tell you otherwise."

"I thought they wanted to make it look like an accident?" she asked from the floorboard. "Shooting at me in the middle of a public place is not an accident."

"Did any gunfire hit the truck?" he asked, keeping his eyes on the road as he scanned for attackers.

"I don't think so," she said, and then with more certainty. "No. Now that you mention it, I don't think any bullets hit the truck at all."

"You can get off the floor now, sweetheart, but stay low in your seat," he said. "I think the shooters *were* after me, not you. That means this was your father."

She eased into the seat, lying with her head on the door below the window, feet on the seat. "Please tell me, no," she said. "If he knows I'm with you, Michael, that hard drive will be it for me. I won't get anything else out of him."

Michael wasn't sure what more she could do anyway with Adam trying to kill her, but he didn't say that. "It's doubtful your father is going to find out I was with you," he said, which was good, if not for the very real threat of a Zodius attack. "Someone killed the shooters."

"I don't understand," she said. "Was it Zodius?"

He nodded. "It had to be."

"Why would they keep either of us alive? And why aren't they attacking now?"

Michael's jaw set, and he reached for his phone to call Caleb. They were going to need backup to make it to Sunrise City. "Adam doesn't want me dead, or we wouldn't be driving away. He wants me alive. So he can torture me. And for whatever reason, the Zodius didn't feel they were ready to stand against me back there."

But they'd be back, sooner than later, and Michael had to be sure Cassandra was out of the line of fire when it happened.

―⁂―

Perched on a rooftop across from Cassandra's condo, Brock's attempt to kill Michael had failed. He'd killed a soldier, which had left him no choice but to kill the other three. If he couldn't kill Michael before he left with Cassandra, no one could live to tell Powell she was with him.

His one last shot at Michael had been a prime one. Michael had opened the truck door, preparing to get in. Brock had prepared to take the shot, when suddenly his weapon had been yanked from his hands.

Brock had whirled around to face his attacker—Lucian. "What the fuck?"

"You will not kill Michael," Lucian said. "Adam wants him alive. You saved him from his attackers, yet you try to shoot him yourself."

"I didn't want anyone else getting the credit," he lied, and quickly drew the attention elsewhere. "I thought we wanted him dead. If you're trying to capture Michael, you're failing, just as you did at killing Cassandra Powell."

Lucian glared. "Michael and Cassandra are about to take a nice long drive on a deserted section of Highway 95. They won't last the night." He raised Brock's weapon and pointed it between his eyes. "And you won't last the week if you don't get me Red Dart." He disappeared into the wind, taking the weapon with him.

Brock punched at the air and took off running. He had to get to the base. He needed to convince Powell to inject him now because if Lucian had his way, Cassandra wouldn't be returning home. Powell had charged him with her protection, but she'd be dead by morning.

Brock climbed into his truck and slammed the door just about the time his cell rang. He eyed the screen. Powell. His gut clenched. He was sitting in front of Cassandra's apartment—four of Powell's men were dead, and his daughter had just left with Michael. That kind of timing screamed of a fly stuck in shit.

He answered. "Yes sir, General."

"Under the Speedway Bridge at I-15 at 2300," he said. "You'll be transported to our facility from there." The line went dead.

Brock sat there in stunned disbelief. A meeting under a bridge in the middle of the night. This damn sure wasn't standard protocol, but then neither was anything to do with Red Dart. Powell was secretive about his lab.

Brock didn't consider himself a wuss, but he was shaking clear through to his bones. He was excited. He was scared. He was aroused just thinking of the power that would soon flow through his veins. This could be the day his life changed forever.

Chapter 15

ONLY A FEW MINUTES AFTER BEING SPRAWLED OUT ON the floorboard of the truck certain she was going to die, Cassandra watched in surprise as Michael pulled off Las Vegas Boulevard and into the parking garage of the Neonopolis Entertainment Center. He cut a hard right to the lower level of the twenty-thousand-square-foot facility.

"Please tell me why we are in a shopping mall?"

"Neonopolis is more than a shopping mall," he said. "It's a full entertainment center with movies and games. It's also a great cover for our inner-city operation in the basement. Crowds discourage wind-walking and battles. Even Adam doesn't want to be known to the public. Not yet. Not until he's ready to take over."

She shivered with that comment. "Don't say that as if it's going to happen. Like it's just a matter of time."

He stopped the truck in front of a steel wall, and then punched a code into his cell phone. The doors opened with rocket speed. He put the truck back in gear. "I'd kill him before I let that happen."

She frowned, realizing the question in the back of her mind that had been niggling with demand. "Why didn't you kill him while you were in Zodius City?"

He pulled into a parking spot next to Carrie, and her chest squeezed with memories.

"Oh I wanted to," Michael assured her, putting the

truck in park and killing the engine. "You have no idea how I salivated to kill that man. Would have done it the day of the Area 51 takeover, but the bastard had enough explosives strapped on his person and planted all over the facility to kill everyone in the place if his heart stopped beating. Caleb and I both figured I'd kill him the minute he unhooked himself, but Adam is thorough. He has chemical weapons set to go off in several major U.S. cities upon his death. I've never been able to find out who holds the remote. That's why he remains untouchable."

This was almost too much to comprehend. "He's frightening. All of this is frightening." A realization came over her, and her gaze snapped to Michael's. "That's why you stayed inside Zodius so long? Trying to find out how to kill him without civilian casualties?"

"Yes," he said softly. "And not just causalities, Cassandra. Mass causalities. Hundreds of thousands of people. I never planned to be gone two years. I was supposed to be in and out—I was going to kill Adam, and the Renegades would attack his followers. It would be over. But nothing is simple with Adam." He shoved open the door. "We need to move. We aren't far enough underground to keep the Trackers from finding you, and the high concentration of people above ground will only mildly dilute your psychic energy enough to slow them down, not stop them."

Cassandra swallowed hard at that announcement and popped open her door. She was being hunted. Would this hell ever end? She stepped to the back of the truck as Sterling exited the elevators a few feet away and approached in a casual saunter, his long, blond hair tied at his neck, weapons strapped to his shoulder, one to his jean-clad hip.

Cassandra listened as Michael replayed what went down at her condo. "Holy fuck," Sterling said, running a hand over his face and then casting Cassandra a teal-green apologetic look created by contacts. Unlike the other GTECHs, Sterling could not mask his eye color from humans. No one knew why.

"Sorry Cass," he offered quickly.

She snorted. "I'm just glad to be alive to hear you curse, Sterling." She'd known Sterling since Area 51 and always liked him. "Besides, I'm fairly immune to soldier talk. All I care about right now is getting that hard drive data decoded."

"I've never met a government code I couldn't crack," he said with a cocky wink. "Michael might be better at scorching someone with a single dark look, but I'm the man with the computer skills."

Cassandra laughed. She'd forgotten the way Sterling teased Michael and the way Michael scowled in return. She'd missed it. And the little hint of light in Michael's eyes told her—he had too. She realized then that those two years inside Zodius must have been hell for him, and she wondered what kind of inner strength it had taken to survive that. For the first time, she felt something more than anger at him for what he'd done. She felt pride.

"I should have it open by the time you two head for the trams," Sterling assured her. "Which better be all of fifteen minutes or the Trackers will be all over us."

"Trams?" Cassandra asked, casting Michael a questioning look and trying not to think about the Trackers.

"We'll travel through a series of hotels by way of the connecting trains," Michael explained. "Then we'll walk through each hotel. It should confuse the Tracker's senses long enough to get a good start on the highway. A team of Renegades will travel ahead and behind us from there."

She bit her bottom lip, her throat suddenly dry. "Because eventually the Trackers are going to catch up to us," she said, and it wasn't a question. Neither Michael nor Sterling denied that statement. They didn't have to. They all knew—the Zodius were coming for both her and Michael.

A few minutes later, Cassandra stood munching on a PowerBar and drinking orange juice in a room full of computer monitors and electronic gadgets. Michael had put down six bars and some sort of liquid supplement drink and was popping the top on a second. Sterling sat at the computer panel, keying like crazy, all kinds of green and white code popping up on the screen.

"How do you feel?" Michael asked softly, studying her.

She nodded. "Better," she said. "Just tired. Wishing I was like you guys right about now and needed only a couple hours of sleep here or there." She really wished for the past right now—to be back at Area 51 before any of this happened, curled to Michael's side after eating a great meal and watching a movie.

He stared at her a moment, as if he too might be thinking of the past, and then cut Sterling a look. "We're on borrowed time here, man. What do you have?"

"Hold your breath and count to sixty," Sterling said. "I need one more minute."

Michael cursed and grabbed the newspaper under Sterling's arm. Sterling cut him a look. "There are similar stories in four states."

"What is it?" Cassandra asked. "What's going on?"

Michael tossed the paper down. "More missing women," he said. "Most of whom are probably already dead."

Bile rose in her throat, and she set her PowerBar on the counter behind her. "Dead? I thought they were just experimenting?" *Just* experimenting. God. That sounded horrible.

"Ava has a new fertility treatment she's developed from her pregnancy hormones," he said. "Problem is — the women only have a 50 percent chance of surviving the process."

"She's pregnant?"

"Giving birth to the devil's spawn," Sterling said, over his shoulder, still keying.

"That was the unavoidable situation that kept Caleb from calling you the night we gave you that phone," Michael explained. "We rescued fifty of the hundred women there. I had to blow my cover to get them out."

"What about the other fifty?" Cassandra asked.

"So brainwashed they stayed," Michael said. "At least half of them are probably dead now." He scrubbed his jaw. "All we did was cause more women to be kidnapped."

"That's not true," Cassandra said. "You saved fifty women, and it will take time for them to replace those women. No matter what, fewer women will die."

"Not unless we stop Adam," he countered.

Sterling turned around, running his hands down his legs. "I'm working with law enforcement to spread certain abduction profiles around the country. Bulletins are going out with public warnings." He shifted subjects. "Okay. The backup data. To start, Powell has two hundred troops headed to Dreamland in a few days."

"That's right," Cassandra said. "All training to fight Zodius."

"I don't like it," Sterling said. "Not with the threat Red Dart represents to the Renegades."

"Agreed," Michael said. "I say Dreamland needs to have a little mishap that keeps those soldiers from reporting."

Cassandra shook her head, pushing off the counter she'd been leaning on. "If anything happens to Dreamland, my father will be suspicious."

Sterling grimaced. "I'll see if I can hack West's email," he said. "I should be able to redirect their orders. Have them sent somewhere else. Make it look like a computer hiccup. That will buy us a few days to find Red Dart."

Cassandra let out a breath. "That should work."

"What else?" Michael asked. "Because we have to roll."

"Powell has Green Hornets," Sterling said. "I'm assuming Brock gave them to Zodius since we know he's in bed with Lucian."

"Maybe," Michael said. "Or maybe it simply means my mother is as big a bitch as my father was a bastard. Selling to our government and the enemy at the same time."

"What?" Cassandra and Sterling said in unison.

"Those bullets are made by Taylor Industries," he said grimly.

"Your family business?" Cassandra asked, cringing in memory of the day she'd looked up Michael's file and realized his family connection, acting on her concern that her father was using that connection for personal gain.

"That's right," he said with a short nod.

Sterling arched a brow. "You're freaking kidding me."

"I wish I was," Michael said. "It's technology that was back-burnered years ago. The bullets imploded inside the weapons and injured the user. Obviously, they found a way around that. And Mommy Dearest doesn't think twice about selling to a terrorist if the money is good. If my mother is involved with the Green Hornets, a weapon being used against GTECHs, it seems highly probable that she is involved with Red Dart, another weapon designed to be used against GTECHs. One to kill and one to control. Powell is being thorough this time. I'm going to need you to find a way into their database, Sterling."

"Jesus," Sterling said. "And here I thought *I* had a F'd up family. I'll get into Taylor's system all right. I want all those bullets. Every last one ever made."

"That means getting the ones on base, too," Michael reminded him.

"Artillery goes in and out of base all the time," Sterling said. "I'll create a shipping order with the Green Hornet coordinates, and we'll intercept the shipment before Powell ever knows they're gone."

Michael nodded his approval. Cassandra couldn't stay silent. "What if my father really is taking a stand against Adam?"

"Those Green Hornets may be the only weapon that allows the soldiers to survive a confrontation." Michael looked at Cassandra—a long, hard stare. "The Renegades, not those bullets, are the best chance this country has to stand against Adam. Your father has forgotten that. I won't let those bullets be used against our soldiers, and they will be if we leave them with your father."

He turned back to Sterling. "Did you find anything on that hard drive about the crystal?"

Sterling shook his head, lips thin. "Nada," he said. "Not one damn word. But at least we have the location of the bullets, and the information on the incoming soldiers who are meant to stand against the GTECHs. Diverting their arrival will delay Powell's plans and buy us some time."

"Zodius," she corrected. "The soldiers are meant to fight Zodius. I still don't believe my father is turning against the Renegades." Determination rose in her. "I know you think he is, just as I know you think Red Dart is about torture, but it's not. I have to go back and prove that. Then we can work with my father and shut down Adam." Then more decisively, "Yes. I have to go back. Tonight. I can't run."

Sterling and Michael looked at each other, and Michael nodded to Sterling who turned back to his computer and began to key again. "Cassandra," Michael said softly. "*There is no maybe to any of this*. Red Dart *is* a torture device, and the Renegades and the Zodius are both the intended targets."

"Damn it, Michael," she said, cursing when she normally did not. "You don't know that."

Sterling rolled his chair back and motioned to the monitor. Cassandra walked to the computer screen and sat down, staring at the scanned paperwork.

Cassandra's world crumbled down around her as she read the documents to the chiefs of staff, the definition of Red Dart, the directives for its use: tracking and remote, intense torture. Her eyes burned, her chest hurt. Try as she might, she couldn't stop the tears from falling.

The past rushed at her and collided with the future. The immunizations. The God-like complex she'd seen glimpses of. Did he ever think they were just immunizations? The lies. The loss of a man she'd considered a hero. Every action he took was to better himself, and every action seemed to lead to lives lost, lives in jeopardy. Her gaze went to that newspaper lying on the counter. All those women already affected, torn from families. Lost forever. And the ones who would be in the future.

Her gaze focused on a certain paragraph, and her eyes went wide. Her father was testing it on humans and GTECHs. She could barely breathe with the implications. If Adam were to use this on humans, he'd rule the world. If *her father* were to use it on humans, he could too. That last thought sickened her more than any other. She had to consider that might be her father's ultimate goal. Oh he'd call it protecting his country, but it was really about controlling it.

She swiped angrily at her tears. There was no time for emotions. Not now. She turned back to Michael and Sterling, but it was Michael she looked at. "I'll help you destroy Red Dart, but I can't do it from inside Sunrise City. I have to be close to my father."

"You're going to the Renegades' headquarters," Michael said, snagging her hand. "You'll be safe in Sunrise City."

"No," she said. "I don't care what kind of danger I'm

in. This is potentially the end-of-the-free-world we are dealing with. I can't go."

Michael eyed Sterling. "We're leaving." And before she knew it, they were in the hallway, her back pressed against the door, his big body in front of hers. Cassandra wanted to scream at him for bullying her. To scream at him for making her see the truth about her father. And she wanted to bury her head in his shoulder and just be safe, if only for a minute.

His fingers laced into her hair. "I know this is hard, sweetheart," he said. "But the Trackers are coming for you. We have to go underground. Then we'll find a way to fix this together."

"How?" she demanded. "How do we do that when you want my father dead, and no matter what, I can't want that. I can't."

"Cassandra—"

"Do you want him dead? Say it. Say it because I need to know."

He bent at the knees, coming eye-level with her. "What I want is your safety. You're my priority right now. You won't survive the night if you stay here. You have to survive if you want to fight."

He was right. She knew he was right. But hiding felt wrong. Guilt was eating her alive. "I helped my father. I stood by him. I—"

He kissed her. A deep, passionate kiss, filled with the gentle strength she'd always loved in him. Gentle. No matter how demanding, how stubborn, he'd always been gentle.

"We'll find an answer," he said. "But we have to leave now. Okay?"

She nodded, unable to find her voice. She was running, but only because Michael was right. She had to survive to fight. And she was going to fight like she'd never fought before.

———~~~———

Lucian found Adam in the center of his coliseum—Tad by his side with a smug look on his face, as if he mattered or something. They stood between a row of thirty wolves and another row of as many soldiers—a formation Adam favored when training the wolves for combat. He planned to use them to herd humans when he was ready for take-over. To herd and kill as needed. Those damn wolves. Lucian would never get used to those beasts walking amongst them as if they were above higher forms of life, just because they were joined with Adam.

Lucian exited a stone staircase as Adam lifted his hand and then threw it down. The wolves and soldiers charged at one another. Adam and Tad backed away, walking toward Lucian, Tad by Adam's side, as if he belonged there instead of at his feet. Tad couldn't see he was just another dog, lapping at Adam's heels. But he would. Soon.

Lucian would see to it. Because Lucian had a plan to turn Michael and Cassandra's time together into their end and his beginning. By night's end, he would not only see to it that Cassandra Powell was dead, he'd frame Michael as her killer. Powell would be furious, devastated—vulnerable to Brock's Red Dart probes. And Michael would be captive, inside Zodius City, ready for his punishment. Lucian would be his replacement, and Tad would be nothing.

Brock pulled his truck to a stop under the bridge and killed the lights. Pitch dark surrounded him, and silence, but for the rush of tires over the concrete highway above. The whistle of the wind came soft and low, and Brock stiffened, flipping open his center compartment and removing a Smith and Wesson. It might be hard to kill a GTECH, but he knew how to make his shot count.

Abruptly the wind gusted. Brock tensed as the truck shook with the violent impact. A roar of thunder followed, providing some comfort that it was Mother Nature rather than a Wind-walker. He relaxed marginally, but with the comfort of that steel weapon against his palm.

From a distance, headlights turned down the street, high beams that cut through the fog. A white van pulled to a slow halt a few feet from his truck, lights illuminating the droplets of rain as they nosedived to the pavement.

He sat there and so did the driver in the other vehicle. A silent standoff of sorts, until Brock accepted with a twist of his gut that he had to get out. He had orders. He shoved open the door and held on to the gun.

Rain fell steadily now, and his shirt clung to his skin, but he ignored it. He aimed the gun at the panel door and knocked. It slid open, and to his shock, big blue eyes framed with long, sleek, raven hair greeted him. The woman was striking, the smile she offered him sweet enough to charm a battalion of soldiers. What the hell was a woman thinking, meeting a guy under a bridge alone?

"Come in, Lieutenant Colonel, before you wash away." Her voice was smooth like whiskey, a throaty sensuality rasped from its depths.

His gaze shifted to the medical bed and monitors behind her. "Who are you?"

"The person who is going to hand you the world, Brock. If you want it. But you can call me Jocelyn."

Slowly, he lowered the gun, and she backed away from the entrance to give him room. He climbed in and pulled the door shut behind him.

"Lie on the bed and roll up your sleeve," she ordered, apparently unconcerned about the water he was dripping all over the place. His nostrils flared with the scent of her; it filled the cabin, the odd but arousing mixture of vanilla and cinnamon.

Jocelyn kneeled by his side and wrapped a rubber tube around his upper arm. Holy crap! This was happening; it was really happening. He was getting his injections. He watched her as she withdrew medication from a vial into a syringe, and his cock stood at attention. He was aroused. By her. By that needle about to deliver him to a new life. She was older than he first thought, maybe in her fifties, but could pass for forties. But it didn't turn him off. No, nothing about this woman turned him off. She was fucking amazing.

Those amazing blue eyes caught his—amazing crystal blue eyes. "General Powell told me you are aware of the risks, but I'd like to hear that from you," she said. "Because there is no turning back. Everything about this program is experimental."

"No risk, no reward," he said, lost in the sea of her stare.

"My philosophy, exactly." She held the syringe up and tapped it. "Ready?"

"I was born ready."

Her lips lifted at the corners. "I'll bet you were." She tapped the syringe once more. "But we'll talk about the side effects a little later."

Something about her words set him on edge. Didn't doctors do that beforehand? But it was too late for questions. She bent her dark head and injected him. The liquid was cold. The anticipation, hot. The darkness, almost immediate.

Chapter 16

AFTER THREE HUNDRED MILES OF STORMY WEATHER and dark highways, Michael pulled the Range Rover that the Renegades had left for them at a Vegas hotel into the parking lot of a storage facility. It was stockpiled with weapons and rarely needed motorcycles, but they'd need a bike tonight to get Cassandra through that canyon.

He was feeling edgy, ready for a Zodius confrontation, certain it was coming the minute they hit the dark depths of the canyon. What he wouldn't do to be able to wind-walk her there. Or even airlift her to Sunrise, but that would make them a big target, one Adam would have no qualms about shooting down.

Cassandra lay on the seat next to him, her blonde hair draped over the cushion as she slept—hair he knew felt like silk and smelled like honeysuckle. He wanted that woman more than he wanted his next breath.

He scrubbed his jaw, silently cursing his sorry, selfish existence. And he was a selfish bastard. If these past two hours of his wandering mind and her silent slumber had taught him anything, it was that. He knew he was a bastard. The selfish part, well, maybe he'd always been that too. Because just like at Groom Lake, he'd convinced himself that he and Cassandra were meant to be together. Talked himself out of it a couple times too, but mostly the opposite. Mostly he'd talked himself right into her bed and into her life all over again. Yeah. Selfish, fucking bastard.

And the danger of getting through that canyon to Sunrise City drove that point home. He didn't want this hell life of war for her. He wanted her back in Germany, happy and safe. *No*. He *wanted* her in bed, beneath him. On top of him. All around him. Smiling at him. Convincing him there was something human left in him. Something worth caring about.

He hit the remote, and the door slid open. Cassandra stirred, groggily sat up, and stretched. "How long was I out?"

"Two hours," he said, pulling into the building. "Which you needed. It's going to be a hard, bumpy ride through the rain, and we need to move quickly." He popped his door open, leaving her to exit on her own.

He needed weapons and a fast exit strategy. They were sitting ducks if they stayed in one place, out in the middle of nowhere, despite the Renegades surrounding them ready to offer defensive action if need be. But they were not human, and she was. Vulnerable.

Michael walked to the cabinets on the wall and yanked one open; at the same time, a voice in his head said *you can fix that*. Lifebond with her. Make her GTECH. Right. And what else would he make her in the process? The only thing he had any business doing was taking her to Sunrise and then leaving, working for Caleb from a safe distance.

He yanked another cabinet door open and pulled out body armor for Cassandra, telling himself to focus, agitated at where his thoughts kept going. The truck door slammed, and he turned to Cassandra, holding up the bodysuit.

"Hurry," he said. "I need you in this body armor and us on the road in the next five minutes."

"It's huge," she said, eyeing the bodysuit made for a man three times her size.

"We'll make it work," he assured her. "I want you as protected as you can be out there." He tried not to think about those damn Green Hornets.

Trepidation flashed in Cassandra's face as if she understood what he was telling her. Nothing good was waiting for them in that canyon, but there was no other way.

He helped her into the suit and then bent down, rolling up the too-long legs and sliding the zippers into place. His hands finally settled on her waist.

Suddenly, they were staring at each other, his heart in his throat. He looked away. So did she.

Their gazes collided again as he said, "I never meant to hurt you." Words he'd spoken before, but he'd say them a hundred more times if that's what it took for her to believe him. He needed her to believe him.

"I know," she said softly. "You just couldn't help it." She laughed, but not the laugh that lifted his spirits. "That's why my mother warned me never to fall in love with a soldier. Because it hurts."

He went completely, utterly still. She loved him? Did she just say she loved him? "What did you just say?"

She wet her lips, that sweet pink tongue glossing her full bottom lip. "I… I said that I—"

A loud crash sounded on the roof followed by another and another. The radio on his phone buzzed. Michael grabbed it.

"A dozen Zodius and double that in wolves," Sterling said. "Come out blazing, and do it now."

Michael snapped the phone back in place and grabbed a helmet for Cassandra. "We'll be okay." He kissed her hard and fast. "Do exactly as I say, when I say it." She nodded, terror in her eyes, and fitted the helmet to her head. He grabbed a helmet for himself and then climbed on a motorcycle.

In seconds, he had the bike cranked and hit the remote to the doors. Then they were flying through the exit, and despite his instinct to use the wind as a shield, he restrained himself. Anything he used against the Zodius he might be using on the Renegades as well.

The instant they cleared the building, rain pounded them, blurring his vision. Wolves lunged at them from all directions. Cassandra screamed as they nipped at her feet, and he was damn glad he'd insisted she wear the armor.

Michael cut and swerved, unable to reach for a weapon and still control the bike. The wolves were everywhere, right, left, front, back. Too close to use the wind without it affecting the steadiness of the bike. But there were no bullets, and he thanked God for that. The Zodius wouldn't dare shoot one of those wolves for fear Adam would kill them. It was a ridiculous, though convenient, weakness he forced upon his men.

Somehow Michael maneuvered through the pack without ending up flat on the ground. The instant he hit the edge of the canyon, he revved the engine and blasted past the trees. Gunfire replaced the wolves, canvassing their path. Michael called on the wind, erecting a barrier until it fell. Then did it all over again.

But the bullets kept coming, and in an unprotected moment, a spray of bullets pierced the tire of the bike.

Time stood still as the bike skidded from beneath them. Michael could think of nothing but Cassandra, and instinctively, he used the wind to cradle their fall, creating a soft cushion over the ground.

The instant they were down with mud splattering around them, terror ripped through Michael as he tore off his helmet, trying to see Cassandra in the rain. He found her a few feet away, sitting up and yanking off her helmet. In a flash of movement, he was on top of her, covering her from gunfire, about to roll to some nearby trees for cover when he heard weapons cock above him.

He turned to find himself looking up at the barrels of a dozen weapons, no doubt loaded with Green Hornets. Wolves growled at the soldiers' feet. Lucian stood front and center, obviously leading the attack. Lucian, who had always wanted power, but had never gained anything more than Adam's disregard.

Behind the Zodius, Renegades materialized, pointing guns at their heads. "These might not be Green Hornets," Sterling yelled. "But they're going right through your men's heads."

"Not before Michael and Cassandra are dead," Lucian assured him. "Back off, asshole."

Michael's eyes latched onto Lucian's, and he could see the panic in his eyes. Lucian was backed into a corner. The only way to save himself with Adam was to shoot Michael and Cassandra, and then fade into the wind.

Michael didn't give himself time to consider the repercussions of his actions, because there was no good answer, no right one. Anything he did with the wind would be temporary, and then bullets would fly. And then they might well die—not only he and Cassandra, but the Renegades here with them. No, there was only one option that gave them any hope of surviving. He grabbed Cassandra, and he wind-walked with her, praying she would survive.

~~~

Coldness seeped into his awareness with a hard bite. So. Damn. Cold. Brock's eyelids flipped open to the burn of bright lights. Pain pierced his cornea, forced his lashes downward as if weighted with cement, granting him the comfort of darkness. Yes. Darkness. He liked the darkness. It was all he could feel, all he could see.

The room shifted around him, shadowy movement almost enough to entice him into another attempt to open his eyelids. A soft voice shifted through the empty space of his mind, a sensual, sweet voice, an angel come to help him.

His lids scraped across his eyeballs, and he blinked into that bright light that splintered through to his brain; it turned the coldness into blistering pain that traveled a fast track down his spine. Muscles twitched in his face, across his eyebrows. He inhaled and forced himself to focus.

White ceiling. He was staring at a white ceiling. His vision faded; spots glistened like water droplets above him, disorienting him. Desperately, he fought for something to hold in his line of vision, but there was only that damn white light. It was all over, surrounding him, consuming him.

Panic expanded in his chest, rose to his throat with suffocating precision, and he jerked upward. A sharp tug on his wrists drew a gasp, pain wrenching them and soaring up his arms. He panted several times, his mind a whirlwind of foggy images that he couldn't make out.

Brock lifted his head, looked around—small sterile room, white sheets, hospital bed. Sharp pains shot through his wrists as restraints dug into his flesh. Desperately seeking freedom, he jerked upward again, finding nothing but more resistance, more pain.

Clarity came to him with the realization that the pain came from the steel pinch of needles, IVs running through his legs, chest, and arms. He glared down at himself, at the tubes and needles around him, in him, and memories weaved a taunting path through his mind. The bridge. The gorgeous female. The injection.

"Powell, damn it! Get the hell in here! Powell!" Over and over he screamed, no concept of time, but there was no response to his demands. He screamed until his throat rasped.

"Easy," came the soft, female voice he recognized from the van, a moment before her lovely, blue eyes came into view. "You're okay." She spoke over her shoulder. "Get Dr. Chin, please." A gentle hand settled on his arm a second before her piercing gaze blinked into focus.

Jocelyn, he thought. Her name was Jocelyn. "You bitch! You tricked me! You were supposed to be giving me the injection, not bringing me here."

She recoiled as if slapped. "No. I didn't trick you!" She leaned closer again. "Brock, sweetheart. The secrecy of our location is a necessity. I know you understand this. You're a military man."

"Then use a blindfold," he snapped back. "It doesn't

require needles or straps. I read the GTECH reports. Don't jerk me around, lady. They weren't tied down. They didn't even know what was happening to them."

An answer slid quickly off her tongue. "Their transformation was gradual. Yours will not be. You're tied down so you won't rip your IVs out as your body transforms. A few days from now when we take them out—"

"A few days!" he shouted, trying to jerk free again. He didn't care about the pain. He wanted free. "I can't stay like this for a few days. I didn't sign up for this. Get the needles out. Let me go." A small Chinese man entered the room, and Brock glared at him. "Who the *hell* are you?"

"I'm Dr. Chin," he stated, reaching for the chart at the end of the bed and then speaking over his shoulder to someone Brock couldn't make out. "Push two milligrams of Ativan."

"Give me that shot, whoever you are, and I promise you, when I get up, I will remember and kill you." The blur of white cloth hung back without approaching, taking heed of the warning. Wildly, Brock swung his gaze from Jocelyn to Dr. Chin. "I'll kill you all."

Jocelyn reached behind her to whoever the white blur was and said, "Give it to me." She spoke to the doctor. "Is he okay otherwise?"

He gave her a nod. "I checked him thoroughly before he awoke."

"Then leave us so I can explain everything to him," she said, and turned back to Brock.

"Give me that shot, and you'll regret it," he warned.

Unshaken, Jocelyn's full lips lifted into a smile, and she reached for an IV attachment. "You're very tough for a man tied to a bed." She pumped the syringe into the tube and emptied it.

"Next time you'll be the one tied to the bed, and I'll have my way with you." She owed him some pleasure for her deception.

She arched a brow. "Promises, promises. But right now, I doubt you could manage to tie your shoes, let alone, tie me down." She tossed the syringe into a trash can and then settled comfortably beside him, resting her hand on his chest. It was warm against his cold skin. "So why don't we talk about what's happening to you, shall we?"

A sudden heaviness thrummed across his eyelids, fusing with the heat of her palm, dragging him into lethargy. "Tell. Me."

"You've been given the GTECH serum—a special serum formula no other man has ever received. You will be the strongest, the most capable GTECH—as you should be as their commander."

Strongest. The word rolled in Brock's drug-laden mind. He liked that word. He liked Jocelyn's voice—all rich and womanly. She continued, "There will be some pain with the transition as your muscles and fluid levels adjust. But when it's over, you, Brock, will be the most powerful man on earth, and we will begin building your army." She inched closer, that crazy exotic scent of hers spiking in his nose as it had in the van, despite his fading senses. "You're going to be a hero, Brock."

Hero, he thought, smiling. He was going to be a hero. The most powerful man on earth. Satisfaction slid into his mind, and he allowed his lids to shut, allowed darkness to overcome that bright light.

Chapter 17

WITH CASSANDRA'S LIMP BODY IN HIS ARMS, MICHAEL reappeared outside the cavern wall of Sunrise City—barely able to breathe and certain he didn't want to if Cassandra did not. Desperate to get her to safety, he stepped to the exact, invisible spot where a scanner tracked his body, identified him. The cavern split in two, dividing into an equally invisible entrance. In an instant, Michael was inside the massive warehouse that served as an entry pod to Sunrise City, the doors automatically closing behind him.

He set Cassandra's dripping wet body down, feeling like a vise was clamping down on his chest as he stared at her pale face and realized his worst fear—indeed, she wasn't breathing.

"No!" he screamed in his mind, even as he scrambled to save her, ripping away her body armor to the waist and beginning CPR. She had to live. *Had to live*. Wildness charged through him, defiance, pain, anger. He pressed his lips to hers. His mind raced with punishing thoughts as he worked to save her. Blame rushed over him. He'd done this to her. He had done this.

Reason tried to save him from the crushing blow—had he lifebonded with her, he couldn't have been apart from her, he couldn't have saved the other women inside Zodius, would never have known about Red Dart, would never have gotten the body armor.

But had he lifebonded with her, he could have given her his full protection. She would not be dying. Or dead. He reared back and yelled at the top of his lungs. She was dead. She was dead. And so was he. Because losing her was the one thing he could not bear, the one punishment this life had given him that he could not endure.

A loud shout spiraling through the darkness consumed Cassandra, and speckles of white touched the black and gray in front of her eyes. She gasped awake, sucked in air, and sat up, head spinning, stomach twisting. But there was only one thing that mattered. The realization that Michael was shouting. Not just shouting. Roaring deep from inside his chest, pain etched across his face. For her. He was shouting for her. She knew it in every ounce of her being.

"Michael," she whispered, reaching for her voice, grabbing him. "Michael. I'm okay. I'm okay."

He looked down at her, instant relief pouring over his features. He grabbed her and held her, then framed her face with his hands. "Cassandra. God. I thought—"

She pressed her lips to his, needing that warm comfort that on some level she knew had brought her back to life. Those lips. This man. A memory—of those guns pointed at them, of being certain she was going to die—washed over her. One minute there were guns, the next… "We wind-walked."

"Yes," he said, pulling back. "I had no choice. They were going to—"

"Kill us," she said. "I know."

He studied her a moment, tenderness fanning his features. "We need to get you down to medical," he said, already pulling her into his arms when an alarm sounded. Her heart jackhammered in reaction, and instantly, Michael's gaze jerked to the cavern wall. Cassandra's own gaze followed the wall as it parted, and Caleb and Sterling appeared in a gust of wind, shadowy figures in black fatigues that faded into the darkness outside the door. Sterling took one step forward and collapsed, blood pooling beside his body. The wind carried three more men to the door, two of whom were hunched over in pain, injured as well.

Cassandra's face riveted to Michael's, and she could see the conflicted emotion spreading across his face. "Go!" she yelled, pushing out of his arms. "I'm okay! Please. Go. Help them."

He hesitated only a moment before he was running toward the injured soldiers. Cassandra struggled unsteadily to her feet, though she was gaining strength quickly. She watched in horror as Caleb threw Sterling over his shoulder and started moving toward the back of the warehouse in the direction of a row of elevators. Blood trailed in his wake. A lot of blood. Leaving no question about the seriousness of Sterling's injuries.

Guilt overtook Cassandra as Michael grabbed another injured man, whose name she remotely remembered as Damion. She'd liked Damion, just as she'd liked Sterling. These men had been hurt protecting her.

"Please," she said softly, her gaze lifting upward, calling on faith she'd perhaps forgotten too much lately. "Don't let them die."

Even as she said that little prayer, she charged toward

the elevators, determined not to be left in the warehouse alone, determined to help anyway she could. She ended up in the back of one of the two, standing behind Michael and Caleb, the injured soldiers hanging across their backs. She looked from one pair of broad shoulders to the other, feeling a silent, yet kindred spirit between the two Renegades in a way she'd noticed back at Area 51. *Renegades*. They were both, and had always been, Renegades. How had she ever believed Michael would really follow Adam rather than Caleb?

The underground elevator moved slowly. Too slowly. A lifetime for these men, she feared, the silence thick with that implication.

"What happened out there?" Michael asked, his voice rigid and low.

"Damion was down, and I was going after him. But Sterling was gone before I could stop him. Windwalking right into the middle of the fucking gunfire and took those Green Hornets meant for Damion. Damn fool. Damn idiotic fool. He knows the Zodius won't kill me. He knows my brother forbids it."

Michael glanced at Caleb. "They might not intentionally kill you, but that doesn't mean you might not have died out there," Michael said. "Your life is too valuable to risk losing. You have to lead us the hell out of this mess. Correction. You're destined to lead us the hell out of this."

"Spare me the talk about the grandness of my life while Sterling is bleeding to death over my shoulder, Michael," Caleb hissed. "My life is no more valuable than—"

"Like hell it's not," Michael countered, "and Sterling knows it even if you don't."

Cassandra squeezed her eyes shut. Shaken. Feeling more guilty. A lot more guilty. Could she have prevented any of this by seeing her father for what he was back when Project Zodius began? Wasn't she here because of him? Weren't they all here because of him?

"This isn't your fault, Cassandra," Caleb said, shocking her with the certainty that he had read her mind. Though nothing should shock her about the GTECHs any longer.

"No," Michael added roughly. "It's mine." Cassandra's heart leaped wildly. "It's mine." Was Michael talking about being the one to bring her here tonight? She regretted that. God, how she regretted coming here, allowing these men to be hurt.

Or maybe for Michael, this was about her father. About allowing him to live. He regretted that, she knew it. That was between them, a wall bigger than any other he'd ever drawn between them, and there were plenty of those.

The elevator doors slid open. Sterling and Damion were quickly placed on the rolling beds that awaited them in a long, narrow stone-covered foyer. Cassandra followed the men and saw other soldiers exiting the elevators on either side of her; all were being attended to or helping others in need.

A whirlwind of activity followed, and Cassandra chased the gurneys down a long hallway that led to the medical facilities. She saw what resembled a large emergency room with a center desk and curtained-off rooms.

Cassandra found herself sandwiched between Michael and Caleb in front of a large window outside a surgical room. And Kelly was inside with Sterling, operating.

She hadn't even known Kelly was with the Renegades.

She'd selfishly shut out everything when she'd fled Groom Lake. Shut out a war that wasn't going away. Refused to fight while Adam became more dangerous. And right now, watching Kelly in there fighting for Sterling's life, as Sterling had fought for all of them— Damion, Caleb, and yes, her—she hated herself for that. She vowed she would make it up. She would find Red Dart. She would destroy it. She'd help get those bullets, too. She wouldn't allow Adam to get more of them. If confronting her father would make a difference, she'd be out in that canyon right now; she'd be charging back to demand he make this all right. But it wasn't that easy, and she knew it. God. If only it were that easy.

She glanced up at Michael, at the hard set of his jaw, the stiff posture. Waves of turbulent emotion rolled off him and crashed over her. Whatever was behind his words in that elevator seemed to be eating him alive. The walls between them had crumbled while he'd worried for her and had rebuilt in seconds as he worried for his friend.

She yearned to strip those walls away, to touch him, to comfort him, but for the first time since she'd met him, she felt she should not. They stood shoulder to shoulder, but it seemed as if he were on the other side of the world, lost with no way home.

"He's crashing!" someone yelled, a moment before a warning buzzer pierced Cassandra's mind.

A harsh breath of air ripped through Cassandra's lungs, and her hands flattened on the glass. She watched as the medical personnel prepared to shock Sterling. And deep in her core, Cassandra knew that this gut-wrenching minute would change this war. Because this moment spilled blood and cut deep in the hearts of those on the front lines. They were not, nor was she, going to sit by and let it be for nothing. These men had saved her life. She owed it to them to fight by their side, to make their sacrifices matter. She stared through that window and willed Sterling to survive, so she could tell him so herself.

～

Michael stood by the surgery window, watching as Kelly worked on Sterling, holding his breath. The instant the monitor by his bed began a steady, stable rhythm, his shoulders relaxed, relief filling him. Those bullets, those Taylor Industry manufactured green bullets had not stolen a good man's life. Nor would he let them. Beside him, he could hear the sighs of relief from both Cassandra and Caleb, the tension in the small enclave of the waiting area immediately easing.

"Caleb." The male voice came from behind.

Michael turned to find Dr. Walker, one of the half-dozen doctors who'd followed Caleb from Groom Lake. A tall, human male with short, dark hair, he was casting Michael a suspicious look. Caleb didn't miss the look. "He's one of us. He's always been one of us."

Michael wanted to bare his teeth and watch the man jump, damn him. Like he didn't feel like crap enough right now without being made to feel he didn't belong here. But then, maybe he did not.

"Do you have something to tell us?" Michael barked irritably, barely keeping the growl out of his voice.

Dr. Walker cleared his throat nervously. "Noah, Cooper, and Jacob have avoided major organ hits. I'm about to take Damion into surgery to remove a bullet near his heart, but I don't anticipate any complications. It wasn't a direct hit, so he should be fine. His body will heal quickly."

Caleb gave a sharp nod, but apparently wanted a few minutes alone with the man, motioning him down the hall as he followed for a little one-on-one private time. And Michael had no doubt that it was about him, which only served to make him more damn agitated.

His gaze settled on Cassandra's mud-smudged pale face, and he motioned to a nurse. "We need medical attention."

Cassandra shook her head, motioning the woman away. "Let them deal with the men who are in life-threatening situations. I'm not."

"No," he said in instant rejection, thinking of those moments when he'd held her lifeless body in his arms. "You stopped breathing. You need to be checked." He raised his hand again and motioned to the nurse who was staring at him as if he were Freddy Krueger from *A Nightmare on Elm Street*. He scowled. "Holy hell, woman. I'm not a Zodius. I'm a Renegade. And we bloody well need medical attention."

"Easy, Michael," Cassandra said, shaking her head at the woman. "I'm fine. I don't need help."

"Like hell you don't," he grumbled.

"I'm okay, Michael. Thanks to you." Her hand wrapped around his arm, gentle, calming. He couldn't afford gentle. He couldn't afford calm. Not when people were damn near dying. The wrong people. Cassandra. Sterling. Not Powell and Adam.

"Don't thank me, Cassandra," he hissed vehemently, anger forming within him like a swiftly thrown blade.

He didn't want her thanks. He wanted... Well. He didn't know what he wanted right now, besides Adam's and Powell's blood, and her beneath him, pressed close, and moaning his name. Giving him a little piece of heaven, an escape.

But she couldn't be that escape any longer. Not without the consequences of lifebonding for her—to a man who wasn't even a man. He told himself to pull his arm away, to break that connection between them, so he wouldn't forget that. Again. He always forgot with her.

But he didn't pull away, and neither did she. Instead, she stared up at him with those beautiful green eyes— eyes that he wanted to remain beautiful and green. Not black. Not spiraling into the depths of obsidian hell with him as they would be if he claimed her fully.

"I cannot imagine what it must be like to be treated like the enemy," Cassandra said softly. "As hard as it was for you to be gone those two years, I want you to know how proud I am of you for everything you did."

His chest tightened with her words, and he cut his gaze to the window. "If you knew what I had to become inside that place, you would not say such things." He'd played his role of Adam's personal bodyguard, of tyrant and terrorist, all too well. All too easily. Sometimes he'd almost forgotten he wasn't that person. But he had prevailed. He'd stayed on his path, reminded himself he did those things, walked those lines because he was capable of doing so, and so that Caleb would not have to. So Caleb could remain a leader of honor, untainted by the likes of his brother and those around him. Someone had to be that person.

"It doesn't matter what you did," she said. "It only matters why."

He cut his gaze to hers. She pretended to understand, but she did not. And he didn't want her to understand. He didn't want this world for her. He wanted to get her the hell away from all of this. Safe. Happy. And so he pushed. Pushed hard. Pushed to make her run. "Is that what you would have said if I had killed your father?"

She sucked in a breath, her hand jerking from his arm. "Killing him wouldn't have solved anything. Adam would still be out there, trying to take over the world."

"Without the lure of Red Dart to aid his efforts," he said.

"So, had you killed him at Groom Lake, the world would be a happy place right now?" she challenged. She held up a hand. "Don't answer. Just don't." She narrowed her gaze on him. "Are you *trying* to upset me?"

"I'm simply trying to prepare you."

She looked stricken, even paler than moments before. She wet her dry lips. "For when you kill him?"

"For whatever the future may hold," he said. "This is war, and I am a soldier."

She choked on that. "Oh, I am fully aware that you are a soldier, Michael." She swallowed hard, shook her head. "No, I don't believe you'll kill him. I know you know that isn't the answer."

"You know less about me than you think you do, Cassandra," he promised.

Caleb's footsteps sounded behind them, and Cassandra squeezed her eyes shut. No matter what her father had done, he was her father. She couldn't wish him dead. Nor could she bear the idea of Michael killing him. It would destroy her. She would lose everything in one fatal swoop. But she didn't say that, not now, not with Caleb joining them.

One look at Caleb's face, and Cassandra backed away, giving the two men space to talk. "I'm going to the ladies' room."

Cassandra rushed down the hall as Caleb said, "The Zodius have retreated for now…" The rest was lost as she turned the corner, seeking her much needed escape.

Once inside the tiny one-stall restroom, she pressed her palms against the cool ceramic sink, letting her head fall between her shoulders. She didn't need to hear more of Caleb's report. "Retreated for now" translated too easily to "more bloodshed to come."

She wanted the bloodshed to end. She wanted to turn back time and do a hundred things differently—to have connected the dots about her father's motives and taken action. But she could only go forward, however daunting it seemed. Inhaling, Cassandra lifted her head, cringing at the raccoon eyes staring back at her in the mirror, the mud slashes streaking a line down her cheeks. She was still sick, feeling pretty crappy to be honest. But worrying about her stomach churning seemed selfish when people were fighting for their lives.

What rattled her in that moment was not the disheveled image or her personal discomfort, but what was underneath it all. For years, perhaps all her life, her identity had been tied to her father's in ways that reached beyond biology.

"You can make this right," she whispered. "You *will* make this right."

Pulling herself together, Cassandra cleaned up a little

and rejoined the men, finding them side-by-side outside the surgery-viewing window. The sight of Michael standing there—legs braced in a V, arms crossed in front of his chest, an unapproachable air rolling off him like thunder—made her stomach clench because she was the cause of his mood.

In a matter of days they'd gone from enemies to lovers, and right now, she wasn't sure what they were. Truth be told, Cassandra wasn't sure Michael completely separated her from her father, no matter how hard he might try or how much he might say otherwise.

She lurked behind the men, leaning against a wall, attention traveling beyond the glass as Kelly dropped one green-spiked bullet after another into a glass container. The tension in the waiting area was palpable; the worry that Sterling wouldn't make it was on everyone's mind. Michael stood like steel, watching every move the doctor made. Caleb, in turn, fell into pacing. He paced to the point of darn near wearing a hole in the solid concrete floor by the time the doctor finally rounded the corner to give them an update. All three of them rushed to greet her.

"He's stable," Kelly announced, eyeing Cassandra with a silent, understanding welcome. Her good news felt like a soft breeze on a hot day. Oh so needed. Kelly continued, "He's not out of trouble yet. He's lost a lot of blood. And he's endured tremendous damage to his body. Whatever those bullets are made of, they do more than penetrate the armor. They shred muscle and tissue. He's in for a long night of healing, and I'm worried about the healing sickness, considering the extent of his injuries. Though untested, I'm of the opinion that C deficiency is creating the healing illness, so I've started a supplement intravenously. That and the fact that he's shown no healing illness in the past make me hopeful."

"When will we know he's out of trouble?" Cassandra asked, before either of the men could inquire.

"A few more hours." Kelly looked them all over. "You should all go clean up and get some rest." She motioned to Cassandra. "Not you. I need to examine you before you get away from me. I just need a few minutes to check on the other patients." She started to turn and stopped. "Oh." She reached into her pocket and pulled out a clear, sealed baggy full of bullets. "Thought you might want these." She dropped them into Caleb's hand and left.

Caleb let them rest in his palm and stared at them. They all did. As if they were the devil in design. And after seeing the other men bleeding to death because of them, perhaps they were.

Abruptly, Caleb did something Cassandra had never seen him do. He lost it. Totally, completely lost it. He blasted out a curse and then flattened one fist against the cavern wall beside the glass, his big body tense, thundering frustration rushing off him.

Cassandra cringed as blood oozed from his knuckles and quickly backed away, hugging herself, unsure of what to do. Not sure there was anything she could do. Caleb had lives in his hands, perhaps the world's future. The pressure had to be immense.

"Adam has soldiers on our perimeters," Caleb growled. "Waiting to unload those damn bullets in every one of my men. And what do we have to beat them back? Nothing. Not a damn thing."

"We can fix that," Michael offered. "Let's go get Powell's stock of Green Hornets now, tonight."

Caleb ran his uninjured hand over the back of his neck, tense, but seemed to calm. "The location is on that encrypted hard drive, and I'm not trusting anyone but Sterling to read it. Finding the bullets without that information would be like finding a needle in a haystack." Caleb leveled him in a stare. "Can you get them from Taylor?"

A muscle jumped in Michael's jaw. "I assume Sterling told you my mother is providing Powell with Green Hornets and that I believe she is helping him with Red Dart. If I'm right, and I show up and do what I have to do to get those bullets, then we've alerted her and Powell with her that we know what they are up to."

"I'm pretty sure we've done that already," Caleb muttered foully. "We need those bullets."

Long, tense moments passed. Michael's expression was unemotional, indecipherable. But Cassandra could feel the emotion rolling off him, the tension eating away at him from the inside out. He did not relish seeing his mother. In fact, he dreaded it.

But he was that soldier he'd reminded her he was—he was going to do it. She knew that even before he finally said, "I'll need a team at the Taylor Facility ready to go the minute I give the coordinates. If they leave with me now, I can get them out of the canyon under the cover of wind." Caleb gave a short nod of approval, and Michael's gaze shifted to Cassandra. "I'll be back in a few hours."

A futile desperation rose inside her. She wanted to yell at him to stay. This night needed to end. The war had already cut too deeply, taken too much from them. But she could do nothing but nod. "Be careful."

His eyes darkened, a flicker of emotion in their depths so fleeting she almost thought she'd imagined it before he turned and started walking. And she realized she feared he was never coming back. That every time he walked away, she would always fear he wasn't coming back. But not because he was a soldier. Not because they were in a silent war. Because he was Michael.

Chapter 18

"HE'S ASSIMILATING 'GRADE 2' SERUM WELL, DESPITE the rapid introduction into his system," Dr. Chin reported, his patient lying in bed a few feet away.

Powell received this report with limited enthusiasm, regardless of the scientific progress that had modified the three-month transformation process and turned it into a few days. He'd watched 209 soldiers transform into GTECHs at Groom Lake before the White House forced him to pull back. But creation wasn't his goal at this point. He'd proven he could create, and he'd stockpiled enough serum for another hundred soldiers, which the government had no idea he possessed. Alignment with the government had given him the men he needed, but it was Jocelyn who would give him the missing element that allowed him to use his new GTECHs—control.

"As it stands," Chin continued, "he's at 70 percent absorption. We should have—"

Suddenly, West jerked, his eyelids peeling back so wide it was as if needles threaded the lashes and stretched them outward.

It was a familiar look, one Powell had seen in the battlefield moments after a soldier was injured, seconds before death. He lifted an eyebrow at Chin.

"It's an unavoidable side effect of the rapid change," Chin explained.

"Oh my," Jocelyn said and rushed to Brock's side, reaching for the face mask on the portable table. "It must be the light." She leaned over, and Brock jerked again.

"Holy hell, Jocelyn," Powell cursed. "You're going to get hurt." Brock was tied down, but he was still wild. "You're not a damn nurse."

Powell cut Chin a warning look that demanded he act. Powell didn't give a crap if West was in pain, but Jocelyn didn't like to cause other people pain, contrary to what one would think about someone who built weapons of mass destruction. That company hadn't been the same since her husband had died. She could kill indirectly, but couldn't stomach it up close and personal, and it showed in financial performance. She was annoyingly female, but he humored her sensitivity simply because he didn't need her doing any last-minute soul-searching, which would do nothing but complicate things.

"Put the damn mask on the man before he ends up hurting her." Indignation flashed in Chin's face that said he wasn't a damn nurse either, but it only served to agitate Powell. "Do it." The order was low, curt. Chin went into motion, placing the mask over Brock's face. Instantly, he calmed.

Jocelyn's brows furrowed with concern. "This is so painful to watch."

"The cornea should fully adjust in the next few hours," Chin assured her.

Jocelyn's concern shifted into a hint of excitement as she pushed off the bed and quickly joined the two men. "Does that mean we can implement the Red Dart application in a few hours as well?" Jocelyn asked, clearly redirecting her sympathy for West into progress. As a scientist and weapons expert, there was no question she wanted to see her work succeed.

"The transformation is the serum's super-powered effort to rid his body of all weakness," Chin reminded them. "We have no idea how adaptable it is during that time. We don't want to risk it building up immunity to the formula you've created. Let the transformation fully complete."

"Cut to the chase, Chin." Powell wasn't in the mood for his long explanations. "How much time?"

"Twenty-four hours."

"Make it twelve," Powell stated.

Chin shifted uncomfortably. "There's still a question—"

"Then go find the answer," Powell sniped. "*Now*." Chin nodded sharply and headed for the door.

Powell had provided all the resources that Chin had utilized at PMI, despite the size limitation of this facility, which was tucked beneath Jocelyn's home and hidden with military-grade technology. A far cry from the state-of-the-art PMI facility, but it allotted a certain element of discretion he deemed necessary for Jocelyn's involvement. He only involved those he knew he could control, those he'd gathered ammunition against. He'd certainly ensured he knew Jocelyn's weaknesses. "Pull it shut behind you," Powell ordered as Chin reached the door.

Powell had kept things all business with Jocelyn, entertaining his sexual appetites elsewhere, but he no longer found those outlets satisfactory. They shared something that reached beyond the Red Dart program. Michael Taylor had disgraced him—slept with his daughter, and damn near sliced his throat. The man had turned his back on his country as he had on his mother and his family years before. Yes. He and Jocelyn both hated Michael. It was a hatred that had become… arousing.

His gaze raked her curvy figure, traced the line of her hips, the swell of her breasts. He skimmed back to her heart-shaped face. "I do believe it's time we opened that bottle of champagne we've been saving to toast our success."

"I thought you didn't consider us a success until Red Dart was implemented?"

He smiled his approval. "Then we will toast the years of brilliant collaboration it took to get us to this point." He held out his hand. "What do you say?"

She hesitated an instant more, but the resistance slid away, her features softening with the promise of submission. Her lips parted, her eyes glossing over. She lifted her hand, her fingers sliding against his palm. Their eyes met, simmering with the familiar, shared attraction, deepened by the promise in the air—he would have her tonight.

Powell led her several feet away to a leather couch and chairs, a desk in the far corner. This was her workspace, and unlike the adjoining rooms down the hall, he'd taken care to add comfort here.

He urged her to sit on the couch. Tentatively, she sat on the edge, watching him with a heavy-lidded stare, her black slacks hugging slender thighs. He walked to the hutch against the wall and pulled out the bottle of champagne and two glasses, filling them. Joining her, he sat down beside her and offered her a glass.

"To us," he murmured softly, and what his words did not say, he ensured that his eyes did.

Her lips parted, cheeks flushed. She touched her glass to his. "To us."

They sipped the bubbly liquid, savoring it. He took her glass and set them both on the table. "Tell me, Jocelyn," he said, boldly resting his hand on her leg. "Does saving the world turn you on as much as it does me?"

***

Brock floated into consciousness with the sound of voices in his head; heavy shadows blocking out the bright light were the last thing he remembered. When was that? Minutes ago? Hours? He blinked several times, tried to focus, felt the heaviness pressing against his face. A mask—he had on some sort of mask to cover his eyes.

He opened his mouth to speak, to call out, but his throat swelled with the effort. He dragged air into his lungs to prove that he could. Pushed it back out. He wasn't dead. A familiar voice pierced the fog. No, they were moans. Female moans.

"General," came the whisper. "*Oh my, General.*" More soft moans and pants. A guttural male growl.

Reality sliced through Brock's mind, possessiveness coursing through his veins. He had no idea why—no understanding of the reason it had to be—but Jocelyn was his. He tried to sit up. Tried to scream out—Jocelyn!—but there was no sound.

Jocelyn's voice carried through the darkness. "General, wait. General, stop." Brock drew a breath and forced himself to calm, clinging to the shattered pieces of her voice. "General, wait!" she repeated. "Brock is awake. General, please stop! He's awake."

The General grunted. "I don't give a damn right about now, Jocelyn."

"We should check on him."

"How about I make you come, and then you check on him?" The sound of kissing followed. "How about that?"

"He can hear us," she whispered.

"Then he can get off when we do," he said. Brock jerked at his armbands again, fighting through the pain thrusting its way up his arms.

The General silenced her with what sounded like more kissing. And more. The sighs and moans tortured Brock far more than the needles in his veins. Wildly, he fought the restraints, fought to break free and stop those moans and sighs until a sharp pain pierced his brow, and he could fight no more. He was forced to lie there and listen to Jocelyn cry out in pleasure, forced to listen to the slap of skin against skin. It went on for long, torturous minutes until finally, silence fell in the room, and Brock imagined with graphic explicitness that they were lying there naked, wrapped around each other. In that moment, he knew he would kill Powell, hunt him down, and make him pay for everything he had done to him. He wrapped his mind around that vow until a loud siren sounded and then turned off.

"Who would be at my front door at this time of night?" Jocelyn said, a scurry of activity following her words, as if she were dressing.

Door? That wasn't a doorbell, Brock thought remotely. Where the hell were they?

"I'll check the monitor," Powell said. "You get dressed."

The sound of a keyboard being punched... followed by Powell's low curse.

"What?" Jocelyn said. "What is it?" She gasped, and Brock imagined she was looking at that monitor. "Oh, my God. My son is here. Michael is here."

The minute his mother opened the door, the scent of sex lanced Michael's nostrils, replacing the storm now fading into the distance. While his keen sense of smell had proven useful in battle, today it turned his stomach. Because there was more than sex mixed with that smell. There was something familiar he couldn't quite identify. Something that screamed of menace and lies, a promise that this meeting was going to prove everything he expected it to be—that she was every bit as malicious as his father had ever been. That she would do whatever it took to be on top, including aligning herself with Adam.

"Hello, Mother."

Jocelyn Taylor stared back at her son with the same crystal blue eyes he'd once possessed himself, with the kind of welcome reflected in their depths that one might give a tiger in the wild—a façade of regal indifference meant to show no fear that masked an underlying desire to bolt. He had no doubt that he looked like an angry tiger, ragged from battle, battered by the rain. But he'd come here with a feeling of urgency, out of some sense of obligation to her as her son to confirm whether she was guilty or not, before exposing her to the Renegades. The minute she appeared at the door, he already knew his answer—she was guilty. She'd always been just as guilty as his father.

"And here I thought you'd forgotten I existed," she replied shortly.

"I'm sure you hoped as much," he said dryly. "We need to talk."

She tilted her head, studying him for several long seconds. The years had been kind to her, despite the demands of leading Taylor Industries—a task she'd begged Michael to undertake. But then, she had plenty of money to ease the effects of age.

"Come in," she said finally, stepping back into the foyer to allow him entry. He entered the house he'd once called home—expensive Italian marble beneath his feet, etched, plate-glass windows lining high ceilings—and wished like hell he didn't have to be there.

"This way," she said.

He followed her down the hallway to the kitchen, a room he'd loved as a child, a place where cookies and milk had awaited him after school and holiday meals had been festive. But age had dispelled fairy tale families, and he'd discovered that his mother had been playing house at the expense of right and wrong, ignoring the immoral business practices of her husband, practices that had permitted that fantasy life. Apparently, she'd decided she was willing to take over where her husband had left off.

In a defensive posture, she placed the eight-foot, navy-blue, kitchen island between them. Neither of them bothered with a barstool.

Michael wasted no time getting down to business. He slapped the bullet on the tile counter. The color drained from her face.

"I see you finally managed to make Green Hornets market-worthy," he said.

"Where did you get that?" she hissed.

"Dug it out of my rib cage," he said. "I see you're up to Dad's old tricks, selling weapons to whoever will buy them regardless of consequence."

"That's impossible," she countered.

"I promise you it's not," he said. "And I have friends, good men fighting for their country, who are now fighting for their lives because of those bullets. I want names. Who you sold them to, when, and in what quantities." He wanted to know how the hell Zodius had even known that Green Hornets existed before they'd approached his mother. But then, Adam was always one to cover all his bases. He'd become like the mob—someone in every operation that might serve his needs.

She laughed without humor, crossed her arms in front of her chest. "That list is short. The U.S. Army. Period. There is no other customer. So if you're shooting each other up with them, that's not my problem."

"You're lying." She could barely look him in the eye, but then, it had been a long time since she could—maybe all the way back to after-school cookies. She wasn't that woman anymore—the perfect housewife and mother— if she ever had been.

She glared at him. "Don't you dare come in here and pretend honor while you judge me, because we both know you've plenty to be judged on yourself. And your day is coming, Michael."

"I want names," he demanded, his tone dogmatic, harsh by design. "Who did you sell the Green Hornets to?"

"I'm not giving you anything," she declared. "You certainly haven't given a damn thing to me."

"If even one more of these bullets ends up in one of our soldiers," he said, "I promise you, I will make destroying you and Taylor Industries my life mission."

That pale, plastic surgery-created face reddened. "What's so pathetic," she said, "is that I believe you. I believe my son would try and destroy me."

"Your son died years ago," he assured her. He'd come here for answers and hoped to find the loving mother he'd grown up with, not the enemy she'd become. Jesus Christ, he was a fool. He'd expected Cassandra to give up on her father, and yet he still hadn't managed to do so with his mother. "Now. Let's move past the talk. Let's go to your computer." He wasn't about to take her word on anything.

Her eyes went wide. "Why would I do that?"

"Because I want more than the names of who you sold those bullets to. I want every last one stocked in your warehouses." Alarm slid across her face, and she looked like she might refuse, so he added softly, "We can do this the easy way, *Mother*, or the hard way."

She glowered, her gaze skittering to the gun and two knives strapped to his hips before she swallowed hard. Without looking at him, she turned on her heels and marched down the hall, turning to the office on the right that had once been his father's.

He was behind her solid mahogany desk at the same moment she was, standing over her shoulder. She wasn't doing anything he didn't supervise. In fact, he reached over her shoulder and punched the HP notebook to life.

"Already logged in," he scoffed. "I'm ashamed, Mother. You should be more careful." He pointed to the visitor's chair across from him. "Sit." Her lips pursed, but she did as he said.

He pulled his gun and set it on the desk, reminding her how easily he could use it, and started typing. A second password screen pulled up the instant he typed in Green Hornets.

"What's the password?"

"Michael," she said, giving him a "go to hell" glare.

He didn't miss the inference that she'd made those bullets to kill him and those like him. She hated him almost as much as he hated her. He typed in the password.

The information he needed quickly appeared on the screen, including storage location and past shipments, which indicated sales to only one buyer—the U.S. Army, just as she had said. Or those were the only sales documented.

He pushed the phone on her desk in her direction. "Call your security team. Clear Caleb Rain to pick up a shipment."

"You won't get away with this," she vowed.

"Just dial," he bit out.

The instant she hung up the phone, he snatched his cell and contacted the Renegade team. Purposely, he set it on the desk next to the gun.

"We'll wait together while they retrieve the bullets," he told her. "That way you can help me clear up any trouble they might run into."

He typed in Red Dart, but came up with nothing. Tried several variations. Considered questioning her, but decided that would only make her bury Red Dart deeper before Sterling could find it. He popped in a backup drive. If she had anything on her computer, he'd get it. And he wanted the specs to manufacture those bullets for themselves.

His nostrils flared with the scent of sex again, and he narrowed his gaze on his mother. It was Powell; he could smell him. "Get up," he said, grabbing the gun. If Powell was here, Michael was going to find him.

Chapter 19

FOR THIRTY MINUTES, HE'D TORN THE HOUSE APART looking for Powell—the man who'd taken Cassandra from him the day he'd decided to lock away the X2s. The man who might well give Adam the power to destroy the American dream of a free world if he gained control of the government as he planned. That man had been in his mother's bed. And knowing that Powell had slept with his mother had sent Michael into a maddening rage. Michael didn't doubt for a minute that he was meant to know.

"Where is he, Mother?" Michael demanded, standing in the middle of her bedroom that dripped of silk, satin, and sex—with Powell. Or maybe that was just her. *She* smelled like sex. Damn, his sense of smell. This was torture. Knowing she'd been with him.

She sat on the edge of the bed, a smug look on her face. "I have no idea what you are talking about."

"I'm losing patience," he ground out between his teeth.

A thin dark brow arched. "And here I thought you were a man of control, like *your father*."

Michael moved his neck from side to side as he drew a slow, agitated breath. "Make no mistake, Mother," he said, low, lethal. "I *am* like my father. And we both know what he would have done if someone crossed him, now don't we?" His father would have found a way to make them pay. Just as Michael intended to do.

If Powell were still here—and every instinct he owned, including his enhanced sense of smell, said he was—he was going to find him. He'd end this now, once and for all. He'd torture him for the location of Red Dart if that's what it took. Screw digging through the trenches for his secrets. If Michael didn't drag it out of Powell, eventually Adam would.

His cell phone rang. Michael snapped it to his ear to hear Caleb speak. "We have the bullets. The men are on the outskirts of Sunrise City waiting for us."

"I'll be there as soon as I can," Michael told him, not about to leave until he was certain Powell wasn't here.

Silence. "I'm on the front porch when you're ready."

Shock rolled through Michael. Caleb was here. He'd known Michael would need him. That shook him in ways even his mother could not. It reminded him he was bigger than this anger. Bigger than the past. He ended the call and attached his phone back onto his belt.

He eyed his mother with contempt and walked out of the room. He didn't stop until he stepped onto the front porch and shut the door. He and Caleb stood there side-by-side for several silent moments. "Everything okay?" Caleb asked, leaning on the banister.

Michael crossed his arms in front of him. "Powell is fucking my mother. Pretty sure he was here when I arrived, but I couldn't find him. I'm thinking he's underground. Otherwise, I would have found him."

Caleb's brow arched. "And you were going to do what if you did?"

"Beat the crap out of him, make him tell me where Red Dart is, and then kill him." It wasn't the answer Caleb, who believed Powell would die before he talked, would want to hear, but that didn't stop Michael from being honest.

"Not exactly the plan we discussed," Caleb said dryly. "At least with Powell alive, we know who has Red Dart. He's the devil we know, as the old saying goes. Better than the snake in the grass we can't see."

Michael turned and eyed the house. Caleb seemed to read where his thoughts were going and said, "We'll bring a team back and do a thorough search." He pushed off the banister. "For now, let's go unload your anger and some of those Green Hornets on the Zodius hanging out at our front door. We need to know our men are safe."

Michael nodded. He was all about a little anger management in the form of killing a few Zodius soldiers right about now. It might be the only thing that would keep him from where he really wanted to be—in Cassandra's bed. And if there was anything a visit to his mother was good for—it was to remind him of all the reasons he didn't belong there. Yet, if there was ever a time he needed that little taste of heaven Cassandra was to him—it was now.

—◈—

"I told you not to use those bullets until after Red Dart was in place!" Jocelyn shouted the minute she entered the lab where Powell waited impatiently. "He's connected me to you! He'll connect me to Red Dart if he hasn't already!" She sucked in a shaky breath, no longer yelling, but still irritatingly shrill. "I told you Michael would know where they came from. We've had this technology for years. He was a stockholder. He saw the reports. My son is ten times more dangerous than his father ever was. He'll help Adam take over the world. He will. And he's going to come for Taylor Industries. He'll take my research. I don't know why he hasn't already."

Holy hell, she was crying. He'd wanted her to fear Michael, to see him as a threat, to use her guilt over the discovery that her dead husband had been a monster and she'd been blind to it, even helped him take innocent lives in the name of money. And it had been easy—she'd wanted a reason to feel she hadn't wronged her son as well by thinking him a monster, by shunning him for most of his adult life. She'd wanted a reason to do something right. And his plan had worked. Maybe too well. A hysterical female was the last thing Powell needed right now. "Control yourself, Jocelyn, and act like—"

"A soldier?" she screamed. "I am not a soldier. I am the woman you promised—"

He grabbed her, shook her. "Get a grip on yourself, woman. I would not be foolish enough to use those bullets and show my hand before we are ready," he said. "They were part of our plan. A double hit. Kill or control. Think about what you are accusing me of, Jocelyn, and you will see it's insanity. Someone deceived us."

"I thought you made sure that couldn't happen," she said and repeated frantically. "You *said* you had ways to make sure."

Powell needed to think. He set her roughly away from him.

"General—"

"Shut up, Jocelyn," he barked. Now, he remembered why he hated involving women in important matters. "I cannot think with your incessant chattering." A look of shock registered on her face, and he turned away before he was forced to endure the tears sure to follow.

He had no time for this. He'd come too far, too close to the realization of Red Dart to falter now. His mind tracked through the possible ways this could have happened.

Powell turned to the bed where West rested. West was the only one who'd had contact with Zodius. The only one who had access to artillery logged in at the base. And the only man who knew what a certain "top-secret" unit contained.

"It was West," he said, fury forming inside him. He snatched up a letter opener from the desk and walked through the open glass door framing West's bed. He stopped by the bed and drove the letter opener into West's leg. West gasped and tried to sit up, his eyes bugging out of his head.

"Oh my God!" Jocelyn screamed. "What are you doing?!" She grabbed Powell's arm.

Powell stared down at her. "Control yourself before I have you controlled."

Shock filtered through her expression, and her grip loosened and fell. Powell turned away and yanked the blade from West's leg whose face was contorted with pain. "You know what I love about a GTECH?" he asked. "All the pain and damage I can cause without killing you. I inflict injury. You heal. I cut some more." He slammed the letter opener back into West's leg. And left it there. "I know you gave Zodius the Green Hornets. Why?"

"I didn't do it," Brock gasped. "I wouldn't do that."

"Lies make me want to cause more pain." He ripped the blade out of West's leg.

"I didn't do it! Please! No more! I hate Lucian. I want him on his knees begging for mercy. *I would not help Lucian!*"

Powell considered him a moment. He would believe him about as readily as he would stick his hand in a tank of piranhas. He shoved the blade back into Brock's leg, reveling at his grunt. Pain would teach him to control himself. "You might think you've buried the records to hide what you did, but I will find proof. You're lying, and I intend to make you pay for it."

He turned to find Dr. Chin standing beside Jocelyn. "Don't even consider stitching him up. And leave the blade in his leg. I want it to heal there. A little reminder about what will happen when he crosses me. Otherwise we continue as planned. We'll use Red Dart to break him."

He cast Jocelyn a cold stare. He despised weakness. She'd proven today she was best kept beneath him, not beside him. "You just make sure you're ready with Red Dart when Chin says 'go.'"

"What about Michael?" Her voice quavered slightly.

He arched a brow. "What about him?"

"He'll come back."

"And we'll be ready," he assured her. "In fact, we will welcome the visit. If Michael comes to us, we don't have to hunt him down. I hope he brings others with him. He will be tagged with Red Dart, then broken and controlled, like all the GTECHs. They will become our protectors, not our captors. It seems only appropriate that Michael be the first to fall, considering the hell he made both our lives." His lips twitched. "His fall will give us another reason to celebrate." His attention

shifted to Chin. "Call me when we're ready to begin."
He glanced at his watch, calculating the time needed to
test Red Dart and prepare before the next nightfall. He
didn't dare delay longer. "You have ten hours."

Powell walked away, his mind on his plans. The more
he thought about Michael, the more he looked forward
to bringing that man to his knees.

Chapter 20

CASSANDRA SAT IN THE SOFT GREEN RECLINER BE-
tween Damion's and Sterling's beds, knees under her
chin. Finally, Damion was resting. The poor man had
been through hell, absolute hell. Throwing up, shivering, and shaking. The same things she'd seen Michael
go through, yet Sterling, who had been injured more
seriously, had experienced nothing but peaceful sleep.

"Knock, knock."

Cassandra looked up to find Kelly standing in the
doorway. "Hey," she said, smiling, glad to finally get
some time with her. Kelly had been so busy earlier.
She'd whizzed in, drawn blood, checked vitals, and
taken off again.

"What happened to my order for you to rest?" Kelly
asked.

"I'll rest when you rest," Cassandra vowed.

"Still as difficult as ever, I see," Kelly teased, claiming the rolling doctor's chair. "And no, before you ask,
I don't have your blood work back."

Cassandra smiled. "I was going to ask."

"I know," Kelly assured her. "I still can't believe you
were wearing Michael's mark for all that time at Groom
Lake and didn't tell me. I would have kept it a secret."

"I didn't want to put you in that position," Cassandra
said. "And I always thought we'd come forward. Things
just... happened."

"Things," she snorted. "That's a good way of putting it."

Guilt fluttered inside her. "I'm sorry I dropped off the face of the earth."

"If you mean Germany and the silent treatment," Kelly said. "I'm not. You should have stayed there. You were safe."

"Safe is an illusion as long as Adam is free." Then she changed the subject, asking what she hadn't been able to when Kelly had been busy. "The final lifebonding process where I convert to GTECH. It hasn't changed—right? The eye color change. The sickness. My symptoms all seem like I'm converting, but we haven't done a blood exchange."

"And these things are triggered by sex, right?" she responded. Cassandra nodded, and Kelly continued, "Could be that his body evolved, and perhaps now the process doesn't require the blood exchange. Maybe a few sexual encounters will do the job."

That wasn't the answer Cassandra wanted. So, no sex or lifelong bonding—there had to be an in-between. Maybe a condom but… "It's not sex. It's orgasm," she said, remembering the restroom encounter in the hotel.

Kelly tucked her hands in her lab coat. "I won't ask details," she said. "But I trust you on that one." She sat there, thought a moment. "It could simply be that you're ovulating. If you are, it's quite possible this is simply your body responding to your mate—a natural need to reproduce."

Cassandra studied her. "I know you, Kelly," she said. "Stop with the good bedside manner routine. You don't believe that ovulation thing for a minute. I *wind-walked* and survived."

"With Michael," she said. "There is a physical bond there that, in theory, might have offered some protection."

"Kelly," Cassandra warned. "Shoot straight with me. Tell me what I need to know, not what you think will make me feel better."

Kelly pursed her lips. "You've had the mark for two years—which I still can't believe you kept from me, but nevertheless—Mother Nature has a way of finishing what it begins. And as I said, Michael may well have evolved beyond needing the blood exchange. There's no denying he has skills with the wind that the other GTECHs do not. Of course, I have no idea why. He refuses to give blood. I think he's afraid we'll find out he's like Adam or something crazy like that. Like we even know what Adam is to compare anyway."

"Because he's X2 like Adam," she said. It wasn't a question.

"Yes," Kelly agreed. "But if he didn't turn aggressive and join the Zodius movement while he was undercover, then after all this time he's not going to. And if he'd let me take his blood—maybe we'd find out he isn't X2. Maybe the test was an error. Or maybe he has something that offsets the X2 violence. I can help him get answers if he lets me. He won't."

Michael didn't do anything he didn't want to do—except bond with her. Panic began to form in Cassandra. She did not want lifebonding forced on her. Or on Michael for that matter. It should be like a marriage—a choice. "If seeing each other again has somehow bypassed the blood bond, can it be stopped if we stay away from each other?"

"Why would you want to do that?" Kelly interrupted. "You love each other. Cassandra. I really don't believe the X2 gene is a danger to you. If Michael—"

"It's not that," she said quickly. "It's complicated. Too complicated to get into right now."

Kelly considered a moment. "If you like, tomorrow we can sit and talk. I'm here if you need me."

Her heart warmed. "I'm really glad I found you again, Kelly."

Sterling moaned and rolled over, bringing another question to mind.

"Why does Damion have the healing sickness and Sterling doesn't?"

"I wish I knew," Kelly said fretfully. "The more developed the GTECH's evolvement, the more enhanced the healing sickness. And the worse their vitamin C deficiencies as well. A good portion of the men now have to inject themselves daily with high doses of C."

A sudden tingling sensation trickled down Cassandra's spine.

"Michael," Cassandra said a moment before he appeared in the doorway, filling it with his broad shoulders and dominant presence. Dominant. Everything about the man darn sure dominated her senses. His hair was tied back, his face brushed with a light shadow of masculine stubble. His dark eyes seemed to spiral endlessly through her soul. The man stole her breath. She should be mad at him for being such a jerk earlier. Instead, she was simply relieved he was safe. Near. There were things to say, things to understand between them. Now they had the chance. Now they were together.

"Did you get the bullets?" Cassandra asked.

"Not only did we get them," he said, "we put them to good use on the Zodius soldiers who'd camped out near our entrance. They're gone. We sent them home to Adam with their tails tucked between their legs."

"If I never see another one of those bullets in one of our men, it will be too soon," Kelly said, rolling her chair so that she brought them both into view. "I was just going to find Cassandra a place to get some rest. We took some blood and hope to have some answers tomorrow." She hesitated and then, "It would help to have a sample from you too, Michael."

Seconds ticked by, his jaw set in a hard line, his expression indecipherable, before he said, "Where do you want me?"

You could almost hear Kelly's jaw hit the ground before she jumped up to offer her chair to him, and in the process, cast Cassandra a discreet wink. "Let me get supplies," Kelly said. "I'll be right back."

Kelly thought Michael's agreement to give blood meant something—though Cassandra didn't know what. But her stomach was fluttering wildly as Michael walked into the room, nearing her with that overwhelming presence of his and claiming the chair, his eyes locking with hers. "How are they?" he asked.

"Damion has been horribly sick, but it seems to have passed."

"How are you?" he asked gently.

Better now that he was back, she realized. "I'm okay." She tilted her head, studied him. Those dark eyes flickered with some unidentifiable something that made her return the question. "Are you?"

A long pause, and then in a barely audible voice he said, "I don't know, Cassandra."

Shock charged a path through her body. He'd never said anything like that to her before. Never. She doubted the man had ever said anything like that to anyone. He needed her. She sensed that, and suddenly all her doubts and worries paled in comparison.

Kelly returned, armed, and ready for action. "Okay. Let's get this done so you two can get some rest."

Michael's eyes clung to Cassandra's for another moment before he turned and offered his arm. Kelly drew the blood—two more tubes than she had drawn from Cassandra—and then packed it all in a pocket. "All set. I told Cassandra I'd have preliminary results in the morning, but really I'd like to keep her for a few more days."

Michael glanced in Cassandra's direction as if he expected her to argue, but she didn't. She was too tired to object. "I'll have to figure out how to contact my father and make up an excuse for being gone that he will buy."

Michael arched a brow at her in surprise.

"You gave up your blood," she said softly. "I'll give up my time."

Understanding flashed in his face before he cast an accusing look at Kelly, his tone gently chastising. "I see you've discussed my distaste for your needles."

"It might have come up," she said slyly.

His expression turned darker. "What's happening to her, Doc?"

Kelly's gaze shifted between the two of them. "What's supposed to happen. I think you both know that." She let her answer linger and then added in her more official tone, "As for the biology of it all... well, we'll see what the tests say. As long as you are together though, I suspect your bodies will continue to try to complete what has started."

"Which means being apart is the only way to stop it," he said.

It wasn't a question, but rather a statement, and Cassandra had the instant sense that it was something he'd been thinking on his own. Unbidden, those words ripped through Cassandra and twisted her in knots. There had been no good-bye last time. He'd just disappeared. She couldn't live through that again.

"If it can be stopped," Kelly replied, tugging Cassandra out of the wildfire of erratic thoughts. "I have my doubts. But I could be wrong. As I told Cassandra, this could be something as simple as hormonal fluctuations that fade when you two are apart. There certainly are scientific reasons not only to want to understand what's happening, but to need to do so. Others will experience this same thing. I have no doubt. We need to know if bonding can take place without a blood transfer. We need to know what bonding ultimately means for the couple. We'll try and find out everything we can as fast as we can." She shoved her hands in her lab coat. "I'll go get the testing started and then catch a few winks myself." Her attention shifted to Cassandra. "I'll talk to you tomorrow. We can grab coffee between me poking and prodding you."

Cassandra smiled. "Sounds good. Well… the coffee part."

A moment later, Kelly departed, and Cassandra was alone with Michael, her heart pitter-pattering against her ribs in a wild, bluesy kind of beat that said heartache was coming.

Michael rolled the chair around to face her. "Ready to get out of here?"

She swallowed hard and nodded. "Yes. I'm ready." He held his hand out to her, and she tentatively settled her hand against his. Warmth spread up her arm, across her chest. He opened his mouth to speak and shut it. She chose not to press. Not here. Not now. She wanted to be alone with him. *To be with him.* God, she wanted to be in his arms more than she wanted her next breath.

Hand in hand, they walked through the sparsely populated hospital and exited a door to a narrow electronic conveyor that traveled through a high cavern. Flickering florescent lights clung to ceilings and walls and seemed to travel onward forever.

Michael pulled her close, his big body surrounding hers, his hands tangling in her hair before lowering his forehead to hers. "My mother," he whispered. "I confirmed she's a part of all this."

She pulled back, brushed wayward strands of his hair from his face. "Oh God. Michael. I was hoping it wasn't true. I'm sorry. Did you see her? Talk to her?"

He inhaled a labored breath, and she settled her hand over his heart, feeling the pounding vibrating through her palm, urging him to calm down with her touch. Finally, air trickled from his lips. "I saw her. She lied and said she sold them to the military." His hand went to hers on his chest. "I expected you to do what I couldn't. Give up on your father. I knew what my mother was, but I still went there tonight wanting her to prove me wrong."

She wanted to cry. The pain in Michael seeped through her skin right to her heart. "Michael—"

His hand tightened over hers. "Hear me out, baby. Please."

She nodded, instant understanding coming to her. Listening was the most important thing she could do for him. "Of course."

"I need to tell you I'm sorry. I'm so damn sorry."

Her free hand went to his jaw. "I'm sorry for both of us." Their eyes held and locked. For long seconds, they were transfixed, entwined together in past and present, in the anticipation of what lay ahead.

The spell was broken by a buzzer sounding the warning for the end of the pathway. They turned and walked off the conveyor and into the most amazing place Cassandra had ever seen in her life. It was a city underground. Quaint little stone buildings with a red brick path. Stores and restaurants, little outdoor tables and chairs.

"Oh my God," Cassandra said. "How is this even possible?"

"Money and a lot of care," he said. "And Caleb wanted this place to feel like home to those who live here. A safe place that wasn't like a prison."

"Is this what Zodius is like?"

"Our city is much smaller," he said. "Zodius City exceeds our population by thousands."

"How did the Renegades afford all of this?"

"Private money from people like myself and Damion, who had it to give. Caleb struck a funding deal with the government as well when we agreed to support them. We've invested with what we have."

"Amazing," she whispered. "Just amazing."

They walked to the left and took another conveyor

that led to a tunneled walkway branching left and right. They turned right to a row of doors and stopped at the very end. "This is me," Michael said, punching in a code and opening the door. He then stepped back and leaned his arm over the door seal. "What's mine is yours. I think you know that. I'll come early in the morning, and we'll get you a phone line to your father, code it to make it look like it's coming from your cell phone. I'll bring you some clothes, too."

She tilted her chin up, stood close, almost touching. "You don't seriously think you're leaving me tonight?" she asked. "Do you?"

"I won't be able to keep my hands to myself if I come in that door," he said hoarsely. "I can barely keep from doing so now."

"Then don't."

"You heard what the doctor said," he argued. "If we—"

She wrapped her arms around him and stared up at him. "You aren't leaving me tonight."

Chapter 21

"WHAT THE HELL WENT ON OUT THERE, LUCIAN?" Adam thundered, charging into the Zodius City hospital where Lucian was placing a soldier on a bed—one of a dozen injured by the Renegades.

"Michael happened," he said, ready for this confrontation. "And he sent you a message. 'Fuck off.' That was right before he took down three of our men with Green Hornets."

Adam all but roared, his face red, eyes half bugging out. "Which he got from where?"

Ava's voice shouted from nearby. "Hurry! Get her to the doctor!" Adam stepped inside the doorway as Tad appeared behind him, a female in his arms, rushing her to the care of a doctor.

Ava scanned the room and pointed at one of the injured soldiers. "Him!" she yelled at the doctor. "He is her Lifebond. Save him, or she will die." She whirled on Lucian, fury in her eyes as she protectively hovered near the female. Tad stood behind her as if he were her guardian. "What have you done, Lucian? Never have we come back from battle with injuries like these. If her male dies, so does she, and so does our chance of breeding them! Already we struggle to replace the lost females."

Tad settled his hands on his hips. "Looks like your contact double-crossed you and sold Green Hornets to us and the Renegades," he said snidely.

"He didn't need Brock West," Lucian said. "He has Cassandra Powell, his Lifebond." He cut his attention to Ava. "He wind-walked her to safety."

"Then he did not care if she lived or died," Tad declared quickly.

"If there is even a slight chance they are Lifebonds," Ava said, "we cannot risk killing her, Adam. We need the Lifebonds too badly. Michael is powerful. His children would be powerful. With Red Dart you will control him and his offspring." She smiled. "Think of the many ways you might torture Michael with both him and his Lifebond in captivity. You can hurt her without killing her. It would be fun. We can do it together."

Adam cast his Lifebond a half-veiled stare. "Perhaps I should go get him myself. Be done with all of this."

"No!" Ava insisted, pressing his hand to her belly. "You risk my life and our child's." She eyed Lucian. "If Lucian cannot get the job done this time, then we'll let Tad try."

Lucian ground his teeth. He was really beginning to hate that bitch.

Cassandra hugged Michael close, refusing to allow him to leave. He stared down at her with turbulent, dark eyes, tormented, hungry—full of passion. And then he kissed her. And it was a kiss that stole her breath, a kiss that made her want to laugh and cry all in one moment.

Michael walked her backwards into the room, kicking the door shut, and turning the dimmer knob on the wall to illuminate the room. But Cassandra didn't care about the room or about the hell outside the room. Not now. All she cared about was Michael, the man, the moment, the kiss.

He tangled his fingers through her weather-tossed hair, kissed her as if he had never kissed her before, as if he would never kiss her again. Need blossomed inside her, more need than she'd ever thought it possible to feel for another human being. Her hand pressed beneath his T-shirt, skimming hard muscle and warm, taut skin. He reached up and tugged the shirt over his head. Before it ever hit the ground, her fingers were entwined in his chest hair, tracing the lines of his defined pecs. He kissed her again, a long, drugging, perfect kiss that brought her to her toes. Her tongue caressed his with soft, hungry licks. A kiss that deepened as his hands bared her waist, calloused fingers rasping against delicate skin with the promise of pleasure that left her shirt on the floor next to his.

Too soon he tore his mouth from hers, his breathing as erratic and wild as her own, and led her into the efficiency-style apartment.

Cassandra scanned the room as they walked. A granite bar framed the small kitchen overlooking a massive open room, the front half the living area with a couch and two chairs and a big-screen television. There was a bedroom toward the back with a king-sized bed and a black leather headboard. There were no pictures anywhere. No personal items. Nothing that said—this was Michael's *home*. Was that because he'd lived in Zodius Nation? Or because emptiness was all he allowed himself? Her heart ached at that thought. She didn't want that for him; she didn't want that for either of them.

They crossed the expanse of the living area and stopped beside the bed, facing one another. Michael released her hand, and they stood there in silent communication, in understanding of a decision between them that was profoundly important.

This was the first time since they'd found each other again that they would decisively choose to get into that bed together, rather than allow passion and emotion to drive them there. It was a signal of acceptance between them, of at least trying to find a way over the walls that always rose between them. And yes, there was a chance it could bind them together; they both knew this. Or rather knew the risk of going forward with so many unknowns, so many possibilities about their bond that they didn't understand.

"I can still walk out that door," he said softly. "This doesn't have to happen."

She reached up and unhooked her bra, tossing it to the side. "Or you can stay."

For an instant, his gaze held hers before skimming downward in a slow, deliberate inspection of her breasts, stark passion etched in his face. Her nipples tightened, pleasure stealing a path from the tips straight to her core. "You have the most beautiful nipples I've ever seen," he murmured softly.

Instant, wet heat clung to her panties. He'd always said bold things to her, things that made her blush, things that aroused her in a deep way, and now was no exception. "And you," she said, "have on too many clothes." Her voice was gravelly with passion, unfamiliar to her own ears.

In response, he unsnapped his jeans. She reached for hers as well, and a frenzy of undressing began. Excitement coursed through her veins, her hands trembling from the intensity. Like the first time they'd been together. Her mind went there now, retraced the path that had brought them here tonight.

Cassandra finished undressing, willing her heart to stop racing, like a schoolgirl on a first date. No one had ever excited her in this way—no one but Michael.

As they faced one another again she admired his body. He was a work of art, the ultimate man in her eyes, rippling muscle and masculine perfection. Her lips parted at the sight of his jutting thick erection; her breath lodged in her throat at the erotic thought of once again having him inside her.

She closed the distance between them, wrapping her hand around the width of him, her eyes meeting his, her free hand going to his chest. He pulsed in her hand, hard, inflexible, veins protruding. "God, I've missed touching you like this," she confessed.

"My restraint is paper thin," he warned.

Her lips twitched. "Ah, now," she teased, leaning closer, her breasts pressed to his side, his arms wrapping around her waist as she flattened her tongue on his nipple. "I'm quite confident of your restraint." She tightened her grip on his cock, and then caressed it with her fingers, stroking the wet liquid tip and sliding it around... kissing his shoulder, his arm.

She pinned him in a seductive stare full of erotic promise and then slowly slid down his body until she was on her knees. Watched the anticipation shudder across his strong features as she made one long lap of her tongue across the bulging head of his penis and then drew it between her lips. She sucked him deeper, harder, the salty-sweet taste of him filling her mouth. She loved the pleasure it represented, the proof that she was stealing just a little of his control. Her free hand went to his thigh, and she could feel him shaking, shaking. Michael was shaking, vulnerable in a way she knew he didn't allow himself to be at any other time.

And she remembered why she loved this so much— because when she drew him into her mouth, when she was on her knees before him, that was the only time Michael ever allowed himself to really take anything. The only time he ever let go and forgot to hold back.

And so she made sure he didn't hold back, working him with her mouth, her hand, her tongue. Remembering what made him hot… what drove him wild. His fingers tangled in her hair, a moan escaping his lips, the sound washing over Cassandra like an aphrodisiac, driving her to give more, take more. His hips thrust as she pumped him, his cock sliding back and forth between her lips. She could feel the pulse of his impending orgasm gathering beneath her hand and feel the urgency in the convulsing of his hips. But he didn't let her take him all the way; his hands went to her shoulders, demanding that she stop. He grabbed her arms and pulled her to her feet.

"When I come," he said, "it will be inside you." With the words, he gently lowered her to the bed, went down on his knees at the edge of the mattress, and spread her wide. She rested on her elbows, watching him. His hands trailed up her legs, caressed a slow, teasing path that told her of his intentions.

She fell back on the mattress the instant his warm breath brushed her clit, his tongue sliding delicately around the tip before he gently suckled. It was Cassandra's turn to cry out as he drew her more fully into his mouth, his fingers stroking along the slick, swollen flesh and then slipping inside her. Her hands grabbed at the surprisingly soft fabric of the comforter, eyes fluttering with the sensation of every lick, stroke, and suckle. At the same time, he stretched to palm her breasts, teasing her nipples.

He gave her everything she could possibly desire, except him inside her. Yes, she so needed him inside her. Whimpering, she felt the flush of orgasm and fought against it. With a Herculean effort, she sat up and tried to move away. He grasped her thighs, held her firmly, stared up at her from that intimate spot between her thighs that only made her ache a little bit more.

"Together," she whispered. "Please. I really want that." She pressed her hands to his shoulders. "You lie down." There was something inside her that said he needed to know in as many ways as possible that this was a choice, being with him, a thought-out decision. There was passion, there was desire, but this wasn't a mad rush of passion overcoming indecision.

His eyes softened and then flared with newfound heat before he rolled to his back. Cassandra wasted no time straddling him, the wet core of her body pressed to his stomach while she leaned forward and brushed her lips over his.

Possessively, he filled his hands with her breasts and then caressed a path down her waist, holding her steady as she reached between them and found his erection. Their eyes held as she slid the tip to the seam of her body, slipping it past her swollen, sensitive feminine lips. Her breath lodged in her throat at the feel of him inside her as her body swallowed the hard edges of his erection. One slow inch at a time, she slid down the hard, hot length of him, until they were one, merged.

They stared at one another, emotions, passion, a web that captured them and would not let go. He moved suddenly, pulling her lips to his, his hand wrapped around the back of her neck, his tongue stroking hers. Slowly, they began to move, hips swaying in a sensual rhythm that sent splayed pleasure to every nerve ending of her body. The kisses shifted from tender to desperate—passionate, wildly out of control. Michael sat up with her, wrapped his arms around her back, rocked with her in this slow, tilting motion that drove her insane. Their lips were close, breath mingled.

Abruptly, he stopped moving, his fingers brushing the hair from her eyes. "I love you, Cassandra," he said. "I love you so damn much."

Her heart skipped a beat, her skin tingled. Those were the words she had longed to hear. The words she needed as much as she needed her next breath. "I love you too, Michael. Even when I told myself to hate you, I knew I loved you."

His hand framed her face. "There are things about me you don't know," he said. "Things I can't, I won't, ask you to live with."

"Stop, Michael," she whispered, her hands framing his face. "Stop judging yourself and then assuming it's what I feel too. Have you ever done anything that you didn't believe was to save innocent lives? Anything you regretted later?"

"It's not that simple," he whispered. "Baby, it's not."

"I know you, Michael," she whispered and kissed him before he declared otherwise.

He tasted of rich masculine spice, devouring her mouth with his. His cock began to stroke the sensitive flesh between her legs. They were lost then, forgetting what had brought them there, what might tear them apart. His big hands powerfully explored her body, touched her in ways no other could. His fingers played with her nipples, tugged in a delicious, rough way that made her cry out and buck against him at the same moment. Made her nip his lips with her teeth and kiss a path to his shoulder. She could not touch enough of him, could not taste enough of him, could not get him deep enough or hard enough. There would never be enough. Part of her yearned to push him back against the mattress, then ride him wildly, take more of him. Take control. But that meant letting go; that meant those strong arms wouldn't cradle her anymore and that was simply not an option.

Instead, she clung to him—with her lips, her arms, her hips. If it could have lasted forever, still it would not have been long enough. Too soon, tension coiled in her stomach, too soon, it spiraled into spasms that milked his cock and left her gasping for air, her face buried in his neck. His grip tightened around her waist, a guttural moan sliding from his lips a moment before she felt his seed spill inside her. They stayed there for long seconds, merged together, as if both were afraid of losing the moment, of losing each other.

It was Michael who broke the silence, sliding to the edge of the bed, still buried inside her. Before he stood up, he brushed his lips over her. "Bath and then sleep for you."

"Only if you come to bed with me," she negotiated.

"I'm not going anywhere." The words rasped across his lips in a hoarse whisper full of torment that seemed to say—not now, but later—later he would leave.

Cassandra clung to him as he carried her to the bathroom. It was true, she'd been afraid of being alone. She'd admitted that to herself. Tonight though, she realized something. She needed and wanted Michael in her life, but he had to want to be there. No Lifebond, no physical connection, would change what was messing with his head. Nor would it bind them together in the most important way—the emotional one.

Michael had to make the choice to allow her inside his life. It could be no other way. Either he gave himself to her all the way or not at all. She might not like being alone, but now that she'd faced that fear, she was prepared to deal with it. What Cassandra wasn't willing to live with was wondering when Michael would decide he was too dangerous for her, or too duty bound, and leave again.

~~~

Michael rested against one end of the claw-foot-style bathtub with Cassandra opposite him, and he stared into her black eyes. God. What had he done? What if they'd fully bonded, and it was irreversible? They didn't even have his blood work back. He had no idea what it would show. He'd been selfish, desperate for the woman he loved.

Cassandra sank lower into the deep tub, her long, blond hair floating on top of the surface. "This is a little piece of heaven on earth."

"Your eyes are black."

Her lashes fluttered to her cheeks, dark circles against pale skin, and then lifted again. "I assumed as much."

Being with her again made him remember why he'd thought he could be a different man when he was with her, how she made him *want* to be a better man. How she found softness in him where he thought there was only steel.

It was clear the GTECH injections enhanced what was there in each man—turned those dark into something much darker. That he'd managed to avoid becoming like Adam was nothing short of a miracle. That he'd gained lethal abilities no man should possess with that kind of darkness inside him shook him to the core. Shook him because he was still changing, still growing stronger. When would the changes push him over the edge? And would he take Cassandra with him?

Concern building, he asked, "How do you feel?"

"I'm fine. Tired. A bit nauseous, but who wouldn't be with hardly any sleep?" She lifted her hand and let water and bubbles drip from her fingers. "I still can't believe you had bubble bath," Cassandra teased. "Bubbles defy the entire roughneck soldier image you wear so well, in case you didn't read that page in my father's macho soldier handbook." Her smile wavered a bit, as if it hurt to say his name or compare the two of them.

Michael lifted her foot, her pretty, pink-painted toes poking out of the water as he gently massaged. She moaned instantly, and he smiled inside. She'd always been a sucker for a good foot rub, and he'd been a sucker for those cute faces she made when he gave her one. "Caleb put one of the nurses in charge of the comfort of the soldiers," he explained. "Emma stocked everything she considered to be the basic necessities in every room, regardless of sex."

Cassandra laughed. "I like this Emma already. Bubbles as a necessity." She moaned a little as he massaged. "You're very good at that." She grinned. "And a great many other things as well."

"Careful," he warned, his cock pulsing with the suggestive tug of her voice. "Or I'll be tempted to come over there and show you a few of those things. And we both know you have to get some sleep." She needed rest. He needed her, but her needs came first.

"Sleep is overrated," she said dismissively and changed the subject, her expression growing solemn. "What are you going to do about your mother?"

He reached for her and pulled her close to his side, under his arm. She was so tiny that she fit beside him easily inside the tub. "I'll destroy her company and strip them of their ability to help Zodius."

Several heavy seconds of silence hung in the air before she whispered, "Tell me what happened tonight."

He drew a deep breath and realized how much he wanted to tell her, even needed to tell her. Though he excluded the parts about her father, the words came easily, rolling from his lips with the relief of a summer breeze rather than the discomfort of a forced wind. She already knew bits and pieces of how he felt about his mother, knew how his mother had shunned him for turning away from the family, from his father. About their long silence. But what Cassandra didn't know was what he hadn't admitted to himself until tonight—how much that silence ate him alive. It had not been until he stood in that kitchen and discovered that he couldn't justify his mother's actions as just those of a misguided housewife anymore, and that realization had ripped him into pieces.

The water was chilly by the time they stood up and turned on the shower to wash off. Michael turned Cassandra away from him, wrapped his arm around her waist, slipped her wet hair away from her neck, and kissed the mark that linked her to him. For a few moments, he let himself believe he could have all of her, tugging her closer, holding her snuggly against his body. The water sprayed them with peaceful warmth, and Michael squeezed his eyes shut, pretending that tomorrow would be as perfect as this moment and knowing it would not.

Chapter 22

A LOUD POUNDING SOUND PERMEATED THE HAZE OF Cassandra's sleep, followed by the jabbing pain in her stomach. Oh God. She blinked awake and quickly squeezed her eyes shut against the agonizing glare of light. Not even natural light. More pounding. She held her head and forced herself to a sitting position, holding the sheet over her naked body.

Michael sat on the edge of the bed, fully dressed in the black fatigues she was coming to know as standard Renegade attire. "You might want to put this on," he said, offering her an oversized blue robe. "Sterling is here to help you scramble that call to your father."

"A robe, courtesy of Emma?" she asked, accepting it. "Because I know you prefer *au naturel*." She attempted a smile, but her eyes pinched, and it turned into a grimace. "And I like *au naturel*."

"Emma is responsible for the robe," he agreed, planting a solid kiss on her lips, warm and sensual. A little sound of pleasure rumbled from her throat of its own accord as he added, "And yes, I do *prefer au naturel*... with you." His mood shifted, darkened. Angst etched the hard lines of his face. "Your eyes are still black."

Her hand curled on his chest. "And I'm sick again, but every second I'm awake it eases up a little." She hoped. Another knock on the door burst through her brain. Okay, maybe she wasn't better. "Please make him stop that incessant knocking." It was killing her head.

She shoved her arms into the robe, and his gaze swept her bare chest, but he didn't touch her. He wanted to, though—it was in the raw sexuality that settled deep in his eyes. Suddenly, he pulled her close again, his lips slanting over hers in a deep, passionate kiss that left her breathless and panting as he pushed to his feet and sauntered toward the door. There was a message in that kiss she frantically tried to decipher, but there wasn't time. He was already at the door, already opening it. Cassandra tied the robe at her waist and scooted to the edge of the bed.

In an instant the room was abuzz with activity as Sterling and Kelly overtook the small space. Michael and Caleb stepped into the hallway, and Cassandra couldn't help but wonder what they were discussing.

"I have coffee," Kelly said, floating through the room in a blossom of jasmine-scented perfume, black pants peeking from beneath her lab coat. "And clothes that probably aren't going to fit well, but they're better than nothing." She held up a small bag with handles. "Emma sent a care package of various toiletries."

"I really need to meet this Emma," Cassandra said. "She sounds like everyone's mother."

"Where's *my* coffee?" Sterling asked, stomping to a halt behind Kelly, looking as good as new in his military garb, a computer case over his shoulder. He gave her a salute. "Thanks for hanging out, bedside, last night."

"I'd say, anytime," Cassandra replied, "but let's not make a habit of hospital visits."

"And no, to the coffee for you, Sterling," Kelly replied, dropping the bag on the floor and then sitting next to Cassandra. Offering her the paper cup of coffee, Kelly cast Sterling a stern look. "You're barely off the IV."

"GTECH, sweetheart." He set the case down on the coffee table and sat down. "I've been off that IV for hours already."

"That's Doc to you, not sweetheart." She cut her attention back to Cassandra, holding up a finger. "One hour off the IV. He thinks he's Superman. At least Damion is taking it easy this morning. He's still resting."

Michael and Caleb returned to the room, the testosterone level in the small space skyrocketing off the charts. They stopped at the edge of the living room, standing side-by-side. Tall, dominant men. Leaders.

"*He's* your Superman," Sterling said, inclining his chin at Caleb, and then he lowered his voice as he glanced at Michael. "And the Dark One, Batman."

Cassandra laughed, feeling a little better thankfully, though she discreetly put the coffee cup on the nightstand by the bed. Coffee and her stomach, not so good. Sterling's observations, terrific. "I can so see that," she said, her attention snagging Michael's, a silent message in her eyes that the comparison, silly as it might be, seemed so true—he was Batman. He was the one you went to when no one else wanted to get their hands dirty.

Caleb broke through their line of sight, claiming the recliner next to the couch. "That makes Sterling, Robin, the Boy Wonder." His mood was light, but a vibe of tension crackled around him. Around Michael, too, Cassandra realized.

Kelly produced two syringes. "The first is to calm the side effects," she said softly. "And I want to take more blood." She tilted Cassandra's chin and inspected her. "Now, while your eyes are black. The sooner, the better. Then I'll need to take samples every couple of hours."

Sterling punched a few keys on his computer. "Boy Wonder needs a few minutes to get set up, so feel free to poke and prod Cassandra. I'm happy that the *doctor's* attention is diverted elsewhere."

Cassandra glanced at the clock. It was eight. "As long as I call him in the next hour," she said. "I'd really like to get dressed, if that's okay?"

"We have some things to discuss, anyway," Caleb said. "Do what you ladies need to do."

"Why don't we go in the bathroom and give them some guy time," Kelly suggested.

Cassandra hugged the robe around herself. "Yes, let's." Michael's eyes touched Cassandra's, dark with concern; remotely, she was aware of Caleb watching them.

"Any results on her blood work?" Michael asked Kelly.

Cassandra took advantage of the shift in attention to inspect Caleb, finding his expression indecipherable, his elbows settled on his knees.

"I'm not prepared to make any conclusions at this point," Kelly replied and then cast him a "dare you to challenge me" look. She grabbed the bag she'd brought with her and motioned Cassandra to the bathroom.

Cassandra could barely contain her chuckle as she sat down on the toilet cover. "You sure shut him down."

Kelly shut the door and set the bag down, her hands going to her hips. "I've learned to hold my own. They were a demanding bunch as soldiers. And now as GTECHs—they're like soldiers on rocket fuel, ten times more intense."

"*Do you* know anything yet, Kelly?" she prodded, steeling herself for the answer.

"You're ovulating. You're low on vitamin C," she said, tapping a syringe. "Which is why I'm giving you a supplement along with the nausea medicine." She glanced at Cassandra's arm. "Roll your sleeve up."

Peeling her sleeve up, Cassandra asked, "What does that mean?"

"Nothing yet," she said, leaning over her and injecting the vitamin C. She set the injection aside and reached for the syringe. "None of the more advanced testing is ready. And I need to compare today's samples to last night's." Minutes later, she finished up. "I'll leave you to get dressed." She sighed. "Now, to talk Michael into giving me more blood. Then maybe I can convince him he's not a monster about to turn you into one."

Somehow, Cassandra doubted that a blood test would convince Michael he wasn't a monster. She wasn't sure anything would.

~~~

Michael stared at the tube that hung from the needle in his arm, holding his breath as he had the night before, waiting for the liquid to appear. Letting out a silent "thank you" when it appeared red—not green, not blue, not anything but normal-looking red. Because it really wasn't normal, not even by GTECH standards. Kelly already knew that, too; he'd seen it in her face when she'd sat down next to him.

With Caleb and Sterling sitting a few feet away in low conversation, Michael lowered his voice to a murmur. "What did you tell Cassandra?"

Kelly's lashes lifted, her green eyes alight with a knowing look that confirmed she'd already seen something in his testing that he wasn't going to like. "Nothing *yet*," she replied, a clear warning in her voice. "Come see me when you get done here to talk about your test results."

Michael's gut clenched in a tight ball of dread. His blood work showing abnormality wasn't unexpected, by him or probably anyone else. He'd known it was selfish to touch Cassandra last night, to touch her period without the outcome of that blood work, without knowing what he might be doing to her—but still he'd touched her, still he'd buried himself deep inside her and enjoyed every last second of her.

Kelly pushed to her feet. "See you gentlemen later." She glanced at Michael. "See you soon." She didn't wait for his reply and hurried to the door in a wisp of white cotton before disappearing outside.

Sterling fixed Michael in a gaping stare.

"What?" Michael demanded gruffly, leaning one elbow on his knee, not in the mood for any crap from Sterling. That Caleb and Sterling had been channeling an edgy vibe from the moment they'd shown up didn't help.

"You gave blood," Sterling said, an astute gleam in his eyes.

"Really not in the mood to discuss my medical history with you, Sterling," Michael ground out. He cut a look between the two of them. "What's going on?"

Caleb and Sterling exchanged a meaningful look of their own, tension crackling in the air. With a go-ahead nod from Caleb, Sterling responded, "I checked out both hard drives, Brock West's and your mother's. Not a single reference to Red Dart. And I can't get into Taylor's servers without you getting me into the facility."

"We might as well take a full team in and be ready to sweep the place then," he said. "The sooner the better."

"Tonight," Caleb said.

"Today," Michael said. "Broad daylight before my mother has time to remove any evidence."

"I'm not sure that's a risk worth taking," Caleb said.

"And why is that?"

The two of them eyed each other again, and Michael grumbled irritably. "Cut the dramatic pauses. What the hell is up?"

Sterling replied, "West manipulated and rerouted outgoing weapons shipments from the base to include Green Hornets, and those shipments never made it to their destination. I see no evidence that your mother sold them to Adam. Your mother may well be innocent."

"Which means any probe of Taylor Industries should include discretion," Caleb inserted.

Michael sat there a minute before a bark of bitter laughter escaped his lips. "Holy shit." He scrubbed his clean-shaven jaw and let out a rough, second cackle of laughter. "This is what you two are walking on eggshells over? You think I'm going to have some emotional seizure over my mother, and you think I need my hand held? My mother is *not* innocent. If she's not helping Adam, she's helping Powell." His attention slid to Caleb. "I told you that last night."

"Maybe you were mistaken about last night," Caleb offered.

"Powell was there," Michael insisted.

"There's nothing wrong with selling weapons to the

U.S. government for national security," Caleb reminded him. "We have no proof she believes she is doing anything but that."

Always one to offer the benefit of the doubt—that was Caleb. "Stop trying to save me," Michael said. "I don't need saving. She is what she is, and I know better than anyone what that is. And if you want proof, I'll give it to you. We have a stock of Green Hornets now. Leave Powell's supply where it is, and hook a satellite to the location. I guarantee you, now that my mother knows I know about them, they'll be moved because she's doing more than selling to Powell. She's in bed with him in every possible way."

The bathroom door swung open, and Cassandra appeared in the crest of fluorescent light, her skin pale against the black T-shirt she wore with loose-fitted, black jeans. Her face was scrubbed clean of makeup, her eyes still black and shining like opals. Possessiveness rushed through him, arousing him with an unexpected jolt of pure, white-hot lust. He'd sworn to himself that he wouldn't touch her today, that he would wait for results on the blood test. How did you not do something as essential as breathing? Because that was what touching Cassandra was to him. How had he survived the years without her?

"I heard you talking through the door," she announced, before hesitating and then casting Michael a tormented look, the rest of the room fading as she spoke to him and him alone. "If my father has involved your mother in this, he's manipulating her." She crossed her arms in front of her chest. "He knows everything about every soldier he involved in Project Zodius. He certainly knows everything about you. Your family owns a weapons manufacturing company that supplies the government. Of course, he knew that when he recruited you. And he knew who your mother was then, and certainly now. There is no coincidence here. I have no doubt that being with your mother is icing on the cake—a message. You were in his world, with his daughter, holding a blade at his throat. Now, he's holding a proverbial blade at your throat. He has your world in his hands. He has control, not you." She drew a shuddered breath and let it out. "I'm done convincing myself he's not the man who would do such a thing. I've tried to justify all of his actions, and I won't do it anymore. And I'm sorry for what he is doing to you and your mother."

Michael's heart froze for a moment before skipping into an angry charge. Damn Powell for what he'd put his daughter through. What he'd put all of them through. "Do not apologize for either your father or my mother," he ordered Cassandra. And it was an order. A fierce, guttural command. He would not let her do this to herself. And he would not let his mother ride under the radar. "We need to operate on the assumption that there is no manipulation of my mother. She knows what she is involved with."

"You can't know that, Michael," Cassandra insisted, closing the distance between them. "Why is the fact that your mother is selling Green Hornets to the government any different than selling them any other weapon?"

His mother knew what she was doing and why—he'd bet his life on it. "She knows," he said, steel lining the words. "Someone was with her last night. A man."

Understanding shuddered across her delicate features.

"You think it was my father," she said. It wasn't a question, but he still offered a nod of confirmation. Her lips parted in a pause, before she whispered, "And you think they're… intimate?"

"Yes," he revealed grimly, shadows of the past rippling through his tone, despite his effort to contain them. "It was your father."

"Do you have any idea where your father's PMI lab is, Cassandra?" Caleb asked.

Her lips thinned, her arms crossed in front of her in what appeared to be a mixture of both disgust and a bit of withdrawal. "No," she said. "He kept that from me 'for my own protection.' His famous excuse."

Caleb cursed and ran a hand over his neck. "We need that location. We're chasing our tails here. He knows we're onto him."

"I'll find the lab," Cassandra offered. "I'll get into his hard drive and dig around his personal space, his office, and his house."

"No," Michael said, his tone implacable. "Even if I'd let you attempt such a thing, which I won't, it's too dangerous."

She stiffened at that, throwing a fiery glare in his direction, as Michael added, "He has cameras everywhere, Cassandra. He'll know what you did."

"And he knows I am nosey," she said. "If I get busted, I'll suck up and make up a lie. I can get by him. If anyone can get by my father's systems, it's me. And it's not like you have a long list of options here."

"We'll start with my mother's place," Michael insisted. "Search it fully. Look for proof that Taylor is involved. Or even a PMI location."

"Whatever we do," Cassandra said, "I need to call my father. It's getting late. He'll be suspicious if I'm not at work without a phone call."

Sterling snatched up the portable phone sitting on the coffee table and passed it to Michael. "What's the number you're calling from?"

Cassandra recited her cell phone number. Michael handed her the phone as Sterling keyed the number into his laptop. She drew a heavy breath when the line began to ring, nerves fluttering in her stomach. "I've never been so nervous calling my father in my life."

It was all Michael could do not to touch her, but Kelly's request that he visit her rang in his mind, and he restrained himself. Any further contact with Cassandra until he knew what the doc had to say was nothing more than selfish. But damn, he felt selfish with Cassandra. "You'll do fine."

"Morning, General," she said into the phone. Everyone knew he hated when she called him General, and thus she teasingly did it often. "Reporting in sick." She listened a minute. "You know how these headaches linger." Pause. "Yes. Really. I'm fine. I just need to sleep off the haze so I'm going to turn off my phone. I…" She listened a minute. "Yes, I should be in tomorrow."

Michael grabbed her hand. *No*, he mouthed silently.

Defiance flashed in her eyes. "Maybe we could have dinner tomorrow night? I feel like we're disconnected, Daddy."

Michael glared at her, and she glared right back, saying a few more words to her father before hanging up. "What the hell was that, Cassandra?"

"Smart," she proclaimed firmly, her spine stiff, resolve steady. "That was smart. No one is closer to my father than me. He'll make time for me. That means he won't be at your mother's house. That means I will go to his house afterward for coffee. I can get his hard drive, and you can get your mother's. I can manipulate those shipments of bullets the same way Brock did. I can get you your ammunition. I'm all you have."

"What about your eyes?"

"If they don't fade," she said, "then I'll use contacts like Sterling does."

"He's too astute for that."

Sharp-witted, she said, "He'll blame the migraine if they look funny."

"What about the fact that Adam attacked you while I was with you. He knows you are with me, which means Brock will know."

"All the more reason to do this sooner rather than later," she countered.

He forgot Caleb and Sterling were in the room, furious at her actions. "Don't you think you should have talked to us about this first?"

Disbelief shackled her words. "Us? *Who* is us? Don't you mean *you*? And no, I didn't consider talking to you. There is no talking to you. You simply blast orders."

"No, Cassandra," he said.

"You don't get to decide for me, Michael." She cut a look at Caleb. "Does it make sense to use me to help?"

"I am your Lifebond," Michael stated flatly. He didn't give a damn what Caleb said. Not about Cassandra.

Her eyes rocketed back to his, Caleb forgotten. "No, you're not," she corrected. "And some biological, physical connection does not give you a license to make my decisions."

Possessiveness ground through his every nerve ending. "The hell it doesn't."

Caleb and Sterling stood up, heading for the door, clearly getting the idea they were intruding. Neither Michael nor Cassandra paid them any mind. "You cannot come in and out of my life," Cassandra ground out, "and then snap your fingers and expect me to obey. You don't scare me, Michael. You've never scared me."

He grabbed her, spread her out on the bed, and went down on top of her. "You should be scared, Cassandra."

Her chin lifted, her full lips close, inviting, all but begging him to kiss them. "I'm not," she declared. "What are you going to do about it?"

What was he going to do about it? Exactly what he'd promised himself he wouldn't do. He flattened her on the bed and spread her legs. Settled the steely length of his cock against the warm V of her body and kissed her, a long, deep thrust of his tongue, followed by a lavish tasting.

She moaned into his mouth, her arms wrapping around his neck, her body curling into his. One hand traveled possessively over her slender rib cage and roughly caressed the high, full mounds of her breasts. Another soft moan was his reward, and it was a damn delicious one that all but destroyed what little restraint he had left. He tore his mouth away from hers, clinging to a thread of control. "You will not endanger yourself," he ordered, his eyes boring into hers. "You will not."

"If I am in your life, I am a part of this war. If I'm not

in your life, I am still a part of this war. Nothing you do can change that."

"Cassandra—"

She pressed her fingers to his lips. "Your bossiness is sexy when you're inside me," she warned, her voice laced with a heady mixture of anger and seduction that about had him over the edge. "It's irritating when you're not. So either get naked or shut up."

"I'm not going to shut up," he said.

"Good," she whispered. That meant he was going to get naked.

He nipped her lower lip roughly, and she gasped, a sweet little purr following. "But when I am naked and buried inside you, Cassandra," he said, "the answer is still no."

A sly smile slid onto her lips. "We'll see about that."

Chapter 23

BROCK WOKE FROM THE DIM RECESSES OF SLEEP WITH A hazy out-of-body experience that had him gasping for air and clawing his way through the decay of darkness. He sat up in a blast of energy, hands braced behind him on a cold, hard surface. His eyes fluttered at the light—long, black lines fading in and out of focus. He blinked again and again, refocused. Bars. There were bars all around him. He was in a massive cage. Cage. Was he dreaming?

Slowly, his head tilted downward, and in stunned disbelief he realized he was as naked as the day he'd been born. Another harsh breath and he scanned the area, memories beginning to rebuild themselves. There were cameras pointed at him on either side of the cage. He squeezed his eyes shut and willed the memories to come back to him. The bridge. The injection. Jocelyn. Her sultry feminine curves, those big, blue eyes. The instant her image filled his head, his dick went ramrod stiff.

His hand went to his leg, a grimace sliding across his face as he flashed back to Powell jamming the letter opener into his leg. The pain. He reached down, touched all over his leg. Saw nothing. Laughed with the realization that it was done—he was a GTECH. He'd been transformed.

His heart tripped with another memory. Powell demanding he admit that he'd given Green Hornets to

Lucian, which, in retrospect, had been a jug-headed decision. Idiot Lucian. He should have known he couldn't keep them under wraps. He inhaled, tracing a path back through the pain and fog—had he admitted what he had done? Relief washed over him with the realization he'd stayed strong. He had not admitted anything that would jeopardize his chance to lead the GTECHs or to crush Lucian.

Adrenaline rushed through his veins, licking at his muscles with a sudden burst of energy. He flexed his hand several times—power chasing each movement, strength coursing through his veins. Leveraging his weight on his palms, Brock leapt to his feet. Power surged through his limbs, and he tilted his head back and roared with the pure joy of it. This was what he'd been waiting for. This was the beginning of greatness.

But then, his hands closed around the bars of the cage—a hard thud of reality punching him in the chest. He was locked up. Computers lined the walls. A long lab table faced the cage with electronic equipment. All framing the *cage*. He was naked. Imprisoned. The high of his transformation churned to a grinding halt.

What the hell was going on? He grimaced. Powell. It was one of his mind games. A control thing. Fine. He'd play his game until he could turn this around—and he would.

A sudden jolt of tingling awareness rushed down his spine an instant before Jocelyn sashayed into the room, a rush of sexy curves and long, dark hair. "I see you're awake," she said, setting a stack of files down on the table facing the cage. Her gaze traveled down his body, settling on his cock. Already half hard, it twitched to life.

"And naked," he said. "You come for the peep show or what?"

"I came to finish what I started," she said, leaning on the desk, her blue eyes blazing at him.

He arched a brow. "Which is what?"

"To make Red Dart a success, starting with you."

"What about Red Dart requires I be naked?"

Several seconds passed. "The General wanted it clear you were being reborn a new man." But she liked it. He could see it in the heavy-lidded stare she cast his way. Something about Jocelyn ripped through him like a raging storm and settled hard in his chest. Suddenly, a memory of Powell and Jocelyn burst into his head.

"You're fucking him." He would not allow that to occur again.

Her expression flashed with surprise before she judiciously countered with, "And you want to, don't you? The minute you're free—you're going to turn on him." Her arms crossed over full breasts.

"If I wanted to fuck Powell I'd have joined Adam," he said. "But if he touches you again—I'll do one better. I'll kill him." He had no idea why the idea of Powell touching this woman turned him inside out. No clue why he wanted to rip the bars away and go shake her until she knew Powell was not to touch her again. Fire licked at his limbs, at his mind. It eroded common sense, tore at him like a blade slicing muscle and flesh.

She studied him, her eyes narrowed on his face. "Why would you say such a thing?" she asked. "You don't even know me."

He pinned her in a tormented stare. "I wanted you before. I want you more now."

"This must be some reaction to your transformation," she said. "I'm going to call the doctor." She reached for a phone on the desk.

Another memory assailed him. "Wait." His eyes narrowed. Michael had been there. Michael. And she'd called him *her son*. "Holy crap," he said in disbelief, tilting his head to study her more closely. "Is Michael your son?"

She set the phone down with a thud equal to a concrete block hitting the ground. "What does Michael have to do with anything?"

Bingo. Hit a nerve. A raw one, too. "Everything, it appears. He *is* your son, is he not?" The uneasiness that flashed in her face was all the answer he needed. "Powell's popping you, and your son is popping his daughter. That's a little freaky, even for me."

"What?" she said. "Michael is seeing Powell's daughter?"

"Apparently they have a long history."

"But Michael is Zodius." She shook her head. "No. That makes no sense. Powell's daughter would not be seeing a Zodius soldier."

"Michael *was* Zodius. He's a Renegade. One of the good guys, supposedly, but then no one really knows whose side Michael plays on, from what I can tell. And really, who are the good guys?"

A sharp, stiff reply followed. "Michael isn't one of the good guys."

Michael sure had a way of twisting everyone into a pissing, little wad. "And Powell is?"

Her defenses bristled. "He's trying to protect this country from Adam."

More like control the world, but Brock didn't care. Not when he was part of that control. "Guess you know Powell hates Michael then. Suppose it's expected with Michael getting down and dirty with his daughter and trying to kill him." He lifted an eyebrow. "You hate him, too, don't you?" Interesting. "What could he have done to turn his own mother against him?"

"Are we ready to get started?" Powell's voice ricocheted through the room a moment before he appeared with Dr. Chin by his side.

Jocelyn whirled on him. "Is Michael with Zodius or the Renegades?"

Powell's gaze flickered over Brock with disapproval before returning to Jocelyn. "He is a GTECH, Jocelyn. They are all GTECHs, and they must all be controlled."

"But he's working with Adam," she said. "You said he's working with Adam."

"Don't go and get a wild maternal hair to save your son, Jocelyn," he chided. "He's far more dangerous than his father ever was and failing to deal with him, I assure you, will result in the loss of innocent lives. And we both know you have more blood on your hands from supporting his father than you can bear as it is." He made a vague gesture toward the computer. "Show me your brilliant work with Red Dart, my dear."

"I'm not sure it's safe," she commented and eyed Dr. Chin. "Brock is having a reaction to the transformation. He's aggressive. Possessive." She hesitated. "Oversexed."

"Whatever he was before the injections, he is more so now," Dr. Chin informed her. "This is nothing to be concerned about. If he has any adverse reaction, I'm here to intervene."

Brock clutched onto the bars so hard he thought either the steel or his arms would break. He was not oversexed. He was not aggressive. And he did not want anyone intervening. He wanted this done and over.

"Do whatever you are going to do, and get me the hell out of here!" Brock screamed, shaking the bars. "He's right, Jocelyn. We are all GTECHs. And I am their leader."

"Get on with it, Jocelyn," Powell ordered.

She hesitated. "I need the crystal."

He pulled a thin silver box from his jacket and opened it. Instantly, a glowing red light emanated from the crystal. Jocelyn removed it and set it inside the electronic device by the computer. Her gaze lifted to Brock's for a tormented moment. A few keys were punched, and there was a cranking sound near the cameras as the barrel of a gun extended. Brock turned toward the weapon, ready for whatever he had coming. All he wanted was freedom.

General Powell stood behind Jocelyn, arms in front of his chest, one finger pressed under his chin, watching West act like a fool about to rule the world. He knew the man had betrayed him, and West would learn quickly who was in charge.

"Here we go," Jocelyn murmured and punched a key. A red dot flashed on his chest, painless, silent, followed instantly by another. Brock stiffened. "That's the tranquilizer," Jocelyn explained. "It's a two-second stun he shouldn't remember."

Sure enough, Brock straightened and turned back to

Powell. "Is that it?" he said. "Am I done? Are we ready to go kick some GTECH ass?"

"Is it done?" Powell asked, glancing at Jocelyn.

She punched a few more keys and turned the computer screen toward him. Powell glanced down at the beeping light on the computer screen. "Walk forward," Jocelyn called out to Brock. He did as ordered. The signal moved with him.

"Excellent," Powell said. "It's holding." He smiled at Jocelyn. She'd always been Taylor's research-and-development genius. Though it seemed a miracle that she'd handled the job of CEO over Taylor Industries, considering her recent displays of weakness. No wonder her husband had kept her involvement with Taylor off the grid. She'd have to be dealt with, controlled fully.

Jocelyn punched another few keys and coordinates popped up. "You will now know his exact location." She keyed again and pulled up a long number. "That is his individual marker. A code we insert along with the tracking material that makes his signal unique. The technology… well… it still amazes me. It is nothing that this planet would have found on our own for centuries."

"And the torture mechanism?" Powell asked, clamping down on his growing excitement. Jocelyn had inadvertently made the magnificent discovery that when Red Dart was exposed with certain silent sound waves, it sliced and diced the nervous system. Unfortunately, any GTECH within a certain radius would be affected, which meant it would have limitations for individual interrogation. But as a mass military operation, it would be irreplaceable. Spray the GTECHs with rays of Red Dart and then bring their entire force to their knees.

"We simply have to activate the sound wave, and the GTECH should respond." She held up a compact remote. "We have not tested this on humans. Dr. Chin and I both believe he needs to be on monitors and stress tested."

"I do have to agree with Jocelyn," Dr. Chin inserted. "We've pulled him from monitoring rather quickly."

Powell flipped the remote over in his hand several times. "If we give him everything we've got, and he survives," Powell said, "then you've done your stress test, and we move on."

"If he survives," Jocelyn quipped. "We need to pull back. To test slowly. We've come too far to blow it now."

He arched a brow. "The man gets a hard-on for you, and you suddenly want to pull back and protect him? And yes, I know he wants you. You forget the cameras. I was watching when you entered the room. I saw and heard everything." He grabbed her and pulled her into his arms, his hand sliding over her ass. She gasped, her hands going to his chest. He yelled out to West. "I'm touching her, West. Who do you want to fuck now? Her or me?"

West screamed in rage, paced the cage, and jerked the bars. "I'll kill you! Kill you, Powell. Skin you alive!" Animalistic snarls slid from his lips.

Powell released Jocelyn, who quickly scurried away like some pathetic rabbit.

"You sonofabitch!" she yelled. "You're intentionally trying to upset him. This is not what science and medicine are about!"

Powell ignored her. "What do you make of it, Chin?"

Dr. Chin scrutinized West, who had stopped screaming

and was now running in circles around his cage. He cut
Powell a look edged with concern. "I've warned you that
faster administration of the serum could lead to a more
primal outcome, especially with the new formula."

Powell fingered the remote. "Even animals can be
trained to obey," he commented dryly. "With the right
discipline."

Dr. Chin glanced at Jocelyn who was hugging herself. "I suspect there is a lifebond connection between
you and West."

Jocelyn gaped with instant rejection. "I'm not even
attracted to that man."

"A Lifebond would be attracted to her mate," Chin
agreed. "We'll have to do some testing."

"I'm not going to become a lab rat," Jocelyn said.
"This is not what I signed up for."

Powell looked down his nose at her. "I thought you
wanted to protect our country?"

She shook her head. "Lifebonding has nothing to do
with protecting my country."

"We must know what makes the GTECHs tick. It
is imperative." Powell considered a moment, his gaze
shifted to Dr. Chin, who, unlike Jocelyn, had a stomach
for necessity. "I wonder what he'd do if we put her in
there with him?"

"What?" Jocelyn grabbed the table. "I am not going
in a cage with that... that thing you created."

Powell grimaced. "Hypothetically, Jocelyn," he said.
"Get a grip on yourself, and be professional. This is a
science experiment, designed to save lives." He walked
toward the cage. "Let's get on with progress."

Expediting his plans quickly was essential now that

the GTECHs knew about Red Dart and Michael was not only inside the Renegades' operation, but sniffing around in Jocelyn's business. Powell had to claim control of the GTECHs and do it now, if not with the sound waves alone, then with Red Dart and the Green Hornets combined.

Losing West would be an inconvenience—his connections to Lucian were a fast track inside Zodius, and his readiness for immediate action, the best possible option. But one had to be willing to take losses in war if one was to gain enemy territory. Besides, he had additional recruits en route, soldiers he'd personally selected for their exemplary track records.

Powell smiled, held up the remote. "This is why you're naked," he said. "Because I'm going to introduce you to death, son, and you will be reborn my follower or not at all." He flipped the remote and West's body began to shake. He turned up the volume, and West slid down the bars and crashed to his knees. Oh yes, he liked this. Easing off the volume, he allowed West to recover slightly.

West lifted himself with his hands, face red, eyes bloodshot. "What did you do to me?" he wheezed.

Powell knelt down to his level. "I didn't do this. Jocelyn did. This was her invention." He tilted his head, studied him. "And you said you didn't mind being under my control. You said you would do what was necessary to be my commander. Now. Why don't you tell me how Zodius got those Green Hornets?"

He snarled. "*I don't know.*"

Powell hit the remote. West's grip on the bars fell away, and he dropped like a rock to the floor, shaking. Powell eased off the remote. "How did they get Green Hornets?"

West pushed himself up on his hands again. "I don't—"

Again, Powell shocked him, left the sound wave on a slow simmer that kept West flat on his face and shivering.

Jocelyn ran forward. "Enough, General! You see it works. Enough!"

"Control yourself," he warned Jocelyn, the snap of a whip in his tone. "Our agenda is bigger than one man's pain."

Defiance flashed in her eyes. "You have no agenda but playing God."

Irritation zigzagged through his body. "Careful now, Jocelyn, my sweet," he said. "You're stressed and saying things you might regret later. Because if making weapons of mass destruction as Taylor does is not playing God, I do not know what is." There was a hidden promise behind those words. He'd discreetly made it clear he knew how many American pine boxes Taylor's foreign relations had created.

He closed the distance between them and stared down at her. "I know how much you want to amend the past. We are a peaceful nation. With super soldiers in our arsenal, we will force peace on others without ever lifting a hand. We are doing a good thing here. Circumstances simply demand we act swiftly." The challenge in her eyes faded, and he settled his hands on her shoulders. "We must know this man's physical and mental limitations, so that we properly gauge their effectiveness against the GTECHs."

She hesitated and then shook her head. "Yes. Yes, you're right. Okay. I just… I can't watch."

"Then don't," he said. "Go to the other room, and we will call you when this is done."

With an inhaled breath, she silently agreed, turning and walking away.

Powell refocused on West, easing up on the remote. West's body went stiff then limp. Then, abruptly he pushed up on his hands again. Blood trickled from his lips. "I was trying to protect our mission," he hissed.

Powell arched a brow. "So you did give Lucian those bullets?"

"They wanted proof that I could be trusted. I knew we'd seize the bullets back when we overthrow Zodius Nation."

"So you did betray me," he said, hitting the remote and turning it to high volume. West shook violently.

He turned it off again.

"No!" West screamed. "No. I was trying to protect you."

"What else are you not telling me, Lieutenant Colonel?" Powell demanded. "Because when I capture Lucian and tag him with Red Dart, I will make him talk. He will tell me what you have not, and Lord help you when he does."

Inhaling sharply, West jumped to his feet, stood there naked and stiff, at attention—prepared for pain. "Right before you called me to that bridge, sir, your daughter left her apartment with Michael of her own free will. Lucian believes she is helping Michael try to find the Red Dart formula to destroy it, and Lucian's plan was to use me as the middleman. Michael would convince Cassandra to find Red Dart, but I'd give her reasons to distrust him. When the time was right, I'd step in and save her from heartache, and she'd give me the information on Red Dart."

Everything in Powell's mind turned red. He hit the

remote, and West fell to the ground like a stone block off a high-rise. Lucian would pay in pain for his plan to manipulate Cassandra. When Brock attempted to stand, Powell would drop him again for going along with the idea and allowing Michael near his daughter.

He hated Michael—hated him for taking his little girl from him, for destroying her trust. For holding that knife at his throat and making him beg for his life. But... an idea formed. Strategy was everything. A good general knew how to turn an enemy's action to benefit. Michael was still a direct connection to Taylor Industries. He was one of the most powerful GTECHs in existence. And he knew both Caleb and Adam well. With the influence of both Red Dart and his daughter, he would be the perfect commander over the GTECHs—on a leash, that was—his leash. He'd break Michael and then built him back up. This was brilliant. Now... he just had to plot how to get his daughter to come back to him, and Michael would surely follow.

Chapter 24

FIERCE, PASSIONATE, HOT SEX. THREE TIMES IN TWO hours. If not for the buzz of the intercom system that had delivered an invitation to Cassandra to attend a lunch therapy session for the women rescued from Zodius Nation, they might still be between the sheets. But that invitation had taken Michael from hot and velvety smooth to distant and reserved, and she had no idea why.

Fifteen minutes after that call, Cassandra inspected herself in the bathroom mirror, applied a little lipstick, and decided she looked somewhat human despite the dark circles under her solid black eyes. She flipped off the light and returned to the main room to find Michael sitting on the edge of the bed watching her, his long, dark hair draped around his shoulders, piercing stare shadowed by half-lowered lashes.

"You should be resting," he insisted.

Cassandra frowned. "The injection Kelly gave me worked miracles. I feel fine."

A second ticked by, two—silence that held yet more unspoken words.

Finally, Michael said, "You should wear the contacts Kelly brought for you."

That drew her back a bit. Her brows dipped. "Why? Everyone else has black eyes in Sunrise City."

"Not the women from Zodius," he said. "They are not GTECH, nor are they Lifebonds. And considering I was one of their captors, I doubt your being linked to me will work in your favor."

"You were the one who saved them, Michael. I don't understand."

"I was their enemy and captor far longer than I was anything else." He pushed to his feet. "We better go if you're going to make it on time." And just like that—a wall slammed down between them, a thick barrier meant to end the conversation.

Oh no, you don't, Cassandra thought, pursing her lips as he started for the door. He could shut out everyone else, but not her.

Cassandra advanced on him with determination in her steps, intercepting him halfway across the room and wrapping her arms around him. "Talk to me, Michael. Tell me what is wrong."

Instantly, he softened, his hand gliding down her hair, his lips pressing against hers. "Cassandra." He breathed her name against her lips, and she could almost swear she felt him tremble. Or maybe that was her? "Just please wear the contacts."

"I'm not hiding my eyes from these women, Michael," she said. "I want to help these women. I can't sit back and do nothing. That's what I did when I ran to Germany. But these women know who my father is. They know he's responsible for creating Adam. I have to get by that and earn their trust. My bond to you shows them that I am a target for Ava's fertility testing, just like them." She kissed him again. "Now take me to my lunch."

He let out a defeated sigh and shook his head. "You don't listen, ever."

She laced her arm through his. "If I remember correctly," she purred, "I listened pretty well the past two hours."

"So I have to keep you in bed to get you to listen?"

She grinned. "Do you have a problem with that?"

"If it were possible to keep you there all the time, no," he said. "But it's not, and you make protecting you nearly impossible."

They exited the room and stepped onto the moving conveyor. "I already told you," she said, "stop trying."

He leaned against the railing and studied her with one of those soul-deep, twist-her-insides-out-in-all-the-right-ways looks. "That's like telling Sterling to stop being a smart-ass."

Cassandra laughed. "It can't be that hard," she said.

"Harder."

She smiled, her gaze following the path of the moving sidewalk, taking in the center of Sunrise City with stores and restaurants, afoot with mostly male activity. "Amazing," she murmured. "All this has been built in only two years?"

"It's a fraction of what Adam has done with Groom Lake," he said. "Caleb held back on construction the first year. He felt building Sunrise City meant accepting that this war would continue. But eventually, he decided the comfort of those who called this place home was too critical to overlook. We have a good number of humans here. Many of the scientific staff fear they are targets for the Zodius. They have their entire families under our protection."

"That's a huge sacrifice for a family to make," she said. "Living outside the world they know."

"Not really," he said. "Adam has a way of hunting down certain talent and demanding they join him. Many of the humans with us are under threat of Zodius capture. Others… we suspected would be targets and approached before they were in Adam's sights."

"That is just frightening," she said.

"More so when you consider Adam has plenty of powerful people in high places silently in his pockets. We've tried to counter that with allies of our own. We can only hope it's enough."

They reached the end of the walkway, and Cassandra forced herself to shake off the grimness of what he'd shared. Soon, they stood at the door of a quaint, little restaurant, complete with a full staff, menus, and cute red-and-green tablecloths. "And here I expected a giant mess hall."

"We have one of those, too," Michael assured her. "No military base is complete without a mess hall and a stash of rations."

"I can't get over how advanced all this is," she murmured. There was an entire world underground. She tried not to think about how far underground, because it made her feel claustrophobic. There was no sunlight, no cars. No easy escape in the event of a disaster. Cassandra could see why Caleb had worked so hard to create a façade of normalcy. There was a lot to overcome.

Michael's dark eyes bored into hers, his focus on her, not the restaurant, not the city. "Are you sure you are up to this?"

Cassandra pressed to her toes and kissed him. "I'm fine, and you know it." She slid her hand along his jaw. He had such a strong, handsome face. Long, dark lashes—eyes that tugged at her soul no matter what the color. "When you left, I questioned if this... us, was real. If you really ever loved me."

"More than my next breath," he said softly, shadows edging the vow. "Cassandra." Her name rumbled off his tongue like distant thunder, low and ominous. "I was Adam's right-hand man."

"Pretended to be."

"Whatever those women tell you I did," he said, "it's true. Listen to them. Then finally you will understand what I am capable of doing."

Challenge bristled within her. "If I listen, and I still love you, Michael—because I will—then what will you do? Will you find another reason to push me away?"

"Listen to what they say," he said. "Then we will talk." He pulled her to an enclave next to the building, out of public view, then dragged her hard against his body and kissed her, long and deep.

She shoved at his chest, tore her mouth from his, and gasped at the torment that bled from the depths of his deep, black eyes. "Don't you dare kiss me like you are saying good-bye," she rasped, angry now. He had no intention of talking later. He'd made his decision, tried and convicted himself for her.

"Cassandra—"

"I'm not telling you there is no good-bye today, Michael," she interrupted. "Because if you cannot love me enough to trust me with everything that you are, then you don't love me enough for me to be with you. And like it or not, you are stuck with me through this Red Dart thing. When it's over—if it's good-bye, then damn it, you *will* say it to my face. Or maybe I'll be the one to say it to you. Either way, we *say* it. You owe me that."

She shoved out of his arms, turned away, and charged toward the restaurant. She felt her heart slide to her feet when he did nothing to stop her. "Damn you, Michael," she whispered.

Leaving Cassandra at that restaurant, knowing what she would learn—about him and his time inside Zodius— was killing Michael. Only minutes later, ripples of energy blistered through him as he entered the administrative wing of Sunrise City Hospital. The low churn of a storm was brewing deep inside him, threatening to consume everyone in his path.

Heads turned as he passed offices—the lab technicians and various scientific minds staring after his passing form, no doubt wondering why he was here. What was wrong that would bring Michael to the hospital? What menace was upon them? It was the kind of dread people embraced when he appeared. The kind of dread Cassandra would find in those women she was lunching with upon the mention of his name.

He didn't want her to see that side of him, and reluctantly, pitifully, he recognized the past for what it was. Leaving her for two years before had been easier than the prospect of seeing the love in her eyes fade and become fear. Instead, he'd forced her hatred, her distrust, forced what he expected from her.

With heaviness pressing on his chest, he rounded the corner to the treatment center where Sterling and the others had been the night before and paused in the doorway.

Kelly stood at the center counter, her gaze doing a sharp snap upward, as if she too sensed the power waving off him. The same power that, under normal circumstances, he controlled as easily as his next breath.

But not now, not on the day that Cassandra would see through the man to the lethal killing machine. His body pulsed with a low hum of uncontrolled energy. His mind jumbled with memories of Zodius, of stories Cassandra might hear about him.

Kelly started walking, motioning toward an exam room, but not before he detected a hint of quickly banked apprehension. Christ. Did he really want to know what she had to say?

Like one of Adam's damn wolves, he followed like an obedient pup, entering the cracker-box-sized room and standing, arms crossed in front of his chest, legs planted firmly on the floor as he awaited the bad news.

"Have a seat," Kelly said, rolling her chair around and motioning to the table.

He arched a brow that silently said she'd lost her mind if she thought he was getting on that table. He'd barely forced himself to come to this room and had done so only for Cassandra. He knew he was an anomaly. He didn't need a test-tube evaluation to tell him so.

Kelly pursed her lips. "Should have known I was pushing my luck." She made a vague gesture at the door with the pen in her hand. "You probably want to close that."

This was the moment, he realized, that he would finally receive confirmation of what he knew was true—that he wasn't like the other GTECHs. It took him several seconds to muster the resources to reach over and slam the door shut. Returning then to his arms-crossed, unaffected, carefree, if-you-believe-that-bullshit stance.

Kelly studied him with an all-too-knowing look. A look that said—no, she didn't believe that bullshit for a minute. "I take it you'd like me to cut to the chase, so let's get to it." She didn't wait for a reply, charging forward with the announcement. "You're still X2 positive, but in addition you have an extra chromosome the other GTECHs do not have. At least, none of the GTECHs we've been able to examine."

She anticipated the question he would have asked once he finally recovered from the blast of shock her words delivered, by adding, "To tell you what that means, exactly, will take time and study, but it stands to reason that this chromosome somehow links to your ability to control the wind. If there are other differences between you and the other GTECHs, it would help if you told me. I can…"

Michael squeezed his eyes closed, shutting out Kelly's voice as his mind spun into a whirlwind of turbulence. White noise echoed in his ears, clamoring in his head, vibrating through his body. My God, what the hell was he? He jerked his attention back to Kelly's explanation. "…an MRI and a series of diagnostic—"

Michael's eyes popped open, and he pushed out the one cohesive thought he could put together in words. "What does this mean for Cassandra?"

Kelly let out a heavy breath. "She hasn't converted to GTECH as of yet. She does have the documented cellular abnormalities we've seen in other females who have the mark on the back of their necks, but hers are more pronounced. But then, none of those women carried the lifebond mark for two years like she has without completing the bonding process." She shoved her pen behind her ear. "We are in uncharted territory here, any way you look at it."

Christ. He had a bad feeling about where this was going. "Her second blood sample. Did it show the changes progressing?"

Kelly's lips tightened. "Yes."

Guilt ground through his bones. "After we had sex." It wasn't a question. He'd known Cassandra was reacting to their physical connection, and yet he'd touched her anyway.

"It's too soon to be sure without more testing, but yes. It seems that with every intimate contact, you come closer to completing the bond." Her eyes lit, and she leaned forward, one elbow on her knee. "The intriguing thing here is that when you were tested at Groom Lake, this extra chromosome didn't show up. It may be why X2 isn't making you aggressive like it has so many others. And I assume you and Cassandra were intimate while at Groom Lake, and yet she didn't have the bonding symptoms she's having now. It's as if you are evolving, and so is the lifebonding process along with you. It's really an exciting discovery."

"I'm glad I've excited you, Doc," Michael said roughly. "Forgive me if I don't go throwing confetti. We don't even know *what the hell* I am. I'm not allowing Cassandra to be linked to that. Fix this. Make it go away."

She bristled at that, stiffening her spine. "You don't just 'fix' cellular changes of this magnitude, Michael. And leaving her in a flux state between human and

GTECH isn't good for her. Her vitamin C is low which is consistent with a GTECH. Her blood count is all over the place."

"If I don't touch her again," he asked, ignoring the cut those words ripped through his heart. "Will the effects fade?"

It was her turn to act agitated. "Cellular changes *do not* fade, nor do they 'fix.' The sickness she is experiencing most likely comes from the cellular changes taking place. As for her eyes—I'm not sure at what point they will stay black. She may already be there."

"If the assumption that if one Lifebond dies, the other does as well, is accurate," he said. "That would only occur if we are fully bound—correct?"

"That's a hypothesis that remains unproven," she said. "However, there have been physical links that create that unproven probability. A bullet wound to one causes physical trauma to the other."

"But she's safe unless we fully bond," he confirmed.

"That's impossible to say," she concluded. "We've never had someone in Cassandra's physical condition to evaluate. As for the rest of your questions... you're demanding answers, and I have nothing to go on. I need to run more tests."

Like hell. He didn't need any more testing to tell him what needed to be done. Nor did he need it to tell him he'd walked a line between Renegade and Zodius that might yet pull him under and her with him. "Stabilize Cassandra. I'm irrelevant."

"And if I can't?"

"Try hard."

"Michael—"

"I will not take Cassandra into this unknown territory."

"Look," she said. "I can't prove evil is inbred yet, but I'm working on it. Adam was always evil. Caleb was not. They are now what they were before those injections."

"You have no idea what is inbred in me," he said. "I do. No lifebonding."

Disapproval mixed with reluctant acceptance touched her features. "I have to tell Caleb about the extra chromosome."

"You wouldn't deserve to be here if you didn't." He turned away and reached for the door.

"Michael, wait." He hesitated, but didn't turn. "What do I tell Cassandra? She's supposed to stop by after her luncheon with the Zodius survivors."

"To stay the hell away from me."

———— ∞ ————

Ten minutes later Michael stormed into the War Room, the heart of the Renegades' operational facility, to find Caleb, Damion, and Sterling sitting at the "Round Table" in the center of the rectangular-shaped room. While Damion's presence wasn't unexpected, considering his family owned a tech firm and he was a tech whiz, Michael could have done without him for this conversation. The guy wore the all-American, Boy Scout image as perfectly as he did a weapon. Michael wasn't in a Boy Scout kind of mood, nor did he want Damion putting Caleb in one.

He towered over the table, a dark demand on his lips. Behind him, strategic maps covered the wall, colored pins marking key targets.

"It's time to stop pussyfooting around with Powell,"

Michael bit out. "Screw alliances with the U.S. government. They're already as much in bed with Adam as my mother is with Powell. Between him and the insiders that Adam has in the government, the Renegades have already been turned into the enemy, or we wouldn't be targets for Red Dart. That isn't going to change. It's time, Caleb. I know all the reasons we approached this conservatively, but we haven't found Red Dart. There is too much to risk. We have to remove Powell from the position where he can initiate this program before it's too late. Bring him here, and lock him up."

Caleb's lips thinned. "You know how I feel about this," he said. "Better the familiar snake in the grass than the unfamiliar one. Once Powell is removed, Red Dart will still be out there in Lord-only-knows-whose hands. We'll be trying to figure out who is in control rather than where Red Dart is located."

"The clock is ticking, Caleb," Michael reminded him sharply. "He knows we are onto him. He'll accelerate his plans—and I might add—we have no idea what they are. We have nothing."

"Turns out we might," Damion interjected. "Sterling and I found a way into Taylor's system."

Sterling arched a brow. "Care to take a seat and help us get inside the head of Mommie Dearest?"

Michael didn't ask how they'd done the impossible. Results were what counted with him. He inhaled and forced himself to calm enough to sit down. Powell had bought himself a few more hours.

Chapter 25

STILL RATTLED FROM HER CONFRONTATION WITH Michael, Cassandra followed the hostess to the table of eight women rescued from Zodius who'd come together in an informal gathering. Already nervous about her father's role in creating the GTECHs, she felt an added rush of self-consciousness over her poorly fitted clothing as she brought the group into focus. Each one of them was spectacularly attractive in her own way. Apparently, Adam's fixation on a perfect race included breeding with certain types of females.

A cute brunette with a bob popped to her feet and greeted Cassandra. "Hi," she said, extending her hand. "I'm Emma. I'm so glad you joined us."

Cassandra slid her palm against the other woman's and blinked in surprise. "You're Emma?" Cassandra exclaimed. Somehow she'd pictured Emma as middle-aged and frumpy, not petite and adorable. "Thank you so much for the care package."

"I'm so glad to help." Emma motioned for her to sit at the head of the table beside her. Cassandra quickly settled into her seat only to find herself the recipient of wide-eyed inspections that bordered on gaping.

"Hello," Cassandra said, feeling dry-mouthed to say the least. She was the only professional in the group. "I'm Cassandra Powell." The last name came out like lead, and her hands flattened on the brightly colored tablecloth. Powell. Her father. The man who'd created the monsters that had tortured them.

"Your eyes." The comment came from the gorgeous blonde at the end of the table. "Emma said you're staying with Michael. Are you his Lifebond?"

"Intended Lifebond," Cassandra said, because it sounded better than unclaimed. "We haven't completed the blood bond." *And might not ever complete it*—a thought that jabbed her right in the heart.

"Wow," the woman said and sat back in her chair as if dumbfounded. "That must be… terrifying." Agreeable murmurs followed.

Cassandra shook her head. "What?" she asked. "Why would that be terrifying?"

"He was Adam's second in command," said one woman.

"They called him 'the Punisher,'" said another.

"Even the other Zodius soldiers feared Michael."

Similar murmurs followed from around the table, and Cassandra absorbed them all with shock. He'd been "The Dark One" and now "The Punisher." What it must be like to be whispered about and feared. Protectiveness rose inside her for Michael. This was the man she loved—a man she knew had put innocent lives above his own, time and time again.

"Did he hurt any of you?" she demanded, not believing for one moment that he had.

A pause ensued. "No," came agreement around the table.

"Did he save you from Adam?" Cassandra demanded.

"Yes," they all said.

Cassandra scanned their faces, challenging them as

she did. "He saved you from that hell, and yet you act as if he is the enemy?"

The blonde at the end of the table spoke again, introducing herself as Jessica, and then made her case. "You have to understand," she argued. "Michael was an extension of Adam. We were not to talk to him or look at him without fear of reprisal."

Another added, "He scared the hell out of us. We went through hell at Zodius."

Another added, "If someone crossed Adam, they were either thrown to the wolves—"

"Or given to Michael for torture," Jessica finished.

Cassandra gulped. Okay, that did sound rather ominous. She shoved her hair out of her face, her hand shaking a bit, but her belief in Michael did not falter. Nevertheless, she was thankful that when the waitress approached, Emma waved her away. Cassandra wanted to hear more.

She was a general's daughter; she understood the rules of war, and she'd never kidded herself about Michael—he was a soldier, and that wasn't always a pleasant job. That's where she came in, helping the soldiers cope with what they had to do—and why they were men of honor, despite the nastiness of their duty.

"But he never hurt any of you?" she asked.

Silence and a skittering of eye contact followed, and a murmur of "no's" followed. "Just the other soldiers," Jessica said.

"But we were sure he would," one girl assured her. "He scared the other soldiers, so we knew it would be horrible to anger him."

Relief washed over Cassandra in a short laugh, a

release of tension, not humor. "Of course he punished Zodius soldiers. He probably wanted to kill them." She leaned back in her chair. "Michael is, and always has been, a Renegade. Those soldiers were not only your enemies, but his. Ladies, this is war. If anyone doubts that, think again." Pride welled in her. "The information that Michael discovered inside Zodius Nation was invaluable to our efforts to protect humanity, and his presence there allowed him to rescue you all." It had been hard to endure his departure, but his actions had probably kept the Renegades in this war—perhaps kept humanity fighting for survival as well.

Silence wrapped around the table, confusion clearly touching many of the women's faces, reluctance to accept Michael in others. Her father deserved condemnation for his actions, but Michael received it instead. *Good Lord*, she thought, *this was so unfair to him*. How could she expect Michael to see himself as anything but a monster—one he felt he had to protect her from—when the rest of the world saw him that way?

"He saved your lives, ladies," Cassandra said, trying to keep in mind how new these women were to Sunrise City, how new to the idea that Michael wasn't Zodius. She was still getting her mind around that idea, and she was in love with the man. "Surely that counts for something."

"It's hard to discount what it was like there," Jessica said. "And it's hard not to associate him with that place."

Emma delicately cleared her throat and set her napkin on the table. "I was never afraid of Michael." An awkward discomfort fluttered through the group. Several women cut their gazes away from Cassandra.

A sick feeling ripped through Cassandra. Her hands

balled on the table. Her breath lodged in her throat, hanging on Emma's words as she continued. "Every soldier close to Adam used us like sex slaves," she said. "We were expected to please them any way they saw fit. Then we had to submit to one medical test after another. Afterwards, we did it again with one soldier after another. Michael came to me. Only to me. How he managed that, I don't know, but then, as we said, Michael was feared. He did what he wanted, when he wanted to do it."

Cassandra almost threw up. Her head spun and her throat heaved. In the two years they'd been apart, she'd tried not to think about him with other women. Now, she was sitting next to her. No wonder Michael was withdrawn before the lunch. No wonder he'd said good-bye outside the restaurant.

Emma placed her hand over Cassandra's, and Cassandra barely kept herself from shoving it away. "But he never once touched me," Emma said. "He made me lie and say he did."

The entire table gasped. Cassandra let out a breath, her shoulders slumping forward, fist to her chest. For a moment, she'd been unable to breathe. She reached up and wiped at one damp eye. "Please say that one more time."

"He didn't touch me or anyone else." Emma looked around the table. "Did he ever touch any of you?" Everyone quickly chimed in with their promises that he had not.

Emma smiled. "He said if I told anyone the truth, it would put them in danger. He didn't want anyone acting suspicious when we plotted the escape. He said everyone had to hate him. Adam expected it." She glanced at her friends. "So I lied to all of you, and I'm sorry, ladies. I was protecting you." She shifted her attention back to Cassandra. "That's why I wasn't afraid of him."

"Thank you, Emma," Cassandra said softly, the seeds of a friendship blossoming in their shared look. Emma had given her a gift. Michael had stayed true to her in the worst of circumstances. Cassandra rested her elbows on the table, chin on her hand. "Tell me what it was like. What you went through."

To her surprise, the stories flowed one after another, and Cassandra could feel their need to talk, to heal. For two hours, Cassandra listened to the horrors these women had been through, starting with how they were lured into being captured.

"Where are the other women?" Cassandra asked. "Why didn't they join us?"

"A lot of them are struggling with being forced into hiding," they said. "Many are afraid for their families, but torn about bringing them here and forcing them to give up their lives."

Cassandra understood. She'd gone to Germany, hiding, feeling like her life had been taken from her. "They need to fight back," she said. "We need to fight back."

"How?" came murmurs from around the table.

"By doing everything in our power to stop the abductions," she said. "The Renegades are busy trying to shut Adam down completely, but in the meantime, the abductions continue. Why don't we play a role in stopping them? We all have skills. We can put them to use. I know trends, chart and graphs, and behavioral analysis."

"I was with the FBI," one woman said.

Several of the others chimed in with skills they

possessed, and Cassandra felt excitement building within her. "We are fifty strong," she said. "We can make a difference. We'll track the trend of how and when the abductions are taking place. We'll talk to Caleb about setting up a team to respond to threats we identify. Find out what ability we have to educate the public and law enforcement without exposing an alien threat and causing more panic. Even if we can't stop the abductions, we can slow them down."

Ideas began flowing as the women clearly shared Cassandra's determination. They were going to fight.

Cassandra had found a purpose, and it felt right. She was not only accepting her circumstances here, she was embracing them. And if Michael couldn't, or wouldn't, do the same, she'd fight him too.

"I got nothing," Sterling said, leaning away from his laptop and folding his arms in front of his chest. It was late, near ten, and they'd been pounding through data for hours.

"Sonofabitch," Caleb muttered a few feet away, his attention on the satellite surveillance monitors that covered one end of the rectangular-shaped room. "The show is on, boys," he said, turning to face them. "Those Green Hornets are moving. You were right, Michael. Your mother told Powell we knew about the bullets."

There it was. Michael's confirmation that his mother was indeed communicating with Powell beyond a simple purchasing order. Not that he'd had any doubt. One more stab in the gut to complete a perfectly screwed up night.

Sterling rolled his chair to the mainframe, punching the keyboard several times to alert their field team into action, before he swiveled around to face Caleb and Michael with a confirmation nod. "Interception is under way. Now, let's hope none of those Green mojos end up in our men's bellies. Powell will be anticipating action."

Sterling's laptop started to beep, and he rolled back to the table, eyed the alarm notice, and glanced up at Michael. "Cassandra is getting a call from West."

Caleb stepped to the table and rested his hands on the back of an empty chair as Sterling hit his volume button. The sound of ringing filled the room, a moment before Cassandra's voice purred sweetly over her voice mail, the soft feminine sound humming through Michael's body and drawing his balls tight. That easily, she reached inside him and set him on fire.

You've reached the voice mail of Cassandra Powell. Please leave a message, and I will call you back as soon as possible.

West's message followed. "Cassandra, this is Brock. I've talked things over with your father, and he's willing to bring you into the loop on Red Dart. I know you are still out with that migraine today, but he told me about dinner tomorrow night. I'll be joining you, but there are some things I want to discuss in advance. Call me." The line went dead, and Sterling punched the sound button to off.

Michael ground his teeth so hard, the muscle in his jaw popped. West was on his list of people to be dealt with, once and for all, right along with Powell.

Caleb's lips compressed into a hard line, and Damion said what they were all thinking. "Is it me?" he asked.

"Or is the timing on that call mighty suspect. The bullets move. West calls Cassandra."

Sterling chimed in his agreement. "I'd like to think it's the real deal, and Cassandra is about to be enlightened, but we know he's working both sides—Powell and Zodius. This could be a trap. A way to lure her out and kill her."

"Brock West needs to be taken out," Michael said. "He's a liability. And it's long past time we accept that we need to lock Powell up. We can keep saying we'll find Red Dart, and that we need him to do that. But what else is he brewing that we don't know about? We left him alone for two years, and Red Dart emerged. We cannot make that mistake again. We need to cut our losses."

Damion shifted in his chair. "We cannot act rashly—"

"While you're sucking your thumb, considering options," Michael interrupted, "Powell could make a mistake that allows Adam, not us, to get his hands on Red Dart. He's scrambling now. Moving bullets. Trying to get his daughter back. Now is the time to move in. We'll find some evidence. We'll find Red Dart. And even if we don't, we'll have rid ourselves of the hazard Powell represents."

He turned to Caleb, and Damion had the good sense to shut up. "I know you worry that we'll create enemies in our government if we take out Powell. But he's creating their fear of us. They think all GTECHs are the same. Walking on eggshells isn't going to make that go away. We take him, and no one knows we have him. We'll hit Powell's house, my mother's place, and Taylor, all in one night. We leave with everything we can, including

Powell. Throw him in a cell here at Sunrise City. Tell him he better help us shut down Red Dart before Adam gets his hands on it and comes after us all."

Sterling's computer buzzed again. He surveyed the message. "Green Hornets are headed to Sunrise City. There was no resistance and no reported injuries."

"Those bullets have leveled the battlefield," Michael said. "Let's get rid of one of the enemies. Let's take out Powell."

Caleb's brow furrowed, and then he nodded sharply. "Tomorrow night."

Chapter 26

MICHAEL REALLY INTENDED TO SAY GOOD-BYE. Cassandra lay against Michael's headboard trying to focus on the DVD she'd popped into the player simply to do something other than watch the clock. She wished with every breath Michael would show up. So much for her excitement to tell Michael about the plans that she and the women had made. That had faded hours ago when he'd failed to appear.

A knock sounded on the door, and Cassandra raced across the room and yanked the door open only to sag in disappointment when Kelly stood there.

"I take it you were hoping for Mr. Tall, Dark, and Incredibly Cranky instead of me?"

"Yes," she admitted dejectedly, stepping away from the door. "I would have welcomed his crankiness right about now."

"I'm convinced that the extra chromosome I told you about earlier makes him incredibly stubborn," Kelly said, entering the room and shutting the door behind her. "I guess you don't want to hear it's time to give up more blood."

Cassandra plopped down on the couch and offered up her arm. "Yes, please take my blood. I can't wait." The extra chromosome. Once she'd heard that news, she'd known she was in for an uphill battle convincing Michael it wasn't a worry. Michael was what he was, and that was the man she loved. Whatever he faced, she was supposed to face with him. She'd made that decision, and she was sticking with it. "When I was in the elevator yesterday, Caleb seemed to read my mind. Can he? Read minds?"

"He reads human emotions," Kelly said, already dipping the needle into Cassandra's arm. "It doesn't work on GTECHs. He senses fear, worry, and happiness. He says it's like seeing a color in his mind."

"So," Cassandra said. "Does *he* have the extra chromosome? Is that what creates unique abilities?"

"He doesn't have the extra chromosome. At least not yet. It is possible that he will, and it has yet to surface. Michael's ability with the wind surfaced very early after his conversion to GTECH, as did Adam's ability to communicate with wolves. Caleb's ability is more recent. I really have nothing conclusive that indicates why certain GTECHs have special skills though it would be interesting to know if Adam has that chromosome."

Cassandra grimaced. "I'm glad we don't know. That would be just one more reason for Michael to compare himself to Adam."

"No matter how Michael demonizes this chromosome or himself, scientifically, I theorize it's a sign of the GTECHs evolving and getting stronger. I'd like the chance to prove that. If you can influence Michael to allow me to do some more testing, that would be helpful. I plan to ask Caleb to talk to him as well, but I can't catch up to him. He's been behind closed doors for hours." She studied Cassandra. "Your eyes are almost back to normal."

Cassandra's hand went to her cheek, her heart twisting. "They are?" Already Michael was slipping away from her.

Kelly's expression softened. "You really don't want to leave him, do you?"

She shook her head. "I love him."

"He loves you too, or he wouldn't be so worried about you," Kelly said, touching her arm. "Just keep telling him. You'll get through." She tapped her pocket. "Let me get this to the lab and make sure I feel good about you heading out in the morning. I assume it's going to be at the crack of dawn. I can't release you until I review the results."

With a nod Cassandra stood up and followed Kelly to the door. "I'll call you in a bit with the results." Kelly reached for the door, and Cassandra felt the shimmer of awareness ripple down her spine. Caleb was standing in the doorway, Michael and Sterling by his side. Kelly looked over her shoulder at Cassandra and winked. "You really have a way of drawing men, girl." She eyed Caleb. "We need to talk when you're done here."

Cassandra's heart fluttered in her chest, and she backed into the room, ever aware of Caleb in the lead, not Michael. "What's wrong?" she asked, her gaze seeking Michael's and colliding with the force of a freight train. He was withdrawn, distant in a way that wrenched her heart.

"We need your help, Cassandra," Caleb said as the three of them took positions inside the room, all in their black fatigues. *Warriors preparing for battle*, she thought.

Her gaze lingered on Michael a moment and then jerked to Caleb. "Anything," she promised.

He motioned her to the couch. Cassandra perched on the edge. Sterling sat down next to her and opened his laptop case. Caleb sat down in the chair beside them. Michael kept his distance, while Caleb told her about Brock calling for her. Despite her attentiveness to Caleb, Cassandra was aware of Michael every second, standing above them, his eyes half veiled by those thick black lashes, his expression unreadable.

"We both heard Brock say in that Washington alley that he wants the serum," Michael said. "He'll get it however he can. There is no way to know if his call is motivated by your father or Adam. It could simply be that one of the men at your condo saw us together, and your father is trying to ensure your return by baiting you with information about Red Dart. But that doesn't mean Brock isn't still trying to kill you. It simply means your father gave him the opportunity."

"The bottom line, Cassandra," Caleb said, "is we're ending this tomorrow night."

Her eyes went to Michael's. "What does that mean?" she asked, willing him to answer.

Caleb replied before he could. "We've confirmed Michael's mother has some connection to your father. We'll search her place, your father's, and Taylor Industries, tomorrow night. And we'll be leaving with your father. He'll be a prisoner in Sunrise City, which we hope will encourage him to tell us where Red Dart is located. We'd like you to return that phone call. Make him feel everything is as it should be. Convince him you're returning tomorrow."

"You say that like I'm not returning," she said, surveying their faces and realizing that was their intention.

"I have to go back. You say my father knows Michael is involved, that he most likely knows I've had contact with Michael. If I don't go back and convince him everything is okay, he'll disappear with Red Dart before you can get to him."

"No," Michael said authoritatively. "I will not allow you to take that risk."

She leveled him in a direct stare. "This is my decision." She glared at Michael a moment and then looked at Caleb. "Let's make that phone call. To Brock first. Then to my father."

Caleb glanced at Michael, arched a brow. "She's making sense," he said. "She needs to return. We'll protect her, Michael."

The room ticked with thick silence before Michael looked at her. "You'll wear a wire and do exactly as I tell you."

"Of course," she said, feeling victorious in a way that held no glory. She was betraying her father. That was nothing to embrace, yet she had no other option.

Sterling handed her the phone, and everyone put some sort of ear buds on to listen to her conversation that he explained blocked out more noise. They dialed Brock first, and Cassandra assured him she was coming to work the next day and thanked him for talking to her father on her behalf. She vowed to be objective about Red Dart, promising she would not make him look bad.

Next up—her father. That was the call she dreaded. "Hello, General," she said, trying not to sound strained.

"Cassandra, sweetheart," he said. "How do you feel?"

"My headache is better, but there's something else. A problem."

A pause, a mere second, but it was there, rich with tension. "What is it?"

"Michael approached me today," she said. "He says he's working for the Renegades now."

"You saw Michael?" snapped her father.

"Yes," she said. "For coffee. He showed up at my door, and I felt trapped so I made the suggestion. I thought a public place was best. But it was horrible. I was a nervous wreck."

Powell inhaled deeply. "Don't you worry, little one. I'll handle this with Caleb and make it clear that Michael is not to be allowed near you. He will not hurt you."

They exchanged a few more words and hung up. Cassandra handed Sterling the phone, her hand unsteady. "Now I have an explanation for being with Michael if one of his men reported seeing us together."

"That was damn convincing," Sterling said approvingly. "That bought us time. I know it did."

"Thank you, Cassandra," Caleb said.

Michael said nothing. He wouldn't even look at her. He was angry. And she had no doubt they would have an explosive confrontation later. Cassandra watched in shock as Michael turned to follow Caleb from the room, and her restraint snapped. She was done playing tug-of-war with her emotions over Michael. "Don't you dare walk out that door, Michael."

He froze, the other two men smart enough to make a fast exit as they had once before that day. Slowly, he turned, the door still open. Her heart raced, pounding in her ears. "The problem with my father ends tomorrow night," she said. "But whatever happens here tonight with us—that's it, Michael. It ends, or it begins here."

—∾—

Brock had done everything Powell had ordered, including the call to Cassandra. He'd listened as Powell talked to his daughter on the phone, hoping *like hell* she didn't say anything to piss her father off. He wanted out of confinement. He'd done as he was ordered. He'd called Cassandra. He'd done his part to lure her back home.

At least he was dressed now in army-green fatigues and standing just outside the cage. Almost human, but not quite. He was jittery, and a damnable muscle in his jaw wouldn't stop twitching—adrenaline hummed through his body like an electric current. Somehow, he kept a steady look, stood tall and proud. He was being tested. Could he be trusted outside the cage? A test he had to pass. He hadn't signed up for bars. He'd signed up for the freedom that being the strongest, the fastest, and the most powerful of all GTECHs would give him.

Powell ended the call and glanced at the tech specialist sitting expectantly in front of a computer panel. The man glanced at him. "The call was scrambled and well done. This wasn't an amateur job."

Inhaling a breath, Powell nodded to the man. "Dismissed, Sergeant." The man pushed to his feet and exited.

The minute he left, Powell glanced at Jocelyn who stood nearby. "Michael has most certainly corrupted my daughter. It is confirmed. She has betrayed me."

Jocelyn inched closer. The scent of her raked through

Brock's senses and stirred some wild beastly lust. "I'm sorry," she said to Powell. "What are you going to do?"

"There is only one thing *we* can do," he stated. "Move forward with our plans and do so quickly and effectively." He glanced at Brock. "You're ready for action, aren't you son?"

He saluted. "Yes, sir." This was a total lie—he could barely focus on anything but the twitch in his jaw and the need to reach for Jocelyn and pull her close. But Brock would say anything to keep Powell—or the techs operating the remote sound signals—from shocking him again. He was pretty damn sure his brain would fry if they juiced him many more times.

"He isn't ready for action," she objected. "He shouldn't even be outside that cage. Not until Dr. Chin figures out what is causing his aggressive behavior."

He held up the remote. "I only have to punch this to control his aggression," he proclaimed. "We do not have the luxury of time. Not with Michael breathing down my neck." He inhaled deeply, as if he were in-haling power. "You will have my laser weapons ready, I assume?"

She hesitated and then nodded. "They're in mass production even as we speak."

"Excellent, Jocelyn," he said, speaking to her, but looking at Brock. One hand went to her cheek, caress-ing it with the intimacy of a lover, while the other went to the remote around his neck—silently daring Brock to challenge him.

"Stop it, General," Jocelyn said, trying to pull away, but Powell slid his hand around her neck and jerked her to him.

Brock started shaking with the effort to control himself. He could feel a little more of his sanity slipping away every time Powell punched that button. Brock turned away, walked to the cage, and shut himself inside, locking the door.

Powell smiled, a smug, "I am God" kind of smile. Then, despite her struggles against him, he kissed Jocelyn. Brock ground his teeth as she finally gave in to the kiss and wrapped her arms around Powell's neck.

When finally Powell's lips released hers, she was panting. "Why must you tease him so?"

"I was simply proving to you how ready he is for action," he said. "You are his weakness and still he prevailed." He brushed his lips over hers again, and Brock cringed at the wild noises filling the room, the grunts and growls he could not control.

"You've done well with Red Dart," Powell said. "We are so close to everything we have dreamed of, my sweet. Do not let the grisly side of war detour you from the greatness of what we have set out to achieve." He brushed hair from her eyes. "I must go now, but I will return tonight to finish our celebration."

The growls slipped into Brock's head, turned into black space. His hands clutched onto the bars. Time stood still.

"Brock." The voice, soft and sweet, pulled him back into the light. He blinked, opened his eyes. Jocelyn stood outside the bars. He soaked in the big, blue, beautiful eyes, and then scanned the room.

"He's gone," she said. "He's been gone for hours."

She stuck the key in the lock. "I made you dinner. You have to eat."

"No!" he shouted, feeling the violence inside him and realizing what he had become. He was an animal, and Powell wanted to create an army just like him. "Do not open that door."

She froze. "You have to eat."

"Slide it through the bars," he said. "I cannot be trusted with you, Jocelyn. I won't be able to control myself." She stepped back as if burned, and for that he was thankful. "Is this what you want to be a part of? Making more animals like myself?"

"Dr. Chin is doing lab work," she said, her voice trembling. "He's going to figure out how to fix whatever is happening to you."

He laughed, bitter and suddenly angry—raging at her. "You bitch. You did this. Every time he jolts me, I get a little crazier. You can't blame Chin. You want to, but you can't. You fucking…" He opened his mouth to speak again, but his mind went black, words lodged in his throat. With a forced breath, he willed himself to calm. "I'm… sorry. I… don't help him. You have to destroy Red Dart," he said. "Stop Powell, before he—"

His eyes widened as Powell appeared behind Jocelyn, and pain shot through his body. Then everything went black.

Chapter 27

MICHAEL'S APARTMENT HAD NEVER FELT SO SMALL AS it did the moment Cassandra cornered him by that door, standing so close that he only had to reach out to touch her. "Is it that easy for you to walk out without a word?"

"It's easier than being near you and knowing I can't have you," he confessed, his voice low, rough. Something savage and wild raked through his body, a demand that he claim his Lifebond.

"The only thing keeping you from having me, Michael, is you," she said hoarsely. "I know about the extra chromosome, and you know what? I don't care. I am your Lifebond. Whatever you are... we are."

Her words twisted the hunger to gut-wrenching intensity. "*There is no we*, Cassandra," he all but growled. "You said it ends or begins tonight. It ends."

Dragging a breath, she leveled him in a challenging stare. "Be sure you mean that, Michael," she said, her voice choked, emotional. "I waited two years for you. I didn't even know I was waiting. I told myself I hated you. But I waited. I know that now. I looked at no other man. I wanted no other man. I knew somewhere deep inside me you would be back, that you had not betrayed me. I will not wait this time. I *will* move on. I will make a life for myself, and I will survive. So... if you say it ends here. It *ends*."

The idea of another man touching her, holding her, making her moan… it ripped through his veins like acid boiling his blood. He shackled her wrists with his big hands and pressed her against the wall, pinning her arms over her head with one hand, the thick ridge of his cock pressed to her stomach. "You will not let another man touch you," he growled.

Her chin lifted. "You cannot have it both ways, Michael. Either you are with me, or you are not. There is no in-between. Not anymore. I won't live like that."

For a moment, he squeezed his eyes closed, reached for control where there seemed none to be found. "Intentionally pushing me is dangerous, Cassandra," he warned. "Didn't you listen to those women at that table today?"

"I listened to them," she said. "And I know you. You did what you had to do to survive inside Zodius. You were trying to save lives. To protect our country. You might scare some people, but you will never scare me."

Lust climbed through every pore of his body. Her lips drew him, entranced him. A taste. One taste. He jerked his gaze to hers. "Will you never stop being a damn fool?"

"Will you?" she half panted, half whispered.

"Damn you, woman," he hissed, his hand gliding over her slender waist to the swell of her breast that fit perfectly in his palm. "Is that what you want, Cassandra?" Her nipple stiffened beneath his touch, and he tweaked it. "You want me to touch you?"

She arched into his touch. "Yes."

"You want me to pleasure you?" he asked, roughly tugging on her nipple. She moaned, and that only made him hotter. Harder.

He abandoned her breast and palmed that plump, delectable ass, molding her hips to his. She rewarded his boldness with a sweet, sensuous moan that vibrated through his body and thickened his cock.

He dipped his head. Inhaled deeply. "You smell like sweet honey." He leaned back, unable to stop his lips from brushing hers, the soft, subtle texture. "I could lick you from head to toe and do it all over again. Spread you wide and taste you when you come."

She shivered. "Do it. Do it, Michael."

He inhaled sharply, grappled again for that hard-won control—held her hands to keep her from touching him. Her touch would undo him. He willed himself to release her. To walk away and allow her the life she deserved— a life away from the dangerous nature threatening to consume him as surely as she consumed him right now.

"I love you, Michael," Cassandra whispered.

"Don't," he raged, his chin snapping down as his gaze locked with hers, his hair escaping the tie at his neck and falling wildly around his face. "Don't love me, Cassandra." With every bit of will he had left, he pushed away from her, distancing himself.

Her head fell back against the door, and Lord help him, his gaze swept the stiff peaks of her nipples puckered beneath her shirt, and he took another step backwards.

"I don't know how to get through to you," she said softly, staring up at the ceiling. "I don't know." Her gaze returned to his, and she stared at him with so much pain, so much helplessness etching her face, he could barely breathe knowing he'd put it there. "I need you, Michael, and I know you need me."

Then she pushed off the door, straightened, walked to

the kitchen, and left him staring after her. She returned a second later with a knife in her hand. *What the hell?*

Before he could stop her, before he had any idea what she intended, she had already acted. She sliced down her palm, blood spilling from the delicate pale skin. "This time is forever," she said and then grimaced. "Ouch. Ouch. Okay, that hurt more than I thought it would."

He was already by her side, picking her up and carrying her to the bathroom. "Are you insane, woman?" He grabbed a towel and wrapped it around her hand. "What were you thinking?"

"I was thinking this would make you see how certain I am about a blood bond," she said, her voice cracking with a hint of agony.

He pressed his forehead to hers, ran his hand down her hair. "Cassandra." He stared into the green eyes that he had so adored. He couldn't steal her humanity, her life. "We have to go get you stitches." The cut was deep, too deep to ignore.

"*You* heal me," she said. "You, Michael. I meant what I said. Whatever you are, we are together, in life or death." She sucked in a shaky breath. "Don't you see? I can't breathe without you."

Michael went utterly still, those words reaching inside his soul and speaking to him. Words he himself had thought about her a million times.

He reached down to his leg and removed the knife inside his pocket, held his hand out, and sliced it opened.

Big pearly tears glistened down Cassandra's cheeks as he unwrapped the towel from her hand.

"And I cannot breathe without you," he whispered. "But once this is done, there is no turning back. We really do live and die together. And whatever monster I become, you will never escape me."

"You are not a monster, and you never will be," she said, grabbing his hand and pressing her palm to his. "If it takes me a lifetime to make you see that, then I will fight for a lifetime."

She sealed their hands together, blinking up at him through her tears.

He trembled with emotion, with the magnitude of what she had just done, with the trust she had in him that he did not dare have in himself.

One by one, he kissed her tears away and then cradled her cheek with his hand, repeating the vow that he never wanted her to forget. "I love you."

"I love you, Michael."

With all his heart and soul, he silently made yet another vow—that he would live up to that love, that he would not let his past, his family, or the darkness within him, destroy them.

Michael kissed her with tenderness, the passion of minutes before shimmering warm and ready, but without any harsh demand—because she was his, his forever, and that was something to savor. He pulled back, stared down at her as black swallowed the green of her eyes, then guided their sealed palms between them and slowly released her hand, showing Cassandra that their wounds had healed.

Cassandra stared down at her hand. Touched her palm. Looked up at him. "Is it done? That easily?"

He closed their hands together again. "It is done," he promised, pressing his lips to hers and lingering there. Their breath mingled, warm and perfect.

She shivered and moaned, a sound so decadently erotic, he had to have more. He delved deeper, his tongue sliding against hers, a caress that turned to long, sensuous strokes, hungry and wild. Clothing disappeared, barriers gone once and for all. He turned her around, facing the mirror, and framed her soft curves with his body, his long, dark hair falling around his face and hers, the steely length of his erection settling between her thighs. The wet heat of her body drenched him in the promise of pleasure and passion.

She reached up and ran her hand through his hair. "I love how you feel."

The thick ridge of his cock expanded, throbbed. It would be so easy to slide inside her, to sink into the deep recess of her perfect body and take her. But this was special. This was their first time lifebonded, and he shackled the urgency within him, focused on her pleasure. Filled his hands with her breasts and tugged her plump, swollen nipples—red, rosy buds that he planned to worship over and over before morning light. She moaned and leaned her head against his shoulder, closed her eyes and shivered.

"Look in the mirror," he ordered. "Let me see how I please you." He continued to roll the hard little buds, tugging with a sharp bite he'd come to know aroused her.

Her legs wobbled, almost buckled. "I can't," she confessed.

He flattened his hand on her stomach and steadied her. "You can," he willed her. "Look at me, Cassandra."

She tilted her chin down, her heavy-lidded stare meeting his in the reflection. His fingers plucked at her nipples. He watched her teeth sink into that full lush bottom lip, dipped his head, and pressed his lips to her ear. "I'm going to give you what you said you wanted," he promised, nipping her lobe and placing her hands on the counter to brace herself. "I'm going to kiss you and lick you from head to toe." He shoved her hair aside and displayed the lifebond mark. "Starting here."

He covered the mark with his mouth, flicked his tongue around the design, his hands sliding down her silky, soft back, his lips following the same trail until he caressed her creamy white, heart-shaped butt. He lifted her hips, spread her wide, and then met her stare in the mirror, letting her see the raw hunger and promise of pleasure in his eyes, before he eased to his knees, the sight of her open for him damn near making him shake. His hands caressed her shapely hips as his lips and teeth nipped at one perfect butt cheek. Fingers sliced a path through the wet heat of her intimate flesh as he reached in front of her and thumbed her swollen nub.

"Michael," she gasped. "I…" She lost the words. He suckled her nub into his mouth. Her hips lifted and then pressed against his mouth, moving with the licks and caresses. He filled her with his fingers, explored her, stroked her, made love to her with his mouth, his hands. She gushed in his mouth, the sweet flavor of her arousal making him lick and suckle with wild determination until she cried out, tightened around his fingers. A second later, spasms milked his fingers, her thighs quaking with her release. Gently, he pleasured her through the release, easing the pressure slowly, until she calmed.

He turned her around, kissing a path up her body until he fit his erection between her legs, tangled his hands in her hair. "You have no idea how much I love you," he whispered, sliding inside the wet heat of her core and lifting her at the same moment.

Her arms slipped around his neck, her body wrapping his cock in warm wonderful sensation, her breasts cradled against his chest. "You have a lifetime to show me," she promised.

Chapter 28

ADAM SAT AT A MARBLE DINNER TABLE ON A BALCONY overlooking the coliseum. Hordes of soldiers filled bleachers to his left and his right, enthralled by twenty scantily-clad females dancing in the center of the ring—new recruits hoping to be chosen by males for their beds and a chance to become a Lifebond.

"You are pleased?" Ava asked, sipping apricot nectar from a silver-stemmed glass, watching him from beneath half-veiled eyes.

He reached for her hand, pressed it to his lips. "Your ability to influence these women's thoughts and feelings is nothing shy of amazing."

She beamed with satisfaction that lasted only moments. "We are up to seventy women again," she said. "Two of the new recruits are now Lifebonds." Considering she'd scaled back her fertility testing and had still managed to kill ten of her subjects, this number spoke highly of Tad's recruiting efforts—if you could call luring women into captivity recruiting.

The crowd roared as the women exited, music blaring through speakers as the real show prepared to begin. The lights dimmed around the bleachers, spotlights glowing around Adam's wolves as they filed onto the stone center floor. Candles flickered on high walls around the ring and on the tables.

Recently captured human soldiers would soon appear

to fight for survival, promised they might earn the serum. Of course, his stock was low. It would take a warrior of great skill to be worthy. Not likely, but it was entertaining to watch his wolves. Adrenaline rushed through him at the excitement, all else but the show forgotten.

That was until the scent of female and fear flared in his sensitive nostrils. His gaze shifted to his right to the stone hallway where Tad entered the balcony, a terrified female in front of him with a gun to her back. Tears streamed down her face.

Irritation grated Adam's nerves as Tad stopped at the far end of the table. "What is it you want, Tad?"

Ava pushed to her feet and walked to the Asian beauty and took her hands. "You're okay," she said, staring into the woman's eyes and then touching her forehead. The female stopped crying, her expression taking on a distant, calm look. Ava gave her another once-over. "She is a good specimen at least," she said dryly.

"She also has an interesting family connection," Tad said, running his hand down her hair. "Tell them who your father is."

"Tan Chin," she said softly.

Ava's eyes went wide. "As in Dr. Chin?"

"That's right," Tad said, his attention going to Adam. "She was living with Chin's ex-wife in China. But I found her."

Adam arched a brow. "Does Chin know?"

"Not only does he know," Tad replied, "he assures me he can get us Red Dart, a stock of serum, as well as both Michael and Cassandra, tonight. He even promises aid with the birth of your child." He leveled his stare on Adam. "I want to be Michael's replacement."

Adam studied him. He was distasteful to the eye, unworthy. Yet, he was resourceful at a time when Adam had been forced to avoid battle for fear any injury would affect Ava and his child. He would use Tad for now. When he had Red Dart, he would force both his brother and Michael to join him. He would not need the likes of Tad.

He inclined his head. "I hear you doing lots of talking," Adam said. "Show me results."

———

Near dawn, with Sterling, Damion, Caleb, and about a dozen soldiers, Cassandra and Michael exited Sunrise City. Nerves jumped in Cassandra's stomach. Instead of sleeping, she'd shared her ideas with Michael to organize the women into a coalition against the female abductions. Talking and making love, of course, had kept her mind off what the day would hold. No matter what the cause, it would be hard to see her father taken into captivity. And then there was the wind-walking.

Cassandra Powell—used-to-be-normal, military girl—was going to wind-walk. Or maybe she wasn't so normal—not for a long time, it seemed. She did, after all, have a father who'd created a new race and a half-alien lover who had now become her permanent Lifebond. Thankfully, there were no morning-after effects from the final phase, considering all she had to face today. She'd been so close to bonding with Michael that the final step had been a piece of cake. For once in her life, she'd had no sleep and still felt like a million dollars.

The doors to the city slid shut behind them, and Cassandra turned and blinked. The mountain looked untouched, as if that door did not exist.

"Not so sure about this whole wind-walking thing," Cassandra said. "My first attempt wasn't such a good one."

"You're different now," Michael assured her.

"You complete him," Sterling joked, repeating a line from the movie *Jerry Maguire* and pressing his hand to his chest. He snorted and then added, "It's addictive. The wind-walking, that is." He inclined his head at Michael. "Not Michael. Or if he is—I don't want to hear about it."

Michael pulled her close. "Ready?"

She inhaled nervously. "I think so."

He didn't wait for a more definite answer. Suddenly, the most incredible force of energy lanced her body, and before she could even begin to react, she was standing in the alley across from her condo.

She blinked and smiled. "Oh my God, that was so amazing. Can we do it again?"

Michael laughed and kissed her. "Many, many times," he promised. "But not now. Now you go inside and change clothes."

She clung to him. "You aren't coming in with me?"

"You bet your life I am," he promised. "But I don't want anyone to see me enter." He slid a cell phone to her hand. "Punch the speed dial '1' button when you get to the door, and let me know it's clear so no one sees me with you, and I'll wind-walk."

"You think it won't be?" she asked apprehensively.

"I'm sure everything is fine," he told her. "The Zodius think you're still inside Sunrise City. They won't know you're here until you show yourself at the base. But I'm not taking any chances with your safety."

He patted her ass. "Now go. Get to that door, and let's get inside." His lips brushed hers as he sent her on her way. Cassandra's stomach clenched, nerves again taking root. The end of this day could not come soon enough.

The path across the street was short, and she was dialing the phone before she even turned into the hallway to her condo. "It's clear," she said the instant she scanned the entryway. Michael was there an instant later pulling a tool kit of some sort from his pocket to pick her lock. Apparently, he'd thought of the fact she didn't have the keys.

He shoved the door open, pulled a gun from under his pant leg, and entered. "Stay here, right inside the door," he said.

Cassandra did as he said, and her heart raced as he scanned the condo. When he reholstered his weapon and pushed the door shut, locking it behind him, she let out a heavy breath she hadn't even realized she'd been holding. "I can't wait until this is over."

He pulled her close. "Soon, sweetheart," he promised. "I have you shielded from Trackers, but I don't like being in this apartment. Go get ready for work. I'll follow you to the base, where you will be safe. Do not, under any circumstances, leave that base without calling me first. You go nowhere without me following."

"You're not making me feel better," she said.

He kissed her. "I'll do that when we get back home to our bed."

"Our bed?" she asked softly.

"*Our* bed," he said, tangling his hands in her hair. "Where I plan to keep you for at least a week when this is over."

She clung to the intimacy between them, to the sweet way he was trying to make her relax. But there was a knot in her chest that clamped down with every breath. Something felt terribly wrong. She told herself this was to be expected; today she would help throw her father into lifelong prison.

Yet still that knot tightened and twisted in her chest with the awful feeling that everything was going to go horribly, terribly wrong. A feeling she didn't share with Michael. He was jumpy and on edge as it was. Her father had created this mess, and she had to help make things right. She felt as if the beginning of the end was upon them, and somehow, someway, she had to stop it from happening.

Lucian stood outside the security gates of Zodius City and called to report to Adam. The instant he stepped on the scanner, the wind shifted, and six soldiers surrounded him. Tad stood front and center, holding a snub-nose .38 special locked and loaded at Lucian's forehead.

"Your service will no longer be needed," he said, grinning snidely.

"Kiss my ass," Lucian said. "You kill me, and Adam will not get Red Dart. I'm the one Brock West trusts."

Tad chuckled. "I have it from a reliable source that West is locked up inside Powell's lab, a nut job jacked up on some new GTECH serum. He's useless to us now."

Lucian's gut clenched. "That's impossible. Powell doesn't have any more serum."

"His attending doctor, Dr. Chin, says differently. See, I have Chin whispering sweet nothings in my ear. Funny how kidnapping his daughter can make things work that way." He cocked the gun. "Would you like the bullet between the eyes or in the back of your head?"

In that instant, Lucian believed that as much as he despised Brock West, they had one thing in common. They both would do whatever was necessary to survive. And Tad… well, Tad was still an idiot. He'd left Lucian unchained, able to escape. Lucian faded into the wind. He'd help Powell before he would die.

Chapter 29

DRESSED IN A BLACK SKIRT AND CRÈME SILK BLOUSE, Cassandra sat in her office near lunchtime, a nervous wreck over both her father's and Brock's absence. Neither was answering calls, and she had a general feeling of unease—a feeling that turned into outright shock when two military officers appeared at her door.

"You need to come with us, Ms. Powell," one of them said.

Heart hammering in her chest, Cassandra thanked God she had her phone in her hand, punching Michael's number and tucking it in her blazer pocket, praying he could hear what was going on. "What's going on? Is my father okay?"

"Your father is fine," the same officer said. "You need to come with us now."

She reached for her purse.

"We'll take your personal items for you," one of the soldiers said.

She froze. "Am I under arrest?"

"Yes ma'am, you are," he confirmed. They advanced on her and confiscated her purse.

Cassandra gently slipped the phone into her trash can and pushed to her feet noisily to hide any sound it might make. "At whose orders?"

"General Powell, ma'am," the lead officer stated.

She was shaking. She knew she was shaking. "On what charge?"

"Conspiracy against the United States of America."

He reached for her arm, and Cassandra yanked out of reach. "I walk of my own free will."

He nodded. "Yes, ma'am."

"And stop calling me ma'am!" She drew in a breath and straightened her spine with a regal snap as she composed herself. Her father would not hurt her. She was not in danger. If she went to jail, she'd get an attorney and fight. And she was wired. The Renegades would find her.

She walked down the long corridor and stepped onto an elevator, but the two officers did not get on. Instead they punched a code on the door, and the doors closed, trapping her inside.

Above the door, the numbers displaying the floors disappeared at ground level, but the elevator kept moving, downward, into an underground area that she hadn't known existed.

Suddenly, a smoky substance floated into the car from the ceiling. Cassandra covered her mouth and tried to block out the fumes, but the effect was almost instantaneous. Her head floated with confusion a moment before her legs buckled.

~~~

Cassandra blinked awake with no concept of time, her chin touching her chest, her neck aching. Presence of mind came with a jolt, and she jerked her head up and yanked at her arms only to find she was sitting in a chair, her arms tied behind her back.

Her father stood in front of her. To his right stood a dark-haired woman she did not know, and Dr. Chin, whom she remembered from Groom Lake. Behind them was a giant cage. She had a horrible feeling she didn't want to know what that cage was for.

Suddenly, she realized her jacket was gone, her shirt disheveled. She could no longer feel the wire taped between her breasts. She was on her own with a man she barely recognized as her own father.

"Hi angel," her father said, his words jerking her gaze back to him. "How's that migraine?"

"Why are you doing this?" she hissed, hardly able to believe this was happening, but she had the presence of mind to scan for a door—one to the far left—and a phone, none to be found. Her purse was sitting on the lab table by her father; it was open, as if it had been grabbed and searched.

"I, my dearest, am trying to secure our great nation," he said dryly. "It saddens me in ways you cannot comprehend that you, my little girl, have chosen to aid our enemies."

"You mean the Renegades?" she asked. "Is it true, Father? Are you planning to use Red Dart against the Renegades? The men who have been risking their lives to protect us from Adam?"

"They are all GTECHs, Cassandra," he said. "All lethal to humanity. I am doing what you wanted me to do. I am fixing what I created. I am limiting our damage."

"My God," she said. "Do you not see you are creating another nightmare? Adam has men inside the government. If he can't get to Red Dart *before* you unveil it, they will take it when you do. You are handing him the ability to destroy the Renegades, and they are all that stands between us and the Zodius."

"Adam will get nothing from me, Cassandra," he growled, showing a rare moment of anger, his face reddening. "When have I ever been foolish enough to show my hand?" He glared at her, his face distorted, before he drew back and straightened. He dumped her purse and searched through her things. "Where is your phone?"

"I left it at home," she said and added sarcastically, "The ringer made my headache worse."

"Where is your phone, Cassandra?" he shouted.

She knew what he wanted—a way to contact Michael. "At home," she sniped back, her gaze slicing to the woman who'd remained silent to this point, her dark hair and facial structure reminding her of Michael. "I know who you are. Jocelyn Taylor. I know you're his mother." The woman's lips thinned, while her eyes flickered with a mixture of guilt and anger. "How could you betray Michael like this?"

"Michael has never been loyal to anyone but himself," she said, her voice lacking the conviction Cassandra would have expected, considering her actions.

"Do you even know your own son?" Cassandra asked. "Michael chooses everyone over himself. Time and time again, he risks his life to save others."

"Have you forgotten the blade he held to my neck?" her father demanded.

Cassandra glared at him. "If he had wanted you dead, you would be dead," she said. "He saved you from Adam, and I think you know that. You just don't want to be the one who needs to be saved. You are out of control, Father. You're going to crash and burn, and take us all with you."

"Enough," Powell bit out. "What is the number to reach Michael, Cassandra?"

"I don't know how to reach Michael," she said. "And even if I did, why in the world would I tell you?"

He motioned to Chin. "Hook her up to the electrical pads, and shock her."

Cassandra and Jocelyn gasped in unison. "You wouldn't," Cassandra declared.

"Tell me the number," her father demanded.

Cassandra was terrified, but she was not giving up Michael. Her chin lifted defiantly. "I don't know how to reach Michael."

Her father glared at her and then motioned to Chin. "Do it."

"She's your daughter," Jocelyn said, grabbing his arm.

He shook her off. "And Michael is your son," he said. "We make sacrifices for the greater good, Jocelyn." He walked to the monitors on the wall and yanked out a drawer, removing a walkie-talkie. "Get an electronic trace on Cassandra's phone, or get me her phone records. I need one or the other *now*."

Chin began sticking electronic pads on her arm. He reached under her hair to attach a device to her neck, and it was all she could do not to jump for fear he would see her mark. The mark.

Suddenly, she thought about her lifebond connection to Michael. Could she be shocked? Would they know when they tried that she was GTECH. Was she stronger now? Could she break that rope?

"We're ready to go," Dr. Chin announced.

The walkie-talkie went off. "Phone records coming to your email now."

—∿∿—

Michael paced the computer room inside Neonopolis as Sterling worked the keyboard, Caleb leaning over his shoulder. "I never should have let her do this," Michael said. "What the hell was I thinking letting her go to the base alone?"

He stopped, eyed Sterling impatiently. "Anything?" The wire signal had disappeared fifteen minutes before. "Either you find her exact location, or I'm going in after her without it."

"I've triangulated her cell phone ping." He leaned back in his chair. "It's still in her office. She must have taken the wire off, afraid she'd be discovered. She knows you can get a basic read on her from your bond."

Michael shook his head. "She wouldn't leave her phone and the wire."

Caleb straightened. "She's still in the building. If she's with her father, she's safe."

"You weren't on that phone with her like I was," Michael said, "I could tell from her tone, she was distressed." He paced some more, stared at the ceiling, and ran his hand over his face. "I should never have agreed to this. I'm going after her."

His cell phone rang, and Michael grabbed it from his belt, answering quickly.

"Hello, Michael." Michael went cold inside. It was Powell. He glanced at Caleb and Sterling and mouthed Powell's name. "Cassandra is here with me. You and I need to have a conversation—alone. You should know that not only do I have the ability to use Red Dart, but Red Dart has the ability to create excruciating pain in the infected GTECH. Anyone who comes with you will find out firsthand."

Michael turned away from Caleb and Sterling, aware that Powell had won. "Put Cassandra on the phone."

A second passed. "Stay away, Michael!" she yelled into the phone. Michael leaned against the wall, pressed his arm over his head, and shut his eyes. What had he done by allowing her involvement?

Powell came back on the line. "I have a little extra incentive," Powell said. "Every fifteen minutes that you are not here, Cassandra will receive an electric jolt." He spoke in the background. "Shock her."

Cassandra screamed in pain.

"No!" Michael yelled, feeling the electrical charge down his spine, a dull, shared pain with his Lifebond that confirmed her torture. "Damn you, Powell!"

Powell came back on the line. "You have fourteen minutes until the next jolt." He recited an address that Michael recognized as near his mother's house. The line went dead.

Michael turned to the other two men, already attaching his phone to his belt and preparing to leave.

"What just happened, Michael?" Caleb demanded.

"He has Cassandra," he said. "I have to go."

"Let's go kick that sorry bastard's ass," Sterling said, pushing to his feet.

"I'm going alone," Michael said. "At best, he wants me. At worst, this is a trap to use Red Dart on all of us. We can't risk that."

"You're not going alone," Caleb said.

"He's shocking Cassandra every fifteen minutes until I get there," he said. "I don't have a choice."

Caleb cursed. "Let's think about this—"

"I have about twelve minutes until he shocks her again," Michael said. "I'm leaving. You stay here and lead the Renegades. Just make sure that if Cassandra and I don't make it through this, you make it worthwhile." Vehemently, he added, "You make Powell and Adam pay, Caleb."

"Is she still on base? Or is he moving her?" Caleb asked.

"I'm not telling you that," Michael said. "I won't allow you to risk your safety."

"If he moved her, it can't be far," Sterling said. "We'll use the satellite and find her. You might as well just tell us."

Michael's attention snapped to Sterling. "Caleb needs someone to do the dirty work if I'm gone. To cover his back. You be that someone if I'm gone." He took off out the door before they could stop him.

Chapter 30

APPEARING AT THE COORDINATES GIVEN TO HIM BY Powell with seven minutes to spare before Cassandra's next shock treatment, Michael found himself at the back of a vacant house. Two soldiers stood in his path. One pointed him forward.

As directed, Michael walked toward the basement entrance, but they bypassed the door. Instead the soldier opened a trapdoor covered by grass and exposed a stairwell leading underground before motioning Michael forward. He walked down several feet before entering a narrow tunnel, the soldiers on his heels. It didn't take him long to surmise that it connected at some junction to his mother's basement. He tested his boundaries, reached for the wind. If there was the tiniest of cracks in the surface above them, he could call on it for aid. But he found nothing.

The tunnel was long, a good mile underground between the vacant house and what he assumed to be a lab beneath his mother's place. He'd barely made it in the door when he saw Cassandra. "Damn you, Michael, I told you not to come!"

Michael would have laughed at Cassandra's ability to challenge him even under duress, if she wasn't inside a cage, and he wasn't so damn pissed. Powell had proven he would do anything to control the GTECHs, and who knew how much more from there, even to hurting his own daughter.

"You know I had to come for you, baby," he said softly, checking the lab for possible exits and finding only the one he had come through. "Are you okay?"

Anguish lanced her voice, tears pouring down her cheeks. "No. No, I am not okay. I would rather be tortured than have you come here." She was sitting with her arms tied behind her, electronic wires attached to various parts of her body. No one else was in sight.

"Step into the cage," came Powell's voice over an intercom. Michael inhaled sharply. Once he was in that cage, he couldn't do squat to get them out of here. "She's on remote control," Powell added. "One punch of a button, and those wires will jolt her. Would you like a demonstration?"

"You sonofabitch!" Michael growled. "She's your daughter!"

Cassandra was crying harder now. "Don't, Michael. Don't come into this cage."

He was going in all right, but he wasn't staying. Michael charged at the cage, crossed the room with the agility of a GTECH on speed, his extra chromosome giving him an added jolt. He picked Cassandra up, chair and all, and then froze. Cassandra gasped and buried her head in Michael's shoulder. Brock stood in the cage doorway holding a gun, his eyes as black as coal. He was a GTECH, which was impossible. That took months of injections.

"Green Hornets," Brock said. "Compliments of your mother."

Michael noted the shake of Brock's hand. Whatever Powell had done to him wasn't going over so well, and judging from the crazed look on his face, the man wasn't stable. "Easy man," he said. "I'm backing up." Slowly, Michael moved back into the cage and set Cassandra down. He reached for the wires attached to her, not about to let her get tortured again.

"Step away from her, Michael," Powell ordered through the intercom.

Brock cocked the gun. "You heard the man."

Reluctantly, Michael did as commanded, holding Brock's stare. "So this is your plan?" Michael said to Brock. "To be some souped-up GTECH doing Powell's bidding? He's using you, man. This isn't going any place good for you."

"Shut up!" he yelled. "Shut up!"

A clicking sound sent Michael whirling around to face the weapon extending from a hole in the ceiling. Cassandra! His mind reached for hers, trying to shield her from whatever was about to happen as he could shield her from the Trackers now that they were life-bonded. Seconds passed as he reached for her mind, used their new bond, and connected, mentally forming a protective barrier around her. And just in time. A red light flashed on his chest. Powell's laughter radiated through the room a minute before Michael's body began to shake. Michael fell to the ground, blackness threatening to consume him. He focused on one thing and one thing only—keeping that barrier around Cassandra. Yet... somewhere in the distance he heard her scream. *I'm going to kill you, Powell,* he shouted in his mind before the shadows consumed him.

⁓

"Michael!" Tears rolled down Cassandra's cheeks as she

watched Michael lying face down in that cage, shaking from head to toe—her fierce, wonderful warrior taken down by her own father. Yet she could feel him in her mind, somehow protecting her through it all. Brock was down too, floundering around on the ground just like Michael. Whatever Red Dart was, it didn't distinguish between one GTECH and another. If it impacted one—it impacted all.

Another soldier stomped into the room and picked up Cassandra, chair and all, and carried her out of the cage, the doors shutting behind her.

"He's going to do that to you, too," she said as he set her down a few feet away. "Do you want that?"

The soldier ignored her, walking away as if she hadn't even spoken. Of course. Her father owned him in some way. Her father, the manipulator.

The sound of a voice had Cassandra looking to the door. Powell, Jocelyn, and Chin all entered the room. Jocelyn rushed to the computer panel and punched some buttons on the computer, speaking to Powell as she did. "You cannot leave him like this without damage." She turned to Powell. "General!"

Her father grimaced. "I left West like this far longer than Michael," he said. "Are you going soft because he's your son?"

"Look at what Brock's become!" She pointed at Brock, her hand shaking. She quickly folded her arms in front of her, as if trying to hide her reaction. "If you want him to lead us to victory," she said, "he needs to be of sound mind to do it."

"Father," Cassandra said. "Stop! Stop hurting him!" She knew it was a mistake, but she was scared for

Michael. "He's my Lifebond. If you kill him, you will kill me, too."

Everyone turned around and looked at her, stunned silence overtaking the room. Powell motioned Chin forward. He checked her neck and then nodded. "She has the mark."

Powell arched a brow and then smiled. A laugh followed. His lifted his hands to his sides in celebration. "This is perfect." He grabbed Jocelyn and kissed her. "Don't you see? Michael will do whatever we wish in order to protect her."

Cassandra's stomach rolled. Her father was sick. Insane. She squeezed her eyes shut against the nightmare this had become, wondering where the Renegades were, knowing they weren't coming. Her father had made sure of that.

The general set Jocelyn back from him, and Cassandra's eyes met the other woman's. To Cassandra's surprise, she saw real regret. Both Brock and Jocelyn were having doubts. That had to equal hope. But then again, Michael was already marked with Red Dart. Hope didn't matter. There was no escape.

Rubbing his hands together, Powell looked at Chin. "We have some time before we move them. Let's test the new creation against the old creation, shall we?" Chin smiled his approval.

"What are you doing, Father?" Cassandra asked desperately.

"Relax," the general said. "Michael heals quickly." He arched a brow. "I imagine you do as well." It was a subtle threat that had her recoiling and trying to work the rope at her hands. Either she wasn't one bit stronger than before her lifebonding, or those ropes were enforced.

Cassandra watched her father turn the dial attached to his neck, her eyes going to Jocelyn's. "What is that thing? What is he doing?"

Jocelyn, to her surprise, answered by motioning to the cage where Michael and Brock were now alert and starting to get up.

"Michael!" Cassandra cried out in relief. He turned to her, awareness washing over his face.

Powell hit a button on the computer and spoke through an intercom. "Lieutenant Colonel West. You will attack and defeat your enemy."

Suddenly, Brock lunged at Michael, throwing punches, kicking, growling like some sort of animal. Michael dodged and maneuvered. "I don't want to fight you, West!" He shoved West against the bars and yelled to the room. "I will not fight him like some kind of animal." Then to West again, "Don't let him turn you into this."

"Help them, Jocelyn," Cassandra pleaded. Jocelyn cast her a helpless look, and Cassandra tried to get through to her. "Don't force Michael to hurt him. Please. Before my father shocks them again."

"I…" Jocelyn whispered. "I can't believe Michael isn't fighting him. I can't believe any of this. It's not what I thought…"

"You will fight!" Powell screamed, stomping closer to the cage.

Cassandra focused on Jocelyn and tried not to think about her father using that remote control again. "Michael is a good man, Jocelyn. He's a *good* man. My father is not. Don't help him."

"Fight!" her father shouted again, and Brock went down with a bloodcurdling scream that ripped through Cassandra's nerve endings and drew her attention to the cage. Brock was shaking, lying face down. Again Michael was not.

"What is going on, Jocelyn?" Powell demanded, still messing with the controller around his neck. At that point, Brock was shaking to near convulsions. Michael didn't so much as flinch. Her father stormed toward the lab table, his face red, fury turning his features to a harsh grimace. "I said... what the *hell* is happening?"

Jocelyn was standing with her hand over her mouth, and her father shook her. "Jocelyn!" her father yelled.

"I don't know," Jocelyn said, jerking into action and racing to the computer, keying some strokes. "I don't know." She pressed her hand to her forehead, and looked at Powell. "It's like Red Dart disappeared from his system."

"How is that possible?" he demanded.

"I'm trying to figure that out," Jocelyn said, rushing to the computers that covered the wall to the right. "I need to look at my research. I need—"

"Where is Chin?" her father yelled, cutting her off. "Chin!"

Nothing. The doctor had disappeared.

"Oh my God," Jocelyn murmured.

Cassandra twisted around to bring the pale features of the other woman into focus. "What?" Her gut twisted in premonition. "What is it? What's wrong?"

"Chin left his email up," she said. "The Zodius soldiers are coming."

—

"We have a green light on trouble," Sterling said, leaning back from his computer. "We have action. Lots of it. Four miles from Jocelyn Taylor's house. At least twenty soldiers who appeared out of nowhere." Which meant Wind-walkers. "Bold bastards. It's broad daylight."

Caleb and Damion appeared over Sterling's shoulder, both mumbling curses before Caleb hit his earpiece to contact the standby team they had prepared to rock 'n' roll into action.

Sterling was already on his feet ready to join them, his attention on Caleb. "You realize this could be a trap," he said. "We could all get tagged with Red Dart."

"I don't plan to worry about a Red Dart trap every time we leave Sunrise City for the rest of our lives," Caleb said. "We came here to end this. Let's end it."

"I love how you think," Sterling approved.

"If we aren't too late," Damion said grimly.

Sterling cast him a hard look. "Stop talking that kind of crap. We won't be too late." He pointed a finger at his head even as the three of them headed to the launch pad of Neonopolis, the area they used to run missions. "You have to think positive, man. We are Renegades." And they were going to bring their men home. Or die trying.

Chapter 31

THE ZODIUS SOLDIERS ARE COMING. JOCELYN'S WORDS had barely left her lips when Cassandra's father darted toward the door, leaving Cassandra to gape after him. Jocelyn was racing around in a panic. "I don't know what to do."

"Release Michael!" Cassandra shouted. "He's our only chance to survive. Let him go."

Survival instincts kicked in, adrenaline firing Cassandra's blood. She jerked on the ropes. Felt them give this time. She jerked again, and she was free. Thank God! She grabbed Jocelyn. "How do I open the cage?" Shouts and footsteps sounded from the hallway.

"Damn it, Mother!" Michael yelled. "Let me out!"

Cassandra grabbed Jocelyn's arms. "He's the only chance we have to survive this. Let him out."

Wide-eyed, Jocelyn stared at Cassandra and nodded. "The blue key above the number pad on the computer."

Cassandra was at that computer punching the key in two seconds, and Michael was out in one. Cassandra's heart about exploded out of her chest as a Zodius soldier appeared in the doorway, his weapon drawn. Michael charged after him, moving so fast he was a blur before he collided with the enemy.

Jocelyn shoved Cassandra away from the computer and started keying. "I have to destroy Red Dart. I have to kill the program. I have an auto-destruct set up on the lab, and everything inside."

Cassandra heard her, but her attention was on that battle in the doorway. Michael forcefully took the other soldier's weapon, planting a bullet between his eyes. Cassandra let out a sigh of relief that it was the enemy, not Michael, who crumpled to the ground.

Michael yanked the soldier inside the lab and went to work removing his weapons. He shoved the door shut as he armed himself. Bullets blasted against the steel door, followed by hard pounding. "We need another way out. It will only take them a minute to blast open the door."

"Hidden panel behind the cage," Jocelyn said, still focused on the computer.

Michael was already moving toward them. "Let's go."

"Wait," Jocelyn said, doing something to the device beside the computer before hitting several more keys. "I need another minute."

"We don't have a minute," Michael ground out, grabbing Cassandra's hand. Voices sounded outside the lab, an argument about how to bring down the door and not the entire lab.

Jocelyn glanced up. "Actually," she said and hit a decisive key, "you have exactly five minutes before everything to do with Red Dart that isn't in my head goes up in smoke along with this lab and anyone still inside." They started toward the back of the lab. A blast sounded in the hallway. The door jerked but didn't come down.

"We can't leave Brock!" Jocelyn insisted.

Michael half growled. "He's a walking tracking device."

"I can use him to make an antidote in case Red Dart ever surfaces again. Please. We need him."

With a conflicted grimace, Michael released Cassandra's hand and was in that cage and out in a second. "He's dead," he announced after checking his pulse. He was already motioning them forward, his gun in his hand as a blast finished off the lab door. "Go! Go! Go!" Michael yelled, firing off a round of bullets.

Jocelyn shackled Cassandra's arm and pulled her forward, punching a code into a panel. Steel doors slid open, and they were inside a stairwell.

Gunfire sounded behind them and above. A semblance of hope found Cassandra. Someone was shooting at the Zodius soldiers other than Michael. Please Lord, she prayed, let it be the Renegades, not her father's men.

Jocelyn was already moving forward, but Cassandra wasn't going anywhere without Michael. She heard him fire another round of bullets and let out a breath of relief as he appeared in the corridor.

Cassandra punched the marked button to close the doors. Cassandra and Michael started running up the steps, Michael yanking his cell phone from his belt as they climbed, checking for a signal. He found one near the exit about the time they heard the door behind them blast open.

"We're in the house," he said into the phone.

Jocelyn called over her shoulder. "Kitchen."

"Kitchen," Michael repeated. Almost instantly more shots rang out from directly above, and the door opened to display Sterling and Caleb. "It's gonna blow," Michael shouted as he pushed the women forward. Sterling grabbed Jocelyn and started running with Caleb behind him. Michael reached for Cassandra to do the same, but bullets sprayed through the tunnel from behind.

Michael kicked the door shut to the tunnel. "Go! Get out of here!" he shouted at Cassandra. "I'll hold them off so you can get out."

"Not without you!" she yelled.

Suddenly, the swinging door off the kitchen leading to the living area burst open, and a Zodius soldier grabbed Cassandra, yanking her into the other room. Michael's heart jackknifed, and he dove for her, but the door slammed shut, bullets coming at him from all sides. He replied with shots of his own and shoved open the door, seeking Cassandra, but it was too late. The Zodius soldier who'd captured her had yanked her out the front door onto the porch. He wind-walked out of the house, intending to cut off Cassandra's capture. He appeared on the lawn right as the house went up in a blast that sent him and everyone within ten feet sprawling to the ground. Michael recovered, flat on his belly, with one thing on his mind—Cassandra. Staying low, he scanned for her, relieved in one instant to find her alive, but—damn it to hell—she and Sterling were in the hands of the Zodius Soldiers, blades at their throats. Caleb stood across from them with Powell as his captive and holding a blade at his throat. On either side of this standoff, Zodius and Renegade soldiers stood toe-to-toe, ready for battle.

Michael stood his ground as the Zodius soldier who he knew to be a cold-blooded killer, Tad Bensen, made his demand. "The general, for his daughter," Tad bargained with Caleb.

Caleb was now put in a position of choosing. If he handed over Powell, then Powell could give the Zodius the Red Dart crystal. If he did not, Tad *would* kill

Cassandra and Sterling. Michael had no doubt about that, and neither did Caleb.

Michael's mother crawled to his side. "Powell can't give them Red Dart, if that's what you're worried about," she whispered. She reached inside her pocket and then handed him the crystal. "I destroyed the data, but I have the crystal. It's yours now."

Michael inhaled sharply, unable to consider the magnitude of his mother's actions now. She hadn't destroyed everything. She'd simply made everyone believe she had. But instead of using the crystal for personal gain, she'd given it to him, and now he was free to end this battle without recourse, with no fear that Powell still held the power of Red Dart.

Michael unleashed his power. Hurricane-style winds whipped around them, wrecking havoc on everyone but Michael. He was on his feet, charging toward Cassandra, well aware that the intensity of this wind was something he could hold for only a minute at most. He ripped the blade from Tad's hand, freeing Cassandra, and then turned to where Sterling was being held. In a quick twist of his wrist, he snagged the soldier's gun and shot him between the eyes. He turned to do the same to Tad, but the wind faded, and Tad instantly wind-walked away.

The soldier he'd killed fell beside Cassandra, and she jumped, a terror-laced scream following, a prelude to the all-out war that followed, Renegades against Zodius soldiers.

Michael spotted Powell and saw the moment he broke away from the group when Caleb had been forced to release him to defend himself. Powell was in a full-out run. He was getting away, and Michael had to choose between him and Cassandra. Which was no choice at all.

With a low curse, Michael let Powell escape, pulling Cassandra to her feet and wind-walking her to his mother's side. "Run!" he yelled.

———~~~———

Powell ran across the wooded terrain, charging toward a tunnel opening a mile away. The sound of wolves howling nearby pierced the air and spiked his adrenaline. Faster. He had to run faster. Suddenly, the wind ripped, and Lucian appeared before him, drawing Powell to an abrupt halt.

"Been a long time, General," Lucian said, referring to his time serving Powell at Groom Lake.

"Not long enough," Powell said, aiming the Glock he'd grabbed from the lab before departing at Lucian. "Careful now, traitor. I'd enjoy planting one of these Green Hornets between your eyes."

"This 'traitor,' as you call me, is your only chance to escape," Lucian said. "Both the Renegades and the Zodius want your blood, General."

"I don't know what game you're playing, but save it for someone who's stupid," the general said. "I know you are with Adam, Lucian."

"I'm a free agent now," Lucian said. "You get the first opportunity at recruitment."

General Powell arched a brow. "And why would I want to do that?"

"Because you don't have a choice," he said. "You will die if Adam gets his hands on you. Or rot in a cell if Caleb does. Agree to work with me, and I will wind-walk you out of here, and we will begin planning a way to show both Adam and Caleb who is really in control."

"Wind-walking might kill me," he said.

"And so will Adam."

"How do I know you won't take me to Adam?"

"Because you are still alive, General," he said. "I could have easily wind-walked behind you and slit your throat. But you have resources I want." Footsteps sounded in the air. A scurry of movement. "Now or never, General."

The general considered only a moment more before lowering his gun. Lucian might think he had control now, but Powell had no doubt—he would easily remedy that. He'd lost the Red Dart crystal in that explosion, but he still had serum and twelve soldiers who were GTECH-ready. Now that he knew what the serum was capable of turning a man into—he wouldn't be a fool this time. He'd take precautions. He'd implant kill switches in their brains before giving them their freedom and come up with a plan suited for limited manpower and resources that involved covert action. This was not over. All he had to do was survive the wind-walking.

"Do it," Powell ordered. Lucian stepped forward and grabbed him. The wind carried them away.

—◇◇◇—

Michael called forth another hurricane-style wind. Zodius and Renegade alike stumbled and struggled, but Tad screamed through the wind. "Retreat!" The instant the wind died, the Zodius soldiers faded into their own gusts, escaping by wind-walking while they still could.

Fire engines screeched into the driveway, men

rushing off the trucks to fight the fire behind them. Renegades faded into the wind before they were spotted, some on a search mission for Powell. Caleb would have to make government contact to explain the fire, and then try and re-create the relationships that Powell had destroyed. A tough task when they had no idea who they could trust.

Cassandra ran to Michael and flung her arms around him. "Thank God, you're okay."

His arms wrapped around her, the warmth of that moment was like none he had ever felt. She'd watched him kill today, and still she accepted him without question. "It kills me to know I did not stop you from being tortured."

"Those two years apart from you were torture," she said.

His mother approached, hugging herself and looking uncomfortable. She glanced at Cassandra. "I'm so glad you are okay. I… well… I don't know how to say I am sorry. I misjudged you. I… misjudged your father."

Cassandra snuggled closer to Michael, as if she knew he needed that warmth right now. "We're alive, and it's over. That's what counts right now."

Jocelyn nodded and cut a tentative look at Michael. "I promise you, I didn't know what I was getting involved with. I thought… well, a lot of things that would appear skewed right about now. Seems I have a bad way of choosing the wrong men."

Michael didn't know what to say to that. He'd spent years believing his mother was as evil as his father, and he wasn't sure he was ready to see her otherwise. Those feelings had defined much of his life and how he saw himself. But she'd come through for him and the Renegades today.

Ultimately, she'd saved Cassandra's life by telling him about the crystal, rather than concealing it. Probably Sterling's life as well. A silent agreement passed between them, and a bit of mutual, if not limited, respect had been earned on both sides. Which was a good thing, considering she was the only living person who knew how to make Red Dart work. She was going to be coming to Sunrise City for protection. Caleb would decide the fate of the crystal. Michael motioned to Damion and gave that order.

His mother accepted it freely. "I can help the Renegades," she said. "I want to."

The sounds of wolves howling in unison shot a warning through Michael. He scanned for Caleb and made eye contact. Adam was here. They both felt it a moment before he emerged from the woods, several wolves surrounding him.

Michael lifted his hand to Damion, who stepped to his side. "Go with Damion, Cassandra," he ordered.

"Michael—"

"I said, go with Damion," he said. "I need to know you're safe."

Reluctantly, she nodded, pushed to her toes, and kissed his cheek. "Be careful."

Michael, Caleb, and Sterling walked toward Adam; there were too many civilian humans nearby to windwalk without exposure. Michael and Sterling lingered behind as Caleb stepped forward and met Adam face-to-face. Two powerful figures, so alike, but so different. One who radiated a magical quality that inspired and motivated. And another who oozed evil and darkness, a promise of destruction.

The two of them spoke, their voices low, too low for Michael and Sterling to make out what they were saying. Long minutes passed before Adam faded into the wind, the wolves howling with his departure.

Caleb turned and walked back to them, a grim expression on his face, a hard set to his jaw. He said nothing as he joined them, stepped between them, and lifted his hand to signal their departure. The three of them faded into the wind—the Renegades' leader and his two most trusted soldiers.

Words were not necessary. Michael and Sterling knew all they had to know. The war had not ended. In fact, it may well have only just begun.

<hr />

Hours after his promise to Caleb that he would destroy the Renegades, one by one, until his brother joined Zodius Nation, Adam sat at his coliseum table and waited for the main event to start. Ava sat by his side. Dr. Chin and Tad sat across from them.

"I'm so excited you're here, Dr. Chin," Ava said, rubbing her belly. "Now I know I will deliver a healthy baby." She smiled at Tad. "And I have you to thank for bringing him to us."

Tad inclined his head. "I am your loyal servant as always." Ava beamed with delight, which pleased Adam. Ava's happiness over Chin's arrival had made any failure on Tad's part easily overlooked. For now. So did the extra GTECH serum that Chin had brought with him from Powell's lab, though it was still limited. Losing the immediate implementation of Red Dart had been disappointing, but they would eventually make it work.

"Perhaps your child," Chin said, "will hold the secret to re-creating the serum."

His child, Adam thought. Yes. His child was the future. There was greatness in the air tonight, Adam thought, as he lifted his glass to Chin and then to everyone at the table. "To the future of Zodius Nation."

He knew that the Renegades believed they'd achieved a victory by destroying Red Dart, but they would soon discover they were mistaken. Adam's plans to spread his Zodius movement had only just begun.

The weak would be destroyed, and Adam would lead a world like none anyone had ever imagined. A world free of divisions. One nation under his command. One *Zodius* Nation.

Epilogue

CASSANDRA STOOD INSIDE THE CONFERENCE ROOM staring at the many maps pegged with colored stick-pens only moments after her group of women, the "Wardens" as they'd begun calling themselves, wrapped up a meeting. Pride filled her that in only a month the Wardens had found a definite trend to the abductions. They had worked through Caleb to set up civilian and military alert systems to act on those trends, and they were only getting started.

Michael's mother was here too, quickly becoming a part of the scientific team. Her father... well, he was missing. The government swore they hadn't heard from him, but none of the Renegades were convinced that was true. She tried not to think about it. And the crystal— locked away somewhere rather than destroyed. Caleb wasn't willing to relinquish a weapon that might one day be needed to save the world.

As for the effects of lifebonding, Cassandra had yet to develop any special gift, like Ava's ability to brainwash others, but she would welcome any skill she could use to aid this war against Adam.

"I have something I want to show you," Michael said, appearing in the doorway, his big body shrinking the small space. She inhaled at the sight of him, always amazed at how easily he impacted her senses every time she saw him. Surprised to find him without his army fatigues, he was dressed in faded jeans and a snug blue T-shirt that hugged his broad chest.

"You aren't dressed for work," she said.

"I took the afternoon off," he said, holding out his hand.

A few minutes later, they were at the peak of a magnificent mountaintop at the edge of the Grand Canyon, a blanket beneath them and a picnic lunch that Emma had packed for them ready to enjoy. Cassandra looked out at the view with wonder, thrilled at the world that wind-walking was allowing her to enjoy.

"It's magnificent," she said, forgetting the war raging around them and embracing this moment with the man she loved. She laughed. "Somehow I doubt anyone but me would believe you would pack a picnic lunch."

He didn't laugh as she'd expected him to, and she did so love making him laugh. Instead, he eased her onto the blanket and leaned over her, raw emotion glistening in his eyes. "You have changed my life in ways I cannot ever explain."

She touched his jaw, her heart squeezing with emotion. "As you have mine," she promised.

He kissed her then, a gentle kiss that filled her with love. Michael made her whole.

Acknowledgments

There are so many people who helped me make this book and this series come to life. First and foremost, thank you to Deb Werksman and the entire Sourcebooks team for their enthusiastic support. It has shown in every step of the process from submission to print. Rachel Dawn Carrington and Cathryn Fox—you are great friends who make the twists and turns of publication a straighter path. Thank you to Janice for living the deadlines with me and reading my work over and over. You make it better. And finally, importantly, a special thank you to Donna Grant for the many special ways she helped this book make it to the shelves. You rock, that's all there is to it.

About the Author

Award-winning author **Lisa Renee Jones** has published more than fifteen novels in several different languages, spanning multiple genres of romance: contemporary, romantic suspense, dark paranormal, and erotic fiction. Her awards include first place in the Romantic Times Aspiring Writers Contest 2003. Before becoming a writer, Lisa lived the life of a corporate executive. Her successful company LRJ Staffing Services was recognized by *Entrepreneur* magazine in 1998 as one of the top ten growing women-owned businesses. She often uses her sales and marketing background for consulting jobs within the publishing industry. She currently lives in Colorado Springs, Colorado.

READ ON FOR AN EXCERPT FROM
THE RENEGADE CONQUEST
AVAILABLE FROM SOURCEBOOKS CASABLANCA
NOVEMBER 2011

He was created, molded, formed from life, love, and misery...

Lethally daring. Ruthlessly passionate. He invites death to his door. Welcomes it with each breath he draws, each step he takes. And thus he *is* danger. A volatile storm that will sweep across the calm realms of humanity and shake it to the depths of its core. And that storm is... Sterling.

Prologue

WITH A SMILE ON HIS LIPS, STERLING JETER WHIPPED his battered, black Ford F-150 into the driveway of the equally damaged trailer he called home and killed the engine.

He leaned back in the seat and pulled the wad of cash from his pocket. Ten thousand dollars. "Yeeha," he whispered. How many twenty-year-olds had that kind of dough? He was liking this new job. Hack a computer, get cash. He snorted. "And they say that government databases can't be hacked. This low-life trailer trash proved them wrong." That's what the kids at school had called him. Trailer trash. Misfit. "Screw you," he mumbled. "Screw you all."

Once Sterling had counted the money down to the ten thousandth dollar, he stuffed the cash back in his pocket and grabbed the flowers on the seat. He'd need all the sweetness he could muster to convince Grandma to head to that fancy alcohol rehab center at Scott and White, down sixty miles north in Temple, Texas. She'd curse and probably hit him. She was good at that, but it didn't hurt anymore. Hadn't for years.

He knew she couldn't help herself. He'd read enough about alcoholism to know she was sick. Yet she'd raised him despite that. Heck, he was to blame, he supposed.

He was why his mother had died—the trigger that had set Grandmom off.

He climbed out of the truck and whistled down the path to the front door. He kicked open the door and went inside. He froze. Grandmom sat on the couch wrapped in the same crinkly blue dress that she'd gone to bed wearing, a big bottle of vodka in her hand. Two men dressed in suits sat next to her.

"Look what these men brought me," she said, grinning, holding up her prize.

"We know how you like to take care of your grandmother," one of the men said, his buzz-cut flat against his skull.

"Kind of like your father took care of his family," the other man stated, a clone of the first one. They had to be army or government. *Fuck me!*

"The resemblance between the two of you is amazing," the first man said, picking up a picture of Sterling's father. His father was standing in front of a helicopter, his blond hair longer than it should have been because he wasn't normal army. He'd been Special Forces, working undercover all over the map. And it had gotten him killed when Sterling was barely out of diapers. The man set the picture back down on the coffee table.

Grandmom grabbed the picture, mumbling to herself. "They're the spitting image of each other." Her gaze lifted, her voice with it. "But Sterling ain't got no clue who his daddy was. Man was never here. Neither was his mama." She took a drink. "They died. Didn't they Ster… ling?"

The Captain focused on Sterling. "We think you're a

lot like him. For instance, you both showed an interest in official government business."

Sterling's gut twisted in a knot. He was busted. Big-time freaking busted and going to jail. "I don't know what you're talking about." He wasn't admitting shit. He wouldn't go down without a fight. He had Grandmom to take care of.

"You know," the second man said, "there's a lot that can be forgiven if you serve your country. Enlistment is favorable in certain circumstances."

The first man took the picture from Grandmom. "I'm Captain Sherman, son." He gave a sideways nod to the second man. "This is First Lieutenant Jenson. We served with your father."

Thank the Lord above. They weren't Feds. "What do you want from me?"

The Captain answered, "Your father was part of a Special Forces unit where certain 'skills,' like say computer expertise, can be useful." He wrapped his arm around Grandmom's shoulders. "In exchange for service in this unit, your family will be well taken care of. It's time you enlisted, son. Be all you can be, like your father."

Grandmom gulped from the bottle, and suddenly Sterling realized he was still holding the flowers—those damn flowers that weren't going to erase his problems any more than the wad of cash sitting in his pocket.

"And if I say no?" he asked.

"I don't remember asking," the first man said.

"I'm not a soldier," Sterling said. He was just a kid in a trailer park who knew how to hack a computer.

"You are your father's son," the man said. "Mark

my words, boy. You will be a soldier when I'm through with you."

Sterling looked at his grandmother, watched as she gulped from the bottle, her teal green eyes that matched his own the only familiar thing left in her. He saw the hint of contempt that lurked in their depths—the blame for his mother's death. The booze could never quite kill that. Sterling realized right then and there that the best thing he could do for her was to leave and give her a chance to heal. To get as far away from her as he could and stay there.

His gaze shifted to the man on his grandmother's right, and Sterling fixed him in an accessing stare. "She'll be taken care of?"

"You have my word."

"Mister," he said. "I don't know you from anywhere. I'll expect that in writing."

A hint of respect flickered in the man's expression. "As well you should."

"Then I'm in," he said. "Sign me up, and ship me out."

Chapter 1

Fourteen Years Later

STERLING JETER SLIPPED INTO THE SHADOWY RECESSES of a dark Las Vegas alley, hot on the trail of a dealer pedaling "Ice," the newest variety of "sin" in the city. The clear liquid slid down its user's throat with a sub-zero effect and delivered a short-lived boost of superhuman strength and speed.

And though users believed Ice to be just another street drug, it was far from it. Ice was alien in origin, its chemical compound unidentifiable by scientists. Its effects resembled those produced by the serum that had created the GTECH Super Soldiers, like himself, under the government program "Project Zodius." Its source—Adam Rain, the GTECH who'd risen against the government and taken over Groom Lake military base three years before, forming the Zodius Movement. Adam fully intended to stomp humanity further down the food chain. And what better way than addicting the population to a drug that had proven resistant to duplication, thus, making him the sole supplier?

"Where's the money, Charles?" asked the young dealer who stood between two burly men, poised as bodyguards. He was the first dealer in weeks who'd been careless enough to deal in the open and risk exposure.

"I won't have it until tomorrow," Charles replied,

hugging himself and shaking. "But I'm begging you, David. Please. Give me a hit. I can... hardly breathe. I need... a hit." He had no idea how true that might be. Withdrawal had killed a half-dozen users so far, their organs shriveling up like prunes.

It was a damnable situation. Warn the public to stop using, they die. Don't warn them, they encourage others to use, and Adam gains more control of the city. Exactly why Sterling wanted to find this dealer, or rather the dealer's source, with two objectives in mind—stop distribution to new users and find out how to safely wean the current users from the drug.

"But you have no money?" David challenged.

Sterling grimaced. Not only was Adam luring the users into addiction, he was taking all their money in the process. Who knew what else they were doing to get their Ice fix, especially if the withdrawal body count grew. "Tomorrow," Charles said, shaking harder now. Even his teeth were chattering. "Tomorrow I get paid. I'll pay you double. Please, man. Please. I need... that hit."

David reached into his pocket and pulled out a vial filled with clear liquid. "Is this what you want?"

Sterling hit the mike by his ear and spoke to Caleb Rain, Adam's twin brother and the leader of the Renegades—the team of GTECHs that had risen up against Adam. "Ice deal going down." Discreetly, he added his location. Caleb's unique abilities to not only read human emotions, but to influence their actions, even clear their memories, made him the perfect interrogator.

"I'm on my way," Caleb said and then added sharply, "*Wait, Sterling.* Don't do anything until we get there." Sterling chuckled. Sure, he followed orders… when possible.

David pocketed the liquid Ice and turned away from the junkie, and Sterling knew this wasn't one of those times.

"Please David!" Charles shouted desperately. "Please! I have to have a hit." Charles grabbed David's arm, but David flung him across the alley with the kind of ease that said David was feeling the super strength of his own Ice addiction.

Sterling cursed, hitting the mike again. "They're on the move and so am I."

"I said, *wait*," Caleb ordered. "You have no idea what those Ice junkies are capable of."

Sterling couldn't hold off now. Sunrise City, the Renegades headquarters, was a good three hundred miles away, which equaled about ten minutes in travel time for Caleb. Sterling didn't have that much time to spare.

"Sterl—" Caleb started, but never finished. Sterling clicked off the mike in the middle of the angry reply.

With as much ease as a normal man walked, Sterling allowed himself to fade into the essence of the wind, hitching a ride to the outside corner of the alley. It was a unique skill GTECHs possessed. One that, thankfully, the "Ice Clanners" showed no signs of developing.

Sterling stepped into the alley, blocking the dealer's exit. "Howdy there, fellas." He ignored the bodyguards, focusing his GTECH black stare on the dealer, his natural eye color gone with his humanity. "I'll be taking that vial of Ice you got there in your pocket. Then you can mosey on along and take the rest of your lifetime off. You know, do whatever retired drug dealers do. Play the casino tables. Watch *SpongeBob* for all I care. Just get the *hell* off my streets."

"Your streets?" David challenged. "These streets belong to Adam Rain, as you will soon find out." He gave Sterling a once-over. "We got us some army wannabe who's been icing too much. Thinks he's superhuman or some shit like that. Thinks he can push us around."

"See," Sterling drawled. "That's where you're mistaken. I already did the 'army' party and left. I'm what you call an independent contractor. We Renegades write our own rules. The good bendable kind that lets me kick your ass all over the curb and then do it again just for fun."

David made a less than successful attempt at a hand signal, and the three men instantly rushed at Sterling. He could have wind-walked away, but what fun would that be? Standing his ground, Sterling kicked one of his attackers in the chest and landed a fist on the other's jaw. The two bodyguards—or whatever the juiced-up bastards were—came back at Sterling before he could make a move toward Charles and David, neither of the guards fazed by his attacks when they should have been.

Sterling punched one of the men and sent him stumbling backwards. Then, taking the offensive, he reached for the other man and did the same to him, but not before the man ripped off Sterling's hat and took a chunk of short, spiky blond hair with it.

"Now you're fighting like a girl," Sterling mumbled irritably. Both men were already getting up as he turned his attention to David, who was running down the alley, leaving Charles lying flat on his face in the middle of the street.

Sterling wind-walked and appeared in front of David.

"How did you—"

Sterling grabbed David and jacked him up against the wall, David's feet dangling above the pavement.

"Give me the Ice."

"Where did you come from?"

"That's what drugs do to you," Sterling said, digging inside David's pockets and retrieving the vial. "They make you see things." Sterling held onto David and turned in preparation to face the two bodyguards, but they had disappeared.

That left only Sterling, Charles, and David in the alley, and Charles was lying on the ground, foaming at the mouth. David threw an iced-up super punch that landed hard on Sterling's jaw.

Sterling grinned. "Feels good," he said about the time the wind lifted, and Caleb appeared at his side.

Caleb took one look at Charles and hit his headset. "Get me an ambulance and a military escort." Every agency and hospital in town had been set up to notify a military hotline about all Ice-related activity, which went directly to Sterling, as the Renegade in charge of the inner city.

Caleb grabbed David from Sterling, then looked pointedly at Sterling. "You don't know the meaning of 'wait,' do you?"

David kicked Caleb who grunted irritably as he turned to the dealer, pinning him in a controlling stare. "Who is your source?"

Sterling was already moving to Charles's side, leaning over the man, who was now turning blue. He cursed. If he didn't give his Ice sample to Charles, the man could die.

David laughed. "Adam Rain. Adam Rain is my source."

"Yeah?" Caleb demanded. "What does he look like?"

"Don't you wish you knew?" the dealer taunted.

Caleb let out a low growl of frustration. "You don't even know who Adam Rain is or what you're involved in."

"I do know!" David said, kicking and punching at Caleb to no avail. "I can tell you!"

"He's my twin, you idiot," Caleb said. "I already know what he looks like." Caleb cursed. It was clear that David was nothing more than a human minion with no real knowledge of Ice or its source.

Caleb lifted the lid of a trash receptacle nearby and tossed David inside with ease, using the plastic cuffs he had on his waistband to tie it shut. "We now know I cannot control Ice junkies, and since it's looking like the world is about to be full of them, that particular skill is pretty damn useless. I can't erase his memory either."

Charles started convulsing. Sterling held up the vial. "What do you want to do?"

"Damn Adam to hell for this."

Sirens sounded in the distance as Caleb kneeled beside Charles and withdrew a syringe from his pocket. Sterling held the man steady as Caleb drew blood from Charles, hoping it might indicate why he was experiencing a potentially lethal withdrawal from Ice.

"We'll give him all but a few drops of the drug," Caleb indicated. "Save some for the lab." They were working on a theory that some variance in the Ice doses might be the cause of the lethal withdrawals. If they could find that variance it might lead to an antidote. Hard to prove considering the dealing had been tightly guarded, and they'd struggled to get samples.

———

A few minutes later, Sterling and Caleb stood with First Lieutenant Chris Riker, a typical buzz-cut, muscle-bound soldier in his mid-thirties who'd become Sterling's contact for all things Ice-related. A good enough guy by Sterling's book, considering he worked for the very government that had plotted, only six months before, to insert an alien-tracking chemical into all the GTECHs, Zodius and Renegades alike, in an effort to track them and torture them into obedience.

The government had blamed their disloyalty to the Renegades, who'd saved their asses time and time again, on General Powell, the creator of the GTECH serum. And now they'd sworn their allegiance to the Renegades again. Right. And Sterling had some swampland for sale back home in Texas. He went along with the uneasy alliance because Caleb felt it was in the best interests of humanity, and for that reason and that reason alone.

"We'll take the dealer in for interrogation," Riker said, glancing at Sterling. "You're welcome to join us."

"We've done our interrogation," Caleb said quickly. "He's all yours." Riker's normally stony face flashed with the same surprise Sterling felt at the hands-off approach. Caleb tended to keep Sterling uncomfortably "in bed" with Riker and his military cronies.

Clearly Caleb had something else on the agenda other than baby-sitting the army. "And here I thought you guys didn't trust me to do my job," Riker said dryly.

"We'll expect video and audio feeds as well as medical records from both men," Caleb assured him. "And I don't expect to find so much as a minute of cut footage."

"Well now," Sterling said dryly, focusing on Riker. "That is more like it. Distrust is alive and well. Familiar territory we all have learned to embrace."

Riker's lips thinned. "My world is as it should be again," he said in mock relief. Someone shouted Riker's name, and he motioned that he was on his way. "You'll get what you need," he said, turning on his heels and heading toward the ambulance.

Sterling instantly focused on Caleb and arched a brow in silent question.

"The body count is rising," Caleb said. "And Lord help us if Adam figures out how to mass distribute it—like in the water supply. We need an immunization, a way to prevent Ice from being absorbed. But Kelly is worried about a fast-track solution leading to other unforeseeable side effects. She needs an astrobiologist who has hands-on experience with the study of extraterrestrial microbes. That list of candidates is small."

Dr. Kelly Peterson was their lead scientist, with whom Sterling had a rather combative friendship. Despite this, he respected the hell out of the woman.

"Four of the five names she considers qualified have disappeared in the last seventy-two hours. Someone got them before we did," Caleb continued.

Adam. It had to be. Sterling cursed. "What's the story on the fifth?"

"Her name is Rebecca Burns, and she's from your home state of Texas. She's been out of the country for two months, which is probably how she's escaped capture. She's returning home tonight. I sent you an electronic copy of her file." His lips thinned. "If we are going to stop Adam from using Ice to take over the city, we need her help. And Sterling—we don't have time for niceties. Convince her to help. If you can't—bring her here anyway."

───⁓───

Twenty-four hours later
Houston, Texas

For the first time in three months, Rebecca Burns accepted that she was going to die. She pulled her blue Volvo to a halt in front of her quaint, two-story stucco house secluded by miles of grassy hills and droopy willow trees. Fear wasn't something she'd entertained in life; she certainly wasn't going to invite it along for her death.

Death. There it was. Her secret. The reality she'd shared with no one. She said the word several times more in her mind, refusing to shy away from it, but still found herself swallowing a lump in her throat.

Becca opened the car door, fighting the strong winds that threatened a midnight storm, her black cotton dress flapping around her knees, her jet black hair lifting around her shoulders. She slammed the door shut. Ignoring the baggage in her trunk for now, Becca confidently traveled a sidewalk hugged by a stone border. The high moon peaked from the cloud cover, casting the path in dull light.

Thirty-four years might not be what most would consider a long life, but they had been good years. Years blessed with friendships, wonderful parents—God rest their souls—and a fulfilling, absolutely amazing job working for NASA. As an astrobiologist, she'd seen things that reached beyond this world, things that people who lived three times her lifespan would never see.

She smiled as she reflected on her life. *Yeah, it had been a good run.*

Her smile quickly faded as she reached the stairs leading to her porch. The motion detectors flickered to a soft glow, revealing a man as he stepped from the corner shadows, the rocking chair creaking with his exit. He was dressed in jeans and a T-shirt, his spiky, blond hair and drool-worthy body, a combination that fantasies were made of.

Specifically, her fantasies. Right then and there, all logic and reason fled. Something inside her flared, and it screamed with life, not death.

He stared at her with eyes so teal green they had to be contacts, and Becca felt warmth magically spray through her limbs. In some far corner of her mind, she recognized that even under normal circumstances—and hers were far from normal—it *was* after ten o'clock at night, and she did not know this man. But there was something about the man's eyes that eased her fear. Besides, if she was going to get herself killed by acting without caution, she couldn't think of a better way to go than by the hands of this incredibly hot guy.

Becca blinked to be sure she wasn't hallucinating. Nope. No hallucination. He was still there, and she blushed with the thoughts that clouded her mind. Never had she had the kind of sizzling, unadulterated sex a girl wanted to have with a made-for-sex man like this one. She'd never dared allow herself such an indulgence, never even considered it.

WARRIOR

BY CHERYL BROOKS

◇◇

*"He came to me in the dead of winter,
his body burning with fever."*

◇◇

EVEN NEAR DEATH, HIS SENSUALITY IS AMAZING...
Leo arrives on Tisana's doorstep a beaten slave from a near extinct race with feline genes. As soon as Leo recovers his strength, he'll use his extraordinary sexual talents to bewitch Tisana and make a bolt for freedom...

PRAISE FOR THE CAT STAR CHRONICLES:
"A compelling tale of danger, intrigue, and sizzling romance!"
——Candace Havens, author of *Charmed & Deadly*

"Hot enough to start a fire. Add in a thrilling new world and my reading experience was complete."
——*Romance Junkies*

978-1-4022-1440-0 • $6.99 U.S. / $7.99 CAN

FUGITIVE

BY CHERYL BROOKS

**"Really sexy. Sizzling kind of sexy...makes you
want to melt in the process."** —*Bitten by Books*

A mysterious stranger in danger...

Zetithian warrior Manx, a member of a race hunted to near
extinction because of their sexual powers, has done all he
can to avoid extermination. But when an uncommon woman
enters his jungle lair, the animal inside of him demands he
risk it all to have her.

The last thing Drusilla expected to find on vacation was a
gorgeous man hiding in the jungle. But what is he running
from? And why does she feel so mesmerized that she'll stop
at nothing to be near him? Hypnotically attracted, their intense pleasure in each other could destroy them both.

PRAISE FOR THE CAT STAR CHRONICLES:

"Wow. The romantic chemistry is as close to perfect as you'll
find." —*BookFetish.org*

"Fabulous off world adventures... Hold on ladies, hot Zetithians
are on their way." —*Night Owl Romance*

"Insanely creative... I enjoy this author's voice immensely."
—*The Ginger Kids Den of Iniquity*

"I think purring will be on my request list from now on."
— *Romance Reader at Heart*

978-1-4022-2940-4 •$6.99 U.S. / $8.99 CAN / £3.99 UK